Silas Crockett

Other Maine books from Islandport Press

Hauling by Hand: The Life and Times of a Maine Island
by Dean Lawrence Lunt

In Maine
by John N. Cole

The Story of Mount Desert Island
by Samuel Eliot Morison

Here for Generations: The Story of a Maine Bank and its City
by Dean Lawrence Lunt

A Moose and a Lobster Walk Into a Bar: Tales from Maine
by John McDonald

Children's Books

When I'm With You
written by Elizabeth Elder
illustrated by Leslie Mannsman

Silas Crockett

by Mary Ellen Chase

Islandport Press
Yarmouth • Frenchboro • Maine

Also by Mary Ellen Chase

His Birthday (1915)
The Girl from The Big Horn Country (1916)
Virginia of Elk Creek Valley (1917)
Mary Christmas (1926)
Uplands (1927)
The Silver Shell (1930)
A Goodly Heritage (1932)
Mary Peters (1934)
This England (1936)
Dawn in Lyonesse (1938)
A Goody Fellowship (1939)
Windswept (1941)
The Bible and The Common Reader (1944)
Jonathan Fisher: Maine Parson, 1768–1847 (1948)
The Plum Tree (1949)
Abby Aldrich Rockefeller (1950)
Recipe for a Magic Childhood (1952)
The White Gate: Adventures in the Imagination of a Child (1954)
Life and Language in the Old Testament (1955)
The Edge of Darkness (1957)
Sailing the Seven Seas (1958)
Donald McKay and the Clipper Ships (1959)
The Lovely Ambition (1960)
The Fishing Fleets of New England (1961)
The Psalms for the Common Reader (1962)
The Prophets for the Common Reader (1963)
Victoria: A Pig in a Pram (1963)
A Journey to Boston (1965)
The Story of Lighthouses (1965)
A Walk on an Iceberg (1966)

Islandport Press
P.O. Box 10
Yarmouth, Maine 04096
www.islandportpress.com

First Islandport Press Edition, June 2003
Second edition April 2006

This revised edition of *Silas Crockett* reprinted by Islandport Press Inc., by arrangement with Simon & Schuster. *Silas Crockett* was originally published by The Macmillan Company, 1935.

ISBN: 0-9671662-2-5
Library of Congress Card Number: 2003103690

Book jacket design by Karen F. Hoots/Mad Hooter Design
Cover illustration courtesy of Dover Publications Inc.
Book design by Michelle A. Lunt/Islandport Press
Photo of Mary Ellen Chase courtesy of Smith College

To the seafaring families of Maine and to their descendants, who still retain within themselves the graciousness and the dignity of their heritage.

As for man, his days are as grass; as a flower of the field, so he flourisheth.

For the wind passeth over it, and it is gone; and the place thereof shall know it no more.

But the mercy of the Lord is from everlasting to everlasting upon them that fear Him, and His righteousness unto children's children.

Psalm 103.

Table of Contents

Mary Ellen Chase

Mary Ellen Chase was not only born and raised on the coast of Maine, she was molded by it; its history, its character and its spirit never abandoned her whether she was standing in the classrooms of Smith College or wandering through the meadows of England, another land she loved dearly. Her longtime companion, Eleanor Shipley Duckett, put it succinctly when she wrote: "Maine made and shaped her."

Less succinctly, Chase herself wrote: "To have sprung from Maine seafaring people; to have spent my childhood and many of my later years on a coastline unsurpassed in loveliness; to have inherited a wealth of thrilling history and tradition; to have been born at a time when great ships, built by Maine people in a hundred seacoast villages, had been for nearly a century making Searsport and Rockland, Belfast and Thomaston, Wiscasset and Calais better known in Canton, Singapore, and Sydney than even New York and London were known; to have been brought up with men, and with women, too, who knew the Seven Seas too well to be bounded in their thoughts by the narrow confines of their own native parishes;—such an inheritance of imperishable values imposes a debt which cannot possibly either be underestimated or even fully discharged."

Mary Ellen Chase was born in the village of Blue Hill on February 24, 1887, the daughter of a country lawyer and school-teacher and the granddaughter of a sea captain. The second of eight children, she could trace her ancestral roots to the original eighteenth-century settlers of Blue Hill, which is located at the head of Blue Hill Bay between Penobscot Bay and Mount Desert Island. She had a strict upbringing and her childhood was steeped in literature and books and religion through the Congregational Church. She attended Blue Hill Academy starting in 1900 and graduated from the University of Maine in 1909. Her college education was interrupted briefly while she taught in one-room schoolhouses in Buck's Harbor and West Brooksville.

Following graduation, she traveled west, teaching first in Wisconsin and then Chicago at Miss Moffat's School for Girls in 1912. She also took her first fledgling steps toward professional writing when she sold her first story, "His Place on the Eleven," a story about football, to *The American Boy* in 1909 for $17.

She moved to Montana to recover from tuberculosis in 1914 and shortly saw the publication of her first book, *His Birthday* (1915), a 48-page children's book about Jesus' sixth birthday. During the following two years she wrote other children's books, including *The Girl from The Big Horn Country* (1916) and *Virginia of Elk Creek Valley* (1917).

In 1917, she began working toward a doctorate at the University of Minnesota. She received her master's degree in 1918, and in 1922 she received her doctorate and became an assistant professor of English at the university.

The year 1926 was an important one for Chase. She published *Mary Christmas*, her first novel, and she moved back east to begin three decades of teaching at Smith College in Northampton, Massachusetts.

In 1932 she published *A Goodly Heritage*, her first of three full-length autobiographical books that touched upon her beloved Maine and her hometown of Blue Hill. (Chase followed with *A Goodly Fellowship* (1939) and *The White Gate* (1954).

In 1934 came *Mary Peters*, the book that launched her career as a successful novelist and established her credentials nationally. Chase considers *Mary Peters* the first of her "Maine" novels—her fictional tributes to her Maine heritage. In writing *Mary Peters*, Chase was greatly influenced by Sarah Orne Jewett's *Deephaven*, which depicts the deterioration of a once prosperous coastal port. *Mary Peters*, set between 1880 and 1920, discusses the shifting nature of some seacoast towns during the decline of Maine's position as a great sea power and the arrival of out-of-state rusticators to Maine.

Chase followed *Mary Peters* in 1935 with the even more ambitious *Silas Crockett*, an epic that follows the lives of four generations of a Maine seafaring family. Reflecting on *Silas Crockett,* Chase said in 1962, "So far as any contribution to the social history of Maine is concerned, I consider *Silas Crockett* the most significant and the most valuable of all my books."

Chase carefully researched *Silas Crockett* to maintain historical accuracy and even took the family name Crockett from a sailor who let her hold the wheel of an old steamboat, *Catherine*, that once plied Maine waters. Biographer Perry D. Westbrook wrote that *Silas Crockett* "epitomizes an era in American cultural history." *The Edge of Darkness* (1957) is considered the final installment of her "Maine" trilogy.

However, other books do feature a Maine setting, including, *Windswept* (1941), one of her most commercially successful novels, and *Jonathan Fisher: Maine Parson, 1768–1847* (1948), a highly regarded history of her native Blue Hill.

Of course, Maine was not her only subject. She also wrote the novels *Dawn in Lyonesse* (1938), *The Plum Tree* (1949) and *The*

Lovely Ambition (1960), as well as several books about the Bible, including *The Bible and the Common Reader* (1949), *The Psalms for the Common Reader* (1961) and *The Prophets for the Common Reader* (1963). She was also hired by John D. Rockefeller Jr. to write a biography of his wife, *Abby Aldrich Rockefeller* (1950).

Ultimately, Chase wrote more than 30 books as well as dozens of essays, articles and short stories. Still, Chase is best remembered for her contributions to Maine literature and her wonderful descriptions both of Maine's glorious past and the powerful forces that transformed it, not always for the better.

Her work gained her significant recognition as both a writer and lecturer. In 1959, Chase received the Hale Award for distinguished writing by an author with New England connections. She also received an Honorary Doctor of Letters from the University of Maine and Bowdoin College, Honorary Doctor of the Humanities from Colby College, Doctor of Letters from Northeastern University and Doctor of Letters from Smith College.

Through it all she never forgot her roots.

She once wrote: "I am daily grateful that I was born of good, simple New England stock, had seafarers among my ancestors, was one of a large family, and can forevermore count Maine as my home. To these circumstances I owe whatever I have accomplished; and whatever honor there is in that accomplishment is not my own but that of the State of Maine."

Mary Ellen Chase died in a Northampton, Massachusetts, nursing home in 1973; she then returned home for good. She is buried in her hometown of Blue Hill, in a family plot that overlooks the coast of Maine.

Dean Lawrence Lunt
Yarmouth, Maine
April 2003

Foreword

In 1999, the historical novel *Silas Crockett*, first published in 1935 by Mary Ellen Chase, was chosen by the Baxter Bibliophile Society for its Mirror of Maine exhibit and accompanying anthology as one of the *One Hundred Distinguished Books That Reveal the History of the State and Life of its People.* After reading the novel, it's easy to see why.

The book *Silas Crockett*, as distinguished from its Maine character, is an ambitious and well-written saga that takes place from 1830 to 1933. A romantic four-hundred page novel that chronicles four generations of the proud and seafaring Crockett family of fictional Saturday Cove, it's also an impressive and realistic account of Maine's dramatic maritime history.

In *The Mirror of Maine*, the editors write: "As the story opens in 1830, Silas Crockett is returning home from a prosperous China Trade voyage, having captained an East Indiaman for Boston merchants … following the lives of Silas, his son Nicholas, grandson Reuben, and great-grandson Silas Crockett II, Chase's novel depicts the social and economic dynamics that accompanied the history of the maritime trade. From the height of the China Trade, the story advances through the heady days of clipper ships, the perilous cold of Grand Banks fishing, the decline of wooden shipbuilding, and the rise of steamships to the time of renewed economic vitality brought by summer residents."

Silas Crockett is as interesting in describing what happens to the generations of residents and the community of Saturday Cove as it is in detailing the maritime changes.

The first Silas Crockett is the embodiment of the legendary and noble Maine sea captain figure of the nineteenth century: handsome and dignified, smart and self-assured, tough and daring, ambitious and worldly, hard-working and resourceful, exuberant and optimistic.

He returns home at 23 to marry Solace Winship, the daughter of an architect and builder of many fine Maine homes and churches, and takes her with him around the world. Silas Crockett, of English Protestant ancestry, has "the right stuff" and he knows it. He's a natural leader of men; and is as restless on land as he is happiest at sea commanding his boat. Of course, the Maine sea captain as God-like figure has long been celebrated and written about in American literature – from Mark Twain's tales (sailing around the Horn with a wild Maine sea captain) to Sarah Orne Jewett's novels, to popular fiction like Sterling Hayden's *Voyage* to today's Captain Linda Greenlaw of *The Perfect Storm* and *Hungry Ocean* fame.

The gallant Maine sea captain, a cousin to the brave seafarers and fishermen from such Massachusetts ports as Salem, New Bedford and Gloucester, embodies the same democratic ideals as the descendants of the first explorers and settlers of the New World, the revolutionary founders of our democracy, and the bearers of America's brand of patriotic red-blooded individualism and spirit. Competitive capitalists to the hilt. The current term "globalization" is nothing new. Maine sea captains like Silas Crockett embraced the concept way back when.

So, in the novel, Silas Crockett feels superior to the captain of the steamboat he's aboard when returning home to get married. Miss Chase muses through Silas, "Of course, if one had no stuff . . . one meandered along the coast in just such a filthy, unseaworthy dugout as this." This unimpressive, unworldly-looking craft of 1830 is a harbinger of the non-future of sailing ships.

Author Chase also reminds us that, "In 1830 the coast of Maine was a thriving place, already on the eve of her great shipbuilding boom." Bangor was becoming the lumber capital of the world, and "There was scarcely a seacoast town or village of any size at all from Casco to Mount Desert which was not venturing upon ship construction of its own."

Because of all the boats coming and going from around the world, the Maine coast in 1830 was "an integral part of the world at large, supplying ships from every ocean and men and boys who knew even the Ultima Thules [the northernmost part of the habitable world] of six continents far better than they knew the wharves and piers of Portland."

Miss Chase adds: "For Saturday Cove, like every other thriving coast town in those stirring days, ate and drank and wore the products of foreign soil and the work of foreign hands and talked more familiarly of the Seven Seas than of Machias Bay."

However, for all his love of his hometown, Silas Crockett does not plan to retire in Maine. "He would not return at forty-five or fifty to Maine as so many men were doing, not to Saturday Cove as his own father had done, there to live in his great white house and look seaward upon a quiet ocean. Not he! The coast of Maine was a good place to come from but not to end one's day on when the whole world beckoned."

Instead, Silas pictures himself retiring to a Boston mansion in the company of other such rich and prominent men.

It was true, even into the 1950s and 1960s when I was growing up in Hancock—a town founded by sea captains similar to Miss Chase's Blue Hill—that a sea captain would return to live in his big house up from the ocean, start a business, and take a strong interest in town affairs and politics where his opinions and theories held strong sway over the locals because of his stature and success in the greater world. The idea seemed to be that any man who could captain a ship around the world could also run a town. Of course, some captains tended to act more like dictators than democratic leaders, telling people how to vote and warning them against selling out to the summer people.

Miss Chase also notes how men like Silas Crockett who returned home only from time to time for short visits provided the local folk with excitement and glamour. His wedding, wonderfully described, is an event not to be missed. "Silas represented to Saturday Cove all its contact with the world at large; and the knowledge that he was to carry his bride with him over the watery face of the earth added a glamour to what was sufficiently glamorous already."

As Chase writes, "Seafaring's a rough life, but when the best of us go into it, it knocks nonsense out of our heads whatever it may put in place of it." Certainly, Silas Crockett was a man of no-nonsense, and so was his son Nicholas; but when it came time for Nicholas to go to sea, times had changed. While in 1850 there were boats still being built in Saturday Cove, by 1860, "There were signs about them of decay, piers rotting here and there; and the best shipwrights had left Saturday Cove because there was not enough money to pay them."

During his first trip aboard a schooner, Nicholas Crockett attends a dinner where this toast is made: "Gentlemen, I drink to the passing of a glorious era! . . . We drink, gentlemen, to the glory of the American clipper and pledge together our fealty to blue water!"

Miss Chase writes: "In 1870, there was little left of the old, far-seeing life which had embraced the world and brought it homeward. The yards and most of the docks had gone, buildings and piers alike."

Being as anti-steamboat as his father, Nicholas Crockett takes a job as a Grand Banks fisherman; and, in turn, Nicholas's son, Reuben, takes a job as a ship's clerk on a coastal steamer. Thus does the Crockett family, like many Maine coastal families (along with summer families, too) degenerate through the years.

After the Civil War and with the Industrial Revolution in full swing, rich folk from the big cities began to invade Maine for the hottest months, to sail, picnic, play golf and tennis – to "rusticate" and enjoy the Maine coast more than most natives were ever able to.

Before the income tax of 1913, grand estates and hotels staffed with servants were built all along the coast. Most of the shipyards were gone by the 1890s, and Chase writes, "Fishing, in fact, as well as shipbuilding had suffered from change . . . (and) . . . by the time the nineties had reached Saturday Cove, it together with scores of other seacoast towns and villages was ready and eager to utilize a new industry — that of supplying the easier demands of a fast-growing summer population . . . master fishermen, who had weathered fogs and gales off Newfoundland, now cleaned and painted their schooners to take out parties for days of deep-sea fishing in the outer waters of Frenchman's Bay, or Passamaquoddy, or Blue Hill, or Penobscot. It was an easy and a pleasant occupation and brought hitherto undreamed-of profits without danger or hardship or even labour."

Silas's mother Abigail worries about these changes, saying, "Folks are bound to get shiftless when the time comes that they can buy everything they need." Abigail, after all, came from a generation of Maine people who prided themselves on being able to do many things well, and remain almost totally self-sufficient. And it was the same with little villages like Saturday Cove which were very self-contained.

Perry D. Westbrook in *Mary Ellen Chase* (1965) writes about Chase's view of Maine character: "In it she saw weaknesses which would lay it open to temptations presented by moneyed outsiders — temptations to discard dignity and even integrity and honor for ready cash, to play the role of servant rather than that of freeman farmer or fisherman. Fishermen discarded their lines and nets to conduct vacationing bankers on picnics; merchants raised their prices beyond enough to ensure a fair profit. Young people, students in the excellent old academies, gave up their plans for college to become the maids and gardeners of the rich."

Thus from 1880 to 1920, parts of the Maine coast switched from seafaring and fishing to catering to the rusticators.

(Miss Chase doesn't write about rum-running during the Prohibition years of the 1920s, but this was important economically for many locals who owned trucks and boats and had access to wharves where they could meet the boats coming in from Canada. Today, we have a lucrative drug trade that has financed any number of new mansions by the sea, fancy boats, and "legitimate businesses" that thrive, at least for part of the year, on the coast.)

This is not to say that these Maine ports completely abandoned the sea. Young Maine men (and women) today still go to sea via the Maine Maritime Academy and work on merchant marine vessels. However, there are less and less American boats on which to work, so they may well be working for foreign companies.

A number of young mariners are also employed on ferryboats and tugboats, especially in the summers.

And there are still many native fishermen who mostly go lobstering. There are also new coastal jobs for would-be fishermen: sea urchin, seaweed, and mussel harvesting, as well as offshore salmon farms. In fact, in Mary Ellen Chase's own Blue Hill, there has been a great protest in recent times from some newcomers over salmon pens in the bay. Some of these protesters are the type of people who seem bent on destroying traditional (as well as non-traditional) Maine industries.

A word about the wives of the Crockett men: Like their husbands, they, too, are forced to change with the times. From the brave, stalwart, and wise Abigail, Silas Crockett's mother, and his admirable wife, Solace, we then meet Nicholas's weaker wife who hates life in Saturday Cove and abandons her own son to run off to Boston with an artist.

Maine coastal women of all classes have always been a hardy breed working alongside their men in both the fishing and farming industries. While few women ever went to sea with their captain husbands as Solace Crockett did, a number of women from prominent families did later run hotels, restaurants and other businesses servicing the summer trade. While "upper-class" native women were mostly adverse to working as cooks, maids, cleaning women, or laundresses for summer people, they did clerk in stores, run post offices, tutor summer children, and even make deliveries to summer cottages. Working-class Maine women were glad to have the summer work to augment family incomes.

Miss Chase's portrait of the faithful servant Susan is one of the most memorable in the novel. Maine coastal history is full of self-sacrificing Susans who attached themselves to a prominent family and stayed with them for a lifetime. Susan even leaves money for Reuben Crockett's son to attend Bowdoin.

In his lovely anthology *White Pine and Blue Water: A State of Maine Reader* (1950), Henry Beston writes, "Maine enjoys being Maine. Something of the eighteenth century gusto of living continues here, and there is a positive enjoyment of adventure, character, and circumstances. Bulwarked by the tradition of an ancestral New England, by the discipline of the wilderness and the ordinances of the sea, the way of life has faced the age of the machine and preserved its communal good will and the human values. Here one still thinks of life as life and not as existence."

Fifty-three years later, one wonders if that's still true. Is Maine indeed "the way life should be"?

Since 1935, Maine has endured the Great Depression and World War II. In the 1947 Bar Harbor Fire, over two hundred homes and hotels burned, and many of the once grand summer estates were replaced by motels and restaurants catering to the tourists visiting Acadia National Park. Passenger trains were discontinued by 1960; and by the early 1970s, the back-to-the-land movement had begun. Add to this the many summer folk retiring to their now winterized summer homes, and it is no wonder Maine's population has doubled along with that of the U.S. It has become fashionable for upwardly mobile middle-class folk to live year-round in Maine.

Small coastal towns like Blue Hill and Hancock have tripled in year-round population, but they are no longer self-contained as they once were. They have become bedroom communities on either side of the city of Ellsworth. Local people are no longer so dependent on the fishing industry nor the summer colonies.

While it used to be the worldly sea captains who once provided glamour for the townsfolk, followed in later times by the summer people, now it's the local citizens themselves who get to travel, take glamorous cruises and trips around the world, at least once a year.

As one of my good friends, himself the descendant of a proud old Maine coastal family, has said about our beloved coast, "Maine native culture is as dead as the old Indian culture." But it's well preserved in Mary Ellen Chase's fine novel, *Silas Crockett*.

Sanford Phippen
Hancock, Maine
March 2003

Original Foreword

In this story of four generations of a Maine seafaring family I have attempted to picture the maritime life of the coast for one hundred years. Needless to say, my work has required much interesting study of the various aspects which make up its background; and I wish to give full credit to the authors of certain books which have been invaluable to me in its construction: to Mr. Samuel Eliot Morison for *The Maritime History of Massachusetts*; to Mr. Arthur H. Clark for *The Clipper Ship Era*; to Mr. Francis B. C. Bradlee for *Some Account of Steam Navigation in New England* from *The Historical Collections of the Essex Institute*; to Mr. Ralph D. Paine for *The Ships and Sailors of Old Salem*; and to Mr. Raymond Macfarlane for *A History of the New England Fisheries*. I am deeply indebted also to Miss Florence Morse of Blue Hill for certain original plans of Maine meeting-houses and for other interesting family papers of which I have made use.

Because of the nature of my subject I have purposely placed more emphasis upon setting and character than upon plot and incident. The characters, however, although typical of people whom I have known all my life, are drawn from no actual persons, living or dead. The dates given are accurate, with the exception of two which I have moved a few months out of place for the purpose of better narrative. To those who know Maine it will be evident that the scene of my story, Saturday Cove, bears no relation to the Penobscot Bay village of that name.

Mary Ellen Chase
Blue Hill, Maine,
September 1935

I

Silas Crockett

1830-1850

Silas Crockett

I

Young Captain Silas Crockett was within one week of his twenty-third birthday when, in the last days of May of the year 1830, he journeyed homeward from Boston to Bath in the steamboat *Pemaquid*. He was hastening to his wedding with Solace Winship at Saturday Cove, which lay still farther eastward where Frenchman's Bay sweeps on toward Passamaquoddy beyond the blue Mount Desert hills. He might have found this first journey under steam irksome had he not been the sort of young man he was and had not his immediate past been so glowing in retrospect and his immediate future so alluring in prospect. For the journey was slow enough in those years, necessitating a change in Bath to the smaller steamboat *Island Maid*, which pursued her walloping course to Boothbay and Owl's Head, Camden, Belfast, and Searsport, Cranberry Isles, and a dozen other ports eastward before she at last coughed and spluttered her way into the deep, spruce-lined haven of Saturday Cove. It meant, in fact, the greater part of four days, the nights being wisely spent at anchor in some harbour or other, for steam travel was still new in 1830 and not held in high repute by anybody, least of all by a young captain who had just commanded his stately ship, *Southern Seas*, around the Horn to Hawaii and thence to Canton.

But young Silas had a thousand things to think about and plenty of time to do it in. The fragrance of the sandalwood he had loaded at Honolulu was still in his nostrils competing with that of the Souchong, the Hyson, and the spices which he had brought safely through the chilly, dangerous waters of Massachusetts Bay. The compliments of Boston merchants and shipowners still sounded sweet in his ears, together with the welcoming shouts which had greeted his ship as, with spotless paintwork, holystoned decks, freshly tarred shrouds, and perfect canvas, she had sailed past

Boston Light with skysails and studdingsails still set, and on up the harbour before a wind he himself could never have improved upon had he been the Lord God Almighty. He still could see himself stalking his quarterdeck in the morning sun as conscious of his buff top hat, blue frock coat, and new side whiskers as of his record voyage. He could still hear the gales off Cape Horn tugging at his taut rigging and his reefed topsails, and feel in his hands the weight of the money which had come from his sale in Hawaii of his cargo of Lowell cottons, codfish, lumber and glass, hardware, needles and threads, and notions such as only the Yankee mind of one hundred years ago could conceive. He could still taste against the roof of his mouth the old Madeira, which had been served in his honour at a banquet in a Summer Street mansion but a few nights before—a mansion whose stately doors had been opened by Chinese servants and whose high rooms were set about with rare pieces of Eastern art.

These things, passing in continuous, bright procession through young Silas' exuberant mind, took time to review, and there were others as well. With these the future crowded quickly upon the past. He liked to remember Solace Winship's fingers as they worked at cross-stitch, crocheting, or tapestry, she sitting in a high-backed chair beneath the white, carved mantel of her father's fireplace, and how large the pupils of her eyes had grown as he told her of a fight he had had off Whampoa with a Chinese junk. They had grown large, too, over his tales of flower-boats, their upper parts carved into the shapes of birds and flowers, and of the great tea-deckers moving slowly down the muddy river with square brown sails above their lacquered sides, and of the coloured paper lanterns which at twilight saw their reflections in the still water. These stories he had told her a year and a half ago, the last time he had seen her. He wondered, at circumspect intervals, whether she would draw in her breath suddenly when he kissed her overlong as he had dared twice or thrice to do, and after such wondering, in order either to quiet or to nourish his excitement, he dashed into his stuffy cabin, which smelled of old lunch boxes, stale tobacco, and salt fish, to examine for the hundredth time the things he had brought her—the perfumed soaps in lacquered boxes, the scent bottles of purple glass, the Canton shawls and scarves, the East Indian damask for her table, the tea-set of fifty-one enamelled pieces, all perfect in spite of his nervous handling, the case of assorted silks and satins in luscious colours, and, as his crowning gift, a dressing-gown of pale blue silk, brocaded with cherry blossoms in rose and gold. When he pictured Solace in this gown over one of the nightdresses she had been fashioning, so she had daringly written him, he got into such a state that he dashed upon deck again, leaving his cabin for the time being in utter confusion.

Nor was the present wholly to be disregarded. There was the coast—the Maine coast now, since ten years no longer that of Massachusetts—slowly unrolling itself hour by hour before his eager, contented eyes. There it was as he had known it all his life, even in far-off foreign waters, its headlands dark with spruce and fir and pine even to the water's edge; its high, rough fields just now green with spring; its snug, clapboarded, white farm buildings complete in a long line of house, woodshed, carriage shelter, and barn; its coves and boulders and rocky beaches. Against the gray log fences of uneven, rock-strewn pastures he could see drifts of white, wild pear and plum and cherry, and on the pasture land itself mounds of purple lambkill. Among the rocks of many a point the new leaves of white birches shimmered in the sunlight against the dark firs. When the *Island Maid* poked her blunt and dirty nose into this and that small harbour, and with much jerking and jumbling came alongside green and barnacled piers to unload her barrels of flour and rum and molasses, her boots and shoes and rolls of cotton sheeting, he could hear the song-sparrows trilling from the sparse orchards where apple blossoms were showing pink and white. The lilacs, already in flower in Louisburg Square and along Mount Vernon Street, were here only in bud. They would be in full bloom, he thought, for his wedding day, and at that realization he felt nervously in the pocket of his waistcoat for the wedding ring, upon the purchase of which in Boston he had spared neither time nor money. Here and there in the sheltered interstices of cliffs he saw crumbling ice and snow, memorials of the winter hard with innumerable blizzards of which Solace had written him. And if his gaze held within it some hint of patronage because of his five years' acquaintance with the world at large, it was none the less one of delight over a long-deferred homecoming.

Not only the works of nature but those of man as well engaged Silas' attention. From Portland, Bath, and Boothbay eastward the coast was a bustle of activity. In 1830 herons did not stand for hours on end in a hundred solitary coves or whitethroats whistle all day from deserted and overgrown farm plots; nor did the occupants of a single summer cottage plan sailing trips over bays dotted only with pleasure craft. In 1830 the coast of Maine was a thriving place, already on the eve of her great shipbuilding boom. He noted at the mouths of countless seaward moving streams the busy mills that sawed the lumber for the yards at Rockland and at Bath; mills flanked by great mounds of sawdust, which flecked the tides moving in and out, and hemmed in over veritable acres by huge piles of logs and sawn timber and lesser ones of staves and edgings. Nor did Rockland and Bath in those years hold copyright upon the shipyards of Maine. There was scarcely a seacoast town or village of any size at all from Casco to Mount Desert which in 1830 was not venturing upon ship construction of its own. Silas noted with pride the skeletons of brigs and barques and schooners being framed upon the shingle beaches of even the smallest bays, saw the blocks of Maine pine with cap pieces of tough Maine oak upon which the ship would rest, watched for a brief hour here and there the framing of her launching ways, the cradle down which she would slide, when all was in readiness, to meet the water. Great pieces of copper sheathing gleamed in the sunlight on many an isolated shore. These to cover her bottom against the worms which attacked the best of wood and against the depredations of the moss and weeds of the far seas through which she was to sail. He smelt the tar and pitch for the soaking of the paper between wood and copper, the tallow and the soft soap for the greasing of her ways, both fixed and sliding, the oakum for the stopping of her seams. Upon the roofs of the sail lofts he saw the spread of weathering canvas to be cut and sewn and set once she was in the water. And everywhere he heard the cheerful sounds of mallet and of hammer upon wood and iron, the calls and cries of shipwrights, riveters and framers, tacklers and seamers, and the excited shouts of boys lingering to watch until the school bell should command their unwilling presence in the white frame schoolhouses or red-brick academies.

From Mount Desert eastward where Schoodic tumbles her red rocks into the sea and the Gouldsboro hills rise in their blue symmetry he saw the building of ships give place in large extent to fishing. As the *Island Maid* dozed in some sheltered cove, he was awakened before dawn by the sound of oars in locks, the flapping of sails, raised and trimmed to catch the early morning wind, the bumping of laden bait-tubs as they were loaded into dories and pinkies and Chebacco boats. In the late afternoon, as they wallowed along their slow, smoke-trailed course, he saw the horizon darkened by the returning boats and watched them make shoreward, the tired men lounging in the stern or upon the small, littered decks, their black, stubby pipes in their mouths. The water of bays and coves was bright with lobster buoys, painted in the distinctive colours of their owners, and the shores for miles as they went eastward were lined with fish-flakes built of stout poles, their lathed tops thickly covered with orderly rows of drying fish. Silas discovered that in the year and a half of his absence the weir fishing, new to the coast, had spread by leaps and bounds. Now, in the channels between islands and ledges or extending from points of land, weir-posts with their horizontal weaving of brown brush rose from the water ready for the runs of herring. Smoke-houses dotted the shores, the smell of curing fish drifting seaward on the land breeze. And in more than one harbour he saw the yards and spars of foreign ships from Liverpool and Cadiz and Marseilles, which had brought to these Eastern Maine fishermen their cargoes of salt and to their sons and daughters the long effects of strange faces and manners and unfamiliar tongues.

The captain of the *Island Maid* was a more loquacious fellow than the master of the *Pemaquid*, who hailed from Boston and rather felt his superiority and that of his steamer over a mere coastwise craft. Captain Gilley, who commanded the *Island Maid*, came from Isle au Haut and had done a bit of seafaring himself, he told Silas, having carried fish to Savannah and Norfolk and once even to the West Indies for a Portland firm. He was a short, squat man of fifty, none too tidy in the fastidious eyes of Silas, who saw with distaste the remnants of his breakfast eggs upon his moustache and the grease spots upon his frayed cravat and blue waistcoat. His berth as commander of such a miserable tub seemed narrow and insignificant enough to one who had secured his captaincy at twenty-one and had four times rounded Java Head. Silas with the arrogance of his successful youth attributed it to lack of any sort of competence. The sea knew no favouritism in its granting of supremacy, he said to himself, as he saw the captain talking to the few nervous women and scornful men who made up his scant passenger list. A man had only to show the stuff that was in him in order to leave the fo'c'sle for an officer's papers. For that fact, witness commanders like Captains William Sturgis and John Suter, who had themselves come in through the hawse hole with pride and risen to Boston fame and fortune. Of course, if one had no stuff, concluded Silas to himself, one meandered along the coast in just such a filthy, unseaworthy dugout as this.

It was obvious to Silas as well as to the other passengers that Captain Gilley looked upon young Captain Crockett with no little obsequious admiration; and well he might, for Silas was well worth looking upon in his six feet of health and strength. His spotless cravats and well-fitting clothes, his light kid gloves and Malacca-jointed cane, his sleek dark hair and perfectly trimmed side whiskers, his air of eagerness and exuberance warranted respect and deference, and respect and deference they obtained. Moreover, his family was known in Isle au Haut as well as in Portland as a family which had for fifty years and more carried the name of Saturday Cove across the Pacific or around Good Hope to Canton and back through the perilous Sunda Straits to St. Helena, thence homeward to the shrewd shipowners of Cape Cod—men who were on the constant lookout for good masters and knew them when they saw them. In the long twilights of the two evenings when the *Island Maid* lay at circumspect anchor and the peepers sounded from inland ponds and marshes, Captain Gilley leaned against the deck-rail with his stubby thumbs in his waistcoat pockets and exchanged well-chosen words with the captain of the *Southern Seas*. He was given to recounting the dangers and responsibilities of his calling as though alike to exonerate it and himself for his embracing of it.

"This coast's a tricky one," he said to Silas, "and the government, if you'll take my word on a serious matter, ain't up to its proper business. I could name on my own fingers, counting them off one by one, fifty reefs and ledges without so much as a buoy. Everyone knows that inshore sailing holds more dangers than open water. For five years now I've seen April and August fogs drifting in thicker than wool off a sheep's back, yes, sir, fogs such as only the Evil One can put together, and nothing to steer by but the compass and God Almighty and your own poor wits. And now that fishing's on the upward take all along the coast and islands, it's worse every year than the last. For you ain't only the souls in your own boat to account for and bring them safe to land, God willing. You've got hundreds of others all slipping across you from the Magdalens and Fundy and the offshore banks, and some in boats not fit for flounder catching. What chance would they have, I ask you, under the bows of a steamer like this? There is hardly a trip that I'm not in a cold sweat by the time I've cleared Machias Bay for Eastport. Good God, I say to my wife, a man don't want murder on his conscience. Every man that commands a vessel has his problems, you, sir, as well as me, and that's a fact. But with steam in its infancy, as one might almost say, and its whole future at stake, the captain of a steamboat has to watch and pray as the Bible says. There's no mistake about that."

He looked toward Silas for commendation but, seeing none, shifted his position uneasily against the deck-rail and put a question to the tall, well-built young captain.

"I suppose as a matter of fact, sir, you've got small faith in steam?"

"If you want to know my views," returned Silas with a proud lift of his head, "I've no faith at all."

Captain Gilley drew from his waistcoat pocket a well-gnawed plug of tobacco and bit off a generous portion of it against his disappointment.

"Well, I don't take overmuch stock in myself as a prophet," he said, after he had revolved the tobacco about in his cheeks until he had it where he wanted it, "but I'm telling you tonight on my own deck that it's coming, same as the last trump. I know you deep-water fellows think there's nothing like over-crowded masts and fair winds, and I'm not saying that a ship before a good breeze ain't the prettiest thing God and man ever put together. But what if there ain't no winds? There's the crux of the matter in a nutshell. What if there ain't no winds? Sailing's a matter of luck if you ask me, Captain Crockett, and if luck's dead against you, what then? Haven't I spent days in the doldrums myself? God, haven't I? Haven't I sat for days on end without so much steerageway as a doughnut gets on a pan of hot grease? Haven't I fidgeted and prayed and bit my nails all to no purpose? There's days coming, young man, when the Atlantic Ocean to a steamer won't look no bigger than Penobscot Bay to a ship with a wind dead against her or no wind at all. But I see plain enough you don't believe it. And it's a free land. Suit yourself, sir. You can leave my words as well as take 'em."

Silas in his top hat drew himself even higher until his shoulders were at right angles with his neat cravat. He wondered why he even bothered to talk to such a chimerical old dreamer as Captain Gilley, and probably he would not have done so had not all the other passengers been within earshot.

"I'm not alone in my views," he said proudly. "All the best commanders I know look upon steam precisely as I do myself. Besides we've history and experience behind us. Look at the *Savannah* only a little more than ten years ago. It took her five weeks and more to make Cork, and she used her engines only eighty hours of all that time. She couldn't carry coal enough, and she'd be floating around today if her sails hadn't done the job. And that Dutch steamer three years ago that the whole world was watching. It took her a month to cross, and she'd never have done it on steam alone. Just compare those voyages with any one of the Black Ball sailing packets, Captain Gilley, or better still with the ships out of Boston for Liverpool. Just look at the *Emerald* in 1824, seventeen days from Liverpool to Boston Light. That's a voyage for you! Show me machinery that can beat a record like that. And when you come to talk of southern voyages, just remember that old steam-driven tub out of Falmouth for Calcutta five years ago—a nine-knot engine that never made over six, and one hundred and thirteen days to do it in. No, sir, I don't stand alone in my feeling about steam, and Boston merchants can talk all they like about a transatlantic line. If they're shipowners, they tell another story."

Impressed by the respectful, even awed silence accorded his words, young Silas cleared his throat and stroked his new side whiskers for his final triumph.

"And you can't tell me a thing about winds, Captain Gilley. I know them all, fair and foul and dead as Lazarus. When a man sails a ship, like mine for instance, he's got to have his stock of patience as well as his stock of wits. Sailing's not just luck. It takes all the stuff a man's got in him, and there's sure to be a wind some time as long as there's a God in heaven!"

He was not an overly pious young man, but the words sounded good ringing out there in the quiet cove with deferential women in shawls, held around them against the cool twilight air, and men staring above their pipes at Silas and doubtless realizing what the coast of Maine could produce in stalwart sea captains not yet twenty-three.

"Steam has its uses, I'm not gainsaying it. I've no doubt the day will come when more ships on the open sea carry it as an auxiliary to sail. And on a coast like this where you're hard put to it to use a wind even when you get it, a craft like yours surely has its uses. But not on the broad Atlantic and Pacific where clouds are the only coaling-stations you can fall back on."

Silas felt pleased enough with himself when after such a conversation as this on the last night of his journey he went back to his cabin to repack his bags and trunks and boxes against his morning's arrival at Saturday Cove. He could not sleep for excitement and kept his smelly swinging lantern burning far into the morning hours. He heard the calling of the peepers give place to the first song-sparrows and felt the *Island Maid* respond to her filthy boiler as soon as the fogless dawn began to outline the dark spruces along the rocky shore.

Now the future crowded out the past, stretching ahead of him with its luminous, endless days. He pictured the faces of Solace's parents and those of his own when they two should burst their secret—that Solace was going with him on the *Southern Seas*. The custom of taking wives to sea in 1830 was not common, even although certain intrepid Salem ladies had successfully undertaken all manner of voyages; and Silas well knew that his announcement would bring surprise and, perhaps, consternation in its wake. He wondered for the thousandth time what the future would hold for him and Solace, to what decisions he should come in order to make it yield its utmost for them both. How many years would he sail? Would he join some great merchant-shipping firm in Boston or Medford or Salem when he had the requisite capital from his voyages, some firm like that of Bromfield and Silsbee, which was known in Canton, Honolulu, and Calcutta as well as in Boston, and direct activities from on shore instead of pacing his own quarterdeck? That would mean a mansion on Summer Street in Boston or on Chestnut Street in Salem, a mansion of warm red brick, its gracious white door framed by sidelights and fanlight, its high rooms wainscotted and panelled, a garden at the rear with Solace in striped muslin from Bombay cutting her own lilacs and larkspur, irises and roses for the Chinese vases on her tables and in the corners of her hallways. Or should he make the boldest move possible and settle at last in Canton, say, perhaps, at thirty-five, become there a respected and wealthy foreign merchant like the Perkinses and Cushings of Boston, with a retinue of servants, an imported Boston coach and horses, and Solace to explain oriental ways to the wide-eyed women of incoming ships? The trouble was there were too many avenues open in those glowing days to a young man of enterprise, whose tight, deep pockets were refilled after each successful voyage and who had never yet known irremediable disaster. Of only one thing he was certain. He would not return at forty-five or fifty to Maine as so many men were doing, not to Saturday Cove as his own father had done, there to live in his great white house and look seaward upon a quiet ocean. Not he! The coast of Maine was a good place to come from but not to end one's days on when the whole world beckoned. Solace was of his own mind, too, he was glad to think, or would be when he had explained his ambitions. Naturally she might have misgivings, especially if the Canton plan seemed best (misgivings were but meet and right in women), only none so strong that they would not willingly yield to his wiser judgment in all matters.

At nine o'clock, after an hour's toilet and a vile breakfast, he was pacing the narrow deck of the *Island Maid*, his belongings in neat readiness, his heart thumping quickly beneath his new buff waistcoat which matched his hat and gloves. There was the thoroughfare, its blue waters cut here and there by lumber-laden coastwise vessels and smaller fishing-craft. Beyond its islands southward, lay the open ocean, northward, the irregular, jutting coastline with the May sunlight over it. There was something odd about Maine coast sunlight, thought Silas, something peculiar to itself. It had a way of outlining all things with itself, so that brown ledges and dark trees, the sails of passing vessels, the line of water against the rocks, even the wings of gulls, were edged with thin gold lines of light. He had never seen its like even under tropical skies. As a matter of fact, Solace had pointed it out to him in her last letter, which he had received upon his arrival in Boston and which now lay in the breast pocket of his new waistcoat.

"Now that the days are long," she had written, "everything shines with light. All the islands are framed in it. I have written for you some poor verses and called them 'The Shining Coast.' "

She had not sent him the verses, thinking them too poor and foolish, she had said, although she might be persuaded to show them to him. But he had generously told her he thought her adjective well-chosen, and now, as the *Island Maid* ploughed her way through the thoroughfare and rounded Sculpin Point, he felt increasingly sure of its aptitude.

Now Saturday Cove was in full view, its hills tumbling northward from the sea, its familiar fields and stone walls, its new white church which Solace's father had designed and built to take the place of the one which had burned two years before. The clatter of its shipyards was borne out to him. He could see the smoke rising from the wide chimneys of its white houses facing the sea along the road that framed its crescent harbour, his own home with wide open green shutters on the eastern point beneath its spreading elms. He could see carriages drawn up beside the wharf houses, and in a few minutes more he could discern the forms of people clustered about the pierhead. They were all there, down to meet him, he knew—to welcome him home. Deep within his new waistcoat he felt the thudding of his heart. The *Island Maid* drew nearer. He heard her engine throb and shorten, her bells sound; he saw her dirty crew crowd the rail with landing ropes ready. And as he wildly gathered up as many of his belongings as he could manage and hurried below, he saw a girl in wide blue skirts and a straw bonnet with blue ribbons hurrying toward the rattling gangplank followed by an older woman in black. At that moment thoughts of Canton wealth and of a Chestnut Street mansion fled and faded into forgetfulness, and young Captain Crockett was swept with dreadful perturbation as to what his mother and Solace might have to say about his new side whiskers.

2

Abigail Shaw Crockett had spent too many of her fifty-five years awaiting the return of some man or other in her family to be perturbed over such a trifling matter as the side whiskers of her youngest son. Of her three she had lost the eldest, Nicholas, at nineteen in 1820 from fever off the West African coast. A stone in the Saturday Cove churchyard recorded that simple and inescapable fact. Beside it a new stone, which she had stoutly deferred erecting for some eight years, was sacred to the memory of her second son, Reuben, who had been presumably lost at sea in 1822 when the brig *Kennebec* had disappeared somewhere in the wide waters she had so safely traversed for a quarter of a century. Even now she had fitful hopes about Reuben when she carried flowers to the yard on Saturday afternoons. Still, she told herself, with his prodigious appetite for her hot apple pies and doughnuts and his fondness for reading in bed during his brief stays at home, he would never have remained away from Saturday Cove had there been the slightest possibility of his return.

Abigail had begun her waiting young. Her father, Captain Reuben Shaw, had indirectly instilled the virtues of patience, serenity, common sense, and humour into his growing Salem family for twenty years before Abigail had arrived as his tenth and last child. He himself had been present at the birth only of his first and had found it a more harrowing experience than an onslaught by pirates off the Guinea Coast. During the successive advents of the nine following he had been "mercifully detained," in the words of his wife, at Surinam or Honduras or in the Mediterranean, returning when cargoes and wind permitted to view with pride the fruit of his loins and, after a brief season of proud parenthood, to depart again with a loaded ship, leaving Eliza Ann Shaw with yet another submissive expectation.

When, in 1775, Abigail had just made her appearance and the West Indian and foreign commerce had received a smart slap in the face by the Acts of Navigation and Trade, Captain Reuben Shaw turned gaily to privateering, adding money to his pockets, fame to his name, and an extra anxiety if possible to his wife and family. With capital of his own and a tenacity that brooked no discouragement, he weathered the lean years following the War of the Revolution when the maritime enterprise of Massachusetts feared its death blow, not disdaining for his part a bit of profitable smuggling now and then; and by 1786, in spite of the fact that few Salem shipmasters entered China by way of the Northwest route, he was hot after the new Canton trade around Cape Horn and the fur trading-posts of Puget Sound, Queen Charlotte Island, and Sitka.

As soon as Abigail could remember anything at all, she remembered above everything else departures and long-deferred returns—the departure of her four brothers here and there as soon as they were in their early teens, shipping before the mast, in accordance with their father's stout injunction, to the West Indies, to Charleston and other southern ports, to Brazil and Sumatra and Ceylon, the delayed or the surprisingly sudden returns of this one or that or of her father. She remembered the bang and clatter of scarred blue sea-chests, the easy, confident farewells, the verses of rollicking ballads and chanties sounding down the long, curved staircase of the patient, well-tried house, the piles of well-knit stockings and mittens against Arctic or Antarctic cold ready on the polished hall table beneath the gilded mirror, the anxious storing with pills and powders of small medicine boxes against Far Eastern chills and fever, the laughing deprecations of her mother's anxious warnings. She remembered the howling of winter blizzards when one or another of them was long overdue and her mother's face at supper in the light of the crystal candelabra, which her father had brought from some great house in Paris and which always tinkled in a summer wind from the garden. She never had forgotten the slow ebbing of the still October day when she had come home from Miss Mercy Pickering's School for Young Ladies to hear from the late return of his ship that her favourite brother Nathan had been killed in an untoward fracas with pirates at Analabu in the Malays. Nathan's prowess in fist-fights about the Salem wharves and yards had availed him little against the methods employed in the South Seas; and his fatal ignorance of Malay offensive and defensive art had left him at seventeen in warm Pacific waters with a Malay kreese between his ribs. In fact, Abigail's life as a child and young girl had been so dictated by the unpredictable circumstances of the most thriving seaport of New England, so well trained against surprise, so fraught with the certainty of uncertainty, that she did not hesitate to prolong its character when in 1796, at the somewhat advanced age of twenty-one, she fell in love at first sight with Captain James Crockett.

Her father had brought young Captain Crockett home with him, as unannounced as he himself, upon a return from Canton one evening in May, a return as casual as though he had spent the afternoon fishing in the North River. Abigail saw them mounting the brick steps between the curved iron railings to the high white doorway and, even before she called her mother, ran to tell the black cook to lay two more plates in the dining-room. With the boys no longer at home the household had missed the confusion which always attended a China return throughout the town, the noise and excitement in counting-rooms and yards and on the Derby wharf. And even if the salutes of answering guns from ship and harbour had greeted their ears, incoming ships in Salem in 1796 were too common to be taken over personally.

Captain James Crockett had himself arrived in Boston but two days ago after thirty months away. He had been bartering with Northwest savages for the skins of sea otter, seal, and beaver which they were ready to exchange for blue duffle trousers, iron chisels, pocket mirrors, scarlet cloth, and blunderbusses; had completed his cargo with sandalwood from the Pacific islands, and had at last made for Canton where mandarins were avid for the glossy, jet-black furs of the sea otter and paid fifty dollars apiece for them. It was a poor shipmaster who could not make a sweeping profit from such a voyage, he told the Shaws after dinner as they sipped their wine in the candlelight of the high, wainscotted parlour. There was no hurry about it, as Reuben Shaw well knew. As one waited for furs, a year, perhaps eighteen months even, there was always the chance of a bit of trading along the coast of Spanish California and the adjacent islands. And a man would be a fool, once in Canton, if he disdained a journey here and there for some Chinese merchants.

He had kept his eyes on Abigail as he said these things, she in a gown of pale green India muslin cut low in the neck with frills of white edging the tight bodice. She worked at making lace with her shuttle and crochet hook as he talked and thought him a fine young man even though he came from a far outpost of Massachusetts, Saturday Cove on the coast of Maine. He wore his hair short and carried his head high above the upstanding velvet collar of his coat of fine blue broadcloth and his ruffled snowy cravat. He had a way of fumbling with the knee buttons of his fawn-coloured breeches or with the single brass button on either tail of his coat which he kept wrapping about his thighs—habits which perhaps betokened, she thought, not all the confidence in self which he was assuming. The lace ruffles, which fell over his brown hands from beneath his coat sleeves, seemed oddly at variance with the fights against Chinook Indians which he had been recounting.

There was a persuasion about him, common to the Crocketts as she was later to discover. He in some unique way penetrated to the farthest corners of the room so that even the shadowy pictures on the walls, the mirrors, the bracket vases, and the flowered chintzes drawn across the windows seemed well aware of him. He was more alive than any person she had ever known, a disturbing lodestone to her thoughts that night in her four-posted bed, so that her future stretched inevitably before her when on an afternoon a fortnight later he had offered her his heart and hand under the lilacs and syringas of the Salem garden. He might carry her body with him to Saturday Cove or to any other place he wanted and her heart to all diverse corners of the world. And as a substantial portion of her dowry she herself had carried to Saturday Cove those very virtues of patience, serenity, common sense, and humour which her life, her time, and her environment had made a part of her.

In a swift, kaleidoscopic train of images these things passed through her mind as she looked upon young Silas on the pierhead in the spring sun and wind. He was standing with his left arm masterfully around the slender waist of Solace Winship whose blue bonnet ribbons fluttered about her pink cheeks, while with his right hand he greeted all the multifarious townspeople down to welcome him. That was like Silas, she thought, to be as bold and adventurous about his love as about his sailing. It was like all the Crocketts she had ever known. She herself held Silas' hat amid the good-natured, bantering comments of their neighbors. She vowed that Silas had grown even since his twenty-first birthday. He towered above his father, himself a tall man with all the shrinkage that invariably attacked one in the sixties. He was thin as a fence-rail, thinner than Nicholas had ever been in spite of all her feeding. Reuben had been stocky like the Shaws with short legs and an inexhaustible appetite. Abigail thought with grateful complacence of her well-stored larder, her pies and tarts, doughnuts and pound cakes, her chickens stuffed and ready for the oven, her roast of beef, her vegetables peeled and waiting in vats of cold water, and of her buttery with its pans of rising cream, its globes of fresh butter and crocks of curd cheese. She was glad that early dandelions had filled with wine the bottles along her neat cellar shelves. Dandelion wine, she knew, not infrequently put an edge on one's appetite. She had not risen one minute too early, she thought, to put all things in readiness. And as luck would have it, Silas had done well to arrive on a Wednesday when the washing and the ironing were well out of the way.

"Your father's in Machias," she said when she could get a word in edgewise through all the chatter. "If this boat ever makes Eastport, which I doubt, he'll come back on her day after tomorrow. He took yesterday's stagecoach though I told him he shouldn't. He said you wouldn't hold it against him, and I could get my talking all done. There's a launching over there—some ship he's taken shares in, though why only he and the good Lord know. They hatch up schemes together, those two, and leave poor women folks to wonder at their nonsense."

As she spoke them, she thought her words perhaps too daring in the presence of the pastor, the Reverend Ethan Fisher, who had himself come down to the pier to welcome home this young man of his flock. Had she uttered them, she wondered, in conscious defiance of the over-long sermon he had preached on Sunday last—a sermon in solemn warning against the jocoseness and blasphemy of many a seacoast town? The world was changing overnight, he had said, and not for the best with its means of transportation growing by leaps and bounds, and its boisterous singing-schools in too many places encroaching upon the evening prayer-meetings. He feared for the future of the young men and women of this perfidious generation, their future in this wicked world, their far more portentous future in the next. His ears had been so assailed by the profanity of the shipyards and the careless, forward speech and behavior of certain young females walking in God's acre on Sabbath afternoons that he had felt the urgent need of supplicating his Saviour through many a sleepless night. She had listened to his tirade without a single misgiving in her mind, glad that she had kneaded her loaves and set her bread to rise on Sunday morning, instead of on Saturday night as was usually her custom. As for James' mind as he sat in the corner of their pew, she knew full well that that was securely anchored to the cradle of the new ship awaiting her launching in Machias Bay.

Mr. Fisher belonged, she had always affirmed, rather to an inland parish than to one on the coast where morals were always more flexible in conception and application, and where men who had sailed the Seven Seas were inclined to take a chance on the vengeance of God against an idle word now and then. Mr. Fisher's two sons, who were delving into theology at Harvard College, were but languid and feeble samples of young manhood when compared with Silas, and she could but wonder if he were aware of the astonishing difference. And if he saw fit to send her an admonition as he had an irritating way of doing, a pious reminder of the influence her light words might imprint upon the budding thoughts of the young people on the pier—well, in that case she was not such a poor hand with the pen herself.

3

Fully an hour had elapsed before Silas helped his mother into the family carriage and picked up the reins to drive her homeward. Solace had already gone with her own parents after some last whispered injunctions beneath her new bonnet to come early for dinner. Besides the manifold greetings there had been hundreds of questions and answers pertaining to his voyage out and back, his ports of call, his cargoes, the ships he had spoken, chance news of this one and that. He had delivered letters entrusted to his earlier passage by Saturday Cove men and boys whom he had met in Honolulu, Whampoa, or Canton on one ship or another, or who had hastily penned their words while he good-naturedly waited in mid-ocean where the *Southern Seas*, heading westward, had hailed them eastward bound. For in 1830 the village of Saturday Cove was neither well-nigh deserted in the winter nor in the summer dependent upon the bank accounts of New York and Middle Western millionaires. It was instead an integral part of the world at large, supplying ships for every ocean and men and boys who knew even the Ultima Thules of six continents far better than they knew the wharves and piers of Portland.

They drove slowly over the clattering wharf-planks, up the rocky road that led behind them to the pier, and along the broad main street between its white houses and beneath its elms eastward toward their own home. The sea sparkled before and beside them, its spruce-laden islands dark in the blue water. In the distance behind one of these a trail of brown smoke gave proof that the *Island Maid*, still afloat, was plunging on toward Machias Bay and Eastport. Silas, still sure that he held the world in his hands, felt his secrets tumbling about pellmell within him, restless for utterance. He was even a bit irritated with his mother who at the outset created the most unsuitable atmosphere for their disclosure.

"There's a new stone for Reuben in the yard," she was saying. "I came to it at last. Your father was set on an anchor, but I held out for a plain slab like Nicholas', and at last he gave in though I never thought he would. I'm not for these fancy, overdone things myself."

Silas, not looking at his mother, felt uneasy. Still some reply was clearly necessary.

"That's right. I like plain things myself. I'll go with you on Saturday to view it. Thomas Winship has done well by the new meeting-house, hasn't he?"

It was great good fortune, he thought, that they were passing the meeting-house at that moment. It stood opposite the grassy churchyard at the top of the hill above the village at just the point where their road turned southward. Only three weeks before, it had been dedicated with a minister imported from Boston to assist the Reverend Mr. Fisher and three barrels of rum to lighten up later the solemnity of the occasion. It was a beautiful building, Abigail Crockett said, suggesting that they stop the horse to look at it, and Silas reluctantly pushed more importunate matters back into his mind and looked with her.

The meeting-house was beautiful. Like many of its date along the coast it had been designed and constructed by a local builder, in its own case by Solace's father, Thomas Winship. A ship's carpenter for twenty years of his life, he had left the sea to satisfy his passion for building, and a dozen or more of the white clapboarded and red-brick houses of Saturday Cove owed their gracious dignity to his imagination and stubby pencil. Into his work he had wrought details of the buildings he had seen throughout the world, Greek temples, English cathedrals, Georgian mansions, Roman columns and porticoes, so that his new white church, looking seaward from Saturday Cove, bore evidence of an assimilation common to a hundred other rural builders along the coast of Maine. Maine pine trees had formed the four Doric columns which gave entrance to its wide porch; Maine spruce had shaped its tapering spire into almost the exact semblance of a certain English cathedral spire which he had once spent hours in drawing after an eager journey by coach while his ship lay in Southampton Water; the notched inner edges of its wide, triangular pediment were reminiscent of the decorative art of churches in Normandy and Aquitaine; and the high, severe, many-paned windows on either side of its panelled doors beyond their grooved pilasters suggested Old England as well as New. In it Sir Christopher Wren lived again,

Samuel McIntyre, Charles Bulfinch, and other builders now nameless whose homes and churches and public buildings Thomas Winship had studied with an eye to shrewd and reverent emulation. For the New England meeting-house in its best and noblest form is an incorporation, a unification, a synthesis of the art and the architecture of many centuries, many lands, and many peoples.

Neither Silas nor Abigail Crockett thought of these things as they looked while the old horse cropped the fresh roadside grass. They knew nothing of the sources of Thomas Winship's plans which had kept him in a fever of excitement for more than two years. They only knew that the meeting-house lent dignity and charm to Saturday Cove and that the Crockett-Winship families would be vastly honoured by supplying the first wedding to be held within its walls. As for Silas, he was relieved by the change in conversation which the meeting-house afforded and waited only an easy and natural progress from the builder to the builder's daughter before he should burst upon his mother the chief of his turbulent secrets.

"As a plain matter of fact," she said as they drove on, "Dorcas Winship has had about as much to do with the framing of that meeting-house as Thomas. She says Thomas has been fairly out of his head for two years, talking in his sleep of joists and beams and what-not, and night after night leaving her to go downstairs to work and figure out something or other. He's not been punctual to his meals for a year, she says. When the last coat of paint was put on a month back, she took the coach for Calais to visit her sister, fair frayed out. But there! She'll not get the credit for so much as a ten-penny nail!"

"It's doubtless been hard on Solace, too," assayed Silas. "I think myself she's looking a bit peaked."

"I shouldn't wonder. A family that's raised a meeting-house and married a daughter within a twelvemonth has had a chore on its hands. But she's been able to place her mind elsewhere, and it's that that counts. She'll freshen up in the summer and fall and when she's settled down for the winter after you are gone. When are you off again, Silas, and where are you bound for?"

"We sail in three weeks," he said, with just a hint of misgiving intruding upon his excitement. He knew that the full extent of his pronoun had not reached his mother. "I've picked up my cargo already, and it's East again I'm going. There's no trade these years like the Canton, mother. I'm doing well and I'll be doing better. Father'll be surprised when I tell him about my profits on this voyage alone."

They were turning then into the driveway of bleached gravel and clam-shells that led to the white house. They passed its apple orchard showing pink among pale green leaves, the budding lilacs of its lawn and doorways. A few moments and the horse was crossing the threshold of the great red barn, whose wide-open back doors framed a view of green meadows stretching to the marshes, cut now by blue lanes of tidewater. The sun was high and warm, penetrating through the windows of the loft so that it lay in shafts of light upon the dusty floor. The mows on either side of them above the weathered timberposts were crammed with sun-flecked hay, and a contented old hen was clucking to her brood as she pecked among the chaff and seed beneath a blue farm wagon in one corner. From the dusty rafters high above their heads some pigeons were cooing, their murmuring, minor notes echoing about beneath the pointed roof-slope and among the dim corners hung with cobwebs.

They sat for some moments in silence in the carriage, looking through the open doors upon the quiet fields where some cows were feeding against the time when the pasture grass was higher. Abigail felt the warm security of the barn enfolding her. It was well, she thought, that the end of one's long journey home should be begun in such a cheerful, familiar place. She glanced toward

Silas, sure that he, too, shared her feeling, but she met instead his major secret coming straight from his eyes into her own.

"I'm taking Solace with me, in the ship, when I sail,"

"To Canton."

She said the words quietly. There seemed no reason to make a question of them against the finality in Silas' statement. She was not even sure that she was surprised by them.

"Does she know it?"

"Of course," returned Silas with some asperity in his voice. "Of course, she knows it. I shan't look upon my wife as something to be carried around just as I please with no thought of her. In that I'm not like many men, I'm glad to say. She's willing and glad to go with me. She says she'd rather go with me to the ends of the earth than wait for me here in Saturday Cove."

"In that," observed Abigail, watching the old hen and wondering how on earth she had ever managed to escape from her carefully placed coop, "in that she is a wise young woman, Silas, far wiser than she knows."

"I suppose," said Silas, "her father and mother are going to be taken aback when they know. Will they mind overmuch, do you think?"

As he put the question, he was divided between concern for the distress of Solace's parents and his own pleasant sense of being the master of an acute situation.

Abigail lowered the carriage steps and gathered her wide skirts about her in preparation for her descent.

"Well," she said, "I don't presume they're hankering to commit their only child to the mercy of winds and water, so to speak, even with you to look after her, Silas. No Crockett's exactly like the Lord in Heaven, you know. There is a little difference between them. But I don't presume either that what fretting's done will be done in the open for you two to see, and people in places like this don't take too much stock in the plans they make for their children, that is, if they've got sense, they don't."

She turned her back on Silas, clutching the seat railing and feeling for the first of the steps. On the last one she turned toward him again.

"Dorcas Winship will say it's the will of God. That woman knows more about the will of God than God Himself knows. And Thomas is building a new meeting-house at Jonesport so he'll be away half the fall and winter. Your father won't be too set up by the news. We were lotting on having Solace with us six months of the year. I told her last winter to save turning some of her sheets and to keep her quilting for us to do together."

She moved toward the door leading into the shed with its neat piles of firewood.

"I'm glad you've got some healthy notions about women folks, Silas, and a few scattering claims they might have. Last winter a fashion book from Boston published an essay on how women ought to know things about their husbands' business, their money and so on. I thought it sound sense myself. I read it to your father. He nearly burst a blood vessel. He said 'twas fortunate only a fashion paper had it so that it would be out of the sight of most men. He said ideas like that were as revolutionary as all this talk about steam propelling ships across the Atlantic."

Silas heard his mother sweep through shed and toolhouse to her kitchen, caught the sound of the oven door opening and closing before her scrutinizing eyes and of her voice giving brisk comments and orders to the maidservant. He stood in the open back doorway of the barn for some minutes after he had called the hired man from the garden to come and look after the horse. The trilling of the redwinged blackbirds swaying on the reeds and cattails of the upper marshes in the sunlight was sweet to his ears, but sweeter far were the sounds from the invisible shores of the cove—the thudding and clanging of the hammers in the yards against wood and iron, the grinding of derricks and pulleys, the distant shouts of shipwrights and labourers.

They were building ships. Ships to cut the waters that encircled every continent, ships which he and Solace would overhaul and hail in passing, ships manned and mastered by the best of men. Their fresh holds would lose the odour of new wood for the fragrance of tea and spices and India coffee, the sharp, acrid smell of lemons and oranges from the Mediterranean, smells of dried fish, of rum and gin and Cadiz salt, of sugar and molasses and Sumatran pepper, of Portugal and Madeira wines, of hides and tobacco, of sperm from the South Seas and tallow from Madagascar. Their white canvas would grow gray and yellow in wind and rain, become patched and mildewed; their straight, untried yards and spars would bend and creak in gales off the Horn, in long, fair days before the trades and northeast monsoons. Their new bottoms above their copper sheathing would grow green and brown and gold from the vegetation of many a warm harbour; the gay colours of their figureheads, angels and mermaids and dolphins, would fade in mighty onslaughts of spray.

It was good to be at home, he thought, but better to go away again beyond the reach of hills and islands, trees and houses, and best of all to see, stretching endlessly ahead, long years flexible to one's strength and ambition, yielding their gifts and treasures as one willed and desired them to do.

4

Thomas and Dorcas Winship did not dampen the home-coming dinner-party by the unbecoming show of any feelings of their own when their future son-in-law made his somewhat peremptory announcement concerning their daughter. He made it from his father's place at the head of the table with Solace at his right in a gown of deep blue challis with silk cordings of rose at neck and wrists. And as he made it, Abigail studied Solace's face and saw therein more pride in Silas than sorrow for her parents. That had been the way, too, with her, she remembered, thirty years and more ago when James Crockett had snatched her to Saturday Cove away from her mother who had no other children left in the great Salem house. That was the ruthless way of young love, especially so when a Crockett fired it within one. Thomas Winship said nothing at all, both because he was by nature a man of few words and because there was clearly nothing to say. He only drank more deeply from his tall glass mug of home-brewed beer, setting it down somewhat finally upon the table. Dorcas paled a little as she fumbled uncertainly with a wing of chicken, then said she presumed that since it was to be, it was to be, and that was that. She did not bring her God into the matter just then, possibly because He seemed out of place at Abigail Crockett's groaning table; but Abigail knew He was in the offing and would appear whenever she and Dorcas were alone together. All in all, the announcement was quickly made and as quickly put out of sight, much as a parcel is hastily opened, surveyed by those interested, and then as hastily wrapped again to be re-opened and examined with greater care when leisure and solitude permit.

The dinner was as bountiful as the Maine coast could produce upon a suitable occasion in the year 1830 when diets and dietitians were alike relatively unknown and when few imaginations could unhappily depict the lurid transformations in the stomach of starches and sugars. Abigail Crockett had arrayed her long, broad table with damask from afar off, a cloth that trailed upon her wide floorboards, and napkins that covered cravats and waistcoats and spread safely over voluminous skirts. Her great plates of blue China ware with mandarins and rivers and pagodas weighed precisely three pounds each before they were heaped with roast beef, sausages and chicken, browned batter puddings, sage dressing, fried apples and onions, mashed potatoes and squash and turnip, currant jelly and damson, all encircled and set about with rivers and pools of thick, steaming gravy. More plates were piled with raised biscuits, brown and light, and golden squares of Indian bannock. There were dishes of pickled pears, spiced crab-apples, and brandied peaches; there were mugs of beer and decanters of port and claret and sherry to fill the manifold array of goblets and glasses at each place; there were pitchers of milk and pitchers of cream and huge bowl-shaped cups to be filled and refilled with the best of coffee. And when an hour had elapsed of partial demolishment, there came from the kitchen mince pies and apple with accompanying wedges of yellow cheese, steamed cranberry puddings with spiced cream sauce, and great slabs of fruit cake encrusted an inch thick with white icing flavoured with almond and bristling with walnuts.

Silas missed his father after dinner was over. Had he been present to take a turn in the fields and pastures and about the yards with Thomas Winship, Silas might have sat with Solace on the haircloth sofa, saying all the things he had stored up to say and many that he had not. But he as the only son of the house knew his manners too well to neglect a guest. He did not propose a walk, feeling that an unnecessary courtesy in the presence of his sweetheart; but he smoked several pipes with Thomas, sitting in their high-backed chairs on either side of the great fireplace, which Abigail Crockett had filled with branches of budding lilacs, while Solace did some fine hemstitching in a corner by the window. Dorcas Winship assisted Abigail in the dining-room in putting away her linen and silver while the maidservant cleared the table and busied herself in the kitchen.

Thomas Winship was not an easy man to talk with, his terse rejoinders being far more plentiful than his sparse assertions. Nor was he given to helpful questioning. But Silas did his best, noting meanwhile how the sun, swinging westward, lay on Solace's neatly parted hair, how her breath rose and fell beneath her tight blue bodice, and how her wide blue skirts made a great semi-circle before the low stool upon which she sat.

"I met a young fellow in Boston," Silas said, "who impresses me as a man with a future. He's barely twenty, I should think. He came up from New York where he's working in the Webb yards, learning his trade, he told me, but he'll go far beyond that. He's a Scotchman from the blue-nose country where he was born and raised. I never saw a man who knew so much about ships in my life. From what he had in his pockets you'd think he spent all his off time drawing models. He came to a dinner in Boston and sat next me, never speaking a word till dinner was over. Then he spread out some papers he had on the table and began to talk about some plans he'd made. He had every man around him in five minutes. Some of the old ones said he was crazy, only they listened just the same, and a builder from a Newburyport yard offered him a place then and there, but he only laughed and said he wasn't ready. He had a lot to learn first, he said. He believes you can build a heavy ship for just as much speed as a lighter one. He's all for sharp lines and high rigging, ships like the Baltimore clippers only with five times the tonnage. He claims that sharper ships can work out to windward in strong head gales better than full-built vessels just as they can use light winds and calm better. He says fair winds don't prove anything—it's the ships that can make record passages with things dead against them that matter. If he does as much in the next ten years as he seems to be doing now, I believe the world's going to hear from him. His name's McKay, Donald's his first name, and he looks like a Scotchman."

Thomas Winship grunted behind his pipe in assent to Silas' long speech. Silas had been, in fact, saving it for his father whose interest he could depend upon, and he felt a bit disgruntled at Thomas Winship's lack of eagerness. Still manners were manners.

"I don't believe he'll stay long in New York," he continued after an overlong silence. "It doesn't seem the place for him. He belongs in Boston or Salem where they care more about the ships themselves than the cargoes they bring in. A Nova Scotian is more at home in New England if you ask me."

As a matter of fact, Thomas Winship had asked nothing at all of his future son-in-law. He sat in his high-backed chair quietly smoking his pipe. He was a small, smooth-shaven man with a peculiarly round head on which his thin gray hair was parted just above his left ear. He wore tiny oblong spectacles with steel rims halfway down a decisive hooked nose, and his small gray eyes blinked keenly above them at Silas. His neat black clothes were poorly made, and as he sat in his chair with his short legs extended before him, one could see that his knees were bowed. His short, square hands were seamed and scarred from many years of handling wood and tools. Silas wondered as he looked at him just where within his squat, capable frame there lodged the ideas and the visions which built meeting-houses and conceived the lines and decorations lending beauty to the roofs and doorways of Saturday Cove. He wondered, too, how such a man could ever have been the father of a girl like Solace. Determined to elicit some response, he plied him with a question.

"Are there blue-noses in the yards here, sir?"

Thomas Winship filled his pipe with undue deliberation while Silas fidgeted with his own.

"Now and again," he said, since there was no escape. "Shivery fellows with eyes that water."

After ten minutes' silence Silas tried him again, this time on the profits which might be indefinitely pyramided from a successful voyage to Canton and back, profits from wages and shares, profits from private adventuring in buying on one's own. Here he made more headway, Thomas Winship's shrewd mind even becoming tempted occasionally to a question. Now that they spoke of money, an invisible barrier shut out Solace and her hemstitching. For in 1830 all matters of gain or loss, investment and expenditure, were, in spite of the daring essay in the fashion magazine, a purely masculine province, as was tacitly proved by a lowering of their voices and a confidential leaning forward in their chairs.

Silas was vastly relieved when at five o'clock Thomas Winship summoned his wife from her sewing in the garden with Abigail and made his laconic farewells. Solace was to stay for a supper of cold joint and chicken, warmed-over vegetables, more pie and cake. Now Silas felt his old exuberance flooding back upon him. He ran up and down the broad staircase which swept in graceful curves from front hall to back, strewed the parlour with his bags and boxes, while Abigail joined them to look askance upon the litter of her tidy room, and Solace's blue eyes grew rounder every moment.

The tea-set first. He spread it piece by piece upon the round centre-table, cups and saucers of rose and green and gold, flowers flecked with sun amid a wilderness of leaves, butterflies of raised gold flake poised above them, fragile plates that became transparent in the light from the western windows so that they made shining globes within the polished table, a teapot with cover and surmounting knob of gold so frail that Abigail felt glad *she* was not called upon to wash it and said so. Then the perfumed soaps that made the warm air sweet with cinnamon and sandalwood, and the tapering scent-bottles for Solace's dressing-table (when she was once at home long enough to have a dressing-table, Abigail thought) and the yards of silk and satin and damask with which

Silas draped the chair backs, holding up each length before he did so for delighted inspection—shimmering folds of satin like moonlight on still water, green and gold and blue, and silks made heavy with sprigs and bouquets and wreaths of flowers. The shawls came next, of finest cashmere, their deep borders woven with strands of blue and orange into dragons and spirals and strange foreign birds with spreading tails ending in fringes which swept the floor from Solace's shoulders as Silas draped her in one after another.

"There's nothing like cashmere to attract moths," said Abigail. "You leave them here with me, Solace, and I'll pack them in cedar and camphor."

"Carry the blue one with you," commanded Silas. "There'll be dinners in Boston before we go. I've already promised your presence. And who knows what in Canton? Those Hong merchants are forever giving parties, and I want my wife the best dressed woman in China. If the moths eat it, we'll buy another for a song."

Abigail left them before the big, canvas-wrapped case which contained Solace's dressing-gown was undone. She had her supper to see to, she said. She discreetly closed the door into the parlour as she went out, knowing full well that there would be secret preliminaries to the revealing of this chief of Silas' wedding gifts. These were so long and tender and foolish that supper was ready and announced by the time Solace stood arrayed in the blue brocaded gown in the middle of the room.

She was all that Silas had ever dreamed of and more in the new gown. Its high collar, richly brocaded in gold and silver, reached almost to the crown of her fair, plaited head; its stiff, billowing folds swept about her over her blue challis skirts; her hands were lost in its wide sleeves, the insides of which were smocked to the elbows in gold and silver threads. Her cheeks were pinker than the rose of its cherry blossoms and the pupils of her eyes even bigger than they had been a moment before from his kisses. As he looked upon her, he saw her, not in Saturday Cove but in the imposing bed-chambers of the homes of Boston merchants in Canton or London or Calcutta, wherever the *Southern Seas* might carry her and him. The swishing rustle of the silk filled the house as, scorning the more direct entrance to the dining-room, he led her on his arm down the long hallway between its candle sconces, its gilt-framed steel engravings of Blenheim and of the Pilgrim Fathers, its shining stands and tables, its multiplicity of mirrors.

Abigail Crockett awaited them behind her second-best tea service, white with tiny sprigs of palest green, which James Crockett had brought her from some foreign port or other. For a moment Silas thought his mother had been crying, but his notion was almost instantly lost in her delighted astonishment over Solace in his gift. Grief of any sort found small soil for nourishment while Solace with her silks rising about her filled the great armchair, which, Silas decided, was the only suitable place for her. And even compassion for youth and its transitory beauty was obliged to take a back seat in Abigail Crockett's mind, which was hard put to it throughout supper to guard Solace's wide sleeves and ample, brocaded bosom from warmed-over chicken gravy and her best blackberry preserves.

5

A wedding of importance in any prosperous shipbuilding town in 1830 was destined by the very circumstances of its time and environment to be something of an hilarious occasion. In this respect the Crockett-Winship nuptials were no exception to the rule in spite of the Reverend Ethan Fisher, who did his utmost to instill into the contracting parties meet solemnity and a proper sense of holiness. In response to his summons and in deference to the uneasy custom of the day, he had received the bride and the bridegroom the evening before in his sombre study, and, with the aid of the Apostle Paul, had enjoined upon them both the sacred nature of their union. Sitting circumspectly apart before him, his black clothes adding rigidity to his searching eyes and inexorable chin, they had listened to the grave accents of his voice reading from the epistles to the Corinthians and the Ephesians:

Let the husband render unto the wife due benevolence; and likewise also the wife unto the husband.

The wife hath not power of her own body, but the husband; and likewise also the husband hath not power of his own body, but the wife.

Defraud ye not one the other, except it be with consent for a time, that ye may give yourselves to fasting and prayer.

Solace felt her cheeks grow pink in the flickering candlelight of the high, austere room, and Silas in his heart of hearts scorned the Reverend Mr. Fisher, who enjoined upon a man aboard a ship such a senseless practice as fasting and such an inconvenient one as prayer.

Wives, submit yourselves unto your own husbands, as unto the Lord.

For the husband is the head of the wife, even as Christ is the head of the church. . . .

Therefore as the church is subject unto Christ, so let the wives be to their own husbands in everything.

Husbands, love your wives, even as Christ also loved the church, and gave himself for it.

So ought men to love their wives as their own bodies.

Small need, thought Silas, to issue such commands to him. In the brief moments when Mr. Fisher refreshed his almost perfect memory by a peep at the holy book before him, Silas glanced furtively at Solace sitting primly in her dark clothes in a corner chair. She looked ill at ease, half-frightened, as the pastor's solemn words resounded through the still room. He would make things right with her, he thought, once he had gotten her away from this rigid, unnatural atmosphere where marriage was made to seem a fearsome state, weak at its best and probably, taken by and large, sinful in the extreme. He could hear the peepers and the tree-toads calling through the dusk, and through the blackened windows could see how the moon, sailing in a clear sky, gave promise of a fair tomorrow.

For this cause shall a man leave his father and mother, and shall be joined unto his wife, and they two shall be one flesh.

Completing his readings with King Solomon's description of the virtuous woman in the *Proverbs*, the Reverend Mr. Fisher slowly closed the book with awe in his very fingers, concluded this rather cheerless visit by half an hour of prayer against all manner of sins, temptations, and perils, the three of them on their knees the while, and at length brought his solemn duty to a welcome close by presenting as his wedding gift a volume of Jonathan Edwards on "Religious Affections." Silas would gladly have thrown the book in the high water of the cove as he took Solace homeward on his protecting arm had she not looked upon the wanton destruction of such a title with a kind of superstitious fear.

Silas knew no fears or superstitions. The day began precisely as he had expected it, the early sky deep gold across the reaches of dark blue water, the marshes and meadows green and still beneath the dawn, a brisk northwest wind rising with the sun to stir and then to toss the fullblown lilacs just below his windows. He watched the distant incoming tide catch the wind and sunlight, saw how the sea broke into sparkling ripples before them both and how the small boats in the cove recovered themselves from the flats and floated straight and clear at their moorings. He could not sleep and, long before the house was early astir, was striding along the field path that encircled the cove, his mind crowded with his dreams of a thrice glorious future.

The shipyards were silent on this morning of the wedding. Captain James Crockett as chief owner had declared a half-holiday with bounteous measures of grog all around and, through Thomas Winship's permission, a general invitation to the reception at which, it was rightly assumed, there would be more to drink and plenty to eat. The old bells in the new church spire began to ring at nine o'clock, sounding out over the meadows and the sea to the islands, from the larger of which boats began to put shoreward. By seven the young ladies of Saturday Cove were flanking the pulpit with lilacs, purple and white, and with great boughs of fresh apple-blossoms.

Miss Serena Osgood superintended the decoration. She wore a somewhat conscious smile of patient resignation beneath her wide straw bonnet and was not unaware of the whispered comments of her assistants. Miss Serena at eighteen had been promised to young Nicholas Crockett, and although West African fever had ousted her claims upon him, she was at thirty still his at heart. A century ago there was no one to diagnose Serena's complaint as a martyr complex or to suggest new interests, perhaps even a *mariage de convenance*, to free her repressions. Instead, her intimates wondered over their needlework at her extreme fortitude in so weathering her sorrow that she had escaped a decline into quick consumption. She was bearing up well, they said to one another, glancing at her with pitying eyes as she stood in the back of the church to survey their carefully placed flowers, although they well knew that a knife must every moment be piercing her incorruptible heart. Nor was Serena's dilemma unique in Saturday Cove or in scores of other seaport villages where yellow jack and breakers, pirates and gales, took their tolls, leaving many a maiden with memories, old letters, and locks of hair to add to the romantic glamour of time, place, and circumstance.

By nine o'clock the young ladies were scurrying down the greensward before the church, their wide, bright calico skirts billowing about them in the brisk wind, their bonnet ribbons fluttering with the fringes of their shoulder capes. They had just time to dress before the pealing bells at ten o'clock should summon them again churchward.

Solace was already dressing or being dressed by her mother and Miss Poppet, the best seamstress in Saturday Cove, who had made a four-day journey to and from Boston at Thomas Winship's expense to study the latest models in wedding finery. Solace's breath was coming and going thick and fast beneath her tight lacing; her cheeks needed no last judicious pinching to make them glow; there was about her the fragrance of perfumed soap from her bath in the Winship kitchen, which had been hurriedly cleared of extra help for the performance of this necessary rite. Once clothed, she would place the tiniest drop of scent from one of Silas' purple bottles in the hollow of her throat.

Upon the quilted spread of her great bed rose her wedding-gown of sheerest muslin, its skirt, which was designed to spread four feet in radius from either one of her dainty feet, flounced in six flounces, its bodice tight over breast and shoulders only to swell out again into the three great balloon-like puffs which formed the sleeves, finest shirring between the puffs, finest lace from elbow to wrist. On either side billowed her petticoats, clouds of cambric and lawn stiffened to give the necessary width to her skirts. Her bonnet of leghorn, bleached to the whiteness of her gown, surmounted one of the posts of her bed, its muslin frill encircling her cheeks set cunningly here and there by tiny rose-buds of satin in palest pink, its broad ribbons pale pink also. Its brim swept high above her parted hair, its sides encircled the curls above her ears; and from its white satin crown there extended into the air a spray of three full-blown roses over which Miss Poppet had spent many a restless night. Her white satin slippers with roses encircling the insteps and bands of pink to cross above her ankles stood uncertainly upon the table by her bed; her plumed fan of palest pink lay beside them with her white kid gloves, wristed in pink satin, and her handkerchief, her mother's gift, edged with a four-inch border of finest tatting. Over a high-backed chair by the door, ready for her nervous departure, was spread a pelisse of white merino lined with pink, its wide-winged cape bordered in swansdown. And over all the great room, streaming through its many-paned windows on the wide floorboards and braided mats, on the rose-strewn walls between their multiplicity of pictures, lay the bright sunlight of a wedding day that had never been surpassed by the favour of the combined heavenly host!

Solace was driven to the church in a closed coach freshly painted in palest yellow with wheels and axle-trees of green, an equipage which had been recklessly bought the year before at an auction sale in Machias by the proprietor of the inn at Saturday Cove. He had designed his purchase for just such an occasion as this and gave thanks as he superintended the attaching of his four best horses that the building of several meeting-houses had expanded Thomas Winship's circumspect mind together with his black-banded leather wallet. The driver of the coach was in full green and yellow livery as at quarter before ten he swung out of the bustling stable yard in delighted view of half the village. So was the footman on the box behind, high-hatted, in yellow breeches and green tailed coat, blowing his red-tasselled horn and laughing all over his florid cheeks as he motioned little girls in pinafores and small boys in tight trousers and short jackets to get out of his cluttering dusty path. The road was lined with onlookers ready to close in behind the coach and to cluster about the Winship picket fence for the first glimpse of the bride before hurrying ahead up the hill toward the church.

Thomas Winship had new black clothes for the occasion and to the astonishment of all, as he solemnly led his blushing daughter to the coach, a fine ruffled cravat. Dorcas was in lilac taffeta with a bonnet of pale gray surmounted and set about and tied with broad lilac ribbons. The bridles and the saddle rings of the white horses leading were adorned with purple lilacs and of the bay horses behind with plumes of white. Their tails were knotted with white ribbons and their polished hooves beat rhythmically through the stones and dust as they trotted along the village street and strained churchward up the hill. The village trooped before them, swaying in wide lawn skirts and bright parasols, hastening in tall hats and tailed coats, bright waistcoats and gold-headed canes. Children in tulle and lawn and muslin, gold-braided coats and trousers of fawn and plum colour threw flowers in the way. These were prosperous days in Saturday Cove, and everyone was in gala attire for a gala occasion.

The wedding itself was all that Saturday Cove had hoped and expected. Silas was an unexcelled bridegroom in his trousers of palest cream strapped neatly below his polished shoes, in his bright blue coat of finest broadcloth and his cream waistcoat of finest satin, in his cream gloves and cravat of cream-coloured silk set with a Chinese dragon in turquoise. He towered above his bride precisely as a man should tower as he led her down the church aisle between the high white pews with their mahogany railings and panelled doors to stand with her before the Reverend Mr. Fisher. Silas represented to Saturday Cove all its contact with the world at large; and the knowledge that he was to carry his bride with him over the watery face of the earth added a glamour to what was sufficiently glamourous already.

Abigail, knowing full well what manner of men were the Crocketts, like too full pots, she often thought, over the hottest of fires, was not in the least surprised when at the close of the ceremony her youngest and only son completely lost his head. Leading his wife from the pulpit steps through the mingled tears and smiles of the crowded church out toward the sunlight and the throngs of waiting villagers, Silas felt all manner of emotions swelling within him. They paused at the door, turning backward to make their low bows to pastor and congregation as was the order of the place and time, in preparation for the lifting of the bride by her husband over the church threshold, the carrying of her in his arms across the porch and down the steps. But once he had Solace close against him, her muslins floating in a fragrant cloud about him, Silas forgot both custom and caution. He did not set her on her feet to receive the jovial good wishes of those without and to await the smiles and kisses of those crowding from within. Instead, seized by some wild fancy, he ran with her in his arms down the grassy hill, across the road, and into the churchyard opposite, her skirts and bonnet ribbons fluttering in the high wind, her deprecating cries and commands lost in the gay shouts and laughter of the people, who, standing for a moment in incredulous astonishment, now followed them in merry abandon.

On they went down one tidy churchyard path, between the sombre tombstones of those once married, now dead, and of those who, deprived in this life of the joys of earthly love, had been presumably recompensed by the higher and more commendable joys of heaven. On they went to the steep slope at the end of the yard where the sea rolled in upon the rocky beach. Silas would have stopped here for his breath was well-nigh spent had it not been for those that followed hard upon his heels. He turned instead, running back along yet another path between more tombstones toward the amazed group of wedding guests that stood before the church. Just before he reached the road, he swayed in his mad race toward one side of the path, so that one of Solace's outstretched feet struck against the last of the tombstones. Its white satin slipper, already loosened, was caught by the stone, stood for a moment in uncertain, incongruous balance upon it, then fell into the grass of the grave which it marked. A little girl picked up the slipper, running with it in high excitement by the side of the confused bride until she was set down at last by her triumphant young husband amid the guests and onlookers staring on the church green.

There were various opinions, to be nursed and nourished by their owners, concerning Silas Crockett's unprecedented behaviour; but even this unique conclusion to a wedding ceremony was clearly not the place for their unburdening. After an interval of gay congratulations the green and yellow coach with many soundings of its horn bore the breathless and dishevelled young couple down the hill. The Reverend Ethan Fisher, as he drove with James and Abigail Crockett to the Winship home, was the prey to grim forebodings concerning the future of a young woman in the hands of a man so obviously influenced by his sojourns in heathen lands that he had small respect for the dead; and Dorcas Winship was not the only woman who went toward the wedding reception uneasily conscious of the white satin slipper balanced precariously upon the old tombstone.

She knew the stone. It marked the early and tragic grave of three small children, one sinisterly named Silas, who had died within a few days of one another in a sweep of fever in the year 1798. She as well as most others in Saturday Cove knew by heart the inscription through many a melancholy cogitation on the mysterious ways of God held on Sunday afternoon walks in the churchyard:

In life they were pleasant though transient their bloom,
Their dust now divided now rests in the tomb,
But in Eden forever their spirits shall shine
With a beauty transcending a bloom that's divine.
So, strangers who pause here and neighbours who stay
To contemplate sadly our frail, sinful clay,
Take heed, look toward Him who hath power to save,
*And grace to sustain thee through Death's chilling wave.**

6

Such dismal reflections, however, must needs give way even in Dorcas Winship's pious mind to the joyous demands of the hours following the wedding. Thomas Winship's careful brain had bidden him spare nothing upon his daughter's last day in her father's house. Its doors were opened wide to the aristocracy of Saturday Cove, the sea captains, the shipowners and builders, the two ministers, the præceptor of the academy and his assistants, the lawyers, the doctors, the chief merchants, the few gentleman farmers; its front garden and great blossoming orchard to tradespeople, yard-workers, and labourers of every sort and description. The polished table and sideboard of its dining-room were heaped with plenty, both to eat and to drink, as were the long boards erected upon trestles in the orchard and covered with snowy cloths. Like the scriptural rain of the Lord upon the just and the unjust, the June sunlight fell alike upon the rich and the poor, the favoured and the unfavoured, upon the Congregationalists and the few despised Methodists, upon those who still styled themselves Federalists and those whose past madness in embracing Jeffersonian democracy

* The first four lines of this inscription are taken from a tombstone in the old graveyard of Wiscasset, Maine.

were now leading them to uphold the equally mad schemes of Mr. Andrew Jackson. All these greeted or re-greeted the bride and groom who stood with their parents beneath a great bell of apple-blossoms suspended from the chandelier hook in the opened parlours—parlours whose panelled doors were grooved and bevelled by Thomas Winship's art and surmounted by his own design, a full-rigged ship carved in wood. They were led within in strict order of precedence by Serena Osgood and her carefully chosen associates and tendered their bows and felicitations as best suited their respective stations in Saturday Cove society.

Captain James Crockett was at his best in the receiving line. In his dark blue coat and trousers of brighter blue, in his buff waistcoat and smart cravat, he towered above the squat, black figure of Thomas Winship, filling the room (as all Crocketts fill rooms, thought Abigail, standing beside him in a gown of pale gray silk) simply by what he had been and was. No one could possibly be unconscious of James Crockett. Every separate episode of his life clung about him, unforgotten by him as it was unforgotten by all who knew him and by all those who, not knowing him, felt it clinging there. He had made his first voyage at fourteen, privateering in the midst of the Revolution under the command of the great Captain Nicholas Danforth of Salem, whose name he had made a household word in Saturday Cove, more venerated than that of Alexander Hamilton, and after whom he had called his eldest son. Captain Nicholas Danforth had taken seven prizes in as many weeks on that hazardous venture; and young James had never turned the white feather even when in a fight with an English frigate he had received full in his face the warm brains of a man struck in the head by a ball shot through the port where James was standing to assist him in loading and firing. It was years before James Crockett even half forgot the splatter of that blood and bits of warm flesh against his hot cheeks. He had early pioneered the

Pacific to wrest otter skins and a subsequent fortune from the Northwest Indians. He had voyaged around the world as one of Captain Robert Gray's young officers in the ship *Columbia*. He knew the Cape Verde Islands, the Falklands, Galapagos, and the Marquesas, which he himself had helped to name. He had fought hard and bloody battles with savages at Nootka Sound and Murderer's Harbour, from one of which he wore over his right temple a long, hairless scar extending to the crown of his head. Every village child knew the story of the Chinook Indian who had given him that scar, only to be flung hurtling through the air from his quarterdeck and drowned like a dog. He carried in the very polish of the brass buttons on his blue coat the ports of all the world. He had known all his life as his intimates the great ship merchants of Boston and Salem—the Perkinses and Winships, the Cushings and Lorings, William Gray and the Bromfields, Josiah Bradlee, the Derbys and the Pierces, all of whom, knowing James Crockett, knew Saturday Cove as well. And as to the new state of Maine, no whit behind its parent Massachusetts in the construction of ships, he knew every yard of consequence from Passamaquoddy to Casco and every ship that graced its blocks. He knew and was known among the seafaring families of the new State, the families of Machias and Rockland, Wiscasset, Belfast, Searsport, Boothbay and Portland, Cobbs and Haskells, Hinckleys and Peterses, Colcords, Pendletons, Nicholses, and Carvers. Even the Sewalls of Bath were at that very hour condescending to James Crockett for advice and capital. What wonder that at the wedding reception of his son his magnanimity and bluff good nature knew no bounds, was extended alike to those who thought themselves his equals and to the meanest labourer in his vast vineyard?

The chatter and laughter in the high, white rooms rose in a pealing crescendo to float through the open windows and be supplemented by that from without. There were comments and questions, hints and suggestions and innuendoes, some perhaps neither disciplined nor delicate, for a seafaring society of a century ago, especially in its masculine element, was as broad in its humour as it was fertile in its imagination. A wedding afforded ample scope for both accomplishments. Tongues were so loosened by Thomas Winship's liberal supply of beverages that the Reverend Mr. Fisher, who, under the stress of Silas' behaviour in the churchyard, had planned his Sunday sermon on the Sanctity of Marriage, was seriously shaken by the claims of James the Apostle on the control of "that little member," only to be later convinced that something should be said at the earliest possible date on the far-reaching evils of intemperance. The Methodist pastor, new to Saturday Cove, stood apart among his more simple brethren, who were relatively uncontaminated by the wider world and its wicked ways, and thanked his God that he and his, although constrained to take the lowest seats at this earthly feast, might well be called up higher when the trumpet should sound its dreadful summons.

And not alone on comments, seemly and unseemly to a wedding feast, were the tongues of Saturday Cove loosened on that early June day in the year 1830. They were set free on other matters as well. Men stood about within doors or under the trees without, in pairs or in groups of three and four, talking excitedly of the burning affairs of state and nation, of New England, the arrogant South, and the new expectant West. There was no end of things to talk about. There was that cataclysmic banquet held but a few weeks ago in Washington on the April birthday of Thomas Jefferson, but four years dead, when President Jackson had faced Mr. Calhoun of South Carolina in his definition of the Federal Union and set angry tongues wagging North and South on nullification and the tariff. There were questions concerning the United States Bank, what it was and what rights it had with the money of the people, and why in the name of high heaven good business should be interfered with by a scatter-brained Democrat who babbled of States' Rights like a lunatic. There were denunciations of the Spoils System and pledges of loyalty to Mr. John Quincy Adams and humiliating recognition of the one electoral vote cast in Maine for the new President. Saturday Cove was in no way responsible for that treacherous vote. It was still Federalist to the core, Adamsite with every breath its leading citizens drew, seeing the prosperous future of America, not in the hogs and hominy of the new frontier but, precisely as its prosperity had been in the past, in the ships and codfish of New England. And just as the charlatans, ne'er-do-wells and ruffians, as Saturday Cove thought all frontiersmen, despised codfish either as an article of diet or as an issue in national politics, so did Saturday Cove despise the hogs and the hominy together with the ill manners and the isolation of the western frontier. There were likewise matters nearer home of close interest—whether Captain Seward Porter was mad or merely reckless in his enthusiasm for coast navigation by steam, and whether all this temperance agitation, nurtured as it was by crack-brained evangelists, might conceivably one day result in a monstrous law against private rights and privileges.

Nor did the past die quickly, if it died at all, on the coast of Maine in 1830. There were old men at Solace Crockett's wedding party, men who had sailed to the West Indies long before the war with England crippled the island traffic, men who had been gentleman privateers in the Revolutionary years and pioneers of the Pacific thereafter. These old fellows preserved their furies with their knee-breeches, furies which blazed afresh under a second or third glass of grog against the Embargo and the War of 1812, which would have ruined any other race of men on earth except New England fishermen and sailors. Even Napoleon was not dead in Saturday Cove, or the Terror, or the perfidy of France in general, or the War of the Revolution, which had all but killed ships and shipping, and allowed the codfish on the Banks to increase in disgraceful millions.

National scandal, too, contributed its well-worn opportunities for the outraged voices of Saturday Cove. In this the ladies could and did add their denunciations, fortified by easy virtue, to the conversation that went on during the afternoon. That the President of the United States should be publicly upholding the immoral life of the daughter of a boarding-house keeper, should be receiving her in the White House and even seating her at the head of his wifeless table, was meet cause for worthy indignation among people whose passion for decent righteousness had since 1620 known as its only considerable rival a desire to get on well in the world. Mrs. Margaret Eaton of Washington was in June 1830 in Saturday Cove styled a strumpet and a baggage in good eighteenth century language, her misdemeanors and general depravity finding rich soil for vilification in the very contrast of young and virtuous love beneath the wedding-bell of apple-blossoms in the Winship parlours.

Once the feasting was over and the bridal pair toasted in innumerable glasses of wine and beer, ale and spirits, cordials and punches and shrubs, foreign and domestic and home-brewed, bottled and kegged, barrelled and jugged and bowled, once old loyalties had been strengthened and rendered again impregnable by new vituperations of all those whose chief crime was that they thought differently because they had been reared differently, once Saturday Cove again knew itself for John Quincy Adams and sound money and the chance to earn it through connection with the wide world at large—in short, once these things had been said and done and felt to everyone's complete satisfaction, some gay dance measures were trod beneath the blossoming trees, with village fiddlers wielding their bows and village young men and maidens, old men and children picking up their eager heels upon the windswept grass. Then Solace, assisted by willing hands, must be dressed in her travelling gown of dark blue silk and travelling bonnet of dark blue straw with ruching and feathers of rose, and Silas must drive homeward for a brief hour with his mother to superintend ably his own exuberant departure. Finally at four o'clock the green and yellow coach came again with more blowing of its horn, and the bride and groom, amid the smiles and flower petals and old shoes of the young, the tears of the middle-aged, and the pious ejaculations of the old rushed to it from the Winships' white doorway. They were away, to reach Ellsworth that night by dint of hard driving and to proceed westward toward Bath where the best of Captain Porter's new steamboats would bear them to Boston, thence after a fortnight of gaiety and preparation to embark for Canton in the *Southern Seas*.

Abigail Crockett, silly woman that she was, spent the twilight and much of the night in memories. Sitting in the doorway beneath her blossoming lilacs while the tide again flooded the marsh estuaries, she remembered Salem and how still the house had been when her father at last reluctantly died after tense days when everybody thought he would beat Death itself. She remembered a pair of tight green trousers she had made for Reuben when he was six and how he had split them from hitching about in church. She remembered Nicholas, how a lock of his hair stood up straight in front above an unruly cowlick and how she had caught him stealing grease from her dripping-pan to control it once he had seen Serena Osgood looking at him at a husking-bee. Serena would never have done for Nicholas, she thought. He would soon have tired of her patient adoration, so perhaps things were just as well. The Crocketts liked spice in women, and Serena was quite spiceless. It was strange how, in spite of all people said about the injustice and irony of life, things seemed to work out fairly well when once one had lived long enough to look back upon them instead of forever expecting and being disappointed. She thought of Silas and Solace and of how life went on, ever renewing itself in some even as it died away in others.

Meanwhile at the dining-room table while the tall clock ticked away the hours, James figured on his shares in the new Machias brig, what his chances were, and whether he was a fool to take good money from the bank and cast it away upon angry water and in the teeth of unpredictable wind.

And Dorcas Winship, while Thomas slept the uneasy sleep of a man who had spent too much money, was torn between the thought of her daughter entering upon a new and strange life and the vision of the white satin slipper balanced on the old tombstone in the churchyard.

7

Solace Winship Crockett never liked the sea, but she adored her husband, so that life upon it with him was preferable to the snug safety of life ashore without him. At the start of every outward passage she stood beside him in the last moments of getting underway, pleased at the deference accorded him by shipping merchants and busy officers, listening to the sharp, quick orders and their prompt reception, the clang and clank of derricks and winches, the sudden plop into the harbour water of cast-off ropes. She saw the sailors running up aloft like so many ants, sprawling on the yards to let free the great widths of canvas. And when the first, almost imperceptible sliding from the pier proved that they were really off, she felt sliding into her own body, almost as though she had swallowed it like her food, a dread that went downward from her throat to her knees, lying like a thin, clinging garment about her heart and stomach and penetrating even into her fingers and toes. It was always there. There was no escaping it. When they were clearing the harbour craft and the water was every moment growing deeper, and the sailors were singing as they sheeted home the topsails, she always wondered (until she looked at Silas' excited face and knew) why she had ever done this overwhelming thing.

We're outward bound this very day.
Goodbye, fare you well,
Goodbye, fare you well.
We're outward bound this very day,
Hurrah, my boys, we're outward bound.

From the very beginning of her sailing she lived in the nagging, unquenchable hope of the blue outlines of land cutting the far horizons. Wanting that, in the knowledge that any land at all was weeks or months away, she hoped for the sight of ships with their promise of assistance against any of the manifold natural dangers which might spring upon them at any hour. Storms paralyzed her with fear so that she cowered, weak and trembling, in her cabin, only to pull herself together upon the appearance of Silas, who only half suspected the way she felt and that at long intervals. In days of high, fair winds when everything was going precisely as it should, when filled sails were straining at their ropes, and canvas was crowded on and on to every possible advantage, and Silas gazed excitedly first aloft and then at the mountains of water hurrying past their half-buried leeward side, she shuddered inwardly at the wet decks and bursts of spray. Only when they floated listlessly on a still ocean and her husband fretted over the time they were losing was she in comparative peace of mind. On such days she wore her prettiest frocks and brought her sewing to the quarter-deck. Silas, sitting beside her, wondered how he had ever weathered such calms on previous voyages, little knowing that while he cursed and fumed, she was praying to some inscrutable God whose ways were past finding out for weeks of just such security.

Nor were dangers at sea in the early 1830's contained within the terrifying limits of merely natural causes. Pirates at large were still a menace in waters like the Caribbean, indeed throughout the Spanish Main, and remained for some years afterward a fear greater than reefs and shoals on the island coasts of the Fijis and of Sumatra. The *Southern Seas* carried guns and ammunition even though Silas was not lured by the Sumatran pepper trade, and Solace knew full well the reason for such grim additions to their freight even as she was familiar with the current happenings of the early years in which she sailed. The tragedy of the Salem ship *Friendship* occurred at Quallah Battoo in 1831 at the butchering hands of Malay pirates; in 1833 the brig *Charles Doggett*, also of Salem, lost six of her men by cruel slaughter in the Fijis; and a year earlier the harrowing tale of the *Mexican*, captured on a voyage to Rio by as bloodthirsty a gang as ever graced a gallows, had penetrated even to the Corn Belt. Small wonder that few captains, even of the Crockett breed, took women to sea with them in those months and years before the United States frigate *Potomac* had brought swift retribution at Quallah Battoo and Boston justice had hanged the worst cut-throats of the *Mexican* disaster.

Nevertheless, the only possible alternative to these perils, namely that she should remain in safety at home and leave her husband to weather alone whatever chance might befall him, never once seriously entered Solace Crockett's mind. She had made her decision when her love was new and untried, and now that it grew miraculously more new with every day and week added to its age, she had more reason than ever to abide by her initial resolve. She came from a race of people whose sturdy aim was to finish what they had begun, who scorned alike cowardice and commiseration, and who held that to keep one's mouth shut in the face of hardship was not the least valuable of social virtues. By upbringing and long tradition she had been trained to expect neither leniency nor favour, and never, even when one fear or another was at its worst, did she entertain the slightest notion either of backing out or of letting anyone know the measure of her dread.

She was a quiet restrained woman, placid to all appearances, not easily moved, yet deep within her ran a vein of passion which held her husband in protective adoration even while it caused her anxious hours of questioning, of wondering whether some occasional pretence of resistance would not redound more to her credit as a wife, dutiful and submissive though the Bible said a wife should be. There was no resisting Silas, either in their moments and hours of complete surrender one to the other or in the more casual hours of their daily existence at sea or in port. The superabundance of his nature lent an edge and a brightness to the most unimportant details and occurrences so that life with him was never dull, fearful though it might be. And the strong strain of common sense within her, together with the recognition that she had taken him for better or for worse, dictated that she keep her misgivings to herself. Men, she learned early in her marriage, could not understand women, try as they might; and women, if they were wise, did not sue for or even expect that understanding.

When five months after their wedding some weeks of illness and irritability forced upon her the stark fact that a child was coming, she began playing a daytime game of pretence which effectually fooled her husband. Only at night when he lay asleep in their cabin or was absent from her when necessity kept him on deck, did she allow herself to be herself. Then she lay in bed, tense and taut as the filled sails of the ship, listening to the creaking of planks and bolts and gear, feeling the sickening swoop and pitch of the vessel as she mounted and descended the swell of the sea, praying frantically, now for calms, now for fair winds, for delays in port, for any conceivable exigency of nature or of time which should allow her baby to be born on any shore at all where there were beds and doctors and other women to look at her with understanding eyes. Her prayers were not answered although Silas had done his utmost to assume the role of God. Two ports had been made and left with every likelihood of making another in ample time when the baby himself set at nought all their care and circumspection, even their loss of profit, of which he had made his father reckless, by arriving a full two months ahead of time in the mid-Atlantic, hundreds of miles from even the scant protection of the Azores.

Marseilles had been their last port of call. Solace was always to remember the mountains of white rock that backed and surrounded its wide blue outer harbour and snug inner one, the old fortresses beetling their summits, the clear sunshine of the June morning when they sailed in before a light wind and came alongside one of its stone piers which gave anchorage to the ships of half the world. Looking beyond the towering forest of masts and yards, she saw the crowded houses where women tended their fires and their children.

She walked that morning with Silas beneath the spring sun along the waterfront under the shimmering plane trees. Everything that happened stamped itself indelibly upon her mind in the exhilaration of feeling once again the safety of land beneath her feet. A funeral passed by, its black-clad mourners self-consciously following the coffin visible within the windows of a rickety hearse; and Silas removed his hat in accordance with the French custom and in common with all the other men upon the street. He made the gesture, she thought, with an almost indecent flourish, so glad he was to see the new colour in her cheeks and the fresh light in her eyes.

"You should show more respect for the dead," she said to him, but he only laughed and bought her violets and roses to tuck within her dress.

The children under foot amazed her, hordes of children, dirty, half-clad, with the races and colours of half the earth stamped upon their faces, Mongolian and African features, Saxon and Mediterranean, a polyglot of children, many of them fathered by sailors at the cost of a handful of centimes and mothered by women and girls who now paid carelessly for their strokes of ill luck.

"I never saw such children," she said to Silas. "In Canton they looked at least as though they belonged there. I'm half afraid to look at them for fear they'll mark the baby."

He laughed at her again and gave her wine in an open café upon the pavement where the waiters wore red sashes and where everyone seemed without a care in the world. He spoke in poor French, she giving him the surprise and admiration which she knew he expected, thinking meanwhile of the odd ways in which men needed women.

There was a rush basket of bread upon the table, bread baked to a crisp brown in tapering, oblong rolls that fitted one's hand. When she held one and broke it to eat with her wine, she was surprised by the tears that sprang to her eyes. She choked them back by eating the bread so that Silas might not see. There was something substantial, reassuring, comforting even, about the very feel of the hard crust within her hand. Were it not a mad thing to do, she would have liked to ask Silas for dozens of such tiny loaves to carry on board with her that she might feel again and yet again as she had just then felt.

They were passing before a stand where a woman sold odd shellfish when one of the ship's officers approaching them drew Silas away for a moment' s conversation. Solace stood alone before the stand with its piles of oysters, crayfish, lobsters, mussels, and other creatures unfamiliar to her. The woman was splitting dexterously with a pocket knife the spiny shells of some circular black fish which contained within itself bits of red flesh apparently in great demand. She was a large, coarse-featured woman, with a dirty red handkerchief about her head, with ugly teeth and with hands that were chafed and bleeding from the shells which she handled and split. The over-full lines of her figure protruded from within the black sacque she wore and from beneath her filthy white apron. Two small and dirty children clung about her skirts, a sickly baby slept in a clothes basket at her feet, and the early addition of another was only too evident to all that had eyes to see. She called her wares in hoarse yet strident tones, accompanying them by what was apparently a volley of obscene abuse to the sailors, stevedores, and wharfmongers who, lounging about, ventured to jeer at her.

In an interval between her small sales and the almost constant splitting of the black, prickly fish she looked at Solace standing near, alone and half afraid of the dark glances of the men who were searching out her secret also, nudging one another with laughing comments. A change swept over the heavy features of the woman as she looked at Solace in her gray dress with the flowers tucked in its front, at her fair face and frightened eyes beneath her bonnet. She turned vehemently upon the men who idled near, letting out upon them such a fury of scorn, upbraiding, and abuse that they slouched away in a dozen different directions, not even staying to buy the bits of fish for which they had been bargaining. The storm over, she looked again toward Solace, a protective, half-embarrassed smile softening her ugly face, leaned across the wet boards of her stand, and said something in a quiet, understanding tone to this strange foreign lady, little more than a child in comparison with her own hardened years, whose fears she had discerned and who had touched her sordid, worn-out heart.

Solace had no knowledge of her words, but she could not fail to grasp that which lay behind them and which had for an instant transformed her ugliness and squalor. She smiled at the woman between the tears that rose again and could almost in gratitude have thrown herself across the piles of shellfish upon her ample, dirty breast. When Silas came hurrying back with many apologies for having left her in such a place among such beasts, all of whom, he said, should be thrown into the harbour without mercy, she turned to smile across his unsuspecting shoulder toward the woman who had befriended her and who knew what she was feeling.

Late that afternoon while Silas was busy with a score of things about the ship and pierhead, she wrapped herself in her shawl, he all unknowing, and went alone down the slippery gangplank and along the bustling waterfront, regardless of the stares from a hundred foreign faces. The low sun was streaming across the harbour, touching idle sails that waited and sails filled with wind, outward or inward bound, outlining spars and shrouds and rigging, lying warm upon the brightly coloured houses, and turning into golden spirals the smoke that rose from nearby chimneys. The woman was gathering up her children and her remaining shellfish when she reached the dirty stand. She turned with a swift glance of recognition, the same piteous smile again softening her dark face, and the blessings she returned for the coins with which Solace filled her hands were unintelligible only in words.

It was this fisherwoman who persisted in Solace's mind on the agonizing day when the baby came, rendering empty and absurd the promises of the English doctor in Marseilles who had known beyond the shadow of a doubt that all was safe and well for another seven weeks at least. It was a day of anguish and terror, of alternate hopes and fears for death, the fourth day of a calm more still than any that she had ever prayed for, a day when the sails hung lifeless from the yards and not so much as a flying fish broke the glaring surface of immeasurable leagues of water.

The baby came at sunset when the late spring light flooded the dishevelled cabin and shone upon Silas' dripping, terrified face as in the last moments he frantically did as the first officer told him to do. Solace, in the brief intervals between the pain that threatened to tear her body into pieces and fling them about the cabin from the table upon which they had placed her, thought how still was the ship—as still, she thought, as was the church at home on Saturday afternoons when she had carried flowers there and had stayed to say a prayer for Silas wherever he might be. She did not know that the news had travelled to fo'c'sle and galley and that the sailors were standing silently about, their pity for her plight inundated by their superstitious fears lest a death on board might at any moment ruin all the luck that a successful birth might bring the ship.

The first officer had studied a bit of medicine in his youth, had even assisted at the advent of a child or two born under more favourable circumstances. He did his utmost while sweat and blood drenched his shirt and the white apron which the anxious cook had lent him. When the baby came at last, both he and Silas tried every method they had heard of both from within and without the ship's medicine book and many they had not to bring a cry from him. But neither he nor they could manage it. And in the awful minutes of confusion and exhaustion he seemed, cruelly enough, not to matter much to Solace one way or another. She never saw him nor did she ask what they did with him, considering that a wholly unnecessary question. A life at sea, as all know who have followed it, does not encourage unnecessary questions.

When a few weeks later they reached Saturday Cove for a month's interim between voyages, her face to Silas' relief had grown a bit less still than it had been. But there was nevertheless an indescribable something about her which forbade any mention of the baby in her presence.

8

Given his chosen profession, Silas Crockett could not have asked of Fate or Fortune gifts greater than they had already bestowed upon him in the very time of his young manhood and in the very circumstances under which he was privileged to live it. The 1830's and 1840's were the golden age of the American merchant marine, the earlier decade speeding up perceptibly like a sound ship before a favourable, ever-increasing breeze into the full-tide prosperity of the later. Silas sailed with the ship and took the tide at its flood. In those full-bodied, spacious years he could never decide from one voyage to another from what continent or what ocean would next rise the clouds to float above his skysails simply because new ventures were being launched over night to intoxicate a man once he was in port again. The foreign trade of New England was in those years at its height, fifteen hundred ships arriving annually at Boston, an average of four for each day, and taking their places in the crowded harbour or along the congested waterfront with easy nonchalance whether they came from Sumatra or Stockholm, Calcutta or Rio. And although Salem as a port now languished in comparison, after a maritime glory which had made her seem the world itself to the natives of the South Seas, although her most successful merchants were moving to Boston and those remaining at home were putting their money into the new shoe factories, she, together with Newburyport and Marblehead, Lowell and Lawrence, contributed her less romantic but quite as necessary share to this glorious era of enterprise by supplying boots and shoes and cottons for the markets of the world.

The good master of a good ship in those years had only to choose the voyage and port he desired from those offered by a score of busy firms. There was the traffic in hides with Mexican California which had come to take the place of the trade in

Northwest furs. For hides there were no years like the thirties as Dana has well told. Maine and Massachusetts ships anchored by hundreds off Santa Barbara and San Diego, swaying in the long Pacific swell, while sailors brought the cured hides from the salt-vats and loaded them into the long-boats just beyond the breakers. The cabins of these ships which had weathered the Horn were fitted up as shops, their cargoes on display as wares for which Mexican señoras bargained, paying fabulous sums for Lowell cotton prints, Boston gloves and underwear, needles and thread, bonbons and parasols, and Massachusetts shoes made out of California leather. There was the growing South American trade as well, ships loading for Rio and Buenos Aires with Maine pine boards for firewood, with boots and shoes, and every conceivable notion that might compete favourably with goods sent thither in British bottoms. These ships brought back hundreds of thousands of hides from Montevideo and Buenos Aires, wool and hair, sheepskins and tallow from the River Plate. Nor was Central America to be despised. Its coast was a haven, after the danger from Caribbean pirates had been weathered, for the small New England brigs and schooners which left their multifarious gimcracks in return for goatskins and tropical woods and cochineal, the last of which coloured the frosting of the cakes on many a church-supper table in isolated New England and lent new spice to cooking as a fine art. Valparaiso sent copper and nitrate of soda; Brazil, millions of pounds of fragrant coffee. And Boston merchants in this heyday of new enterprise, finding South American ports an excellent market for China silks and India shawls, opened a direct trade from Canton and Calcutta to Rio in Boston vessels.

In the flourishing forties the Boston ice trade was extended to every large South American port and to the East Indies as well. Conceived by young Frederic Tudor as early as 1805, the carrying of this questionable commodity into tropical waters required thirty years of patient experimentation and of imperturbability against the scorn directed upon it in its earlier years before it reached success and the preservation from ruin of Boston's East India commerce. But heaven-made ice from a hundred New England ponds and lakes once it reached Calcutta and Bombay, once it had slipped down the parched and suspicious throats of nabobs and rajahs and commoner folk in all varieties of cold drinks, could be sold for almost any price and in return could purchase indigo and other dyestuffs, jute and hemp, saltpetre and gunny cloth, which was needed for the packing of Western corn and Southern cotton.

The small brigs and barques of Boston when Boston was literally the hub of the universe in those banner years of her maritime supremacy navigated the island-strewn Ægean drawing her Mediterranean traders farther eastward for figs and olive oil to complement their fruits and wines. Their New England captains and officers, their common sailors from the villages of Maine and Nova Scotia, rounded the Peloponnesus and gazed with eyes perhaps more homesick than those of Sophocles' exiled sailors upon the white columns of the temple of Poseidon crowning the level summit of Cape Sunium. Sailing still further eastward past Andros and Chios, they came at length to Smyrna at the head of its blue gulf; and there in the narrow, noisy streets and bazaars, gray and grimy with Asia Minor dust, they rubbed shoulders and drove hard bargains with Turk and Greek and Armenian. Lowell cottons found a market there, and West Indian rum, clocks and umbrellas, straw hats and bonnets, buttons, cooking utensils, every sort of hardware and toy; and the Central Wharf in Boston received in due time enough packed figs to supply the whole of North America, Turkish carpets for the wealthy, and innumerable sponges for many a Saturday night bath from Maine to the new West.

As less tangible but perhaps more lasting cargo these small, adventurous barques brought back to New England the memory of Rhodes and Cyprus, Patmos and Samos, their angular outlines softened and made lovely by the luminous haze of the Ægean, their mountains of sheer rock rising from sapphire or opalescent water. Such memory and such knowledge, brought homeward as it was from perhaps as complete a cross section of society as it was possible to obtain into another as complete, lent to New England a hundred years ago a subtle dignity and culture that has by no means passed away. The young supercargoes of the Mediterranean and Ægean trade, fresh from Harvard as they often were, felt their classical learning assume a light as clear as that which bathed the islands and peninsulas of its own home. And boys in their teens, mingling in the fo'c'sle from every sort of home America could produce, looked upon the barren, precipitous slopes of Patmos and wrote to their Bible-reading mothers and grandmothers that even they had seen the place of the Apostle's vision.

So vast and abundant, indeed, were the gifts of those years to all who in any way partook of their maritime richness, so ample, so spacious, so widespread was the world which they embraced, that Silas felt an almost angry regret filling his mind and taking the place of natural grief when in the autumn of 1837 he received in Canton by a ship that had followed his own the news of his father's death. He was resentful against Fate that James Crockett should have had to leave a world so limitless and far-flung, so pregnant with new undertakings, for one at its best, at least in Silas' mind, vague, problematical, and lifeless. It was impossible even to attempt to imagine his father in a place where he could not bluster about shipyards, could not speculate upon gain and loss, could not review the glorious hardships of his past. All his sorrow was for the earthly possessions of which James Crockett had been summarily deprived, his work in the world, his eager concern in its interests, the honour in which he was held by all who knew him, his robust enjoyment of food and drink and laughter. He had loved life with a passion akin to Silas' own. It was monstrous and unjust that he must leave it, even at the age of seventy-three.

James Crockett, Abigail's letter said, had suffered a shock in his own yards at the close of a hot August day when she had tried in vain to keep him at home. He had been much worried during the past month over reverses he had sustained in the loss of the Machias brig with all hands aboard her. He had not been an easy patient during the fortnight he had lived, impaired in body but more active than ever in his mind. He was rebellious in the extreme, as Silas might know he would be, and after she knew there was no hope for his recovery, she was relieved when the end had mercifully come in a long, quiet sleep.

"I myself am well," she wrote in conclusion, "and I beg you both to have no concern about me. After sixty one learns to expect such things, and I am only glad he did not have to live and suffer, which would have been a sore trial to him and to us all. My neighbours are extremely kind, and I find enough to busy myself about in the house and garden. I prove daily that hard work is the best antidote for sorrow, and, although I grieve for myself and for you, I have no useless regrets. He lived a full and a good life, and he left you to carry on his work. I have faith to believe in another and better existence beyond this one, although I fear not as Mr. Fisher enjoins me to picture it, for I think such a one entirely unsuited to your father."

9

They spent the late winter and early spring in Saturday Cove after James Crockett's sudden and reluctant death. After a long and hazardous voyage of head winds and a score of mishaps, each of which threatened disaster for nerve-wracking hours and days, the snowbound village spelled thrice welcome security to Solace. She was grateful for every delay in the settlement of James Crockett's affairs which kept Silas from his ship and tempting contracts from one busy firm or another.

The harbour was frozen in the bitter February cold even to the outer islands. The village was buried in snow. During the long nights in her old room in her father's house or in Abigail Crockett's best chamber, she lay in bed, rejoicing in the protection of four walls and of the very cold itself which had frozen the sea and kept people within their homes, warm beneath their home-made covers. She was glad to awake in the night, for then she could realize to the full the stillness and the safety—no motion of the wide bed in which she lay, no sounds of ship's rats scurrying about the interstices of cabin walls or in the hold below, no creaking and groaning of planks and gear, no continuous swish of water, no sharp and staggering impact of waves. Sometimes during the late hours of the night or in those of early dawn, she saw passing in slow shafts of light across the walls and ceiling of her room the reflection of the lanterns on sleighs or sledges and caught the reassuring whine of runners and the crunch of hoof-beats against the surface of the snow-packed roads. She loved the slow, certain striking of the clock in the spire of the church.

In the morning she watched the cold, pale sun darken the still island spruces and bring into sharp relief the ice-bound shores. She saw the blue smoke curling upward from the wide chimneys of the village houses where women prepared breakfast in decency and order. She heard the sound of sleigh bells cutting the frosty air and understood that she was among people who knew where they were going and when they should arrive at warmth and shelter.

She took pleasure in the neat and thorough unpacking of her trunks, in the sight of her clothes hanging from the high hooks of wide, clean closets. She built fires and cooked, taking the management of the Winship house over from her mother, although Abigail Crockett still held the reins of her own home in her own capable hands and allowed Solace's assistance only because of her welcome presence. She got out her own china and linen and set the table herself as though she could never have enough of placing napkins at proper angles and refilling salt and pepper shakers, vinegar cruets and sugar bowls. She felt an exhilaration in the very shaking of a dust cloth from the front doorway between the bare sprigs of the half-buried lilacs. There was the cold morning air, there were the lines of white houses with their green shutters, the chance greeting from someone who passed at that moment, the friendly sight of other dusters shaken by vigorous hands from the hastily raised upper windows or from quickly opened doors.

She helped her father with his records and accounts during the alternate fortnights when she left Abigail Crockett's great empty house for her own home. Thomas Winship was as meticulous with paper and pencil as he was with plane and square and chisel; and now that winter had once again put a stop to outdoor building and rendered even indoor work precarious against the expanding of wood and plaster in warmer weather, he busied himself with his plans and papers, binding carefully the great sheets upon which he had drawn the details of meeting-houses, homes, and public buildings. He talked more that winter than Dorcas Winship had ever heard him talk in all his life before. She was hard put to it not to feel an occasional twinge of jealousy when, during the long evenings while Silas read or was with his mother and she sat with her workbasket, she heard him talking in low tones to Solace by the big dining-room table. He fingered the great sheets of brown paper before him as he spoke.

"I don't know that all this is of much account to anybody but me, but I'd like to set down a record of what I've done in my life. It's not much, perhaps, but I did it, and I've not let much grass grow under my feet since I left the sea at thirty years. When a man's nearly sixty and more than half his working life has gone, he likes to take stock of things he's done. These big sheets I've got together here are the plans of the meeting-houses I've drawn and put up. There are fourteen in all, and not one of them had any other architect but me. I'm laying them away in a safe place for what they're worth. Maybe somebody will see them some day, but if they don't, I'll be neither the better nor the worse for it."

Solace watched him gather together the sheets with his stubby, calloused fingers. First, there were his drawings of the finished churches as his eyes had foreseen them, each different, each dignified by care and thought, knowledge and vision, each the product of his assimilation and interpretation of the things he had seen in his own and other countries. Upon every one in turn he pinned or pasted carefully his smaller sketches and specifications of the details which made up the whole, columns and porches, pediments and pilasters, spires, roof-slopes and steps, pulpits, pews, windows and doors. They spent hours gathering these together, making sure that each was in its rightful place and that all were labelled accurately.

"These are the main things," he said when that portion of the work was completed. "The meeting-houses may stand long after I'm dead and gone. I may say without boasting that there's some that strike me as fair jobs for a plain man like me. But there's odds and ends of other things that I thought might be put down, all sorts of things that have filled in my time when meeting-houses weren't called for. I've kept records all along as I've worked, and I guess I have them all. Your hand is better than mine, Solace, at writing plain, and I've got a book here that I bought to put them down in."

From the slips he held in his hand he dictated to her one cold evening, as they sat beneath the whale-oil lamp at the old familiar table, the introduction to these lesser records. On the first page of his new memorandum book she wrote:

Thomas Winship began his joiner work in May of the year 1807 in the counties of Hancock and Washington in the then State of Massachusetts. He has designed and built in all fourteen meeting-houses without assistance in planning by any save himself and what he has read and seen with his own eyes. Of these he has made separate record for whoever may follow him.

She wrote the last words uneasily, reading her mother's fears and his own anxiety lest there should be no one.

In addition he has worked as superintendent and labourer alike on
84 dwelling-houses
83 vessels of various builds
12 school-houses
18 barns and sheds
12 vessel heads
5 stores
14 taverns

He has made besides in thirty years 197 coffins with burial boxes to match at the cost of $2.50 each.

This work has been done in fourteen different towns and villages.

The account of each job together with time, cost, and profit, will be found truly described on the following pages.*

As she wrote each evening in the record book until all was complete, she thought of all the nails driven by his own careful hands or by those of others whom he had trained and watched, all the boards sawn, all the joists hoisted into place, all the bits of carving with which he had embellished their own and other homes. She was proud of her father in those evenings.

* These figures are accurately given from the diary of a Maine village joiner and builder of this period.

Her life at Silas' home was different from that in her own, in one sense more curtailed, in another far more free. Abigail Crockett set her own table and managed admirably her own kitchen; but she was a far easier woman for Solace to talk to than Dorcas Winship, in spite of all the closer ties of blood that bound her to her mother. One could do little for Abigail in material, manual ways, but one could give her much and take from her even more.

James Crockett had not been alone in bequeathing abundant life to Silas. Abigail had done her share. Nor had she impoverished herself by so doing. At sixty-three she was still young and eager, taking her husband's recent death not as a blow singled out for her alone, but only as one of those ceaseless results of time which knew neither favour nor mischance. She was at once too wise and too rich in nature to be resigned to her common lot, knowing as she had known all her life that in acceptance rather than in resignation lies the freedom of the spirit.

"Once a thing is over," she said to Solace as she went briskly about her ways in kitchen, buttery, or sitting-room, "and you know it is, you don't keep on fussing and working yourself up all to no purpose. It's hanging on to things that hurts you most in this world, not just letting them go. I've known that for years, but it took Reuben to bring it home to me. Now I've learned it for good and all."

Solace loved her afternoons with Abigail. Once dinner at twelve was finished and they themselves and the house were tidied up, they sat down with their sewing in the sitting-room. The afternoon was before them, serene, uninvaded, until the early lighting of the lamps should set Abigail again in motion. The snow without, crusted and glittering in the February cold or melting and settling before a high March wind, only increased the confidence and satisfaction which Solace felt within herself. Such hours to her were ample, replete, sufficient, like the bread on that June morning in Marseilles. The tall clock ticked on as they worked together; the birch logs crackled in the great fireplace. From the clean, orderly kitchen they could hear the singing of the teakettle, the occasional snapping of the fire, and smell the warm, rich smell of the beans baking in the brick oven.

Their talk, interspersed by comfortable silences, was that desultory, intimate talk of women who have earned the right throughout the morning to busy themselves idly with their fingers in the afternoon. On one such day they talked of Silas, knowing that they understood him far better than he could ever understand himself.

"Silas," said Abigail, "hasn't changed a mite since he was in his cradle by this very fire. These Crocketts somehow don't change. It seems as though they were born with everything complete, all done up so to speak like a bundle. Silas never kept still a minute even when he was a baby. He hitched and twisted even when he was asleep. Amos Crockett, his grandfather, was just like all the rest and his uncles, too,—always scheming and planning and taking the world as their own, never thinking anything could beat them. When James heard he'd lost his money in that Machias brig, he just sat in that chair you are in and stared as though he couldn't believe such a thing *could* happen to *him*. And the queer thing about it is the way they've always attracted luck just by expecting it round every corner. Look at Silas, now. He's got everything he wants just where he wants it. And you and I and all the rest of the world like nothing better than giving it to him."

Solace reached for the scissors to cut the wool-ends of the tapestry she was weaving. The colour rose in her cheeks as she glanced at Abigail, comfortably knitting socks for Silas.

"He hasn't children," she said. "I almost wish he'd stop expecting them. That doesn't seem to happen his way with all his hopes and plans. I've—failed him there."

She had never before mentioned this to Abigail, but with the quiet room shutting them in together, anything seemed easy to say.

"Get that notion out of your head," snapped Abigail. "It's unhealthy and won't do either of you any good. You haven't failed him, and there's yet time in plenty."

Solace stretched her tapestry tight across her knees. She was weaving in needlepoint a footstool for Abigail, a wreath of roses on a black background. Just now she was tipping one of the petals and it required careful attention.

"You don't suppose?" she began, and then hesitated, searching for a better beginning. "Mother's never said a word to me, but I know what she thinks. I see it in her face over and over again. She thinks it's because of what happened on our wedding day. You remember. She thinks it's a judgment of God upon us or a—a curse from the dead. She thinks that's why the baby died. And sometimes—well, sometimes I get scared about it myself."

Abigail dropped one of her shining needles on her polished floorboards and let it lie there while she leaned forward almost fiercely in her chair and glared at Solace.

"Stuff and nonsense!" she cried. "Are the women in this village plain crazy with their old wives' tales and trappings? The dead wreak no vengeance on the living. They're too glad to be free from the troubles of this earth to concern themselves with poor mortals like us. And as for God—well, I never! Whatever God is, I don't believe He's that kind. Silas may have been a fool—most of us are—but God isn't. Your mother's a good woman and a smart woman, Solace, but who is she to know about God or the dead either? You can't do much with the old, but the sooner young folks get rid of such stupid thoughts, the better for all concerned."

She stooped to pick up her needle, puffing a bit from exertion and disgust.

"You've seen too much of the world, my dear, to put any faith in such clap-trap notions. And if your mother had come from different stock, she wouldn't. Seafaring's a rough life, but when the best of us go into it, it knocks nonsense out of our heads whatever it may put in place of it."

They worked on in a silence broken only by the sharp click of Abigail's needles and the dull punching of Solace's canvas. The afternoon sun was setting. Soon the lamps must be lighted and Abigail busy with beans and brown bread, chili sauce, and Washington pie.

"I've always wondered a bit," said Abigail after fifteen minutes had passed, "about the way the Crocketts stick to their women. Given all their high spirits, you might expect them to do their bit of gallivanting with all the world to pick from and scores of silly fools idolizing them. But I must say I've never known them to lose their heads in that way." She smiled at Solace. "Perhaps," she concluded, "they've had their luck there, too,—in finding somebody fit to stick to."

Solace liked her mother-in-law's terse way of giving rare compliments. This one lay warm within her, taking the place of the foolish notions which Abigail had so stoutly dispersed. Silas would come in soon, ruddy and alive, filling the house with himself and her and Abigail as well. And if, perchance, he was to say that things were shaping themselves so that they might soon be off, she could bear it better now than at other times she had known.

10

In 1839 Silas disposed of the *Southern Seas* to one of the owners of the new yards at East Boston, which already were giving promise of surpassing those of Nova Scotia, the Mystic and the Merrimac river-yards, and even those of Scotland along the Forth and Clyde. In her place he ordered built at Saturday Cove the *Solace Winship*. Her bows were less bluff than those of the *Southern Seas*; her water lines were more graceful, her rigging loftier; and her added length and depth in proportion to her breadth, which increased her carrying capacity, gave alike proof of innovation in building and prophecy of greater speed. Her permanent lashings were made of iron instead of rope; her sails were of the best Lowell duck obtainable; and the jauntiness of her appearance was a hundredfold increased, Silas said, by her bright blue ports which lent spice to the sweeping dignity of her clean-stripped black hull. Wanting his father's alert supervision, he stayed again at Saturday Cove a full four months to see her finished, spending ten hours every day beneath her hull or upon her decks, while Solace lived in a second blissful dream now at her own home, now at his. She was launched on a September afternoon when the red maples were glowing among the pines and spruces on the headlands, with Solace to christen her. She slipped into the full tide like the thoroughbred that she was with all Saturday Cove cheering itself hoarse; and Silas swore, glowing in his pride, that they two would sail her into the ports of half the world.

His prophecy proved not far from true. They sailed for ten years thereafter, now to one far harbour, now to another. They took the *Solace Winship* to Rio, deeply laden with flour and lumber to exchange for coffee and sugar. At anchor two miles seaward from the city they saw the mountains towering above the purple hills, the peaks of Gabia and Corcovado, and smelt the fragrance of the orange trees borne to them by the land wind. It was sunset when they anchored and the bells from tiny churches which crowned the harbour islands were ringing, for Vespers, Silas said. They saw the lights come out in the distant houses, and Solace felt fear passing out of her body and mind until she could almost see it go, leaving her once more unafraid.

She never tired of the land excursions which Silas was forever taking her upon whenever he was free. He had an insatiable desire to show her the places he knew and to discover with her the places he did not know. There was no tiring him, no exhausting the prodigality of his nature. When they landed at Havre and were waiting for cargo, he took her by train and coach to half a dozen cities and towns, to Paris, where he bought her new gowns and took her to see numberless pictures and statues because, he said, it was the thing to do in Paris, to Rouen, to Chartres. She remembered the lumbering oxen on the flat French fields, the willows and tall poplars by the slow streams where the women washed their clothes, the far horizons cut by sharp church spires. She remembered her astonishment over the cathedral at Chartres, how cold it was on a hot July day and how the jewelled windows repeated themselves in motes and gleams of colour on the gray pillars and arches. Silas was forever saying jocose, unexpected things. Cathedrals were no deterrent to him, nor the presence of black-robed priests and nuns. The long white finger of Salome in the row of transept windows touched his humour.

"Women were dangerous in those old times just as now," he said. "Look at her eyes and hair, Solace, and think how she's been here all these centuries flirting with those black-faced heathen kings beside her. But she's not so dangerous as you in that Paris bonnet. All the priests cast eyes on you. Don't you suppose I see them doing it?"

In the early mornings she lay beside him in their hotel, hearing while he slept the deep, echoing tones of the great bells calling the people churchward. She never forgot those grave, resounding notes reverberating through the still air, nor the clatter of sabots on the pavement and through the cobbled streets. For moments of such peace and security, she thought, she would endure any number of dangers. And if one waited and endured long enough, they were sure to come, dispelling all fears, blotting them out as though they were not.

Like the bells at Chartres some one particular or salient feature of the many places to which they journeyed was likely to impress itself upon her mind and glow there when other memories had passed into confusion. In Barcelona she remembered less the sumptuous dinner to which some Boston merchants resident there had invited them than the great boughs of mimosa in the dark market-place through which they drove at dawn from their hotel to the ship. The country folk were bringing their cluttering wagons full of produce to the dirty market square in the half-light of a winter dawn, and the yellow of the mimosa everywhere gleamed like sunlight. From the snug harbour of Soller in the Balearics where they put in once for repairs after a Mediterranean storm she saw the tight, close walls ascending and encircling the rocky slopes of the mountains, miles of walls rising one above the other, giving depth and safety to the roots of the olive trees. She wondered how many centuries they had been built and what hands had held the patience to pile and repile their stones.

"Time is nothing to these peasants," said Silas. "They've nothing to do but pile walls and pick olives in the sun. Probably not one in a hundred has ever been out of this very village."

"Happy people!" she thought, but she did not say so to him.

In Sicily where the snow glowed on distant Ætna beneath a blue, sun-filled sky and the lemons hung in countless thousands from their shining trees, she saw a tired woman making lace before the cloisters of an old church. She plied her needle with incredible swiftness above a sleeping, naked baby face downward in her lap.

"Too many children in this island," said Silas. "It's a pity they can't be more evenly distributed."

She bought yards of lace from the woman and thought about her afterward in all sorts of odd moments when there was seemingly no reason for it.

They went to the Baltic by way of the West Indies leaving their mixed cargoes at Havana and loading there with sugar for St. Petersburg or Riga. She remembered the dull, cold Russian skies, the gray, forbidding shores, and the silent workers who loaded Russian hemp and iron for the shipbuilders and the harpoon-makers of New England. These men had impassive faces with eyes that seemed filled with guarded secrets.

She had added reason to remember the silence of those northern shores and skies, for it was in St. Petersburg that she heard of her mother's death, three years after James Crockett had passed reluctantly to whatever reward awaited him. She was not surprised when the news reached her, many weeks after Dorcas Winship had gone. The brooding land itself in November together with the gray sea that lay before it seemed in complete accordance with such stark and unequivocal knowledge, ready and waiting to acquaint one with it. Moreover, her life had inured her to surprise of all sorts. She sat on the deck that afternoon well-wrapped against the early cold, and wondered at the quietness within her, deeper than grief. She found herself involuntarily setting aside the beliefs in which she had been reared, the faith in, even the desire for, the survival in some happier sphere of those who had been lost to earth. The very fact that people had passed from confusion and fear into stillness and the security of complete unconsciousness should bring in itself, she thought, a peace and an order to those who were left. There must be a healing in the very recognition of silence, making as nothing all importunate demands which wrongly conceived life itself and all its concerns to be so desirable a thing. In those hours, under those still skies, she could not feel grief for her mother; but in the night, when her mood of the afternoon was over, the thought of her father weighed upon her. There was a dignity in death which saved it from too many tears. Its very isolation from human affairs spared it the pathos of life and living, before which men alone were more helpless than women or even than children.

Thus her years unfolded, marked now and then by swift changes, again, in spite of a multiplicity of fresh experiences, seemingly changeless like a wide span of time rather than of periods neatly marked off by weeks and months. She looked with interest upon the world spread before her, but her interest was given largely because it was more the world of Silas than of her own. And since it was the world common to all the people whom she knew, even to most of those among whom she had been reared, her life within it grew to seem neither novel nor strange. Even when she returned to Saturday Cove as she did each year, or at most two, for a brief visit between voyages, she could not lose or even loosen connection with it as she had done during her longer sojourns at home. For Saturday Cove, like every other thriving coast town in those stirring days, ate and drank and wore the products of foreign soil and the work of foreign hands and talked more familiarly of the Seven Seas than of Machias Bay. She never overcame or outgrew her fears, but she grew accustomed to them, and they bred within her a kind of fatalistic acceptance, enlivened only by the seeming impossibility of her husband's being vanquished in anything he set out to do. He had such abundant life and strength, his dreams were so easily accomplished, that she came to look upon him as someone invulnerable against the disasters that befell others of his calling, someone set aside by the capricious favour of Fate from the slings and arrows of outrageous Fortune.

Only in the matter of sons to inherit his vitality and to sail like him to the uttermost boundaries of the earth did he seem to be playing a losing game and she to be failing him. She accorded her failure in this respect to the terror of her body before the suffering it had once endured. Even though she herself was willing and eager, in spite of any cost, to make it subservient to their common desire, it overcame her, now granting harbourage to her fears, lodging them so securely within itself that her will was powerless, now refusing to submit itself to greater torment. She was constantly in rebellion against it, and it was as constantly asserting its supremacy over her mind and spirit.

Silas' early dreams of one day settling in Boston or in Canton never matured beyond their gay and easy birth. The maritime world at large between 1830 and 1850 was too engrossing a place for one to leave it lightly, even to attempt to control a fraction of its destinies from somewhere ashore. He wanted, he told Solace, to drink the brimming cup it offered him to its last quickening drop. At thirty-five and forty he was wiser and more far-seeing than when at twenty-three he had arrogantly expressed his views to the untidy captain of the *Island Maid*. On a voyage home from Liverpool in late May 1840, the *Solace Winship* had been overhauled in mid-Atlantic by Mr. Samuel Cunard's pioneer steamship the *Unicorn*, on her maiden voyage to Boston. She was the first outward and visible sign of Mr. Cunard's soaring dreams, which had the year before founded his North American Royal Mail Steam Packet Company. The picture of her approaching clouds of smoke, catching slowly but inevitably up upon his full sails, the sight of her pulling slowly but steadily away from him toward the western horizon, gave Silas some bitter food for thought to be substantially increased a few years later when a fortnightly schedule of side-wheelers was established between Old England and New. Mr. Enoch Train might have his line of Liverpool sailing-packets, built in Newburyport and East Boston by Donald McKay, who, true to Silas' prophecy, was in the early 1840's beginning his work to astonish the world. His beautiful ships of the Train line, the *Joshua Bates* and the *Ocean Monarch*, might continue for a season, but the time was surely coming when they must give up their glory and be ousted from the seas by the black smoke of these walloping interlopers.

Silas was not the man to welcome these evidences of approaching change. His world and his profession in it in his eyes wanted for nothing. He was at once suspicious of innovation and noisily remonstrant against it. In moments and hours of irritation over a bad or delayed passage he nursed his disappointment over his deprivation of children by declaring to Solace that he would rather have no son at all than to see him unable to prove himself a man in the high vocation of sail. And yet, as is ever the case with persons of plenteous nature whose hopes and misgivings leap ahead of those of more average makeup, his fears were maturing long before there was actual reason for them, were over-reaching their own time and place. Sail was doomed, it is true, but it was not to know its condemnation until two decades and more after Silas' initial fears. In 1849 by the repeal of the English Navigation Acts, which threw British markets open to the products of New England shipyards, such competition arose as to which nation should market the new China teas, as to which should excel in the Australian trade, that New England shipbuilders lay awake nights to devise ways and means of satisfying the insistent demand for more and bigger and faster sailing ships. Before such a renascence in building and such new eagerness to sail beyond every horizon Silas in large measure forgot his restless dread. And when in the same year the California gold fever attacked New England with a frenzied sweep and men must be gotten around Cape Horn speedily in greedy thousands, ships and more ships became the cry—a cry that was to bring Donald McKay to his long-deserved fame and set at rest in other minds than Silas' the nagging terror lest sail had received its death blow.

11

It was in 1850 that Silas and Solace watched the launching of the clipper-ship *Surprise*, fully rigged with colours flying, from the East Boston yards of Samuel Hall, then the most eminent builder of the Massachusetts commonwealth. They had a special interest in her launching. Silas had lent his encouragement and faith to her designing by a young friend of his, a boy of twenty-three, whose daring experiments in line and rigging had brought upon him the scorn and skepticism of hundreds. Moreover, her first commander was a Maine man from the Gardiner-Hallowell family on the Kennebec; and Maine men then as now felt a peculiar sense of integrity toward one of their own number.

The new ship might have been Silas' own from the excitement and nervous interest which aroused him at dawn on the day of her launching. He had cancelled a voyage to China to be present, so sure did he feel that a new era in sail would begin with her swift cleavage of the harbour water. He paced the floor of their hotel room, hurrying Solace with her dressing, for once careless of what she looked like. They were hours early at the waterfront, in ample time to see the crowds gather, the flags flung out from nearby windows and roofs and hoisted to the main trucks and along the shrouds and stays of every anchored vessel. Half of Boston was at the waterfront, hanging from windows, swarming over house-tops, perched in trees. They waited in the brisk wind, listening to the prophecies of onlookers, both confident and faithless, watching her upon her ways in readiness for the signal shot which should sweep her toward the water, to capsize as hundreds said, to stick her sharp stern into the mud and be a total loss, or to initiate a new and glorious and golden age in marine architecture.

The shot came at length. The crowd became breathless and silent until she began to move down her smoking ways, faster and faster amid a cloud of dust and splinters and flying timber, until her stern cut the water and she shot out into the harbour, to gather herself together for one awful moment, then to pause erect and magnificent with colours flying.

Then cheers shattered the air, doubling and redoubling. The bells from church towers pealed out a welcome. Bands burst into triumphant music. The sun came from a cloudy sky to touch her lofty rigging and accentuate the long curving lines of her sharp bow and slender sides.

Silas felt his heart swell within him. His throat pained him. Tears sprang to his eyes. It was for such a moment as this that he and others like him had lived their lives. This ship, riding the water before him, was no dead thing but a living glory, an achievement equal to the artistic triumphs of other and older lands in stone and paint and marble. In her and in others like her, which would now be built, the art and the romance of a restrained, hard-headed, practical people had burst into splendid manifestation. No other country could have conceived and built her; no other race of men could sail her. He looked upon her and saw defiance in every line of her, contemptuous rebellion against any contrivance of man and machinery which should attempt to take from her the sovereignty of the seas, to sever her from her God-given alliance with wind and water. He saw her rounding Java Head, weathering the Sunda Straits, sending spray masthead high as she tore through the roaring forties, riding at tranquil anchor in London Pool while half of England looked upon her with envy tearing at their vitals. And as he looked and saw, all his fears were for the time completely swept away before the conviction that this new burst of genius which had framed her daring hull and conceived her breadths of added canvas would prove more than a match for anything that steam might do.

In those moments of conviction he saw his sons and grandsons on the quarterdecks of such ships as this, seizing proudly and as proudly handing down the tradition of his family in bold seamanship. Crocketts had sailed for two centuries, he was thinking. In the earliest Colonial trade to the West Indies, to the Mediterranean, to Madagascar they had sailed their tiny, home-built vessels, laden with fish and lumber, vessels so small and unwieldy that only men with wits to learn the secrets of the ocean, with courage to weather her perils through good and ill fortune, would have dared venture upon their decks out of sight of land. Through the eighteenth century they had followed every rugged avenue, shaping all to their purpose, triumphing over every obstacle by which wars and parliaments might have put less stalwart men to shame. Now in the nineteenth they were reaping their hard-won reward in the chance to man and to master such ships as this one that rode so magnificently and so insolently before him.

Solace watched him standing there, unconscious of her, of the cheering crowds about them, of some heavy raindrops which had come suddenly from a dark cloud above them. And as she watched, she knew as she had not known before the supreme devotion of his life before which even his love for her was blotted out. There followed an understanding equally as swift when she looked from him upon the ship, waiting eager and triumphant upon the harbour water. The thoughts within his mind suddenly translated themselves into her own; the revelation of a vision, which all her years at sea had never given, now swept upon her. In that penetrating flash of comprehension all the dread from which she had been powerless to free herself became as nothing. The past loosened its claims; the present made way for the future. When she sailed again, she thought, her body would no longer hold her in slavery. She was like those of whom the prophet had spoken, those who had once sat in darkness, even in the shadow of death, but who now were shined upon with light.

Ten years were to pass, however, before she was to experience the truth which those moments had granted her. For in three months Silas sailed alone for Australia leaving her willingly in Saturday Cove to await the long delayed coming of his son.

II

Nicholas Crockett

1850-1875

Nicholas Crockett

1

Nicholas Danforth Crockett was named a full month before his father took ship for Australia in early September of 1850. Silas, needless to say, had named him. The disquieting suspicion that a daughter might conceivably be the portion of the inheritance allotted to him had never once seriously entered Silas' expectant and delighted mind, although the fear, together with manifold apprehensions of a lesser nature, lay heavily upon the mind of Solace. Twenty years had not sufficed to blot from her tenacious memory all that had happened on that flat sea in the month of June of the year 1831.

She was glad to be alone with Abigail during her long months of waiting. Abigail was one to quiet apprehensions of all sorts in so far as they could be quieted. At seventy-five she seemed to have entered upon a second middle-age, much as middle-aged persons sometimes experience a recrudescence of youth. She stoutly affirmed again and again to Solace that she felt better than she had at fifty, that so far as she could see nothing whatever was wrong with *her*, and that she had not the slightest notion of consulting a doctor until she was flat on her back for her last illness, which she prayed the Lord might be short and soon over. It was impossible not to take heart from her brusque cheerfulness.

Moreover, she was inclined toward Silas' unshakable faith that a son was inevitable.

"The Crocketts run to boys," she said when she detected misgiving on the part of Solace. "And as for the Shaws, they're betwixt and between. As regards your own family, that don't cut much ice, there being only you, though your father was one of six boys, a good sign enough, and your mother had three brothers as well as three sisters. Some folks say that thinking makes a difference. Praying, too. It don't seem sense to me, but there's no harm in trying it. The main thing in all this business is not to get all flustered up, no matter what happens."

While Solace hemmed innumerable diapers on still, warm September afternoons on the wide porch, crocheted sacques, and feather-stitched foot-blankets, Abigail got her own store of things ready. She was not one, she said, to wait until the eleventh hour. She made half a dozen draw-sheets for Solace's bed of good, unbleached Lowell cotton, which, when finished, she spread upon the grass of the field in the full sunlight and allowed to remain out for two nights in order to get the smell of the mills from the tough yellow fabric. Some people might be contented with four or even two, she said to herself, as she ran her hot iron over the crinkled surfaces preparatory to putting them away, but she was not one to skimp, she was glad to say. Biding her time and chance, she got at last a new silver half-dollar in some change handed to her, and took it to the blacksmith to have a hole bored through it. This was for the baby to cut his teeth on. She crocheted in close chain-stitch a stout cord of red wool to hang it from. Red worsted, she had always been told, was proof against croup, and, although she did not really believe it, the coin might as well be hung on red worsted as on anything else. She procured three yards of the best red flannel she could find and finished her hemming of it with a firm border of cat-stitching in white. She would swathe Solace in this once her pains had begun. There was nothing like it for warmth and a good, secure sense of tightness and strength.

"There used to be an idea of charm in these old swathing-bands," she said to Solace as she put in her cat-stitch. "When I and all the rest of us were born, my mother was all done up in one that was embroidered in white letters. 'Wait on the Lord,' it said. 'Be of good courage.' My grandmother used to say it kept off bad luck with those words on it, and my mother did have her ten without any of the fuss that so many women make in these latter days. But I'm not one that believes such things myself. All the same I wish we had kept it. It's a shame to throw away old things like that that meant something once. When the boys went off to sea, my mother cut it up and gave it to them for chest protectors. Nathan, I remember, had the piece that said 'the Lord' on it, but it didn't keep him from the Malays."

She saved the wood ashes from her fires, sifted them, and with lye and her best lard made some specially prepared soap in wooden butter molds, one placed on the other. She perfumed her cakes of soap, some with lavender, some with rose water, wrapped them closely in thin paper, and laid them away in the drawer where she kept all her things in readiness for the great event.

"They're pure," she said. "That's one thing. I know every dite that's in them. They're not like these prepared soaps that are made nobody knows where or by who just in order to get some profit out of folks that buy. I like things myself that your own hands make in your own kitchen. There are too many mills and factories coming into this world these days to suit me. Folks are bound to get shiftless when the time comes that they can buy everything they need."

She made a healing ointment of lard and mint and tallow for the initial greasing of her grandson; she brewed and bottled essences for croup and colic. She searched circumspectly about her hen-yard whenever she went for her eggs for quills of just the right width and texture and laid away half a dozen perfect ones in the drawer. When Solace was once in labour, these would come in handy. Inserted in her nose, one by one as she needed them, they would induce sneezing and immeasurably assist the necessary contractions. She went through her linen closet, tearing her soft, worn sheets into pads and bandages, cutting her old blankets into tiny ones for the baby's cradle. In the field before the house on a still, windless autumn day she dismantled an old feather-tick, airing and sunning its contents before she filled with them the small pillows and bed-cushions which she had made. And she did all these things with such assurance and confidence, such eager expectation, that Solace, thinking of Silas somewhere on the high seas, found shallow ground in which to nourish her worst fears.

All Saturday Cove felt an excitement tinged with foreboding over the coming of the baby once the early news had traversed the village. There were prognostications and forecasts gloomy enough in all conscience. Travail at forty, after twenty years of God-sent barrenness, was a ticklish business at best. Experience and the Bible seemed dead against it in spite of the eclipsing triumph of Sarah, the wife of Abraham, at the age of ninety! Old women, still unforgetful of the slipper on the tombstone, muttered grim prophecies while they gave thanks to God that Dorcas Winship had been spared this last and crowning anxiety; the middle-aged at quilting-bees and church sewing-circles recalled a hundred disastrous incidents, whispering decorously in pairs across their needlework, for such subjects were not bandied about recklessly in 1850; the unmarried young, presumably in chaste ignorance of Mrs. Crockett's "condition," found their Sunday afternoon strolls in the churchyard immensely enlivened by a topic of conversation blushingly ventured upon between closest friends and judiciously withheld from their mothers.

Yet the fingers of many belied their thoughts and their tongues. Never was a baby so lavishly prepared for as this latest and last of the Crocketts. Yards upon yards of sheerest linen were drawn and hemstitched, shirred and embroidered, smocked and tucked and feather-stitched for his dresses, which measured four feet and more from neck ruffles to the deep hems of their wide skirts. Bobbins and shuttles and crochet hooks made filet and Valenciennes, picot and Limerick and tatting for the edging of his petticoats and his wide, long sleeves. He had sacques of pink and sacques of blue, bonnets and socks and foot-blankets, slips and shirts and bands, carriage robes, counterpanes, mittens, arm-warmers, and bibs, capes and cloaks and knitted boots, lined with the finest quilting. He had throws of butter muslin for the hood of his cradle to keep too much air from him and squares of fine netting to cover his face against flies in summer.

His grandfather was not the least among those who laboured in his premature behalf. Thomas Winship, living alone in the downstairs rooms of his house, was deaf and shaky at seventy-four. He had lived a hard life and his muscles were in meet rebellion. But he puttered about his shop nevertheless, fashioning a cradle for young Nicholas. It was a cradle of cherry wood with the triangularly sawn boards of its hood fitting so closely and neatly that not a nail was needed to strengthen the glue that held them in place. The foot was hooded, too, and the rockers were so cleverly designed that the whole could be entirely stationary at will. When it was done to his complete satisfaction, he rubbed it inside and out for hours each day with oil and finest sand, moving the palm of his hand with the grain of the wood until it felt like satin even to his experienced touch. And one December morning when the air was clear and cold and there was no suspicion of dampness anywhere, he carried it himself on his shoulders, through the village, up the hill, and eastward to Abigail Crockett's house, quite unconscious that his behaviour in so doing was unseemly in the extreme and bound to cause deplorably intimate questioning by children of their disturbed parents.

All in all Saturday Cove in the year 1850 was surging with excitement. What with three new ships for California taking shape within its yards, with a fleet of twenty-five vessels leaving for Fundy and the Magdalens whenever fish were running and every boy turned fourteen advancing three times a day the best of reasons why he should leave school at once, with the neighbouring town of Eastport clamouring for lobsters to be put up in cans by seven busy firms, which already were curing fish by eighteen thousand quintals annually and putting up each year twelve thousand barrels or pickled herring, and with the discovery in Hancock County just to the west (and by a woman at that!) that the despised porgy contained oil worth thirty-seven cents a gallon, the arrival of another Crockett was an event well-timed in an era of surpassing richness when the sea was yielding its heavy fruit yearly even though the tough land might be obdurate.

News from Silas was far-spaced but consoling. A Boston ship brought letters from Madeira telling of a favourable voyage; another, two months later from Sydney, announced his safe arrival after a commendable passage around Good Hope. His thoughts were all at home, he said, where he hoped, cargo and weather permitting, to arrive by early summer. His assurances, like those of Abigail, were high; he did not allow himself to be anxious although he found sleep difficult and set-backs more irritating than formerly.

Solace accused herself of heartlessness as the days came and went, slipping almost imperceptibly into one another, over sharing Abigail's honest relief at his absence. It was easier to wait without him. She and Abigail were daily drawn together in a world, which, though occasioned by man, was mercifully without his intrusion. It was a woman's world, patient, unhurried, self-contained, a world of letting well-enough alone until the time should come for action.

"Men are bad waiters," said Abigail. "At least on land they are, and the Crocketts are worse than most. My mother was forever thanking the Lord that my father was away when her children came, except for the first. Her eldest was nervous as a cat, and she always said 'twas because of his father stumping up and down stairs and saying things ought to move faster. He nearly drove her crazy, well-intentioned as he was. If Silas was here now, he'd be bouncing around this house like a pea on a skillet and suggesting a dozen things that we could do better'n we're doing. You can't hurry Nature, and women know it. You'd think men would learn it at sea if anywheres, but the Crocketts at least never brought much of it ashore with them."

Abigail was right, thought Solace. You could not hurry Nature. Every day fulfilled its purpose, quietly, invisibly for the most part; yet within itself, she knew, the earth, itself pregnant, must be conscious of the passing of time, rhythmic, inevitable, unerring. She began to feel herself a part of it, in an odd sense in league with it as, like it, she waited until her own time should be fulfilled. Except in the coldest weather Abigail encouraged her being out-of-doors as much as possible. In October and November, when the hazy skies bent close above the land, she bent above the garden rows, gathering the best of the seed-pods and sacs against the spring sowing, cutting back the dried stalks of hollyhocks and larkspur, pulling the stout, corrugated roots of the dahlias and wrapping them in burlap for storage in the cellar. It was good to get up and down, Abigail said, to bend forward and straighten oneself again. It was good, too, to feel the earth beneath one's body, the soil in one's hands. Wholesome, sustaining things came from the earth, she said. In the short December days Solace walked across the brown, withered fields, noting the close hold of the hardening loam and clay upon the grass roots, the swift yellowing of the marsh reeds and cat-tails. After such hours outside, the warmth of the evening fire seemed not so much to shut out the cold and the frost-bound earth as to translate them into heat and light, the flaming logs to give out the sun's long gift of heat, the glowing embers the colours of sunrise and sunset and autumn trees. Even the murmur of the fire became the sound of wind. She had not realized before how akin people are to the earth, how they come from it and go back within it to add themselves to its eternal cycle, its never-ending round.

She loved Silas; the thought of him quickened her senses after twenty years even as at first; but she became increasingly glad as her time moved on toward its completion (or its beginning, she sometimes thought) that he was not with her. He would worry over her, disturb the even flow of her quiet days by the very turbulence of his thoughts and plans for her, for the baby, and himself. For herself, as January gave place to February, she seemed less and less able to look either ahead or behind. She had heard it said somewhere that there was no such thing as the present, that it was only an instant between the two eternities of the past and the future. But now with her the present seemed all in all, the present of Monday and of Thursday and of Saturday, not cut into hours and minutes that fled but instead enclosed in a motionless sphere in which she moved, never reaching the end of one spent day, never actually beginning upon a new. And since the past had moved backward into oblivion and the future refused to picture itself, fears became absurd and futile. Perhaps the earth, she thought, as she looked out upon the snowy fields and meadows, had become like herself, was now quiescent, even somnolent, unconscious of the future, unable to summon up the past. Only when the child moved within her with increasing strength, as the marsh willows in late February and early March began to put out their catkins, was the even balance of her existence disturbed. Then the changing face of time began again to make itself apparent and she to be aware of the days as days.

"I'm coming to life again like the earth," she thought, and she said to Abigail as they sat sewing together,

"I believe I've been half asleep all the fall and winter. I haven't thought or decided anything. I'd begun to think I'd lost any mind I ever had. At first I could remember all the things that scared me most the other time, but for six months I haven't been able even to remember much of anything."

"That's good," said Abigail. "That's the way it should be. You can't expect to make a life out of your own body and at the same time have your brain crackling away like a soft-wood fire. It's not sense. There's seed time and harvest, as the Bible says, and there's a long, slow space between them."

Solace looked gratefully at her mother-in-law. If her years rested on her at all, they rested as fulfillment and completion, a good finish of a job well done, not as any threat of impending change. Even her hands as she quickly shifted her knitting needles were not the hands of an old woman. They were smooth, deft, and pliable, almost untouched by the usual furrows and blotches of age.

"And I've not been really frightened," continued Solace, "at least beyond the first few weeks. You can't know what it has meant not to be frightened, even with all the things people say happen to women when they bear children late in life. The time before," she shuddered in sudden remembrance, "the time before—oh, it was terrible from start to finish! Sometimes I thought I'd just have to give way and tell Silas I couldn't stand it."

"It wouldn't have done any good," said Abigail. "And it would have cheated you out of remembering one of the few times when you were able to keep your mouth shut. It's a help as one goes on to have those times to remember."

She had risen from her chair to place another log upon the tall brass andirons. She stood with the log in her hands as she spoke, erect by the great blackened fireplace. She looked oracular as she stood there, like some ancient prophetess in her wide black skirts and spotless white apron.

"No, it wouldn't have done a mite of good," she repeated. "Women are forever saying that they'd like for men to suffer just one hour some of the pains women suffer for days on end. That's nonsense. We have our portion and they theirs, and I often think theirs is the hardest for just the reason that there are some things they can't grasp, no matter how they'd try. Suffering without understanding in this life is a heap worse than suffering when you have at least the grain of an idea what it's all for. They say the world's bound to change a lot in the next fifty years. They say there'll soon be schools and colleges all over where women will learn all the same things that men learn. Maybe so. But learning won't alter the fact that women are women and men are men." She smiled a bit slyly at her daughter-in-law. "Sometimes I'm that bold to think," she said, "that if the Lord God had been born a woman, there'd have been more wisdom among men."

She threw the log on the fire with a fine, free sweep of her arms, then slapped her hands briskly together to clear them from dust and bits of bark before again taking up her knitting.

"Some things and places are unnatural to women. The sea's one, though I'm not saying it hasn't had its part in the raising of certain of us. It takes the fretting out of one, that's sure, and makes you know you can't hurry along the Lord's good time. But women belong to earth, not to water, and it's best for all concerned when their children are born on it."

It proved best for all concerned in the case of young Nicholas. He came in the late afternoon of the last day of March after twelve hours of what Abigail termed only a moderate hard time for his mother. Not one of the grim catastrophes, which were all day predicted about the village when once it was learned that Solace was in labour, occurred. The doctor, leaving the house at six o'clock was just in time to meet the town crier starting on his sunset rounds throughout the village and give him the welcome and unexpected news. So that Nicholas Danforth Crockett began his sojourn upon this earth with the stout ringing of Mr. Hosea Horton's big brass bell and the sonorous tones of his voice sounding up hill and down through the drowsy streets in the early spring twilight:

"A son is born to Captain Silas Crockett and his wife. And all's well!"

The sexton took matters into his own hands and rang the church bell; the vessels in the harbour ran up their flags although the sun was setting; and women everywhere neglected their suppers to call upon their neighbours and rejoice.

Solace did not hear the crying of her son by Mr. Hosea Horton nor yet the ringing of the church bell. She was sleeping away her exhaustion and her pain in the big bed of Abigail's best room where Silas himself had first seen the light and yelled lustily at his greeting of it. But when she awoke at eight o'clock between her clean sheets and saw the tidiness of her room in the light from the candle sconces and heard the spring wind tapping the twigs of the lilacs against the window sill, she caught the cheerful accents of Abigail's voice rising from the distant kitchen.

Abigail was signing to her grandson whom she had laid, well greased and wrapped in old blankets, across her knees. She was accenting her song both with her voice and with the firm tapping of her heels against her yellow floorboards:

Róck-a-bye, báby, upón my fond knée,
Thy fáther's a sáilor and sáils the deep séa.
Thy móther's a lády, her shúttle doth ply
With her fáce toward the tíde and a teár in her éye.

Solace drifted back again to sleep, the most perfect sleep she had ever known; and while the well-pleased nurse stirred corn-meal gruel plentifully sprinkled with raisins in the iron kettle over the fire, Abigail studied her grandson by careful peeps within his blankets.

The baby had been born with a caul, a perfect one well drawn over head and face. Abigail could scarcely wait for Solace to be strengthened by her corn-meal gruel before she broke upon her this stupendous fact. For free as Abigail was from most of the manifold superstitions that beset her place and time, she had never eschewed nor cared to do so the faith that such a child was in some mysterious way singled out from the beginning for rare gifts and achievements, a thrice glorious future.

Óh! The oák and the ásh and the stúrdy pine trée
They máke all togéther the shíps on the séa.

He was long like Amos and James and Nicholas, like Silas himself, like most of the Crocketts. He had a well-shaped head with a mass of dark hair. She could swear he would have a cowlick on the right of his broad forehead like his uncle Nicholas. He had long fingers which he held straight out, the sign of a generous nature. His ears were inclined to stand a bit too far from his head, but that could be easily corrected by a thin indoor bonnet of net. She had never seen a better forehead on any child. If the promise of intelligence did not lie within that skull, then she was at a complete loss to find it anywhere. He was of a fine shade of deepest red, which always betokened a better whiteness later on. She was always suspicious of pale babies. And his knees, she was relieved to think, did not show the slightest trace of the Shaw and Winship tendency toward too great width and stockiness.

But the ápple and the háwthorn and whíte lilac trée
Will béckon thy fáther back hómeward to thée.

2

Nicholas was five months old to a day when his father first saw him. By the time he had reached the age of five years he stoutly maintained with an early stubbornness that distressed his mother and amused his grandmother that he remembered the event—how his father had torn up the wide staircase three steps at once to his mother's room where he lay on the bed in his best clothes, which spread out like a great fan over the quilted counterpane, how he had laughed until the room rang with his laughter and shouted, "Well, I'm blessed, Solace!" how he had given him then and there a gourd from Australia that rattled, a tiny, full-rigged ship in a glass bottle, and a monkey that ran up and down a red string, and how he had lifted him on his wide shoulder and run downstairs with him and out into the sunny garden.

"You cannot remember, Nicholas," Solace patiently repeated. "Little babies cannot remember things. You only think you remember because we have told you so many times. It is not true to say you remember, and you must not tell untruths."

He always appealed to his grandmother.

"Your mother is right," she told him. "Your mother is always right, and you must not contradict her. If you do, you must be punished."

He glared at them both then with his wide blue eyes, so like his father's, full of angry tears, in the kitchen or the sitting-room or garden, wherever they were, fear keeping him silent, frustration feeding his rage. Then he ran wildly away from them both, through the woodshed and into the great barn in the winter, out into the fields in the summer.

"I do! I do! I do!" he shouted there, to the windy trees and blowing grass, to the sea that every day came rushing in to right the harbour boats. It made him feel immeasurably better so that he could return to the house and smile at them again.

His real and earliest memories were centred about his grandmother rather than about his mother. His grandmother set him safely on the top of the old chest of drawers in the kitchen, tied him securely to its tall, upright posts, and let him sit there and watch her while she worked about the great sunny room. He remembered the sun lying on the yellow floor in great shafts of light, the red geraniums in the window, and the smell of ginger cookies baking in the oven. There were always cookie-boys for him with currants for buttons across their wide, fragrant stomachs and short, stout legs which he ate first. Or there were rabbits and ducks which he could not have until he had counted the row of them on the kitchen table far below his high perch. Through the bright window-panes in spring and summer and autumn and above the sparkling, uneven line of the frost in winter he could see the water with ships moving over it, inward and outward, until the ice closed it in and the snow covered the fields. His grandmother said endless rhymes to him about Jack and Jill and Tommy Tucker and made him say the last words of each when he once began to talk. She sang to him, too. Whenever she sang, she stopped what she was doing, stopped the spoon which she was moving round and round in a great yellow bowl, the iron with which she was smoothing the white sheets, the round mass of dough which she was folding and kneading with vigorous pushing of her arms and hands. She pointed her finger at him while she sang and tapped one of her feet against the floor. She had a wide variety of songs, yet they all seemed to swing to the same tune, which she apparently liked because she could swing her finger or her spoon up and down before him.

King Ne-bu-chad-nez-zar, that wily old fox,
God sent to the fields to eat grass with an ox.
Said the ox to the king, "You're an odd king to me,
But I'll lend you my grass and the shade of my tree!"

When she had finished one song, she was given to explaining it.

"He was a kind ox to be good to a king who had torn out people's eyes and burned them up in fiery furnaces. Animals are good, Nicholas. You should be kind to them."

Old Móses went úp on a hígh mountain tóp,
Said Gód unto Móses, "Right hére you must stóp."
Said Móses to Gód, "I don't líke it up hére,
Cold wínd blows my beárd, in my éye there's a téar."

Said Gód unto Móses, "Stop fússing at mé.
I'm the Lórd and you're Móses, so stáy where you bé.
I've commándments to gíve you, in áll there are tén?,
They're for yóu and all péople, both wómen and mén."

"What's commandments?" asked Nicholas when he was four and had been moved from the chest to walk about the kitchen and clean the frosting-bowl with a big spoon.

"They're rules to live by," said his grandmother. "You will learn them presently on Sundays. If you break any one of them, there'll be trouble for somebody. So just remember that."

Solace was distressed sometimes over the familiar, even sacrilegious tone of Abigail's songs. She thought secretly that Abigail improvised them as she worked. Their nature was surely not in keeping with the scriptural teaching which Solace had received or with the Bible instruction usually given to children in the 1850's. She accused Abigail of this practice one morning when she had caught such light treatments of Joshua and Gideon echoing through the warm, bright kitchen. Abigail's defense of herself was as light as her songs.

"Well," she said, "I caught the tune from my grandmother. It's an easy tune and words fit into it well. They can't hurt him, can they? He'll remember the names at least."

"I don't presume they'll hurt him," ventured Solace, "but they don't seem—well, exactly in keeping with the Bible."

"Nonsense!" said Abigail. "The Bible always did need to be livened up a bit in some parts, at least in my opinion."

His grandmother, too, devised his punishments and mercilessly administered them. In this his mother was sadly lacking. He early learned that he had but to look beseechingly at her and cry for his absent father, upon which behaviour she would, in all probability, relent. But Abigail was obdurate.

"The Lord," she said, "has spoiled all Crocketts from the first by His gifts and graces. I'm not the one to continue with His bad work."

When Nicholas screamed at the table and refused to eat his porridge or his baked potato, which would make him into a strong sea captain like his father, his grandmother summarily lifted him from his high-chair and sent him shrieking into the dark hall closet, no matter how his mother quivered. She did not carry or lead him there. He had to walk himself, stumbling half-blind in his fury, his bib tight against his face. Nicholas learned a good deal in that hall closet, sobbing against the old greatcoats of his grandfather and his father. He learned that it was far easier to decide to eat what was on his plate than to put there in the closet a cheerful smile upon his face when all the strange things inside his body were rebelling against the smile. But since it was the only condition upon which he could return to the table, he learned to put it there.

Abigail was unique and original about her methods of correction and discipline. She had one punishment which Nicholas detested above all others because it so hurt his superabundant pride. When he was disobedient or saucy or above all else whined over some deprivation (for Abigail could not tolerate a whiner, she said) she put a stout roller-towel around his neck, crossed it over his chest and under his arms, and hung him to a convenient knob or to the wide, jutting corner of a window sill. She arranged him so that his toes just touched the floor and left him to his solitary contemplations. Such a position was ignominious in the extreme and most efficacious of all her contrivances for the decent moulding of his character.

From the time he could remember anything he remembered Wednesday and Saturday afternoons when he went to see his grandfather. After he was five, he went by himself unless the snow was too deep for him. When dinner at noon was over, he had his nap and was then "cleaned up" in the kitchen according to the rigourous term and custom of the time and place. Cleaning up meant the scrubbing of his neck and ears with a rough, soapy cloth, the washing of his hands and face in a tin basin, and the careful brushing and parting, well on the right side, of his unruly hair, which, true to Abigail's prophecy, grew in a cowlick like that of his Uncle Nicholas. It meant, too, the changing of his morning clothes into his second-best suit, a suit whose short blue coat met his long buff trousers behind in a tiny peak and buttoned close around his neck inside his starched white collar. This for fall and winter. In spring and summer he wore white trousers of duck or merino and a short jacket of blue linen.

Once dressed, he set forth at two o'clock with a present from his grandmother in his hand, in summer a bunch of flowers, in fall and winter a loaf of bread warm from the oven or a bag of dough-nuts. He was always slow in his journey once he was out of sight of his mother and grandmother, who stood at the door or window and who had warned him not to stop at all on the way. Nicholas loved stopping. There was so much to see along the familiar way to his grandfather's. The road ran beside the shore, and he was forever loitering in spring and summer and early fall to scan the harbour and look out between and beyond the islands to see what craft were visible. There were always lumber-laden schooners for the yards and by two o'clock some inshore fishing-boats were coming in, lying deep in the blue water. Sometimes—oh, glorious sight!—

his eyes caught a ship under full sail cutting the horizon and making landward. He learned with incredible swiftness whether she was a foreign ship or not. If she was, laden with salt for the fisheries or with hemp for the rope-works at the yards, he knew how interest would quicken about the village with the arrival of dark men, jabbering in strange tongues, wearing outlandish handkerchiefs about their necks and sometimes gold rings in their ears, and frequently carrying parrots and monkeys about on their shoulders. When the tide was out and there was nothing else to stay his feet, he left the road and wandered along the shore, turning over the crabs to watch them kick their ungainly legs or walking as close to the flats as he dared to make the clams spit at his unwelcome presence. In the village street people were likely to stop and speak to him. He had friends among the storekeepers who gave him sweetmeats to be eaten hastily and never confessed at home.

When he at last reached his grandfather's white house, he trudged past its austere closed front behind its white pickets to the back door, which was flanked by lilac trees and enclosed by a curving green lattice with a honeysuckle vine weaving itself in and out of the square holes. There his grandfather always met him with a good deal of formality, extended a shaking hand with big blue lines standing out upon it to meet his small one, and led him through the kitchen into the back sitting-room. Nicholas never knew how his grandfather had prepared himself for these visits, how after his solitary dinner he had shaved carefully with a good deal of peril to himself and put on his good black suit and a clean low collar, which in his old age he had substituted in place of the cravats he used to wear.

The visits were always divided into three distinct parts. First, there was a solemn quarter of an hour in the sitting-room with Nicholas on the edge of a red plush chair at one side of the center-table and his grandfather in one with broad arms on the other side. During this time Nicholas was formally offered an apple from the plate always on the red cloth table-cover. Sometimes it was hard to eat the apple and keep his balance on the chair for his feet were fully twelve inches from the floor, but he always managed it. He had to shout to his grandfather whenever a question was put to him, which was not often, for his grandfather was a silent man and the questions were usually the same ones to which he knew the answers he was expected to give.

"How is your mother today, my son?"

"She is very well, I thank you, sir," shouted Nicholas across the big room with its high ceiling, its heavy gilt-framed pictures, the shiny haircloth sofa with its curved back, and the what-not with shells and a rose-jar and a little full-rigged ship, which his grandfather had made and which, he always vainly hoped, might one day be offered to him to take home.

"And your grandmother, I presume she is as usual?"

"Yes, sir," shouted Nicholas again. "She sends you some doughnuts and says you are not to eat them just before bedtime."

There was always a pause then in which Nicholas while he munched his apple studied his grandfather. He never could understand why his throat was divided by two flabby pieces of wrinkled skin that lay upon his collar whenever he bent his head and why his hands trembled as they did upon his black knees or the arms of his chair.

"Your mother and grandmother are good women and bring you up well. I trust you are a good and obedient boy to them at all times."

"Yes, sir," shouted Nicholas once more, often with misgiving at the very back of his mind. Yet the reply seemed necessary and invariable.

"Is there news of your father?"

Sometimes at this question, as in the autumn of 1857 when Nicholas was six and a half, he hitched himself carefully down from his chair, laid his half-eaten apple on the center-table, and crossed the room to shout into his grandfather's ear.

"He said there was a big wreck on Sydney Heads. A great ship from England called the *Duncan Dunbar* ran on them in the night and split herself in two. There were people and people drowned, like rats my father said. It was a terrible wreck."

His grandfather nodded his head slowly at this terrific disclosure, but he did not seem so surprised as Nicholas had hoped. He always seemed to know by some strange process forbidden to little boys everything that had happened. Nicholas stood on the very tips of his toes then and shouted still louder into his grandfather's ear.

"Only one man was saved and there were over one hundred in all on board her. My father thinks the captain was at fault, sir."

"Doubtless," said his grandfather, still sagely nodding his round, bald head quite as though he had known the master of the *Duncan Dunbar,* his family at home, and what he had had for his supper on the night of the disaster.

Nicholas stood back then on the flat of his feet surveying his grandfather. Clearly something should be done to make him realize the size of this event. Nicholas had not meant to tell him the words that had been ringing in his ears ever since his mother had read his father's letter aloud to him. She had warned him against repeating them carelessly, but the time had surely come. Now he raised himself on his toes again and shouted at the very top of his lungs.

"The captain, he cried when he left Plymouth in England, 'Hell or Sydney in sixty days!' That's what he cried, sir! My father says it was a—a *vain-glorious* boast. My father says it was not Sydney that captain reached!"

His grandfather then leaned forward a bit in his chair and chuckled from somewhere far within his collar, and Nicholas felt a little more satisfied.

All in all, except on the days when there was something like the *Duncan Dunbar* to impart, the first quarter of an hour was trying to Nicholas, but he bore it, knowing what was to follow. For after it was over his grandfather was sure to draw from the kitchen chest two aprons of blue and white ticking, one large and soiled, one small and clean, and bind them about himself and Nicholas. Then they went through the kitchen and the long wood-shed into his grandfather's shop where in winter a small black stove was crackling and where in summer the door was always open upon the blowing fields. They spent an hour there, sometimes longer.

Thomas Winship taught his grandson to drive nails straight and sure into square white blocks of pine, little nails first with a quick stroke of his own small hammer with the red handle, then larger ones.

"That's the first thing a builder has to learn," he said, "to drive a nail straight."

"I like to drive nails," shouted Nicholas, "but I shall not be a builder. I shall be a sailor like my father."

Thomas Winship looked steadily at his grandson. He knew that he had not many years to look at him, and he did not wish to lose any time.

"That's well and good enough," he said. "I was a sailor myself. But it's good, too, to build things."

It was good. Nicholas at five had his own small chest of tools which his grandfather gave him and his own bench upon which to work. He stood beside it in his apron and learned to use his plane and saw and chisel as well as his hammer. He made a square footstool for his mother to use in church and a box with two partitions in it for his grandmother's knives and forks and spoons. He wanted above all else to make boats, but his grandfather would not allow him to begin before he was nine. By that time Nicholas had learned a great deal about boats from being on one himself, and his grandfather had gone where there was no need of boats, at least if the prophet on Patmos had been right in his vision.

It was pleasant in the shop especially in spring and summer. The fields stretched before its open back doors to the pastures which in their turn rose toward the hills. Bobolinks swung on the grass-tops and sang; the wind blew the daisies and buttercups; in July the men bent to their scythes.

When their hour there was over, his grandfather fetched his hat and cane, and they started on their walk to the yards. This was for Nicholas the crowning hour of the afternoon. His grandfather did not take his hand as his mother and grandmother, or even his father when he was at home, were always doing. Instead he walked sedately, if a bit uncertainly, on the right of the board or cindered sidewalks and expected Nicholas to keep to the left. He rarely spoke as they went through the village street and down the gravelly road that led to the docks and yards, although he watched carefully to see that Nicholas did not forget to take off his round hat of black beaver or white straw whenever they met a lady or an old gentleman. But once they were upon the scene of thrilling action he became more talkative. He was forever introducing Nicholas to all kinds of gentlemen who were tending to this or that, captains and owners, master shipwrights and foremen.

"This is my grandson, Nicholas Crockett," he would say, even though they had seen Nicholas a hundred times already. "You remember his grandfather and his father. He will one day command a ship himself like the others of his family."

"That's right!" they said to Nicholas, who knew it was right, the rightest thing in all the world.

The yards and docks were the most wonderful place that Nicholas knew. Ships were everywhere, the great skeletons of new ships, only their bare ribs showing upon their blocks, the closed-in hulls of ships in such further process of construction that their deck furnishings were already being made, their rails and hatchways and fo'c'sles, their officers' quarters, their capstans and winches. There were foreign ships, too, lying at the docks, a brig from Cadiz just unloading her salt, a barque from Rio. There were others preparing to leave, their decks bustling with activity, their officers yelling commands and men swarming about to carry them out. There were dingy schooners with patched sails, their decks piled so high with lumber that the sailors scrambled up and down, in and over and out, to get anywhere at all. To these Nicholas paid small attention, since at best they were only from Nova Scotia and did not count for much. There were intoxicating smells all about, of wood and tar, new rope and old, pitch and oil and canvas, the smells from the fisheries on the western shore of the cove, from the curing-sheds and flakes and barrel of cods' livers—all mingling with the smell of the sea or made heavier by the warm wet mist of late April evenings or August dog-days. And there was such a din and clatter and racket everywhere, such poundings of hammers and top mauls and mallets, such clanking of chains and groaning of tight ropes, that he could hardly hear what his grandfather was saying.

"Two for Californy this very year and a score of lesser ones for who knows where. That's a record for a village like this. But even so it's not what it was two and three years ago, Nicholas. There's a change even now, what with Californy being overcrowded and the gold giving out and Old England waking up about her own ships and hard times on us all. If you'd been born twenty-five years ago when you should have been, my son, you might have raced round the Horn to the Golden Gate in 1850 or 1851 with the best of them. Those were the days. Yes, there's a change. You ought to grow faster else the old world may beat you yet and send you to the Banks or Savannah instead of Sydney and Canton."

Even at six Nicholas did not like to hear his grandfather talk in this vein. Although he did not understand all that his words meant, he knew that he was suggesting that fewer great ships were being built everywhere, and that when he grew up there might perhaps not be one for him to sail to foreign lands where men were black and yellow, not white, and where there were wild animals and pirates. But when his father came home, he would tell a different story; and meanwhile there *were* the ships before his very eyes. Someone must sail them, he thought; and he was growing so fast that his grandmother marvelled with every Saturday night bath she gave him before her kitchen fire.

3

From the time he was four or even three he knew about other ships than those that were building and docking at Saturday Cove, many other ships. When his father was at home, and he was there for a blissful few weeks or so once every year, the talk was nearly all about ships and their captains, those new and splendid clippers, the ports to which they sailed, the races they entered upon and won, the record passages they made, smashing in less than a hundred days around the Horn to California in gales that split their high sails, to feed the men who were digging gold from the hills and washing it from the rivers and to carry more men who wanted more gold as quickly and easily as they could get it. In fact, when the talk was of anything else, Nicholas felt distinctly uneasy, fussing about the sitting-room, a nuisance to everybody, standing at the window and killing flies for poor sport, sighing and coughing now and then in the hope that someone might soon pay attention to him. Frequently his father seemed to forget him altogether, sitting in the garden or by the fireplace in his big chair and talking to the others in discouraged tones, the laughter quite gone from his face. Nicholas hated these times.

"If things don't pick up pretty soon and lively, too," his father would say, "I declare we might as well scrap all the ships or let them rot where they lie. They're rotting fast enough as it is. Captain Josiah Eldridge told me that when he left Hong Kong four months back, there were eight of the best lying there, doing nothing and nothing to do, idle as a dory at low water, no cargoes for any place at all, no agents taking any chances, money tight as a sound anchor rope. With freight dropping from sixty dollars a ton to ten dollars what's one to do? I declare I never thought a time like this would hit us."

"There've been hard times surely before," said Nicholas' grandmother. "It seems to me I've known more than one in my eighty-two years, and the talk was always the same. Anybody with sense might have known that folks even in California wouldn't keep on forever paying fifty dollars for a barrel of flour. Times are bound to get better, they always have, and you seem to be keeping afloat yourself, Silas."

"That's just about what I am doing!" cried his father, getting so upset that he walked around the room in his excitement and still paying no attention to Nicholas. "I'm afloat and that's all. I'm losing money every voyage, and where it's going to stop I can't for the life of me see. I might as well take on passengers for a fancy yachting cruise, only no one's got any money to pay for a voyage from New York to Sandy Hook. I've seen hard times myself, but they didn't hit shipping this way. In 1837 I didn't see a whit of difference."

Nicholas' mother never took any part in these conversations. She just sewed on or sat quietly with her hands in her lap as though she thought that if she said nothing and sat still, other people might do the same. But they didn't.

"Well, we're not paupers yet," said his grandmother. "I guess we'll weather through somehow and the world, too."

Nicholas did not know what paupers were, but from his grandmother's cheerful tone he assumed that, bad as they must be, they would escape being them a while longer. And after all his father did not always or even often talk thus, at least when Nicholas thought about him afterward in the dull days immediately following his departure. He never could reconcile these long, slow days with the quick ones when they had been expecting him, looking every day in the column of the state paper that said *Marine Intelligences* for news of his ship, when his grandmother had been cooking, cooking, always cooking, it seemed to him, and his mother had been singing, and he had gone more often to his grandfather's shop to finish some surprise he was making for his father. After all, when he thought about it afterward, he remembered most clearly the hours when he and his father had been all to themselves, shutting out everyone else, who did not seem in those shining days to count for anything at all.

His father took him to the docks and yards, stepping more briskly than his grandfather could ever step. He took him on the very ships themselves, those being built and those waiting at the piers. He taught him to name all the different places and parts as they walked about, beginning with the large things like the main deck and the topgallant forecastle, the jib-boom, the bulwarks and scuppers, some of which he knew already and could startle his father with his knowing, and coming down to capstans, winches, belaying-pins, and a dozen others.

Once when a ship was getting underway from her anchorage in the waters beyond the cove, he rowed Nicholas out in a dory and explained all the manifold confusing things they were doing on board her until Nicholas' head fairly swam with his father's explanations, with all the orders he heard from the mates and the scrambling about below and aloft. He saw the sails loosened fore and aft, the courses, topsails, topgallant sails, royals and skysails fluttering in their gear, the great ship feeling the breath of life. He had braces and halyards, buntlines and leechlines, gaskets and clew-lines and sheets pointed out to him until he was dizzy with all the words. He saw the three topsail yards go aloft with the sailors singing their throats hoarse. His father, standing up recklessly in the rocking dory, sang with them:

Then up aloft that yard must go,
Whiskey for my Johnny.
Oh, whiskey is the life of man,
Whiskey, Johnny!

Oh, whiskey killed my sister Sue,
Whiskey, Johnny!
And whiskey killed the old man, too,
Whiskey for my Johnny.

Then the ship looked like some great seabird ready for flight, and fly she did with her yards braced sharp to the wind, the water curving back from her sharp bow and closing in behind her. And when she had gone at last so far that only the gleam on her sails came back to them rocking there, his father taught him the song and they sang it all the way homeward with his father pulling on the oars to the rhythm of the refrain.

Evenings were perhaps the best of all. Then, as soon as he was six and had had some lessons for a week, they played a game of questions and answers before bedtime, on the porch or on chilly nights before the fire. Nicholas stood between his father's long legs for this game, for he liked that better than sitting on his knees, and he always wanted his mother and his grandmother to be present, for it was more exciting to show what he knew when there were more to hear.

"Now, young Nicholas," his father always began, "we will see what you know this evening. Stand at attention and answer like a gentleman and a sailor."

"Who is the greatest builder of ships the world has ever seen?"

"Mr. Donald McKay, sir."

"Name his best ships."

Nicholas drew a long breath and stood up very straight. This was the worst question of all.

"The *Flying Cloud*, the *Flying Fish*, the *Bald Eagle*, the *Sovereign of the Seas*, the *Great Republic*, sir."

"Good! Which was the largest?"

"The *Great Republic*, sir."

"Launched when?"

"In 1853, sir."

"What happened to her?"

"She was burned, sir."

"What ship has made the fastest passage around the Horn to San Francisco?"

"The *Flying Cloud*."

His father glared sternly at him.

"You know better than to answer that way. Give that answer again."

"The *Flying Cloud, sir*."

"Better. In how many days and when?"

"Eighty-nine, sir. In 1851."

"Name a great Maine captain."

Nicholas always wanted to name his father then, but he said instead what was expected of him.

"Captain Philip Dumaresq, sir."

"What ships has he commanded?"

"The *Surprise* and the *Bald Eagle*, sir."

"Are those all?"

Nicholas felt his throat grow dry and his ears pink. He thought hard, but nothing came.

"Do you know?"

"I'm afraid I don't, sir."

"Don't be afraid of saying promptly you don't know a thing when you don't know it. It's the mark of an honest man and a gentleman. He commanded the *Romance of the Seas*. We'll have it in your lesson tomorrow. What ship is he commanding now?"

"I don't know, sir."

"That's better. He's commanding the *Florence*, and she's not so good a ship as the others. Now who is another great builder of ships?"

"Mr. Samuel Hall, sir."

So it went on with his cheeks growing redder and redder, his heart beating faster and faster, his mother smiling, and his grand-mother putting down her knitting to stare at him.

"Name one other great commander, young Nicholas, and that's all for tonight."

"Captain Nathaniel Palmer, sir.—But aren't we to have the sails tonight, father?"

"It's long past his bedtime, Silas," began his mother, "and he's so excited already he won't sleep a wink."

"Oh, mother, I'm not!" pleaded Nicholas. He said it carefully, being sure that it was not said like a contradiction, for his father would not stand a contradiction of his mother.

"Well, the sails then," said his father, smiling at his mother in a way Nicholas knew she could not resist. "And that's positively all."

Then Nicholas fetched the pictures from the drawer in the sitting-room table, and they went over the sails, skipping agilely about from one to another until he could hardly draw his breath between his quick answers. His father carried him up to bed when it was all over. They went up the stairs two at a time singing together at the top of their lungs *Whiskey, Johnny* or *Blow the Man Down*.

One evening when he was seven and his father on a longer stay at home than usual had talked overmuch to his mother and grandmother, to Thomas Winship and the gentlemen about the yards, about the frightful state of affairs, Nicholas put an anxious question to him just at the moment when, after kissing him good-night, he was at the head of the stairs. It took courage to ask it, but a greater fear conquered lesser ones.

"Father," he called from his bed in the room which he now had for his own, "will there be a ship for me to sail when I'm a man?"

His father came leaping back into his room then in great strides of his long legs, and stood towering above him. Nicholas remembered always how he stood there, looking down at him in the summer twilight, and how he shouted,

"A ship for a Crockett to sail? Well, I'm blessed! Yes, there'll be a ship, my son, as long as there's an ocean, and don't you forget it. We're too good a race not to make ships and sail them, even though we sail in ballast half around the world!"

So he did not worry any more even after his father had gone away again and the days were dull with school under Miss Serena Osgood, who was growing old and creaked from too tight stays when she bent above his desk. Miss Serena singled out Nicholas for especial attention, did not glower at him so blackly as she glowered at the others when they banged their slates, and always spoke his name in lingering accents which annoyed him, for the other boys were given to twitting him about it. She taught him to read, although he knew how already, in the schoolhouse which was on the grassy hill above the docks, too close to them for comfort when the hammers sounded through the long, slow mornings. She used large charts for reading, and everyone must read from them whether they knew the words or not as everyone did because the charts were never changed. They began when he was five to read:

God is our God. He will be our God even unto Death.

When he was eight and a new chart had miraculously made its appearance, they read in addition to the words about God and His watching over Saturday Cove even unto its end:

Our country is undivided and indivisible, and no state has the right to secede therefrom.

4

On a certain Friday in April of the year 1859 when Nicholas had just turned the exciting corner of his eighth birthday, he left the schoolhouse in a hurry to go to his grandfather's. Beneath his cape of black oil-cloth, which his grandmother had fashioned to keep the spring rain and dampness from his clothes, he carried with some solicitude the chromo he had just received from Miss Serena for what she termed a perfect rendition of his afternoon recitation before the school of some stanzas from John Greenleaf Whittier. He did not care much for the chromo since it pictured some water-lilies which were being pulled by a young man in a top hat and a young girl in white muslin leaning somewhat languidly from a frail-looking boat. Nevertheless, it did prove that he had said his poem well and might elicit a more material and valued reward from his grandfather.

Nicholas meant to give his recitation before Thomas Winship. He knew his grandfather would enjoy with him the spirited rhythm of the stanzas and the fine roll of the words. He meant to stand straight beside his grandfather's chair and scream them with all his might. He said them over to himself as he descended the hill far in advance of the others who were still gathering up their slates and fussing with their rubbers:

God bless her wheresoe'er the breeze
Her snowy wings shall fan,
Beside the frozen Hebrides
Or sultry Hindostan!

Where'er in mart or on the main
With peaceful flag unfurled
She helps to wind the silken chain
Of commerce round the world.

Her pathway on the open main
May blessings follow free,
And glad hearts welcome back again
Her white sails from the sea.

It was a gray, soft, wet afternoon with the chill of lingering winter side by side with the promise of spring. The lacy twigs of the village elms sent showers of drops before a vagrant wind. A light fall of snow earlier in the day increased the muddy flow of the roadside ditches. The full harbour water stretched to the fog and mist that overhung the islands and obscured the far horizon, colourless, still water except when the wind blew across it in little ripples and eddies. The small boats at anchor rode still and neglected, and the sounds from the yards were muffled in the sombre air.

His grandfather did not meet him at the back door, and the kitchen was chilly and fireless when he had once lifted the latch and passed through it to the sitting-room. His grandfather was asleep on the haircloth sofa next to the window below the iron brackets on either side where the oxalis could catch the sun. He had the newspaper spread over his face, as he often did when he fell asleep, and Nicholas, not wanting to disturb him suddenly, stood and looked at the paper, which was, conveniently for him, open at the very placed marked *Marine Intelligences.* He did not even have to lift it from his grandfather's face to read all that he wanted.

It was no use looking for his father's ship. That, he knew, was somewhere on the far seas, near St. Helena, perhaps, or Ascension Island, or even as far north as the Cape Verdes on her long way homeward. But he saw amid the manifold notices of this vessel and that the desultory cruising of a "trader," due to stop at ports along the coast, heralded as having left Boston a fortnight earlier. That was a notice worth remembering. A trader carried all sorts of merchandise, toys and school supplies, odd candies, curiously wrought marbles, tops and kites, sling-shots, pop-guns, ring-toss and pea-shooters; and if his grandfather *should* give him even so much as a dime for the successful reciting of his poem, what glee was in store for him when once she had docked at the Long Wharf and spread her wares on her main-deck for the gloating, youthful eyes of Saturday Cove!

He stood reading *Marine Intelligences* for fully five minutes before he so much as thought of his grandfather. Then something about one of his hands, extended in an odd way across his black waistcoat, caught Nicholas' attention. The hand looked blue and stiff. Nicholas laid his own warm hand upon it, partly because he was curious about it extended there, partly because he thought it a polite way to wake his grandfather, who like most deaf people never liked to be startled suddenly. The chill of the unresponsive hand went straight through Nicholas' body, warm beneath his oilcloth cape and flannel suit, widened his eyes, and made him feel afraid there in that silent room with the dish of red apples on the table and the tall clock ticking away the minutes. Then he saw his grandfather's feet, straight and stiff in their worn black slippers; and at last, with the strangest feeling he had ever had clutching at this throat, he saw his grandfather's face beneath the newspaper, which in his fear he lifted inch by inch, peering under it upon that still, set nose and mouth and tightly closed sunken eyes.

Nicholas never knew what happened next only that he found himself in the cold front hall of the house cowering in its farthest corner beneath the leaded sidelights of the great front door. It was colder there than in the room where his grandfather lay. The curved balustrade of the carpeted staircase went up and up to the cold, silent rooms above where nobody went now that his grandfather was alone. The braided rugs on the wide floorboards of the hall lay flat and stiff, their bright colours dull from the gray light without. There was a lonely smell about, the smell of chilly, unused rooms where no fresh air came, the smell of cold paint and plaster damp and dank from the rains and wet snows of March. Not even the smell of apples penetrated where Nicholas was, crouched there below the sidelights. There were three closed doors, panelled and shining in their white paint, that led to three closed, cold rooms, one door on one side of the wide hall, two on the other. The door into the sitting-room from which he had escaped stood open, and the sound of the old clock came through it, measuring off the minutes and the hours. Within the old house there was no other sound anywhere at all. Outside, the bare twigs of the lilacs in the white corners of the high doorway tapped against the wood, reaching even to the leaded glass of the sidelights. Outside, the gray, misty air lay over the bare, cold garden, the wet white fence pickets, and the deserted street.

Nicholas never knew how long he stayed there in the cold hall, listening to the clock within, to the lilacs without, and to the surging murmur of the silence which beat upon his ears. He tried the latch of the front door and found it securely locked. He tried it again and found it just the same. He knew that some time, somehow, he must go back through the sitting-room, past his grandfather on the sofa, past the newspaper on the floor and the apples on the table, on out through the kitchen with the sound of his feet against the yellow boards echoing through the house, past the table where no supper had been laid for his grandfather, past the wood-box and the green pump in the sink, out through the door into the gray, soft, wet afternoon. He knew that he must walk quickly through the village street, up the hill past the church and churchyard, and down the long shore road by the sea to his own house. He knew that he must open the side door upon his grandmother or his mother preparing supper in the warm kitchen and tell them that his grandfather was dead.

He did all these things which he knew he must do. Edging his way along the high white wainscoting of the hall, he went quickly through the sitting-room, pausing at the door into the kitchen to look once more at the still, straight figure on the sofa. He did not want to look, but in an odd way he felt that it was neither right nor polite to leave his grandfather without it. Then he opened the back door softly, closed it as softly behind him, and went out into the misty daylight through the wet brown grass of the yard. His feet felt heavy as he lifted them up and down, and the chill of his grandfather's hand still stayed within his own.

The wind was rising now and driving cold slants of rain through the air; the fog was rolling in, obscuring the islands; the still water of the harbour was now ruffled and gray; the village street had never seemed so deserted. Everyone was probably inside preparing for supper. But when he reached the post-office on the corner where the muddy road led to the harbour and the docks, he saw the town-crier beneath his big umbrella talking with the postmaster. Mr. Hosea Horton was holding the clapper of his big bell in his hand. There was no hurry about his rounds, for the church clock was only just striking five. Neither noticed Nicholas, trudging along in his black cape, but when he passed them standing securely there, he heard the town-crier say to the postmaster:

"Duty is duty, but it's a dull enough town these days. Few ships in, few out, nobody born of folks that count, nobody dead, and little to cry but 'All's well!' "

5

Things were looking up early in 1860. Nicholas knew they were, not only by the way his father talked when he came home but by the way he carried his head and shoulders, the extra presents he brought them all, and the genial air of well-being which he scattered all about him like the bird-shot flying from Nicholas' new gun and hitting everything but birds. Most wonderful of all, information which made Nicholas the centre of an envious group every day at recess from school, his father had bought a new ship with money that he had and some that he hadn't. How one bought a ship with money that one hadn't got was a puzzle to Nicholas; but he assumed that this feat was only another of the accomplishments peculiar to his father, and he shut his ears to the comments made sometimes by his mother and grandmother when his father was out of the house.

"It doesn't seem a wise move to me," ventured Nicholas' mother, "sinking money that way when it's just not going again. But there! Silas never asks advice of me about money matters, and what can I say?"

"Nothing," said his grandmother. "Nothing at all. Money's a closed province to us women. I learned that long ago. And wisdom never was a quality of the Crocketts. Startling people is more in their vein. They've been up to that rinktum all their lives. There's nothing you can do except not to worry. It'll doubtless come through all right. Things do with Silas. I'd have less misgivings myself if only the parts of this country would stop picking at each other's throats. If there's a war, it won't do much good to shipping. I've seen wars before in my long days, and they weren't any of them too healthy for folks that get their living from the sea."

Nicholas did not really know whether he wished the throat-picking would cease. It made things vastly more exciting at school. Now they had a flag draped above the teacher's desk, and they saluted it every morning standing at strict attention. In the early afternoon when they were all drowsy from too much dinner they inscribed over and over with purple ink in their copybooks

United, we stand; divided, we fall!

an exercise which was far more awakening in its nature than the inscribing of

God is our refuge and strength.

Moreover, with no picking at each other's throats there could never have been the stirring sequence of events which had followed quickly upon the visit of a boy from Virginia to Saturday Cove. His name was Calvert Carter, a silly name everybody thought, and he had come peaceably enough to visit his grandfather, whose daughter had married a plantation owner. His grandmother had in an ill-advised moment sent him to school where his Southern voice and bearing had made him the butt of every boy in Miss Serena's domain, in spite of her morning talks of manners and the behaviour expected daily from Christian boys and girls. Matters had reached a climax one morning on the way to school when Jonas Norton, who was Nicholas' idol among the older boys, threw Calvert, ruffled collar and all, into the village horse-trough. It was not a duck but instead a complete throw-in with Calvert sending rivers of water down the hill from his sleek clothes when he had once scrambled out and stood glaring at them all, speechless from fury. Jonas took for this a mild chastisement from Miss Serena's ferule and a terrible licking at home from his father; but he bore both with the trappings of victory floating about him, not in the least as one bore an ordinary punishment, striving at concealment and praying frantically at night that the Lord in His mercy would not let it get bruited abroad.

None of these things, however, touched the new ship in the dimensions of their importance. She had been built in Boston two years before, when things looked none too good for ships and shipping, and had been waiting ever since for someone to sail her and for a cargo to carry in her spacious hold. Nicholas secretly wished she had been built at home like the *Solace Winship*; but the yards at Saturday Cove were not what they had been even four years ago and certainly far from what they had been when Nicholas' grandfather, James Crockett, had owned and operated them. There were signs about them of decay, piers rotting here and there; and the best shipwrights had left Saturday Cove because there was not money enough to pay them.

She was not precisely like the California clippers, her spars a bit less lofty perhaps and the amount of her canvas somewhat reduced; but she was a clipper all the same and, his father estimated, could outsail the *Solace Winship* by a good four knots an hour, which meant something to a sailing day as Nicholas well knew. Her hull was black from her metal up, but she carried a stripe of crimson which lent her vigour and dash, his father said. Her bowsprit and yards were black, her lower masts white with the tops and doublings brightly varnished. As a figurehead she bore an eagle with outstretched wings and splendid head, which gave in itself the appearance, indeed the prophecy of speed. She was named the *Four Winds*, although every sailor knew there were a deal sight more than four scurrying and sweeping across the heavens. Her name sounded good in Nicholas' ears as he said it over and over. She was for Australia, one of the thirteen ships bound thither that year from Boston alone. She would carry clothes and canned food, farm implements and machinery, books and clocks and furniture to Sydney, and bring back wool and hides for the busy factories of Massachusetts.

For a week before his father left for Boston to board the *Four Winds* Nicholas was conscious of an odd tension about the house. He knew that everyone was thinking of something from which he was left out. He was sent out to play more often than usual, and when he came in from Prisoners' Base or Mutiny on Columbus' Ship, he was aware that earnest conversations stopped suddenly once he was in the room. He did not like the atmosphere over-much, but he did not venture upon questions which were obviously not his to ask. And one morning, the morning of his father's departure, all mysteries were gloriously solved, and he entered upon a world which "hard times" had placed outside even his dreams for four years and more.

He came down to breakfast on that last morning earlier than usual. He had been wakened by a curious and unaccustomed clatter in the attic above his head, the noise of something heavy being dragged across the floor and carried down two flights of stairs amid sundry warnings from his grandmother at the bottom about paint and paper. When he reached the dining-room, there was the family at the table. There was an air of expectation about them all, his father in blue broadcloth paying small attention to his codfish balls, his grandmother rattling her cups and saucers, his mother passing muffins to them both although they were clearly not interested in muffins. And there on the floor by his father's chair was a sea-chest, blue and old, scarred and dusty with a fresh new rope neatly coiled upon it. In the middle of the coil of rope he read his name in faded white letters, NICHOLAS D. CROCKETT.

"Well, young Nicholas," began his father, trying in vain to measure his words and failing completely because of the excitement in his voice, "here's your chest. Your grandfather Winship made it for your Uncle Nicholas when he was fourteen and first went off to sea. No Crockett ever boarded a ship with a trunk, and we're not going to begin with you. You'll get your things together and put them away in here, for you're leaving in a week with your mother to join the *Four Winds* in Boston for Australia."

"Come, Nicholas," said his grandmother then, for Nicholas, standing there, was staring, first at his father, then at the sea-chest, then through the wide windows at the sea itself beyond the marshes and the meadows, "come, eat your porridge. There are days coming when you'll wish for porridge like that. And you can't go to school without it."

So he ate his porridge though he thought he never could. And every day for a week thereafter while he sat at school, he stared at the map of the world above the blackboard, noting how much more water there was than land upon it, neglecting the sums on his slate and the words in his speller.

They went, Nicholas and his mother, leaving his grandmother cheerful in the great house, journeying to Boston by coach and train, boarding the *Four Winds* smart and spruce in her new paint and in her canvas ready to be set and braced to the wind once she was towed into clear water. They went. Far out into the mid-Atlantic they sailed on the beginning of making their easting, through sullen gray or green water under gray skies, working ever south into the genial northeast trades where sky and water became blue and sunny, and long days succeeded long days with everything shipshape on board, with time for the sailors to loiter and smoke and spin their endless yarns, and with hardly a change in the sail they carried. On south through the variables where for days on end as they neared the equator the sun bounded up from the horizon to blaze upon the surface of a glassy sea, where the sailors worked with might and main to make use of the slightest puff of wind, wrinkling the still water in the distance like a school of silver fish, where the heat melted the pitch from the deck seams, and where drizzling hot showers or sudden downpours of warm rain sent Nicholas in his underwear to take a bath on the quarterdeck. Once over the line the southeast trades took the *Four Winds*, took her with all her sails set through more days and even weeks of bright weather, sailing ever southward with Brazil somewhere beyond the far western horizon and Africa somewhere beyond the eastern. Then the blue faded from the water, the sky became overcast, great winds began to blow, the roaring westerlies, his father said, winds that would carry them booming and smashing around Good Hope and well over to Australia itself.

Nicholas had never known such winds could blow. They kept him and his mother in the cabin playing his games at the table when they would stay on the table, keeping his father forever on deck, howling and tearing at the few sails, driving tremendous seas to pound and thunder against the groaning timber—mountainous seas hoisting the stern and driving the ship's nose down with thudding blows into the desolate waters before her. They brought with them squalls of sleet and icy snow before which the *Four Winds* drove on and on, now ever eastward, until one morning two months and more after they had left home, his father led him on deck to see in the distance some rocky islands rising from the waste of black tossing waters.

"The Kerguelens, Nicholas," said his father. "Two weeks more and the voyage is over."

Nicholas never wanted the voyage over. Even the worst days held their excitement for him, quite apart from the roar of the wind and the thunder of the water. He had never in his life had such delightful friends or so many of them. The officers were all his friends, telling him fabulous stories at the table, explaining the chart to him at night. The carpenter allowed him to follow him about on fair days and on bad ones to sit in his stuffy shop with the spray drenching the tiny windows. The bos'n took him for walks in the second dog-watch, forward where in good weather the sailors lounged and sang.

The sailors were the best friends of all. They all had names for him, many of which he did not understand and all of which his mother disliked when, in a thoughtless moment, he told her of them. His mother disapproved of sailors in general and did not in the least like his stealing away to the fo'c'sle when he had grown to know them better and sitting about while the off watch ate their supper.

The fo'c'sle was distinctly a man's world. Nicholas loved to sit there in the smell of drying clothes and stale tobacco, in the dim light of the swaying lantern which cast their great, ungainly shadows on the walls and floor. Outside the wind roared, making them all seem more snug and comfortable within. He loved to watch them sitting about the mess-tub with their spoons and tin basins, ladling out the thick pea soup with dumplings and bits of pork, swilling down their cups of steaming coffee, gnawing great fistfuls of hardtack.

The oldest of them all was called Rats. There was no place in the world where he had not been and no kind of ship that he had not sailed on. He had hairy arms, which were tattooed from shoulder to wrist with ladies' faces, all different. When Nicholas asked him who the ladies were, he said they were his daughters who all lived in different places. The others roared at this answer, some saying that he should have a hundred arms to picture all *his* daughters. Rats had so much hair on his chest that he could braid it and tie a red ribbon on the braid. He swore before God and the Devil, too, that the hair had all sprouted in one dreadful instant of a dreadful night off the Malacca Straits when from the lookout in his watch he had spied close by a ship manned completely by skeletons, skeletons on the decks, skeletons scuttling up and down the rigging with their loose bones snapping and cracking in their bare sockets, skeletons hanging to the yards as they bent ghostly sails. The biggest skeleton of all sat astride the jib-boom, glaring up at Rats with fire in his eye-sockets, and screamed through his empty mouth and clacking teeth that he was Rats' own father and that he alone could teach Rats how to escape the Devil. It was then that the hair sprouted! But just as the skeleton was about to tell him, Rats clean lost his senses up there in the lookout and never came to until he was relieved at eight bells. And the worst part of it all was, Rats solemnly told Nicholas, that he had never been able to escape the Devil, try as he *had* tried all his life.

There was another sailor named Joe who played a mouth organ, lying in his bunk once he had finished his supper. He had a bosom companion called Mike who sang to his tunes. They had one song which kept ringing in Nicholas' head both because of its catchy music and because of the wide and odd experiences which it suggested from all over the world. And when sometimes they all joined in, slapping their knees and stamping their feet in time to the tune, he was fairly dizzy with joy.

This incomparable song ran:

I've a plum in Honolulu,
She's named Kanaka Whore,
She's better than my Zulu,
Or my sweet in Singapore,
Or my wife in Valparaisy,
Or my wife in County Cork—
But she's nothing to my Daisy
Saving kisses in New York.

There was one named Bloody Ben, who could go aloft faster than any man on the *Four Winds* in spite of the fact that his feet were flat with no anklets at all and that he always threw off his shoes before he took to the ratlines, coiling his stockingless toes around them like a monkey. He was an ugly-looking man enough with half his nose gone and the other half wedged into his face; but he was kind to Nicholas and taught him to tie any number of difficult knots and to splice a rope so that the splicing hardly showed at all. Once, at the mess-tub, when things were more hilarious than usual, Nicholas felt such an excitement buzzing within him that he forgot his manners and asked Ben about his nose.

"Where did you lose your nose, Ben?" he yelled, putting his arms smartly akimbo and balancing himself on the high fo'c'sle stool, though the *Four Winds* was even then pitching through the first of the westerlies.

"My nose?" yelled Bloody Ben in return. "You ask about my nose, young feller? I lost it in a bull-fight in Pernambuco. I killed that bull and sat on his head with all Brazil a-cheerin' of me and the ladies throwin' roses. But when I wasn't lookin', the bull raised one horn in the last move he made on this earth, my sonny, and took my nose off!"

"He's lying to you, kid!" bawled Mike. "A hussy bit it off his mug for'm in San Diego!"

Nicholas did not ask then and there what a hussy was, but, his curiosity conquering discretion, he inquired at bedtime of his mother. She said she did not know; it must, she thought, be a word peculiar to sailors. He regretted his question, wishing many times thereafter that he had asked it of his father or saved it for his grandmother, since it kept him from further visits to the fo'c'sle until they reached Australia.

Nevertheless, there were still the walks forward with the bos'n or the carpenter; there were long talks with the sailmaker as he sat punching the stout canvas with his heavy thimble bound across his palm; there were hours at the wheel in fair weather when he helped the helmsman spin the brass-topped spokes, down and up, up and down to keep her on her course. On sunny days when a fair wind was with them and they flew along with every inch of canvas on her, there was an exhilaration in the very sense of taut rigging and filled sails, in the water racing past. There were ships to speak and sometimes to overhaul—a packet ship with the passengers waving their hats and handkerchiefs, a big-bottomed whaler, an odd steamer or two spouting black smoke into the wide, clean sky, British tea-clippers racing home, the *Falcon* and the *Fiery Cross*, smart ships with shining rails and bulwarks and polished brass that caught the sun. There were flying-fish and porpoises and birds that circled about far from land. And in the dog-watch when supper was over and he was sleepy, there was the secure sense of the three of them together, smiling at one another across the table or walking arm in arm up and down the deck.

"Land ho! On the port bow!" cried the lookout early one bright morning, and there ahead was the blue outline of Cape Otway, the southernmost point on the Australian mainland. Not many days now before they would slide through the straits between Tasmania and Australia and head northeast for Sydney. Nicholas watched the surf ringing the white beaches and crashing upon the headlands, jumping nimbly out of the way while the crew holy-stoned and scrubbed, painted and varnished, so that the *Four Winds* might enter Sydney Harbour with no apologies for her appearance.

Nicholas never forgot the month they lay in the beautiful harbour of Sydney with ships from all the world as their neighbours. Before he had been there a week he knew their names and from what countries they hailed. The first officer taught him to distinguish quickly those from home by their house flags, the crimson field and yellow beehive of Sutton and Company; the red and yellow horizontal bars of A. A. Low; the red cross upon the white field of David Ogden. It was a gay month. His father and mother dressed up for dinner almost every evening and went to drink good wine and eat rare foods on some ship or other that lay at anchor, swinging idly to the tide, her lights twinkling in the darkness beneath the flaming southern stars. Ships had hostesses in plenty in 1860, for many captains now brought their wives to sea and some their children. On rare occasions Nicholas, too, went to dinner, wearing his long new trousers of blue and green plaid and his short black velvet jacket over his starched white underwaist with lace collar and cuffs. Sometimes he stayed with the gentlemen at the table after the ladies had withdrawn; and he listened with all his ears to the talk that went on and on.

There were many things for the masters of sailing-ships to talk about in 1860: the sudden disappearance of the McKay clippers, the *Romance of the Seas* and the *Bald Eagle*, sailing from Hong Kong and never reaching their ports; the recent voyage of the new steamship *Great Eastern*, whether she threatened sail or whether she was singled out for mishaps because of her clumsiness proved at her unfortunate launching; the action of the Southern States to cripple the American merchant marine; Britain's sudden spurt in building and the superiority for shipping of Free Trade over a protective tariff. These things at times widened his eyes with excitement; at other times they sent him homeward to the *Four Winds* with worry conquering sleep.

For these men knew things, thought Nicholas. They were the finest men in all the world. And when one of them rose in the dining-cabin of his stately ship, raised his glass and cried, "Gentlemen, I drink to the passing of a glorious era!" Nicholas knew uneasily that, whatever an era was, it was surely passing away.

"Fate is against us," went on this gentleman at the grandest dinner of all, when ten of the best commanders known to the sea sat around a sumptuous table with candlelight shining softly on wineglasses and silver, on snowy linen and black clothes and white satin waistcoats. "Fate is against us, and every sailor bows to Fate. The screw steamship is against us, and the perfidious South, and the iron and coal of Old England. The *Romance of the Seas* and the *Bald Eagle* are now no more, a dark sign of our passing. But we drink, gentlemen, to the glory of the American clipper and pledge together our fealty to blue water!"

Nicholas, sitting next his father, rose with the others and raised his cup of milk, drinking it as they drank their wine. But he was sad and heavy within him until the same gentleman, spying his anxious face, cried again,

"A further toast, gentlemen, to the young lad in our midst. He comes of a glorious race. May he sail his father's ship to the uttermost seas and prove himself victorious over time and chance!"

So he felt better as he went homeward, snuggled close to his father in the stern of the boat while the third officer pulled the oars and they wound in and out among the ships toward the high, dark side of the *Four Winds*. He *would* fight time and chance, he thought. When he was older, he would, of course, know better what they were and what was the best way to conquer them both.

6

The year after he came back from Sydney, the year he was eleven, Nicholas fell in love, doing it even at that age with the completeness characteristic of the Crocketts and keeping it staunchly to himself. He fell in love with Deborah Parsons at her soap-bubble party. Deborah was ten and had come to live in Saturday Cove because her father had recently been elected præceptor of the academy, a stately red-brick building with white columns, just below the church on the hill. The academy had been built by Thomas Winship in 1810 and administered strict doses of the classical languages, mathematics, ancient history, and a few odds and ends not felt even in the eighteen-sixties to be of much importance. Deborah like Nicholas had been born somewhat late in the life of her parents, her father being well past fifty when she was ten, and neither of them knew exactly how to cope with her superabundant spirits or to steer her firmly into the paths of modesty and comeliness, which in the eighteen-sixties were held to be the chief of womanly attributes.

Deborah had not made the slightest dent upon the consciousness of Nicholas until the day of the party. She had just been another girl in the village school, her sex substantially counteracting her newness; and although she could draw amazing pictures of Miss Serena on her slate when she should have been studying her tables, such talent was, in Nicholas' mind, little enough compensation for the multitude of things closed to her and to all the others like her. But the bubble-party depicted Deborah in a new, disarming, and wholly delightful way.

The party was held one Saturday afternoon in late May in the orchard behind the præceptor's big white house. It was an early spring, and the apple-blossoms were a cloud of pink and white above Deborah and her guests, who had at last been allowed to shed their winter flannels and serges and alpacas for cotton frocks and suits. Deborah's mother being absent, the stout and capable maidservant had arranged the big table under the trees with its white washbowls of soapy water, its basin of soft soap for more suds, its row of new clay pipes each gaily tied with ribbon. Deborah had sketched in pencil on the bowl of each pipe a clever drawing of the guest who was to claim it; and there was much hilarity at the beginning while all found themselves.

The stout maidservant, whose name was Susan, was not in the most equable of tempers. First of all, she disapproved of parties in a time of war. Sugar was dear and so was flour, and so were all the other ingredients of the cakes which she had refused to make for Deborah. Cookies were to be the refreshments at this party, thin ones at that, and cold molasses water. Susan had two brothers in General Sherman's army, and she knew well how they were being starved to death though they did not dare to say so in their rare letters. Secondly, she saw little sense in parties at any time and especially in the absence of her mistress, who, although she could not always manage Deborah, was at least responsible for her and might have been able, although Susan had her doubts, to keep Deborah's new blue muslin securely locked in the closet until the night of the church concert a week later when Deborah was to speak a piece if she could be kept still long enough for her to learn it. But Deborah had wheedled both the party and the dress from her father, who was at this moment reading some outlandish tongue upstairs and paying no heed to the rowdyism messing up his premises, which were, as a matter of plain fact, not his premises at all, though some folks were born with no idea of what belonged to other folks. So there was nothing for it as Susan saw, being a woman of common sense, but to weather through the party as well as she could and keep some outward show at least of law and decency and order.

The pipes having been sorted and claimed with great glee, and ease for that matter as Deborah's drawings were unmistakable, the blowing began. It was a lovely party as anybody but Susan, standing stiffly under a tree with her arms tightly folded across her black and white calico, might have seen. The pipes were dipped in the warm, thick suds, cheeks were distended, and the round, clear bubbles began to float singly and in tiny, diaphanous chains from the clean white pipe-bowls. They sailed through the soft, still May air, up and up among the apple-blossoms, the biggest reflecting the rosy petals in their transparency. The children danced about under the trees, jumping to catch their bubbles, marvelling at the biggest and brightest, dashing to the table to refill their pipes and to spill soapsuds over Susan's clean cloth with which she had been no end of a fool to cover the table.

It was like Deborah, thought Susan, to be the most thoughtless hostess possible. There she was, prancing about like something fair possessed, blowing more bubbles than anyone else, crowding her guests out at the table. Manners had simply gone gallivanting since Susan's day. There weren't no manners any longer, and what this world was coming to, Susan, unaided, could not tell nor the Lord either!

Matters reached a climax at last, at least in Susan's mind, when Deborah, who had already ladled enough soapsuds on her new blue muslin to ensure the necessity of a washing of it and an ironing of half a hundred ruffles before the church concert, broke her pipe fairly into smithereens by pertly striking it on Nicholas Crockett's head. Susan's exhausted patience at that moment ran quite out of the orchard and left her not knowing in the rage that took its place that she had missed it. She bore down upon the excited Deborah, who was now gaily picking bits of clay from Nicholas' stubborn hair, and administered some smart slaps and some shakes that untied Deborah's blue sash and sent it whirling on the orchard grass under the strong arms of Susan.

"Shame on you to treat one of your visitors so!" screamed Susan, now holding Deborah at arm's length and glaring first at her and then at all the others who stood aghast and staring. "You're a naughty, ungrateful girl who ought to be properly spanked and put to bed if your folks had any sense. Now, you little sauce-box, you'll stand and watch your party with never another bubble for you! No one's to lend you a pipe either, so mind that, all of you!"

Deborah was not one whit behind Susan in her own fury. She did her best to kick Susan's legs, safe within the ample folds of her calico, but the arm that held her was inescapable. Her cheeks grew redder and redder, and the black pupils of her eyes extended until they almost hid the blue around them. But though her arms and legs were useless, she still had her voice.

"You mean, hateful old thing!" she shrieked at Susan. "Who are you to spoil my party? You're a nasty, horrid old skinflint, that's what you are, and all my friends think so, too!"

Deborah's friends thought nothing at that moment. All stood in their places, the youngest too frightened, the eldest too embarrassed to move. Nicholas thought he ought to speak up and to say that he liked pipes broken over his head, which, indeed, was true at that moment as he looked at Deborah, somehow triumphant even in her ignominious plight; but the necessary words to convey this information would not come. At last when the littlest girl began to whimper and start across the orchard grass toward the security of her own home and her own mother, Susan thought retirement on her part the wisest move and retreated to her kitchen, her broad back swaying from side to side in her indignation.

It took but a minute for Deborah to comfort and lead back her departing guest, another for her to tie her sash and push back into place her disordered curls. Then she made an appropriate face at the back door, which had just been slammed with gusto, and turned upon her friends the most charming and subtle of smiles, reserving the long conclusion of the smile for Nicholas himself.

"Now the party will go on," she said. "I'm sure you would all lend me your pipes, but I don't need them, thank you. I can blow better bubbles than anyone without the sign of a pipe. Watch me, all of you!"

Upon which, while they all stood about recovering themselves, she marched to the table, dipped one hand into the basin of strong soft soap, the other into one of the great bowls of suds, and began to cover her mouth and nose with the heavy white lather.

Well up into her nostrils she forced it (how it must sting! thought Nicholas) well between her parted lips. Then she stood in their midst beneath the blossoming trees with the sun shining on her fair hair and dripping soap-covered face.

"Watch me!" she cried again.

There was no need of the command. They were all watching her, small and half-sized girls in ginghams and muslins, small and half-sized boys in white ducks. They drew silently together to make a half-circle before her, their fear giving place to wonder as they watched.

For Deborah, wrinkling up her crimson face, began to blow gently from both mouth and nose, and fast upon her gentle blowing there came wreathes of bubbles to float away with the spirited tossing of her head. How long can she hold out? thought Nicholas, lost in delighted admiration. Deborah held out far longer than anyone thought she could. Her concluding triumph was a mammoth bubble which she held poised on the end of her nose before it, too, sailed away for one overwhelming instant and broke amid a chorus of admiration and applause.

Deborah had magnificently transcended her disgrace into triumph, cast a glow over impertinence and insubordination, brought the young world of Saturday Cove to her feet. As they trailed homeward at supper-time, there was not one among her guests who did not long to emulate her behaviour and yet not one who did not regretfully admit that such deportment would not work acceptably under their allotted roofs. As for Nicholas, he had for the first time in his life seen girls in a new light. Deborah, he said to himself in bed that night, after his grandmother had extricated divers bits of white clay from his thick hair with questions that were not answered, might conceivably be equal to any occasion. She might even, like Mrs. Joshua Patten, command a clipper ship around Cape Horn and take her safely into the Golden Gate, as

Mrs. Patten had done for fifty-two days when her husband was ill and the first officer under arrest for neglect of duty.

7

By the year he was thirteen Nicholas had learned something about time and chance, although because of them both he never learned that they were unconquerable by any might or power save by the might of the human spirit reaching out toward That which had made it in the beginning. He learned about time through watching his grandmother, less steady on her feet than she had been, more willing to sit down and let his mother do things, more transparent in her hands and face, less interested in him and his doings. He understood vaguely that the war, bursting at Fort Sumter upon them soon after they had returned from Sydney, was hard on his grandmother. She watched it as one from afar off, and yet he knew that she suffered while she watched. As she neared ninety she became given to repeating herself, and there was hardly a day that he did not hear her say to his mother:

"I never thought I'd live to see another war, and God knows I'm not hankering to watch this one to a close. There's something wrong in the way things are. Old men should fight and not the young, for things don't matter so much to the old."

The war was hard upon his father, too. The *Four Winds* with hundreds of other good ships was hauled up in Boston. His father was away a great deal of the time, sitting on commissions in Boston or New York, engaged in endless deliberations which came to little or nothing, he said when he came home, tired and half ill from his own and larger anxieties. When he was at home, he sat on other commissions, too, among men who met in the village hall to interview younger men and boys, to decide whether they should go or stay, and to send those who were to go, to larger towns where they would get their blue uniforms and rifles and knapsacks. He fretted and chafed about the house, deploring his age, insisting he was better than half the men on ships or battlefields or in the camps. Like Nicholas' grandfather Winship he wished that Nicholas had been born when he should have been, for then *he* would show them. His mother, Nicholas knew, was glad that he had been born when he was born.

School became preferable to home on the days when his father was there. Miss Serena at sixty-two had reluctantly given place to Sergeant Peasley, who had lost his right arm at Bull Run and been sent home without it and with a hole in his side as well. Sergeant Peasley was perhaps not much of a teacher, but he was admirable, the school overseers thought, for the time at hand. Deborah drew amazing pictures of him on her slate. She was decent about the pictures, always tactfully drawing him with the arm he had lost and allowing her genius full scope only on his face, which was funny enough in all conscience. Lessons did not matter much. They droned through whatever was necessary, indefinitely lengthening the morning exercises so that they might hang old Jefferson Davis to a sour apple tree and go marching on with John Brown's soul though his body was mouldering in the grave. After school and on Saturday mornings the boys were drilled in the school yard by Lieutenant Simpson, who had done nothing but jig mackerel on George's Bank when he was a boy but who had distinguished himself for two years in the Navy until a cannon ball had taken his leg clean across the deck and over the side of his ship. He managed wonderfully on his wooden peg, and Nicholas and the others drilled for hours on end with wooden guns while Deborah and her friends watched respectfully from well on one side of the yard.

Chance first showed its arrogant and imperturbable face to Nicholas in 1864, when Jonas Norton got a stray bullet in his heart. Rejoicing that he was at last eighteen and could join General Grant's army, Jonas had gone merrily through the May campaign, crossing the Rapidan, fighting the Battle of the Wilderness without a scratch, weathering in early June the crushing defeat at Cold Harbour. And now in June, after the Petersburg siege was quite over and the war was surely wearing itself out, he was killed in no battle at all, simply struck by a stray bullet shot by an unseen and unknown sniper. He had been sitting under a tree when the siege had ended and things were quiet again, writing his mother about the blue Virginia hills, when the bullet got him. It was like Jonas to sit all by himself under a tree, thought Nicholas, when the news reached Saturday Cove. He had always liked to spend long days fishing by himself or reading flat on his stomach under the elm trees at the foot of his father's field.

Apparently, thought Nicholas, trying to figure it out in his muddled head as he trailed slowly homeward that evening along the shore road, apparently one could not know beforehand with any degree of certainty what was going to happen to one, or prepare against it, or even be ready for it. He wished the town-crier might have cried Jonas' death, given to it something of the importance it held for Nicholas' and Jonas' family. But the town-crier was now no more in Saturday Cove, having been voted down in the last March town-meeting as a worn-out and expensive institution, useless now that newspapers were an everyday affair for everybody and national matters rightly of greater importance than mere local tidbits.

"So the town-crier's gone," his grandmother had said when she heard about the town-meeting, "and the telegraph has come. Common as common telegrams are now. And I've lived to see the passing of one and the coming of the other. Well, well!"

Her words had made Nicholas think suddenly of time, of the gentleman's words at the dinner in Sydney harbour, how it took away one thing and brought another. Now with Jonas gone in such an odd, unexpected way he was beginning to think about chance, over which he must somehow be victorious even though no one in the world could beat time.

That chance bullet, which, singing through the warm southern air, found a lodging in Jonas' heart, did not stop there. It had its repercussions. Jonas had a dog, a setter named Captain, who had been Jonas' faithful slave ever since he was ten and Captain was a puppy. It seemed as though the dog knew all about Jonas. After the telegram had come, he sat outside Jonas' room and howled long, dismal howls. Whenever he could, he lay on Jonas' bed, sniffing at the covers or wandered all about the room, sniffing at his books and at his old shoes on the closet floor, looking beseechingly at anyone who tried to drive him out of doors. When July came and school was out, he began howling at Jonas' fishing-tackle in the woodshed. Mrs. Norton told Solace Crockett that she couldn't stand it another hour. She gave Captain to Nicholas together with the books and fishing-tackle, which soon began to take on Nicholas' smell so that Captain ceased his howling and felt at home once more.

Nicholas loved Captain both for Jonas' sake and for his own. He had never had a dog before, in spite of his father's perennial threats to buy him one. Dogs were hard on rugs and furniture, Abigail Crockett had always said, and they smelled no matter how you scrubbed them. She would do anything else in the world for Nicholas, but she did not see how she *could* have a dog about the house, shedding hairs over everything. Now, however, that dogs together with many other things were slipping to the bottom of her mind, she had made no objection to his coming, especially since he had belonged to Jonas.

The dog made up, at least a little, for Jonas. Not that Nicholas had known Jonas closely, but he had adored him from afar. Jonas had been decent to the small fry in the village school, seeing that they got their rights and sometimes joined in the games of the older boys.

Even when he went to the academy and studied Latin and Greek, he did not forget Nicholas. Sometimes he had even come to the house for an evening to play anagrams or to help Nicholas with his boat-building on the kitchen table. Nicholas had dreamed long dreams about Jonas, how some day when the war was over and shipping had picked up, they would sail together, for Jonas' father was a captain, too, and he himself had had long thoughts about the sea.

Jonas, dreamed Nicholas, would command the ship, and he, after he had worked his way up, would be Jonas' first officer, call Jonas "Sir," and execute his orders more quickly than any other officer could ever do. Some morning when they were clipping along on the starboard tack with the starboard leeches of all square sails well forward, Jonas would take a quick look around from his deck and shout:

"Get all ready for about ship, Mr. Crockett!"

"Aye, aye, sir!" Nicholas would cry, and then to the men on watch,

"Furl the crojik!"

"Haul up the clews of the mainsail!"

"Stand by the main and mizzen braces!"

The men would cry, "Aye, aye, Sir," to him in turn, and with Jonas and him both seeing to things, and not losing a moment, the great ship would come about and drive forward on her new tack.

Now that this dream had to be put away, the dog helped no end. They ranged the woods together, scaring up rabbits and partridges. In chilly late August evenings they lay together before the fire with Captain's nose snuggled between Nicholas' shoulder and elbow while he read *Two Years Before the Mast* or *Mr. Midshipman Easy*. Within a month the dog seemed to have forgotten Jonas completely in his new faithfulness to Nicholas.

Then one September afternoon when his father had just come home for three short days and even Captain in comparison lost interest for him, he, remembering Jonas' generosity to him as a smaller boy, lent Captain as a playmate to some youngsters who had long begged for him. There was, as a matter of fact, another and more powerful element that stimulated his generosity. Deborah was with the younger boys, and he could refuse Deborah nothing that she wanted. They took him to the woods where he ran afoul a porcupine, and at nightfall they tearfully brought him home, not knowing what to do with the quills which protruded in dozens and scores from the tender skin about his nose and mouth, and which made him mad from pain and fright.

Nicholas did not know what to do either, but his father did. They stretched Captain on an old rug in the shed and went to work to extract the quills. It was hard, slow work. The quills were nasty things to handle, and the suffering dog was nastier. Nicholas lay upon him, holding his head as his father directed, while Silas did his utmost to get out most of the quills. Deborah stood in the doorway of the shed while they worked. She had summarily sent the small boys home, but she remained, contrite and sorrowful, with tears running down her cheeks. There were blood and howls of pain from Captain and well-directed snaps at Silas' patient fingers and hands; there were tears from Nicholas, too, and blood all over the rug, some from Captain, some from Silas. They kept supper waiting while Nicholas' mother stood anxiously about, more concerned for Silas than for Captain.

Silas laughed at her fears as she bandaged up his hands and arms after they had treated the dog's mouth with hot water and some healing ointment. But the next day he did not feel over well, and on the third he sent a telegram to Boston that he could not come back to the men who were awaiting him.

Nicholas, lying beside Captain on the sitting-room floor, could not believe that his father was really ill, and yet he knew it from his mother's face. He had developed a high and stubborn fever, the doctor said, which did not look too good. He called another doctor from the nearest city who said it did not look too good to him either. Nicholas was frightened on the fifth evening when the new doctor had gone and the other stayed on in his father's room. The sitting-room was still, but from upstairs he heard the creaking of his father's bed as he tossed about, and now and again the sound of his voice, not in protest against his mother's hands but against the war and steam and the loss of money and the ruin of the sailing ship. All the things which had worried his father most were now being made more plain than he had ever made them even in his most discouraged hours. In her chair in the sitting-room his grandmother sat as though waiting for something which was coming whether or not anyone desired it. He wondered as he lay there before the fire, unable to read, whether all old people waited for things, whether he, too, would wait for things when he was old.

His grandmother said at ten o'clock, "It's long past your bedtime, Nicholas."

She did not seem to realize, he thought, that it was long past her own.

He crept upstairs with Captain at his heels. He looked into the room where his father was and where his mother and the doctor sat by the bed. His father was more quiet now, his mother whispered, beckoning to him. He and the dog stood by his father's bed, but his father did not know either of them. He lay staring at the ceiling where the lamp cast a shadow, and he did not look at Nicholas when he bent to say good-night.

The next morning while he lay drowsily awake, looking at the blue water filling the harbour and at the bright autumn trees that had begun to fire the headlands among their dark pines, his mother came in to tell him quietly that his father was dead. He did not believe it at first, but he came to it at last after his mother had talked to him. The house was more still than he had ever known it, more still even than his grandfather's house when he had lain dead on the haircloth sofa. It held a silence that again murmured in his ears. Even the day outside was still, the September sky, the still water. Captain at the foot of his bed awoke and sensed the strange stillness, greeting it with a whine of distress. Nicholas thought he could never be kind to Captain again. But there he was, not in the least to blame, his mother said, having merely followed what had been the instinct of dogs from the beginning.

That night, hours after he had gone to bed it seemed, he awoke, hearing voices in the sitting-room, the voice of his mother crying now although she had not cried before him, that of his grandmother steadier than usual. He got out of bed and went quietly past the closed door of the room where his father lay. He sat down on the topmost stair, wrapping his long night-gown about his bare feet. He heard his mother say:

"It's harder for you than for any of us. It's not right that you should see everybody through like this. First, Nicholas and then Reuben and then Silas' father and my own mother and father. I'd hoped it would be different for you."

Captain joined Nicholas then, sitting on his haunches and staring, his eyes big and brown in the light of the candles in the sconces on the wall. He was whining a bit as though in puzzled wonder, and he would have howled there in the still hallway had not Nicholas slapped him well and drawn his erect head down across his knees.

"You're wrong," he heard his grandmother say, her voice strong and steady as it used to be. "You're all wrong, Solace. It's just as it should be, for once. The hard thing about bearing children is not the bearing of them or the bringing them up. It's the knowledge that ten chances to one you can't live to see them through their lives, that you've got to die while you're still anxious about them. That's been spared me. I've lived to see them all through and safe, and now I can go any time, knowing that my work's done, finished with no loose ends to it. Somehow or other, I've always hated loose ends."

They did not say any more, and Nicholas crept back to bed past the closed door. His room was flooded with light from the harvest moon, clear and bright in a cloudless sky, transforming the harbour water into a golden sea, mirroring within it the dark lines of the fishing schooners that lay at anchor, their hulls and masts and rigging. Something in his grandmother's words had taken away his fearful awe over the stillness in the house. The confusion and the sadness of the day, the bitter questioning of why such things had to be, were for the moment lost. Young though he was and quite unconscious of the nature of his experience, he was as he lay there understanding something of what those who looked on ancient tragedy had understood, something which, freed from the perplexity and disorder of the actual world and transcended by a poet's vision, gave to them a sense of rightness and of peace.

His grandmother was old, he thought. If she said things had happened as they should happen, then there must be at least a chance that she was right. Perhaps his mother, now that his grandmother had told her, would wish to see him through as his grandmother had seen his father. For just an instant before he fell asleep he felt sorry that, because he had been born so late, it could never be.

8

Nicholas went to the academy at fourteen and weathered four years of it with an ill grace that troubled his mother. He could not see that any of it counted for much toward the things he was burning to do once he was old enough to do them. He neglected his lessons to follow the great contest of 1866 when nine British tea-clippers raced from Foochow around Good Hope to London, three ships doing the passage in ninety-nine days and slipping up to London docks on the selfsame tide. He deplored the fact that there were no more races by American ships around Cape Horn to the Golden Gate, but even British tea-clippers were better than Greek and Latin. Had he been born earlier, he thought, in place of his brother, who had died before he had really lived, he would not have had to render poor translations of Cæsar and Ovid and Sallust, or to dig away at his geometry, which, however, he undertook with a bit more interest than he accorded his other studies when he had once found that it helped him with his boat-building. Had he been born then, in 1831 instead of twenty years later, he would have packed his sea-chest and shipped before the mast, not having to bother with higher learning, which at best fitted one only for the law or medicine or the ministry. None of these professions held any lure for him. Not many boys on the New England coast in the forties and fifties, if they came from seafaring families, had bothered with the narrow world of school when a wider one was beckoning. But time had wrought its changes and that other dark enemy, chance, which thus far he had not been able to withstand.

Fate was clearly against Nicholas, he said in sullen, self-conscious moods to Deborah when he was sixteen and had begun to take her home from Sunday night prayer-meetings and church suppers on Thursday evenings. Deborah at fifteen was far too young to be seen home, her parents said, but Nicholas saw her home all the same. They stood as long as they dared before her white gate on summer evenings and on winter in the dark hall of her father's house. The nearness of Deborah made him tingle from his head to his toes and sent him home to dream dreams about her which frightened him and made his books duller than ever on succeeding days at school. Deborah had not the slightest intention, she told

Nicholas, of remaining in Saturday Cove once her days at the academy were over. She intended to go away and learn more about drawing and painting and sketching. Some day, she said, even though Fate was against her, too, in making her a woman when she longed to be a man, she would astonish Saturday Cove and the larger world with her art. Deborah at school was always drawing something or other; but since she learned her lessons by merely looking at them, no valid objection could be made to her drawing.

Sometimes, when an examination was pending, Deborah brought her Latin books to Nicholas' house and helped him with his translation. She had beautiful manners when she was away from home, and both Solace Crockett and old Abigail, sitting now in her chair and waiting to slip away any hour without any fuss, she hoped, were won by them. Nicholas approached such evenings with dread and delight alternately tearing him in shreds. He was stupid compared with Deborah, and he always seemed more stupid when he sat beside her at the table.

"You make such work of it, Nicholas," she said. "It's really easy. All in the world he says is, 'If you are well, it is well, and I am well.'"

Or, "That's wrong, don't you see? It's a command. What Æneas says is,

" 'Cease to stir up my sould and thine with thy complaints. It is not through my own wishes that I steer forth for Italy.' "

She had a way of commenting on what they read.

"She was an idiot to take on so through all these lines. Catch me throwing myself at the feet of anyone who treated me like that!"

This was said with a spirited toss of her head which sent Nicholas' blood racing in his veins.

When they were respectively eighteen and seventeen and both in their last year at the academy, Deborah increased Nicholas' worry about his future by recklessly steering their evening conversations at her gate into more personal veins.

"I'm going to Mt. Holyoke Seminary just to please father, but I shan't stay there long. I'm sure it's a dull place full of queer, blue-stocking girls. There's a new art school in Boston that lets women come as well as men. That's where I'll likely go in a year or two. At any rate I'm not coming back to Saturday Cove to marry any fisherman that asks me. There's nothing more in this village any-way but fish!"

When she talked like this to Nicholas, he kept his hands close at his sides or gripped securely about the gate railings to keep them where they belonged. He wanted at these times to seize her and hold her close against him, to kiss her and tell her that if only she would believe in him, he would prove to her that there was something even now in Saturday Cove besides fish, or at least someone with ambition enough to leave it. But he never did what he wanted to do, partly because he was afraid of Deborah's power to hurt him, partly because he knew there was sombre truth in what she said. As he went homeward along the dark shore road with the water sucking at the pebbles and few if any ships at anchor, he could take comfort only in the thought that she bestowed her favours upon no other youth in the academy and that there was yet time for him to prove himself worthy of the Crocketts.

There was truth in what Deborah said about Saturday Cove. In 1870 there was little left of the old, far-seeing life which had embraced the world and brought it homeward. The yards and most of the docks had gone, buildings and piers alike. The long wharves upon which Nicholas had walked with his grandfather and his father little more than ten years before had been shortened by neglect and disuse. The sea was nearer the land than it had been. Already burdocks and rank grass were growing on the very spots where the yards had stood, spots marked by rusted and forlorn pieces of what machinery had been left as useless. Foreign ships came no longer to Saturday Cove. Nicholas could hardly remember when he had last felt a leap within him at the sight of square, sun-washed sails bursting upon the horizon. Square sails themselves were passing away to give larger place to the stout, schooner-rigged vessels that plied between coast ports north and south. Now at Saturday Cove the craft that beat their way in among the islands and slid into their places at the dismantled wharves were schooners from Nova Scotia or sometimes from so far away as Norfolk, Savannah, and New Orleans. The war and its tariffs, the building of railroads, the opening of the Great West, the perfection of the steamship, the competition of European shipyards—all these and more had at last dealt to shipping under sail its death-blow. The master-builders of Maine and Massachusetts and Nova Scotia, "reluctant to raise barnyard fowls once they had reared eagles," were dropping off one by one; merchants who could make high percents by exploiting the new West were, wisely enough, turning their attention away from slow sailings in old ships. Maine, it is true, was to keep the American flag floating at the spanker gaff longer than any other state; and yet the Maine men who still embraced the old life, taking the long eastern passages where sail with lower freights yet had its chance, were for the most part men of middle or later age who had put their all into their ships and to whom little else was left to do. These would continue to sail until age had taken them from the seas. Silas Crockett would have been among them had chance not intervened; and had everything been different, Nicholas' early dreams might yet have come true in a measure. But, as thing were, there was not much hope of their flowering. Decent berths to Canton and Calcutta were not easy to obtain even by the most ambitious of youths; wages were low and uncertain; and the men who now made up the crew of a sailing-ship were not the stuff that had prevailed in the forties and the fifties when sailing was a gentleman's calling and when the best families in New England sent their sons before the mast.

There was still the fishing as Deborah had said. Nicholas scorned fishing, but there it was. For a decade both before and after the war the deep waters off the New England and Nova Scotian coasts swarmed, even surged with an abundance of cod and haddock, mackerel, halibut, and herring. Now that shipbuilding was virtually no more and the trade by sail with foreign ports had practically ceased, the fisheries of Saturday Cove, indeed of all Eastern Maine, were bearing the palm and carrying off the victory. Ships from Cadiz and Rio might no longer loom upon the clear horizon; but the fishing boats darkened it by scores when the offshore fleets bore in from the Banks. Within a day's journey eastward of Saturday Cove factories were packing herring by train loads and turning over yearly millions of dollars. And boys who had once dreamed of pacing their quarterdecks while their ships swung majestically into the muddy harbours of China, and who could not get the necessity for the sea out of their bones and blood were becoming glad to pack hip-boots and oilskins and set forth for Newfoundland or the St. Lawrence Gulf. That at least was a better calling than throwing coils of frayed and dirty rope from the gangway of some miserable coastwise steam-tub to draw her nudging, sooty side close to village wharves, better than trundling freight-barrows up and down the slippery planks of small landing-stages to supply village grocers with their wares and the earliest of the summer visitors with their trunks and baby carriages.

9

Nicholas graduated from the academy in June of 1870 and gave in the village church a spirited oration on *Donald McKay, Master Builder.* He had refused to write a farewell essay on *Time and Tide Wait for No Man* or *Trans Alpes Italia Est,* subjects more in vogue in 1870 than eulogies to men who had built sailing-ships and who like their ships were, if not dead, already half forgotten. His mother sat in the corner of the old Crockett pew in the church where forty years ago she had been married and looked upon him as he gave his speech. He was handsome, she thought, tall and spare like his father, his blue eyes eager and yet anxious below his stubborn dark hair, which would never lie straight and smooth no matter how he brushed it. She knew as his voice rang out in the crowded church the things that were tearing his heart and making him an uneasy companion in the great house. And she at sixty was powerless to help him.

For matters at home lent their anxiety to Nicholas. Some were the result of his having been born too late. His mother was no longer young, and he was all she had. There was not much money left of the thousands that China teas and porcelains, India shawls and silks, shared profits and private adventuring had once brought the Crocketts. It had gone with lost ships and the decline in the yards, with the results of panic and war and of his father's too hopeful nature. True there were two great houses, his grandfather Winship's and their own, stately memorials of better and more gracious times; but houses took money for care and upkeep. Nicholas, in point of solid fact, must soon bear a man's portion in a world which at present favoured ill for his talents and desires. He was adamant against college and any subsequent profession which might yield him an irksome livelihood; and Solace, knowing full well the determination characteristic of the Crocketts, always men of single minds, gave up one by one the arguments with which she had attempted to banish his moody discouragement.

"I'd rather jig mackerel all my life," he said to her when graduation was over and only the long summer stretched ahead with chores about the garden and barn, with haymaking in the meadows and odd jobs that he could do for her about the house. "I'd rather do that than bump around back roads with a doctor's kit and not know what to do for people. I'd rather freeze to death off the Banks than sit all my life at a lawyer's desk. And school-mastering's no good, at least for me. I'm not much at books, you know that. But I know ships and a bit about navigation, and I'm going to try those examinations they're giving in Portland in August. It might be even that I'd show I was better than an able seaman."

Nicholas took the examinations and proved he was far better than an able seaman. The hours that he had neglected his Latin for Maury's *Wind and Current Charts*, his *Sailing Directions,* and *Physical Geography of the Sea* began to prove that his time had not been unwisely spent. His neat, accurate drawings and his quick, intelligent handling of the problems set before him had their just reward. In September he was offered a lesser officer's berth in a ship bound from Boston to San Francisco for wheat.

She had no glorious name like the clippers, being called only the *Mildred May*, which he thought foolish enough; she had lost her splendour aloft, and her square sails were supplemented by fore and aft rigging. The port to which she sailed, as his grandfather had prophesied, was neither Canton nor Sydney. But she was the best that was offered, and Nicholas was fast learning that one must adjust oneself to the exigencies and changes of time. At all events, she was rounding the Horn, and since he could not race through the roaring forties as he might have done in 1851 had things been different, her course was at least far ahead of that of a fishing schooner for the Banks.

Best of all, Deborah, on the eve of leaving for the seminary at Mt. Holyoke smiled upon the *Mildred May* and Nicholas' officership thereon. He pictured his ship in glowing words to her. She might have been the *Flying Cloud* or the *Bald Eagle* from the way his voice rang out in the September woods as they walked together on Deborah's last afternoon. The trees were already bright and the birds were gathering to go—thrushes scurrying silently among the undergrowth, towhees and phoebes and whitethroats. A soft haze lay over everything and there was no wind.

Deborah was kind on that last afternoon. All her sudden complexities, all her incomprehensible ways, all her arts of making him uncomfortable and bewildered, were mercifully absent from her. Even her vaulting ambitions seemed for the time asleep. Nicholas put his arm tightly about her waist, and she played with his long, strong fingers. If she did not tell him in so many words that she loved him, her behaviour suggested that fact and overwhelmed him with adoring gratitude. Nor did she laugh once at his own ambitions and high purposes. She even said as they rested against a boulder with her wide blue skirt spread out upon it and her feet and ankles peeping out from beneath its ruffled hem:

"There's something about you, Nicholas, that keeps you in my mind for hours after we've been together. You even make deciding about my future difficult. Sometimes, do you know, I wish I'd never seen you?"

Nicholas told her then about the bubble-party, how from that day to this she had never once been out of his mind, not only for hours but for days and weeks on end. He had never believed he would dare say all the things he was saying in a torrent of confidence to Deborah, there in the quiet of the September woods and in the warm glow of her unfamiliar graciousness. He told her that he would carry her picture every moment high in his waistcoat pocket and that it would keep him from all the temptations which beset men in port and of which she, he was glad to say, knew nothing. Perhaps Deborah did not know, but she knew how to give him back his kisses, surprising and intoxicating him so that he went homeward happier and more secure in his mind than he had ever been in all his life.

10

The voyage to San Francisco was long and hard, nearly five months of ploughing through bad seas which even the less successful clippers had traversed in four and less. Nicholas slaved early and late, helping to kick and beat into shape a motley and sullen crew of ne'er-do-wells and to exact from them a minimum of labour. The pumps were busy for at least half the time, for the *Mildred May* proved herself leaky and unstable long before they had rounded the Horn. The winter rains and fogs made of San Francisco a far more dismal place than he had ever pictured it; necessary repairs in port lost them two cargoes; and Deborah was unsatisfactory in the one letter which he received from her. Only the memory of that September afternoon in the Saturday Cove woods kept Nicholas storming about the decks, a whirlwind of good-natured and reliable activity, and won for him a second officer's job on the long way back.

It was late July when they at last reached Boston and mid-August before he was free to travel homeward, a freedom hastened by a sudden message from his mother which said that his grandmother was fast slipping away. She had been dead for three days when Nicholas reached Saturday Cove. They were waiting only his return before they placed her in the churchyard with Reuben and Nicholas, Silas and James, Amos and Amos' wife Mary, who had been born when King George's War was making the backwoods more unsafe than ever and who had died without knowing that the Revolution had ended and that shipping was free once more.

Nicholas stood, tall and brown and rugged, unquestionably years older, Solace thought, by his mother and looked upon his grandmother lying in the front parlour, between the two great windows looking seaward, her coffin placed against the wall from which the gardens and fountains of Versailles looked down upon her. Amos

Crockett had bought that paper in 1793 in Paris while the Terror was raging. There was little demand for things which had to do with Versailles in 1793, and Amos had bought the paper for little. He had always regretted that Mary could not have lived to see it, once it was spread upon the walls that he had built. Now Abigail lay below it among all the things which the Crocketts had owned for generations and which marked their proud voyaging to the far ports of the world: the portraits of Judah, James, and Amos and of Amos' brother Benjamin, self-assured, contented, eager men in gilded frames; the painting of Amos' ship *Mary*, full-rigged with colours flying leaving Marseilles, and that of Judah, his father, named for Judah's wife, Sarah, who had lived so long ago that not even a vestige of her remained in anyone's memory, although she had been a prime housekeeper and a woman of many other parts as well; the carved, high-backed chairs of English oak which Amos had brought from London; the highboy and chests and cabinets with their multiplicity of knick-knacks; the Heppelwhite table and the fire-screen with Chinese dragons, which Eliza Ann Shaw had found time to work in imported silks between bearing her ten children.

Abigail Crockett lay among all these things which she had dusted twice a week and closed the door upon except on the rare days when, as a wife, she had entertained her husband's guests or given a neighbourhood party and, as a widow, had come in quite by herself to look about her. She seemed to have shrunken pitiably in death, Nicholas thought, lying so deeply within the stiff, unreal folds of satin that he, towering above her, felt somehow as though he were already looking into her grave. He could not discern any familiar line or expression in her still face, not even carelessness of death which he, knowing her, had half expected to find. She had so completely gone that he, gazing upon her with his arm about his mother, found himself summoning frantically back all her countless mannerisms, tricks of voice and hands and speech, all her sudden spurts of life, all her words and thoughts that had betokened her wisdom and humour and made her so incontestably what she had been. When they had once come back to him, clear and shining, her punishments, her frosting-bowl, Moses and Nebuchadnezzar, her Saturday night scrubs, it was as though he heaped them all in the coffin with her to combat her loneliness and give life to her nothingness.

"She went without any fuss just as she always wanted," Solace said, "in her sleep; I don't even know when. I found her gone when I went up in the morning to take her a cup of tea. I'm sorry she couldn't have seen you. She grew brighter somehow for two weeks or so before and talked about you and how she knew you'd command a ship like all the others before many years. She even took up her knitting again and began some socks for you. I think she knew she was going. The last few days she talked a lot about the things in here, how she wanted you should have them all and how some day they might fetch money if you were ever in need. She was what I call a big woman, Nicholas. This world won't make a finer one no matter how it goes on and on making people. I've thought since she went how there was nothing she didn't know about or have sensible thoughts upon."

His mother's words about his grandmother kept coming back to Nicholas, now comforting, now reproachful, during his next voyage around the Horn and back as second officer of the *Mildred May*. Like the former it was a hard voyage in a ship ill-fitted for the sturdy demands of her course; and it was made harder for Nicholas because of Deborah, at home for the summer and far less gracious than the year before. Deborah had her own problems, she had told Nicholas, quite as insistent as his. She might even go away from Saturday Cove for good and all. The new trustees of the academy, who had recently taken the place of older, more conservative men, held that the academy needed a younger head, one more urgent as to discipline and more alive to the needs of the young who were beginning to feel the lack of relationship between their antiquated studies at school and the demands made upon them by a new world. Deborah did not blame the trustees. She herself thought her father antiquated, she told Nicholas. And it *was* a new world, she said, a world of land rather than of the water *he* persisted in sailing upon. Look at the New West, she said, with rich land for the asking and with cities springing up over night, some even now with art schools like Chicago. She had come to think, she told Nicholas with a hard glint in her eyes which hurt him worse than her frequent refusals to let him kiss her, that really all the up-and-coming young men were going West—young men who dared to strike out for themselves instead of stubbornly pursuing a lost calling just because their fathers had pursued it. But she did not know that it concerned her one way or another how Nicholas felt about one's work in the world or for that matter whether her father stayed on in Saturday Cove with his musty old Latin and Greek. She might even go West herself, she said ominously to him when he had come to say goodbye.

It was a rainy afternoon when he called for the last time upon Deborah, such a downpour that he had worn his oilskins over his blue clothes and looked more like a sailor than ever when he entered the Parsons' sitting-room. He had walked through the village and to the fishing-wharves before he had mustered up courage to turn back and mount the hill to the præceptor's white house. He sensed foreboding in the dark, windy day, the fog that lay over the harbour, the wet filth about the piers where the laden boats were discharging their messy freight. Young men whom he had known in school were standing in the holds of the fishing-boats knee-deep in herring, shovelling these by great slippery shovelfuls into baskets on pulleys, which bore them either to the larger schooners waiting to carry them away or to the new canning factory recently built in Saturday Cove. The men and boys who stood in the thousands upon thousands of fish were bronzed and tired. Fish scales clung to their hair and to the stubble on their faces. They lived a hard life and were working only to get home for a late afternoon supper and sleep before earliest dawn summoned them again to their outgoing boats.

The rain was beating against the panes of the sitting-room when he at last sat opposite Deborah, who was sorting out some sketches before the fire. She wore a gray dress with a broad white collar about her neck and had never looked more beautiful, Nicholas thought. When he said so, she did not seem to notice overmuch, being busy with the papers and cardboard on her lap. It was a difficult afternoon. The memory of it rankled in Nicholas' mind throughout every hour of his long voyage, lying there to torment him with the uneasy knowledge that something was wrong and then suddenly raising its head to confront him with what the something was.

There was a young man in Boston, Deborah said—it seemed only right that she should tell Nicholas, seeing how he felt—who had asked her to share his life and fortune. He was a lawyer, already settled in business, although he was sensibly thinking of pulling up stakes and going where there was more business. To speak frankly, Deborah was not quite sure in her own mind exactly how she felt about him, but there he was. She thought it only fair that Nicholas should know, nor did she think it fair to encourage him in any behaviour with which in ill-judged moments she might have encouraged him in the past. Better for them both, thought Deborah, to forget the past and let time take its own course.

"It's no use making plans, Nicholas," said Deborah's icy voice, "when I don't even know yet how I feel. I thought I did last year, but now I'm sure I don't. No, there's nothing wrong with you. You're just what you've always been, and always will be. You're not the changing kind. I'll always like and admire you, but that's all I'm ready to say. You don't need to feel so bad about it. There are plenty of girls in the world, and men, too, for that matter."

The remembrance of Deborah's quiet, indifferent voice and of her fingers forever sorting and resorting her sketches never once left Nicholas as they sailed down the slopes of tossing water toward the Horn and up again toward San Francisco. It burned within him, making him hot and breathless within his heavy sea clothes in icy squalls of sleet and snow, now firing anger and resentment, now hurting him with an ache beside which weariness and the manifold irritations of an old, poorly manned ship were as nothing. The voyage seemed never-ending, monotonous in the very evenness of its consistent ill luck. When they at last reached San Francisco after five months of infinite desolation, there was no word from Deborah even although, now that the Union and the Central Pacific had united their lines to make transcontinental travel and mails an easy certainty, there had been time for half a hundred letters.

Nicholas lost his head then, doing this also with the completeness of the Crocketts, Silas and James, old Judah and Amos, who under like circumstances would have behaved (and perhaps did if the more intimate records of them were not lost) precisely as the last of their line. He met a woman in San Francisco, or rather she met him, overtaking him quite by chance on the last night of their stay in port when the hope for letters had gone for good and when everything else had left Nicholas except bitter resentment and fury. The woman, who was old enough to have borne Nicholas, banished these emotions by supplying for the moment a tumult of others more bearable, which in turn left him with nothing but disgust and self-loathing and the restless memory of insane promises when he boarded his ship at dawn.

It was then and during succeeding days that he thought of his grandmother, now that he had proved himself unworthy of even a memory of Deborah. He might, he told himself as he paced the pitching decks and fought his way forward and aft through engulfing seas, have told Abigail Crockett had she been anywhere to tell. He had a feeling that she might have returned even his anxious confidence with a sympathy in which reproach, although rightly present, would have seemed as nothing compared to her quick understanding of what had made him do as he had done. Now that he could look back upon her, review his boyhood with her, she fulfilled in his mind the truth of his mother's words that there was nothing she did not know about and think sensibly upon. But since her understanding was closed to him, since the brightness had now quite gone from his world, he experienced a bitter relief as they stumbled homeward through gray seas (Nicholas for once careless of delays and ill luck) that he was free at least from the necessity of telling Deborah what she, in common with most decent young women in the 1870's, could never have understood for the fraction of a second.

11

The necessity of telling Deborah did not dissolve itself so easily. For when he reached home once more, there was Deborah, more winning and needful of him than she had ever been. She was sorry about not writing since he had evidently been anxious, but she had thought it best and kindest in the long run to leave him as free as she herself had wanted to be. Now Saturday Cove, she said, seemed to be her portion whether she would or no. The trustees of the academy had been spared an embarrassing interview with her father, for he had died suddenly while Nicholas was in torment somewhere off Brazil. She and her mother were already preparing the præceptor's house for a younger and more up-to-date man; and they themselves were moving in a few weeks into the old Winship home, which Solace Crockett was glad to have occupied against the dampness and mould sure to attack unused dwellings. Her mother with a tenacity amazing to Deborah had refused to leave Saturday Cove. Her friends of eleven years were there, she said, and at over sixty one could not pull up stakes and transplant oneself. Nor had Deborah's father on a salary of five hundred dollars a year left them too well off. They would best leave well enough alone, said Deborah's mother, and thank the Lord daily for their many blessings.

Nicholas thanked the Lord fervently as the autumn months wore on and Deborah constantly warmed toward him. He was even grateful that the *Mildred May* was undergoing extensive repairs in Boston before taking to sea again. She would not be ready before January, her commander wrote. He only hoped that Nicholas could wait for her and him. Nicholas waited. Now when he saw Deborah as he did almost every evening, he said good-night to her in his grandfather's old sitting-room. It was good to see her there. She kept red apples on the table and oxalis in the window-brackets. The wide hall was no longer cold and still, and the doors of the rooms upstairs stood open.

The subtle, persistent change creeping over Saturday Cove was evidenced even in the fact that Nicholas did his courting of Deborah in the Winship sitting-room whereas Silas had sat with Solace Winship in the front parlour. The doors of the front parlour were closed now upon its former light and grandeur as were the doors of the front parlours everywhere in Saturday Cove now that great ships came no more, now that entertaining of their commanders was a thing of the past when talk had flowed on about half the world. Back parlours did very well now; for not only did front ones take extra wood to heat them, but housekeepers of a second generation were wont to guard priceless possessions against daily wear and tear. Indeed, after those sweeping changes in shipping in the sixties and seventies, changes social as well as economic, there was a gradual shifting from front to back parlours along the entire coast of Maine.

The knowledge that he must one day tell Deborah about the woman in San Francisco still weighed upon Nicholas, but he pushed it ahead into the future as far as it would go. When one was living in Paradise, it was monstrous to descend into Hell. He shrank from the suffering of Deborah once regained and then perhaps irretrievably lost. If he could but make himself necessary enough to her, she might forgive him when the wretched hour came that he must tell; and although his honesty reproved him for what he felt to be an unfair game, he was swept on by a tide that he was powerless to resist.

The woman in San Francisco was mercifully silent. No word came from her to Nicholas. She had, in fact, forgotten all about him; his young promises had meant nothing to her no matter how they nagged at his honest nature. She recalled his visit only to laugh at his inexperience when men wiser in the ways of the world sought her favours. Her careless, mirthful confidences to them would have made Nicholas' cheeks burn with humiliation could he have heard them. But as things were, he was grateful for her silence which in a measure healed his fears if it did not effectively quiet his conscience.

Deborah that cold winter in Saturday Cove was irresistible. She set at nought his worries over the long-deferred sailing of his ship and consequent loss of hard-earned money. When the ice closed the harbour and the fishing-boats were hauled up and the village fell half asleep, she made it for him a place of warmth and light. Nicholas dutifully played cribbage with Deborah's mother in the long evenings while Deborah, now forgetful of her sketches, sewed by the table till the old clock sounded nine. Then he had

Deborah to himself for an hour and a half before he took the dark shore road for home.

On Sundays Deborah and her mother dined at the Crockett home, coming together from church where the Reverend Ethan Fisher, for twenty years in the churchyard, had been superseded by a younger man, who, ardent though he was in the yearly seasons of revival and in the cause of temperance now sweeping New England, did not feel called upon to concern himself quite so vitally with the private affairs of his parish and the strict keeping of the Sabbath day. Nicholas and Deborah spent an unconscionably long time in Abigail Crockett's kitchen doing the dinner dishes on Sunday. A great cook stove there had long since taken the place of the brick oven which Abigail had used for years. Only a wall of red brick showed where the fireplace with its pots and cranes once had been. Tin kettles now took the place of iron ones, and the wood-box by the side of the stove held smaller lengths of birch and spruce than the logs which had in the thirties and forties still fired the old oven. Deborah was fussy about dish washing. New and ingenious soap-shakers gave her plenty of hot suds, and the kettles must be kept filled for her careful rinsing of glassware and silver. Nicholas was in heaven while he dried the dishes for Deborah. He wore a great apron of his mother's over his Sunday suit and followed Deborah's directions to the last minute of hanging the scrubbed dish-towels on the clothes line in the back yard.

In April the *Mildred May* was ready to sail again, loading her cargo this time not for San Francisco, as both her owners and her commander had at last come to admitting that with all her overhauling she was unfit for the stormy passage around the Horn. She was now routed for Norfolk and Savannah to carry fish and manufactured goods and to bring back coal to Boston, or perhaps to go to New Orleans in season for cotton, although new railroad lines and steamships were in stout competition against sail for that purpose also.

Nicholas' threatened departure brought matters to a head between him and Deborah. One late April evening when the moist spring air came through the windows of the Winship sitting-room and some branches of wild plum which Deborah had gathered before their time of flowering were showing buds of white on the mantelpiece, Nicholas, sitting beside her on the old sofa, told her about the woman in San Francisco. He had asked Deborah to marry him when the spring came around again to mark his twenty-third birthday, and he would not claim her promise until she knew. Deborah on the whole was decent about the story, which Nicholas stumbled through with his long brown hands covering his face and fumbling in the heavy air above his forehead. She was even disposed to kindliness and a partial understanding when she saw his pathetic wretchedness and remembered how she herself had felt beneath the stress of his kisses.

He went home late that night with the weight of a long year mercifully gone from his mind and body. He left the next morning to rejoin his ship, which under Deborah's forgiveness was transformed more miraculously than new paint and cordage could ever have effected. Even Savannah, Norfolk, and New Orleans took on the outlines of Calcutta and Canton. Their low, dishevelled wharves, their hot suns and filthy blacks, rolling their eyes under cotton bales and canvas buckets of filthier coal, had no power to depress him. Life and the world had given Nicholas more than he had dared hope; and time and chance no longer loomed ominously before his re-opened eyes.

12

Nicholas and Deborah were married the following spring after Nicholas in a year of coast sailing had risen to the first officer's berth on the *Mildred May* and at least partially replenished his flat pockets. They were married on the forty-fourth anniversary of Solace's wedding day and in the Saturday Cove church where she had swept up the aisle on Silas' arm, strong within its folds of best blue broadcloth, her shaking hand held close against the cream satin of his fine waistcoat. Neither Deborah nor Nicholas had wanted so simple a wedding as theirs to be held in the church, but they consented to it to please Solace. Nicholas wore a new blue suit with the buttons and braid which proved his recent promotion, and Deborah was quite beautiful enough in a gown of pale green silk with a piquant hat to match sitting high upon her fair head. The church was quite as well filled as on Solace's wedding day although the guests were more sombre in appearance and although social distinctions were far less closely marked. Miss Serena Osgood was there, shrunken and feeble, still faithful in her fading memory to an old romance, which only a scant handful in Saturday Cove so much as dimly remembered.

The Winship home was again open for a wedding reception, its front and back parlours again made into one great room. Lilacs once more banked the fireplaces, and the sunlight fell upon the polished furniture below Thomas Winship's carved ships above his white doorways. Deborah and Nicholas with their mothers received their friends in the front parlour; and although there was no wedding-bell above the heads of the bridal couple and far less ceremony in the presentation of those that wished them well, there was no less cordiality and good humour. There was plenty to eat and an abundance of coffee and good fruit punch to drink. The temperance agitation of the seventies banned the more vivifying beverages of 1830 just as their social seriousness in general discouraged any dancing upon the unkempt orchard grass. Nor did the talk now include the world in its scope; nor were the ladies' costumes so costly and picturesque; nor were there men about in satin and broadcloth, gold-headed canes and buff top hats—prosperous, self-assured men home for a season with the magic of China and India about them and their ships perchance riding at anchor in the very harbour.

But it was a beautiful day all the same and a fully satisfying occasion; and if the velvet on the chair was a bit faded and the muslin curtains a bit less fine and the house in general less spruce than it had been, there were few there who could remember acutely enough to note the difference. Miss Serena, it is true, kept repeating from the chair in which Nicholas had placed her that times had surely changed; but since the fact was obvious and everyone had grown used to it, more pity was accorded to Miss Serena than to time.

Nicholas and Deborah did not drive away in a coach. The green and yellow one had been scrapped as useless twenty years before. They did not drive away at all, but after everything was over and their guests had gone and they themselves had helped to put the house in order, they walked in the early evening to the Crockett home and under the syringas in the garden ate the supper which Deborah had prepared.

Deborah, it had been decided, was to make her home (and Nicholas') with Solace Crockett. It seemed the best plan all around. Deborah knew that she would get along better with her mother-in-law than with her mother, and from long experience her mother knew it, too. Mrs. Parsons was quite able, she said, to make out by herself. No house was large enough to hold two families, she wisely concluded; and when the autumn came, she would take in for the winter some country girl who wanted to attend the academy and who for her board would help with household chores.

Deborah did get on better with Solace Crockett than with her mother. Indeed, she got on very well. She had Solace's idea of her to keep untarnished, and a thorough respect for her mother-in-law stimulated and strengthened her resolve. She might have her ups and downs with Nicholas; his very adoration of her and his annoying patience made them inevitable; but they were not to reach his mother's eyes and ears. And when Nicholas was away, as he must be most of the time, Deborah would like the dignity of awaiting his return in a house which bespoke a larger world than that of Saturday Cove even though that world had now withdrawn itself homeward across the seas.

There were no ups and downs during their first weeks together in their new life. Solace Crockett stayed on with Mrs. Parsons in the house where she had been born and left Deborah and Nicholas to themselves. They lived those weeks on a pinnacle of breathless happiness where their own future and that of Saturday Cove had no part. They did the things which they had done as children, picked wild strawberries from the thick meadow grass, fished for flounder in Nicholas' old dory, pulled their lobster-pots and dug their clams, picnicked on the boulder in the woods where Deborah had once told Nicholas that she could not get him out of her head for some hours after she had seen him.

The ups and downs came when Nicholas had gone to the *Mildred May* and Deborah was left with Saturday Cove as background and foreground, past and present and future. And because Solace must be kept inviolable from Deborah's moods, they were all the more heaped upon Nicholas once he was at home again. Before a year was up, Nicholas approached his homecomings with a stealthy dread creeping insidiously into his expectations and desires. Fear made inroads upon his longing to see Deborah, the fear that in their hours together there would be upbraidings of his stubborn determination to stay under sail when there were steamships in plenty, Deborah said, and numberless berths on them for men with half the spunk of Nicholas, if he would only think of her and not entirely of himself. Steamships made quicker passages and more money; and, after all, they *were* ships and they moved in the sea, which was clearly more to Nicholas than was Deborah herself. An officer's berth on a steamship might mean a home or at least rooms in Boston or New York during the winter months where Deborah might conceivably take up her art again and not decay in Saturday Cove as she most certainly was doing with no one to teach her anything that she did not know already.

Nicholas was always slow in replying to Deborah's impatience. First of all, he was perplexed by the fact that Deborah never could be made to understand how he felt about a sailing-ship and his family's connection therewith, a connection so long that to Nicholas it was indissoluble. And while he was honestly endeavouring to understand why she could not understand, Deborah's impatience was sure to progress into reproach and continue into anger. Against her anger Nicholas had no weapons. It was one thing to feel anger against Deborah when she had kept him upon tenter-hooks before she had made up her mind to marry him; but now that she was his, anger was as impossible as was the abrupt changing of his life to comply with her pleading. Nicholas' wounded stubbornness acted but as a spur to Deborah's ready imagination. She could think of a hundred things to say to Nicholas to which he had no answer. When all else failed to move him, there was always the woman in San Francisco to fall back upon in order to make him aware of his unworthiness. To this last and final goad, which always plunged Nicholas into black humiliation and remorse, there was clearly no countercharge.

Fate seemingly dealt winning cards to Deborah in the fall of 1875. The *Mildred May*, bound adventurously and unwisely to Bermuda, capsized in a gale off Hatteras. Things looked bad enough from the start, but almost certain peril swiftly became disaster when she caught fire and within three hours was a blazing wreck. The boat mastered by Nicholas was the only one to reach shore and safety after three days of frightful privation and suffering. Nicholas lost two men from burns too terrible to weather the thirst and exposure demanded of them and returned home himself so haggard and ill that Deborah, even while she bided her time, was swept by tenderness and pity.

Nicholas was cited in the papers for his hardihood and sense, and companies and captains began once more to know of Saturday Cove and what it could produce in men. While he rested at home in the short November days, offers came to him. New steamship companies were proving eager for officers trained thus under sail. The successor to the great Charles Morgan, who in his long life given to steamship building and navigation had built and managed one hundred and seventeen craft of every conceivable description, came forward with the captaincy of a new steamer of seventeen hundred tons built to traverse the dangerous waters of the Gulf of Mexico. The newly organized Savannah Line, itself boastful that its steamboats were designed, built, and engined against Cape Hatteras weather, offered, nay urged upon Nicholas the command of one of its best.

When letters and telegrams of this nature reached Saturday Cove, Solace, dictated by her pride in Nicholas as well as by her anxiety for his future, joined her forces with those of Deborah. Nicholas might as well face facts, she said. It was no use beating one's head against a stone wall. She was all for sail herself as her life witnessed, but if there was no sail, what was one to do? A stubborn determination like that of Nicholas could not raise up sailing-ships.

Nicholas sat in his father's chair by the fire until Christmas and listened to his mother and Deborah, holding off meanwhile the southern steamship lines although he knew well what he would say to them. He was standing with his back to the wall, fighting desperately against being overwhelmed. Time had beaten him and so had chance, which had wrecked the *Mildred May* and brought him to the unwelcome notice of companies and courses which he despised. His only allies were a worn-out tradition and a cause already gloriously lost.

On the last day of December when he felt his powers of resistance waning like the spent year—a year that had left him poorer in pocket and more distressed in mind than he had been since his marriage—two things, leaping suddenly above his horizon, confronted him with the promise of a new world. The brief day was dark with flurries of icy snow when he went outside in the afternoon to look upon the still open and forsaken harbour. The brown, snowless fields and ridges were gaunt and lifeless. Indecision nagged within him, an emotion rather than a state of mind, making him worn and half ill in spite of his mother's attempts to build him up again with food and sleep. Deborah had gone earlier to the village, declining his company, and he wandered about awaiting her return, miserable without her, more miserable in her presence. The sun was lying low and pale above the western spruces when she at last came home.

She told her news when she was once in the sitting-room. She sat on a low stool with her long hands stretched out before the fire. Solace had made her some hot tea, and she held the cup far from her as she told them. The doctor had confirmed her alternate hopes and fears, she said. There was a baby coming in the early summer.

When she had told them with her eyes on Nicholas' face, Nicholas rose and walked about the room, not saying a word to Deborah. He was tingling all over his body, feeling as he had felt when they had studied their Latin lessons in this very room. He was half glad, half sorry that Deborah had not waited to tell him when they were alone. The baby's coming, he knew, could not now be an isolated fact, complete and triumphant in itself. It was swathed and circumscribed by the necessity for quick decisions, by offers for steady and higher wages, and by Deborah's loneliness and fear. One could not make a simple statement of pleasure in the face of all these things which made a natural, long-desired happening so complex and bewildering.

At last he came and stood by Deborah after his mother had gathered up the tea things and gone to the kitchen. Deborah leaned her head against him while the early darkness settled outside the window and the sharp snow flakes began to click against the panes. She said:

"There's some one else to think of now, Nicholas, besides just you and what you want. You'd best telegraph Savannah, don't you think? They're holding it open for you until tomorrow."

He bent and kissed Deborah then and got his coat and cap from the hallway. He went along the shore road, stumbling over the ruts of frozen ground now fast filling with snow. He felt as though years had passed over him since Deborah had come home.

When he reached the village post-office, the stage had just arrived with the evening mail. He went in to wait for its leisurely distribution, glad to defer his visit to the store which also held the telegraph office. Most of Saturday Cove was waiting for the mail, the Bangor and Portland papers, the *Farmers' Almanac* for 1876, the few letters, the overdue Christmas packages. The small outer enclosure of the office was filled with men and boys, women and girls muffled against the cold. Nicholas stood in one corner, returning vaguely the greetings of his neighbours, wondering if any among them beneath their hoods and wraps were faced with problems like his own or were burning within themselves from a secret akin to his.

Once the slot was opened, he crowded forward with the others for the contents of his box. There was a letter from the Savannah Line, repeating its offer, urging upon him a quick and favourable decision; there was the Boston paper; and there within the folds of the paper and hidden from his first inspection of what the mail might offer, was yet another letter addressed to him in a cramped, decisive, unknown hand.

He retreated to his corner to open and read the letter while those behind him in the line continued to harass the postmaster, labouring to empty the half a hundred boxes which he had recently filled. Nicholas forgot everyone there and elsewhere as he read—Jonas Norton's father, who had retired and was growing old, Lieutenant Simpson, who now used his wooden leg in skippering one of the best schooners on the Banks, a small boy to whom he had promised one of his earlier ship-models and who was gazing at him with admiring eyes, even Deborah and Solace waiting for him by the fire with supper ready. He saw only the long seas stretching southward from the equator to Good Hope, the still glassy water of the doldrums splattered by driving slants of hot rain, the fair, rolling clouds of the southeast trades, the tearing gusts and squalls of the westerlies.

"I have a first officer's berth to Hong Kong to offer you," he was reading, "on my own ship, one of the best as you may know, knowing ships. We are just now in and sail again from New York on the first of March. I knew and admired your father, and I took my first orders as a mere boy from your grandfather. I hope you may see your way to joining us. I have a good crew, mostly of home men and boys, rare in these days, and the second and third officers are first-rate stuff. There are those that think that to follow sail in these days is to waste a good man's time; but knowing your family and reading the record of your recent disaster off Hatteras, I am constrained to believe that you are of different mind."

Nicholas' telegram went not to Savannah but to Searsport, to a name known throughout New England as that of a master mariner and commander. A half-hour later he burst into the dining-room upon Deborah and Solace waiting at the supper table, the tired lines erased from his face, his eyes again lighted by the old glow as he told them. His mother watching him thought of Silas twenty-five years before at the launching of the *Surprise*, and all her misgivings faded into nothingness as they had faded then. But Deborah, although she saved her main offensive until she and Nicholas should be alone, still harboured her own.

"You don't mean, Nicholas, that you're turning down a captaincy to keep only what you've had for two years."

"Yes," said Nicholas. "I suppose it looks like that to people who don't understand. But there's not much in commanding a thing you've no respect for. Everyone knows the ship I'm taking. She's the best of those that are left. I'd rather sail on her as cook than to pilot a Morgan steamer through a Galveston swamp or to carry fancy passengers from New York to Savannah."

"What about your future?" went on Deborah's still voice, so still that Nicholas, knowing what smouldered beneath its stillness, fidgeted uneasily in his chair. "You've got to think of that more than ever now."

"I know. That's just what's made me do as I have done. I'll be proud to have a son of mine know I helped command such a ship, and he'll be proud, too."

"Is the voyage long?" asked Deborah after an uneasy silence. "If you sail the first of March way off there, when will you be back?"

Nicholas' eyes fell before the steady gleam of her own. "It'll be seven months at least," he said, "with all things going right. Most likely far longer. I'm sorry, Deborah."

"You don't mean!" cried Deborah, and then stopped, remembering her reserves kept tightly in check for Nicholas' ears alone.

Nicholas appealed silently to his mother.

"I'm afraid you don't quite understand, Deborah," said Solace. "Women whose husbands go to sea expect these things—or worse. And you'll be glad he's away. Men are no good at such times. I've never ceased to be glad that Nicholas' father wasn't here with me."

"I suppose," said Deborah finally, after another silence that completely took everyone's appetite, "I suppose that that's all in the way different women look at it. Times have changed and women, too, since Nicholas was born."

Deborah's main offensive lasted well through the night. There were tears and upbraidings, sobs and threats, cleverly drawn pictures of her sacrifices and of Nicholas' stubborn unworthiness. By dawn even the southeast trades had lost their lure, and Nicholas was wondering as he lay beside Deborah, at last asleep, how two months were to be weathered before the Searsport ship sailed on the first of March.

At half-past six he stumbled down the stairs to light the fires for his mother. Snow was falling, and the fields and meadows stretching to the slate-coloured harbour were white and still in the pale light of the winter dawn. He stood by the sink in the kitchen watching the sky slowly brighten, glad of the stillness in the house, fearful of breakfast. He heard the muffled, distant tones of the clock in the church strike seven; and as the last one died away and the day became inevitable, he saw a well-bundled man limping through the unbroken snow to the back door.

It was Lieutenant Simpson, who had once taught him to drill with a wooden gun on the school playground, now Captain Simpson, successful skipper of the schooner *Lydia*, a "high-liner" in the fresh halibut fishing on the Grand Banks. Captain Simpson did not apologize for his untimely call as he entered the kitchen upon Nicholas' surprised invitation. For a man who habitually breakfasted at four A.M., seven doubtless seemed well on into the day. He stood upon Abigail Crockett's yellow floor with his legs, real and unreal, well apart, shook the snow from his heavy cap, tugged at his muffler, looked appraisingly, perhaps admiringly, at Nicholas. He himself came from no family like the Crockett's, and yet he had used his time and talents well. A pension in payment for his leg had been wisely spent and substantially increased in the one thing he understood, namely fishing. Now he owned and skippered a stout new schooner of one hundred and twenty tons and, unlike most Maine fishermen, had had the foresight to desert cod and mackerel for the more lucrative, if more perilous, pursuit of halibut.

He was not disposed to preambles or to unnecessary explanations. Standing there in the kitchen with the sticks of spruce crackling in the black stove and the snow falling steadily without, he said to Nicholas:

"I'm not callatin' on how you'll blow, Nicholas, but I'll come to the point straight on. I've lost my best man for this month's trip: he's been took sick; and we sail with this afternoon's tide. I've six dories and I need twelve men. When I saw you last night in the post-office, I had an idea that seemed even better once I'd slept on it. It's no summer picnic, my job ain't, but there's money in it. We aim to make the trip in twenty days at most, there and back to Boston. We'll bring in some ninety thousand pounds of fresh stuff, and each man'll stand to make his two hundred dollars or more. We don't have no fancy ranks aboard as you know. Each fellow does his share. But I've known you and what you come from, and if you're favourable to go along, I'll give you a half of my own turnover, which ought to mean nigh four hundred dollars to you. I've some good strong fellows, but I need another man with a head on his shoulders for bad weather and with wits that jump in a fix. And I thought if you was layin' off waitin' till spring for somethin' more in your own line, you might consider my offer till that somethin' shows up—in the interim, as they say, so to speak."

Nicholas looked at Captain Simpson. Although he knew nothing of all that was passing through Nicholas' mind, he seemed at that moment to have come in the guise of a saviour. Nicholas felt fog in his face, cold air in his lungs, wide free skies above and about him. He felt money in his hands against new necessity. Upstairs he heard his mother and Deborah moving about in preparation for another day, the first of many days until March should come, days which would beat steadily against him with their weight of opposition and reproach. He stood leaning against the old chest where he had heard his grandmother's songs and eaten her gingerbread-men. He heard Captain Simpson say:

"Like as not I've kind of taken you off your feet, so to speak, but the fact is I ain't much time left. I can't wait much beyond ten o'clock to know."

"You don't need to wait," said Nicholas then. "Not an hour. I'll be ready. And—thanks."

13

Life returned to Nicholas once they were anchored in the bitter gray waters of the Banks. He had felt it coming back during the five days that they worked northeastward, using head winds as best they might, stamping about the narrow decks to keep from freezing, and on off hours clustering about the fire in the stuffy cabin. Order was slowly taking the place of confusion in his mind; assurance was banishing the blackness of indecision; the rightness of his allegiance was again establishing itself. Perhaps even now, he thought in the cold hour of his watch, he might begin, late as it seemed, his victory over time and chance.

The fishing itself at once stabilized and increased his renewed faith and confidence by the very rigour of its demands. It left no hours for misgivings, no moments for questioning as to one's course of action. From the first hint of dawn until the last shadowy gleam of daylight it gave, in return for monstrous labour, at least the negative peace of a mind unable from utter weariness of body to be anxious.

By five o'clock in the darkness and cold of the January mornings they were rolling from their bunks, numb from the heaviness of their sleep, stiff from cold and from the dampness of clothes that served for night and day alike. They drew on their great boots over the heavy socks in which they had slept, buttoned on their extra shirts, their pea-jackets, their oilskins, spread mutton tallow from the common can over and within the worst of the cuts and bruises on their hands. Before or after, between or among these operations, they breakfasted, the starboard gang of six in one lot, the port in another, crowding the galley, drinking down cups of scalding coffee in which hardtack might be soaked, devouring great bowls of corn-meal mush sweetened with molasses or brown sugar and slabs of platebeef wedged between slices of soggy, unbuttered bread. Then the dories must be inspected and made ready, the gaffs and gobsticks tested by smart whacks upon the stout gunwales in the dim light of the lanterns, the allowance of water stored. When the first rays of light began to penetrate the obscurity of gray, lowering skies and the more mighty obscurity of winter fogs, the dories were made ready for lowering without delay, for the day was brief and precious and no time must be lost.

Nicholas' labour on the *Mildred May* was as nothing to this. So exacting was it, so stealthy in its every moment of danger, that he felt as though his life heretofore had been spent in sleep in comparison with the omnipresent vigilance demanded of eyes and ears, hands and back and legs. When the dories slipped away from the vessel and started through the cold, tossing seas for the trawling grounds where the great lines with their baited ground hooks had been set the afternoon before, there was not the fraction of a second in which a man could be safely off his guard. There was fog to watch; there was the wind, the slightest shifting of which must be noted and reckoned with lest the position of the *Lydia* might be lost in fog or darkness and the dories lost in their turn once they had mistaken the home and shelter to which they would hasten as soon as the trawls had been hauled. There was danger from heavy, breaking seas ready to slide over their gunwale, level with the water when the great fish were gaffed; there was danger from the fish themselves unless they were stunned by the gobstick before they were thrown into the bottom of the labouring dory; and there was danger from ice which sometimes appeared suddenly as though rising from the sea, ghosts haunting a ghostly waste of water, jagged cakes, any one of which might smash them into bits, indiscernible in fog, often unnoticed in the blank whiteness of the winter atmosphere even when fog was mercifully absent. And always there was the more stealthy danger from exposure and from the cold that surrounded them as though, Nicholas thought, they were but pulsating, living cells, the only life of a vast, lifeless world which was encircling them and gradually extending to them also its overwhelming cold.

Nicholas felt his muscles, unused to such strain, tearing beneath his chafed flesh as he hauled in the trawls, heavy with fish each weighing from forty to two hundred pounds. And then there was the long task of rowing homeward through stormy seas, sleet and hail and snow, fog and menacing ice, and the equally long and laborious task of landing their fish once they had reached the side of the *Lydia*, hauling them in with their long-handled gaffs, one man in the tossing dory, the other on the rocking schooner. There was dinner then, a quick meal of more platebeef and coffee and hardtack, eaten, if they had been lucky, long before noon; and after it was over and one longed to stretch, drenched as one was, if only for half an hour in a sodden bunk, there were thousands of pounds of fish to split and clean and throw into the ice-lined hold. In passable weather the trawls were rebaited as they were pulled, and sunk again; but in bad the baiting was done after the fish were cleaned and stowed away. The tired men squatted by the trawl and bait tubs on the deck, cutting into hunks the by-products of their catch, cod and haddock and menhaden, which would serve for halibut food, and securing the hunks to six hundred hooks for the trawl-lines, each of which in its full length extended a mile and three quarters between the anchoring buoys. Then in what daylight was left the dories slipped away again to lay the baited trawls, helped back home where there was fog or when darkness overtook them by a conch-shell blown by the cook or skipper or by the firing of the *Lydia's* warning gun. When the darkness fell over the face of the desolate sea, and the dories were piled on deck ready for the dawn, and supper had been eaten, there was at last time for a pipe or two in the cabin before sleep settled upon them where they sat or lay, sleep so numbing that few had time or inclination to take off more than boots and outer coats, sleep so dreamless that no one recognized it as sleep until one must be wakened for his watch or to begin again the terrible and yet healing monotony of another day's labour.

All night through from early darkness at five until late daylight at seven watch must be kept turn and turn about, an hour to each man, cook and skipper included. It seemed impossible to climb the frozen, icy shrouds to the lookout, but one did it, mechanically as though some hidden machinery within was hoisting heavy legs and feet, enabling cold fingers to clutch upon colder security. Drowsiness must be shaken off, the dark sea scanned and watched, mast lights scrutinized seemingly at every moment, for other schooners were passing on the way to and from Gloucester and Marblehead, Nantucket, or ports nearer home. Ice was an ever-present menace;

and now that steam had won its tough foothold, ocean ships might come looming from the darkness across their very anchorage.

But at most the labour, terrific as it was in its strain on mind and body, was of short duration. In that, the halibut fishing was more lenient than the cod, in spite of the fact that skippers thus engaged could not wait to ride out gales or to lay off their fishing while they awaited decent weather. The *Lydia*, in common with other vessels chartered by the fishing companies, lost her profits unless she could deliver her fresh cargo in quick time. A fare of eighty thousand pounds of fine white halibut, which would fetch seven and one-half cents, meant a wallet full of money to every man, provided he lost no time and balked at no hardship.

Captain Simpson had chosen his men well. After six days of labour that brooked no delay and made allowance for no peril his hold was stocked with close to a hundred thousand pounds of the best fish he had ever taken on the Grand Banks. They had reached the grounds on January seventh, and late on the night of the fourteenth after a day that exceeded any they had yet spent because of its steadily increasing cold they were ready to hoist anchor and start southward.

Nicholas was aware of an almost peculiar sense of relief when he felt the *Lydia* respond to the icy wind in her sails and bound forward through following seas—peculiar in that he had experienced, at least consciously, no sense of dread while he had laboured at the fishing. Now, however, as they drove through the darkness he was grateful for their escape from a desolation he had but half perceived in the increasing rigour of their days. He lay in his bunk, half asleep, awaiting his watch at ten o'clock, and listened in a weary stupour to the talk of the tired men who lay about the narrow quarters. The air, cold though it was, was heavy with the smells of wet and dirty woollens, the fumes of cheap tobacco, the strong not unpleasant odour of the liniment with which some were rubbing the swollen muscles of their legs and arms, now freed for a season and in consequence more tortuous from pain. They were talking of less successful trips than this one when the smaller work had yielded smaller profits, spending their money more cautiously since it had been earned at dearer cost. One of them was saying:

"I've got a new kid at home. Likely enough he'll get a baby carriage now."

Another was good-naturedly receiving banter upon his approaching marriage to a girl in Machiasport. He was stripped to his waist in spite of the cold and was rubbing salve into his joints, which responded so generously that his body was black with filthy grease.

"If she seed you now, Bill, she'd sure give you the go-bye."

"Not her!" cried Bill. "She don't turn a man down for cuts and sores when he's worked like Hell for 'em. No, nor for bow legs neither."

Others were asleep in their bunks, their heavy, stertorous breathing adding its weight to the closeness of the air.

Nicholas was more weary than he had ever known a man could be. His back ached, the pain running down his thighs to his knees and ankles with sharp stabs of anguish. He shivered from the cold, wondering why the sweat stood out upon his face even as he pulled his dirty blankets more closely about him.

At ten he dragged himself to his feet, put on his heavy shirts and fleece-lined jacket, his cap with ear-laps and his mittens, and made his way up the icy stairs to the deck. The cold was steadily falling over the sea, beneath the clearest of skies, shot and pierced with stars and with the long streamers of the northern lights. Five below it had been at noon when they brought back their laden dories after the last great haul; ten below at their four o'clock supper; fifteen at "mugging up" time. There was no reason for looking at the deck thermometer, he thought, as he pulled himself up slowly and cautiously into the lookout; there was small sense of adventure in this cold.

Once at his post, well-propped against the stout wood of the mast which shielded him somewhat from the wind, he began his watch. He was glad to be away from the cabin and alone, weary and ill as he was. The thoughts which had been dulled by labour or waylaid by the necessity for constant vigilance came back to him there, high above the black sea, in the immensity of space. In seven days if the wind held good he would be at home, bathed and in a clean bed; in five weeks he would be leaving for New York and the Searsport ship, his life at last beginning after its long span of incompleteness. Even the hardest and least propitious of voyages in comparison with his experience of the past days would seem a yachting cruise. And after a rest at home with the money he was bringing smoothing the way for everybody, he would be at the height of his powers, able to impress the finest of commanders with the knowledge that sail could never entirely pass from the seas since there were young men left who, like their fathers, were worthy of it.

At brief intervals he swung his arms violently across and against his chest, although the pain of his action was almost less easily borne than the fear that prompted it. He began to do this once he had fully realized the cold, of which the man he had relieved had warned him. He continued to do it, soon not so much in fear of the cold itself as of the drowsiness which crept over him, dulling his mind and silencing the pain of his body, bringing with it the terror of sleep.

Now the future closed down before him, black and opaque as was the dark wall of the night beyond his shortened vision. He could not pierce it, try as he would. In its place the past came back, not thronging upon him, gay and bright with memories, but gleaming fitfully through long stretches of darkness as fireflies gleam over Maine meadows and through tangled roadside thickets on warm July evenings. Once he mistook the *Lydia* for the *Duncan Dunbar* rushing on through black waters for Sydney Heads. He even roused himself with painful suddenness at that instant by hearing his voice cry to the cold stars above him, "Hell or Sydney in sixty days!" The cold became transferred to the cold of his grandfather's house on the day when he had died, and the tapping of the frozen reef-points against the taut sails the tapping of the bare April lilacs against the leaded panes in the sidelights of the old front doorway. And last of all, deep down in the bottom of his slipping mind, there came one by one the sight of soap-bubbles, brighter than the lights that streamed above him, the warm May sunshine, and Deborah in a blue dress, cookie-men with currants for buttons, and the words of an old song:

> *"King Nébuchadnézzar, that wíly old fóx*
> *God sént to the fiélds to eat gráss with an óx.*
> *Said the óx to the kíng, 'You're an ódd king to mé,*
> *But I'll lénd you my gráss and the sháde of my trée.' "*

It took four men to get Nicholas down from the lookout and all the rest to work over him with panic in their stiff fingers. But it was all to no avail. The *Lydia* tore on southwestward through the cold; and in the morning the sun was bright and the long seas stretched ahead, their blue fully as deep as that of those that rolled south before the trades.

III

Reuben Crockett

1875-1910

Reuben Crockett

1

One warm July afternoon in the year 1886, when the haymakers were busy in the Crockett meadows, a little boy was watching them through the high open doors of the loft in the old barn, his eyes swollen from many recent tears. They were just finishing the raking of long swathes of well-dried hay into mounds which, he knew, they would soon pitch into the waiting rack. He could see the rack under the big elm trees in the lower corner of the field with the oxen standing beside it out of the rays of the hot afternoon sun. He wanted to join the men who had been working hard all day to beat some angry clouds threatening rain and thunder from the western sky; but he felt shy because of his tell-tale cheeks and eyes. They always good-naturedly allowed him to help tread down the load, he stumbling back and forth over the hay which they pitched up in great, fragrant forkfuls until the rack was filled, crowned and streaming, and ready to be drawn by the labouring oxen over the shorn, uneven meadowland and into the back driveway until it stood just beneath the loft doors where he now waited.

He did not think he *could* give up making the hay, for it was one of his chief summer pleasures. It seemed the worst of ill luck that his mother's letter with its crushing disappointment should have come that very afternoon, brought from the post-office by Susan, who had got herself cleaned up after the dinner dishes were washed and gone to the village in her black and white calico beneath her black umbrella. Susan had spared him his cleaning-up, deferring it until just before supper on account of his working in the meadows. He could hear her now in the distant kitchen rattling some tin pails and cups, wielding the green pump handle in the sink with many quick strokes to be sure she was getting the very coldest water from the bottom of the well. Susan always filled pails for the haymakers with molasses and ginger drink, which would refresh them before they began their gathering in. Reuben was accustomed to carrying it to them himself, a pail in each hand and the cups tied to the handle with stout twine. Once he was in the meadows, resting with them under the trees, one of them was sure to propose that he remain to tread the loads and then to ride toward the barn exhausted and stretched to his full length on the very top above the straining oxen.

He was not crying any more, he was glad to think, and he knew he would never have the courage to resist Susan's shout which he expected any moment now. It was rather a long walk to the meadows, and the breeze from the full harbour water might conceivably work wonders with his face before he reached the haymakers. He did not mind Susan's seeing the traces of his tears, as more might burst out at supper or afterward when he told his grandmother, although he meant to try as hard as ever he could to keep them back. His grandmother, once he had learned to read, had never asked to see his mother's letters, waiting only for what he chose to tell her; and she was quite unaware of this one in the pocket of his blouse. He did not read it again as he awaited Susan's call before descending the ladder from the loft to the barn floor. He knew it by heart:

"Dear Reuben" [it said],

"I am very sorry, indeed, to have to disappoint you a second time about your visit to Boston. Mr. Sawyer and I should have been glad to show you the things you want to see, and I am anxious to see how much you have grown in two whole years. You must be a big, tall boy by now, and I feel sure you are a credit to your father and me, as your grandmother tells me you are. But your stepfather has been called away to Charleston in South Carolina to make some paintings of some old houses there, and he wishes me to accompany him. I hope that you will be patient and bear your disappointment manfully. You will surely come next summer, or perhaps even at Christmas when you are free from school, although I do not like to have you leave your grandmother alone, especially in the winter when it is harder for her to go about.

"Mr. Sawyer has bought you a fine new box of paints which we hope you may enjoy. We shall send them to you tomorrow.

"With love to your grandmother and best wishes to Susan, I am, my dear Reuben,

"Ever your loving
"MOTHER."

Now, as he said it over again, no more tears were forthcoming. Perhaps, he thought, there were no more left to come. Perhaps, indeed, his grief had been pushed aside by another feeling which he did not quite know how to name. It was not exactly anger against his mother, who after all could not be blamed for wanting to go with his stepfather to South Carolina—a far-away place, which held the lure of all far-away places to Reuben and which he knew well from his geography book as a pale green southern state on the Atlantic Ocean. It was rather a half-formed feeling of resentment that she did not seem to mind much about not seeing him. He remembered his shyness when he had last seen her, beautiful and dainty though he had thought her in her city clothes. She had made him feel ill at ease when she remarked on his shortness as she helped him undress at night and when she had fussed about the way his stockings had of crumpling untidily below his thick little knees. He did not grow tall fast enough to suit her, he knew, and, since he had not made much progress between eight and ten, perhaps it was just as well that he stayed in Saturday Cove with his grandmother who never embarrassed him. He did not at all mind not seeing his stepfather, who never knew what to say to him and who was always painting something or other all over the disorderly Boston flat. But to give up seeing Bunker Hill Monument and the Minute Man, the site of the rude bridge that arched the flood and even the possibility of Plymouth Rock, and above all else the docks where two of his grandfather's great ships had been built was a disappointment cruel enough, especially in view of the fact that he had told all his friends at school, including the teacher herself, that he was actually to see these things with his own eyes. He was a shy boy, and the realization that he must soon admit he was to see none of them at all made him quiver with embarrassment up there in the loft and helped to increase the resentment he felt. But since even in his short life he had learned that plans must often be set aside and that people must try for the sake of others to conceal what they really felt, he leaned farther from the loft doorway and hoped that the breeze from the incoming tide was helping his eyes at least a little.

Susan's call came just as the haymakers had joined the oxen beneath the elm trees where they would rest for a quarter of an hour before the gathering-in should begin.

"Master Reuben," called Susan. "Where are you anyway? The swipes is ready."

Susan had odd ways, he thought, as he answered her call and began to descend the ladder. She always called him Master Reuben out of respect for his father whom she had known as a little boy and for his grandfather whom she had greatly admired. Susan knew her place, she often told Reuben, and even though she ate at the table with him and his grandmother and sometimes even carved the meat for his grandmother, who was poor at such things, she never forgot that she was their servant and was proud of it.

"Wherever have you been?" she asked a bit irritably when he had come through the shed to the back door and stooped to take the pails from her hands. "In the loft, I'll be bound, all this nice afternoon with hay and chaff all through your clothes and the Lord alone knows what else. You'll get a scrubbin' tonight and don't you forget it. Now don't slop the swipes whatever you do, for the men can't spare so much as a pint on a day like this."

Reuben felt immeasurably relieved as he started for the meadows, bending well forward so that he could carry the heavy pails without spilling them. If Susan had not noticed his eyes, then his chances were good with the haymakers who did not know him so well as she. The path that he followed was a well-trodden one leading straight to the shore. He would leave it once he had reached the stone wall that separated the meadows from the field directly behind the house. The field years before had been part of the lawn and garden; but now that he and his grandmother were alone and big lawns and gardens cost money (which they did not have) to be kept in proper shape, it had been allowed to merge into the orchard and like the orchard to be mown only twice during the summer. The elderberries on the stone wall were flaming red now that July was half over, and the wild clematis a mass of fragile bloom. He was careful about the wall, lifting the pails in turn well over it and setting them securely upon the newly shorn ground of the meadow before he himself climbed over and resumed his journey toward the elm trees where the men were resting with their pipes.

They were glad to see him. They roused themselves from the haycock against which they had been lying and took with thanks the cups which he offered them. Then they sat with their backs against the hay and their knees drawn up, holding their cups low between their legs until they drank off their cold drink with long and satisfied swigs. Reuben went about among the four of them, refilling their cups from the long-handled dipper which Susan had placed in one of the pails. They had pushed their wide-brimmed straw hats to the back of their heads; they were wet and hot, and there was dust and dirt in the seams and wrinkles of their necks and arms; they smelled of sweat and labour there under the trees. The light, intermittent breeze from the sea only made more apparent the odour of their bodies which mingled with the dry fragrance of the hay and with the warm, rich breath of the patient oxen, switching their tails against the tenacious flies upon their flanks and sides.

When they had drunk their first fill and had returned to their pipes, Reuben set the pails each within reach of two of them and stretched himself before them on the ground with his own cup near at hand. Now that the sweat was running down his flushed face from his exertions in their behalf, he was no long anxious over their detection of his tears; and even if he had been, he could not bear either to rest upon the next haycock, where they might conceivably forget all about him, or to intrude himself upon a vacant spot of the one where they rested, lest they should think him too familiar. So he lay before them on his stomach, his compact, thickly set little body looking uncomfortable enough in his close knee pants of corduroy, his blue denim blouse, his ribbed stockings and heavy shoes, which Susan would never let him shed, even on the hottest days, except on Saturday when his weekly bath was imminent. He silently chewed a long piece of hay, watched the thunderheads rolling up in the southwest, threatening rain and yet never quite obscuring the sun, and wondered how soon one of them would mention his treading of the loads.

They were all four kindly disposed toward Reuben as they regarded him between short puffs on their corncob pipes and long drinks from their tin cups. When they had first seen him coming slowly toward the meadows under the weight of his pails, they had been put in a good humour toward him by one of their number, who did Solace Crockett's milking for her and saw to the place in general. He was called Seth Tucker, and he had been in school with Reuben's father.

"That little fellow's a good one," he had said to the others, "and no mistake. His grandmother, she tells me how he's her right-hand man round that big place there, and time and again he works along o' me, capable as capable, and never beggin' you to do something for 'im like some young ones. Seems like it's kinder hard for 'im to live along just with them two women, good as they be. Seems like he'll grow old before his time. Look at him, there, liftin' them pails over the wall, careful as careful. He ain't much like what his father was, and that's a fact. My mother says he don't favour the Crockett side at all. Far back as she can go, they was all tall, fine set-up men. Nor his mother's side neither. She says he's like a brother of his grandfather—that Reuben who has a stone in the churchyard sayin' he was lost at sea."

"An' your mother's right," said the oldest of the four, a man of more than seventy, who had sharpened so many scythes in his life that on July nights he dreamed uneasily of whetstones against steel. "I mind him myself, that Reuben Crockett, an' how my father come into the kitchen where we was havin' supper an' said what a stew Cap'n James Crockett was in because the boy's ship hadn't been heard from. That was way back somewhere long before any of you young fellows was so much as thought of—in the eighteen-twenties, shall we say? My father worked in the Crockett yards in them days, an' we was taught to look up to the Crocketts. I was just a shaver then—knee high to nothin' atall—but I remember it all the same, an' how I went to bed thinkin' of drowndin' alone 'way off to sea somewhere. Yes, I mind that young Reuben. He was short an' squat like, not favourin' the first Nicholas or Silas or their father or uncles. I mind them all, an' what a prime lot o' men they was in the good old days when this village counted for somethin'. An' I mind James' wife Abigail—she's not been dead so long, take it by an' large, to an old fellow like me. There was a woman for you! I've sat in this meadow many a year as a young chap an' as a man o' middle age an' seen her come sweepin' through that field there which was a lawn then, her muslin skirts all billowin' out around her an' a basket on her arm full o' stuff for us, doughnuts an' pressed veal an' bottles of ale that nobody sees nowadays, but that used to be as common as they was right for a thirsty man."

He had looked appraisingly at Reuben as he drew near, stumbling a bit on the uneven surface of the freshly cut ground.

"Yes," he concluded, "he's a sight like that first Reuben who never even got to the churchyard, cheap end for a man's costly life as 'tis. An' when I see him comin' along here from that old house that's seen fine days, an' remember how his grandmother rode off in a coach on her weddin' day an' how his great-grandfather gave a glass o' grog an' a new dollar bill to every man in his yard, my own father included, without so much as a thought as to the price, I says to myself, I says, as David said about Saul an' Jonathan, his son, 'How are the mighty fallen!' "

The old man's words had had their effect upon the others as well as upon himself, and all the four who had received Reuben gratefully now looked upon him with friendliness.

"I hear tell, young Reuben," said one, breaking the warm, close silence in which they lounged for the last possible minutes, "I hear tell from my boy at home that you're to take a journey before many days are over. Goin' to Boston, is it? You'll doubtless come back so full of knowledge about the world that you won't want to tread no more hay for us."

Reuben lay closer against the ground to still the jump within him. So intent had he been upon concealment of his disappointment that he had not reckoned on such a crisis as this. It was lucky that the last doubt had vanished about treading the hay else he did not know how he could have answered. But his reply was so steady and straightforward that only Seth half suspected all that had been passing through his mind and hurting his body, since Susan had brought the letter.

"I'm not going just yet, I'm afraid. My mother has to go away when she wasn't expecting to. So I'm likely to wait awhile, maybe till next summer. And I'll always want to tread the hay, thank you."

To Reuben's relief as well as to his joy they began then their preliminaries to making the great loads. They all rose with one accord and stretched themselves, raising their brown, hairy arms above their heads, settling their torn old hats, and giving an extra hitch to their galluses, which, when they were suddenly loosened before being tightened once more, revealed wet and dirty lines upon their cotton shirts. Once their baggy overalls and trousers were hauled up tightly, their empty pipes and tobacco cans stowed in their hip pockets, they began to gather together their long wooden rakes from against the haycock where they had thrown them, their stout, three-tined forks from the floor of the rack. The metallic clatter of the forks as they were drawn over the rough boards of the empty rack was music in the ears of Reuben as he stood about, waiting and watching for some chance to be of service himself. He found it in holding up the heavy pole of the rack while the oxen were backed about, one on either side, and fastening it firmly with iron pins within the cross-piece of their rattling wooden yoke, polished to the lustre of satin by years of wear against their necks and shoulders. Once they were yoked to the great blue rack, and the man who was to drive them ready with his goad-stick across their necks, and the other three with pitchforks in the hands of two and a rake for cleaning up in the hand of one, Reuben slid along the warm red side of one of the oxen, jumped upon the pole, and pulled himself between two of the round rack uprights to the knotted, chaff-strewn floor. Standing there above the oxen with his arms just long enough to reach the stout horizontal bar that held firm the rungs inserted into it, he was gloriously ready for his part in the best of the haymaking.

The oxen started; the empty rack lumbered and clattered, bumped and swayed to the farther side of the meadow where the hay had been longest cut and piled; the men followed behind, using their forks and rakes now and again as giant walking-sticks. Reuben wondered why they did not ride when they could have done so as well as not, but they seemed to know their own minds. The hot sun continued, in spite of the thunderheads, to beat down upon the newly cut ground and the rounded yellow haycocks; the harbour just beyond, so near that one could hear the shouts of some rusticators on a pleasure sloop, was filled with blue, sparkling water; the marsh stretches, where toward the east the meadows fell back before the sea, were cut by still, full lanes of the rising tide. The gulls were quiet, settled drowsily upon the high rocky banks, only a few circling above the sloop which had the empty harbour to itself.

All the emotions which had hurt Reuben in the loft became as nothing in the warm, bright completeness of that afternoon in the hayfields. When they reached the last haycock, just before the meadow began to lose its dryness in marsh water, the oxen stopped, the man driving them substituted his goad-stick for the pitchfork which had been clattering about in the rack with Reuben, and the real work began. Now great mounds of hay came tumbling over the high railings, sometimes two at once, often smothering Reuben for the instant before he could extricate himself and go on stumbling back and forth, forth and back, treading down the forkfuls, stamping in the corners, kicking the hay about so that the surface should be as compact and as even as he could make it. They went from haycock to haycock, the sudden starts of the rack hurtling him backward or forward on the soft hay where he lay panting until they reached the next, the man behind raking up the odds and ends that the forks had left and the few trailing bits that fell from the load and throwing these in upon Reuben just as they stopped again. When the load was half-made, one of the men joined Reuben to help with his added heaviness and with the use of his fork to distribute the hay that still came as quickly as before though only two were pitching. And so fast did everyone work that within half an hour the rack was laden far above its railings, and Reuben lay hot and happy in the very center, ready to ride to the barn, to wait there until the hay should be stowed away in the loft, and then to return to the meadow for yet another load until the grass was clean and free and ready for the rain.

The sensation of being on top of the load was always unparalleled by any that Reuben had experienced in his ten years. From there he could see nothing that belonged on the ground, not the oxen, or the men walking behind or beside the rack, or the grass itself. Instead when he lay face downward, he looked straight into the seemingly trunkless orchard trees, straight above the harbour to the green spruces on the islands, straight into the beams and rafters of the great barn, floorless now to him; and when he lay on his back, there was nothing between him and the sky but the waving green veil of the highest elms.

When they had once creaked and lumbered up the driveway to the barn and come to a standstill directly below the open doors of the loft, they freed the oxen, who stood in the barn floor, their sides heaving from their labour. Then Reuben pumped deep water from the well, and the men stood about the curb, drinking it from the dipper, which always rested on the square, flat top of the pump. And after the hay was stowed away, two men pitching it high in great streaming forkfuls and the two others drawing it from the doorway and stowing it tightly beneath the cross-beams and over and among the brown rafters, they had another drink all around before they started again for the meadows.

It was supper-time before they had quite done and the men had started homeward, now sitting in the back of the empty rack with their legs hanging downward. Reuben saw them go with regret. He stood at the barn door and watched them out of sight down the hill that led to the shore road, hearing, even after they had passed from his view, the clatter and the creaking through the summer dust. It was a treat to him to have men about, doing the work of men, saying the things that men say to one another in men's voices. He did not know what a treat it was until he saw them go away before the gathering storm. Seth Tucker stayed for the milking, and Reuben was loathe to leave him and go indoors when Susan called him peremptorily to come and have his scrubbing up before he was fit for the supper table.

That evening while Susan did the dishes and heated still more water on the stove for yet another scrub, the storm broke in jagged streaks of lightning and a savage downpour of rain before a frightful wind. His grandmother was clearly nervous. She did not like storms and looked upon this one as especially sinister since it had broken all expectation and custom and come up on an ebb tide. She did not remember, she told Susan, whom she had sent throughout the house to close all windows, more than three storms in her life which had ever come once the tide had turned; and each had been a caution. So agitated was she that Reuben did not add to her anxiety his own disappointment. Instead, while she and Susan moved from room to room, keeping wary eyes on the barn, the great trees, and the church spire just visible from the side windows, he got the ink bottle from its place on the shelf in the dining-room cupboard and wrote his mother a letter. His hands and arms were stiff from the haymaking so that it was hard for him to keep his lines straight and his words clear. He had to copy his letter three times before he decided that it would do to send.

"Dear Mother," he wrote,

"It is a terrible storm. I am glad we got our hay in. I tredded five loads this afternoon.

"I think it is very nice for you to go to South Carolina with my stepfather. I will come to Boston some other time when it is better for you to have me.

"Thank Mr. Sawyer for the paints.

"I am not so tall as you want me to be.

"Your obediant son,
"REUBEN CROCKETT."

2

Solace Crockett had named her grandson. She had chosen his name directly she had seen him in the early morning of a July day which had finally come after six dreadful months of waiting. She did not even consult his mother. Deborah had longed for a daughter, saying even that only the slender chance of a little girl had kept her alive to endure her grief and suffering. A little girl, she said to Solace, could be depended upon to stay at home and comfort them for all they had gone through. Moreover, a little girl, unlike a boy, even though she bore the Crockett name, could hardly give promise of sorrow in the future because of any family loyalties which she might inherit.

Deborah had said these things in her most bitter hours. For the most part, she had been a companion to Solace rather than a drain upon her spirit. She was honest and intelligent enough to face squarely the truth, both that Nicholas' death had brought more suffering to his mother than to her and that she herself was in measure answerable for it. She was honest enough also both to realize and to acknowledge that Solace Crockett was a finer woman than she herself, and that, ironically enough, it was Solace who was paying a heavy toll not for the willfulness of her son but rather for the selfishness of her daughter-in-law. Deborah acknowledged these things and suffered genuine and bitter remorse over the part she had played in the tragedy of Nicholas' death. But just as she was unable, because of a limitation within herself, to realize the more poignant tragedy of his life, so she was unable to build upon her suffering and remorse any structure of mind and spirit in which she might continue to live in some degree of dignity and order. She gave to Solace without stint consideration and affection, gratitude and admiration; and except for moments and hours of bitterness when she railed aloud against the injustice of life and in secret deplored the impossibility of escape from a future she could neither endure nor transmute, she had borne the anxiety of waiting for her child with a fair measure of fortitude.

Solace, remembering the strength and serenity which Abigail Crockett had lent to her, had done her utmost for Deborah, losing sight of her own grief in concern for Deborah's present and in the troubled thought of her future. She herself had lived her life and, on the whole, had small complaint to make against whatever had determined it. But Deborah was young. It was hard to see her at twenty-five throttled and thwarted by circumstances, tied hand and foot, and unable, by the very imperiousness of her nature, to adapt herself to things as they were and must be. Solace joined her hopes and prayers to those of Deborah that the baby might be a girl. When a boy came and his grandmother held him before the kitchen fire precisely as Abigail had held his father, she named him Reuben Shaw Crockett on the spot.

There was a great deal in the name which Solace could not explain to Deborah. First of all, there was the desire to recompense Abigail for a grievous loss, even although Abigail was either far beyond the need of recompense or else had received it already, pressed down and running over. Abigail, in common with other women of seafaring families, had felt the loss of her second son more complete and summary than as if he had gone to earth in the churchyard. A sea change differed from an earth change in that it was less natural, more comfortless. Who could know these things better than Solace herself? In this child which lay on her lap the elder Reuben, she had thought, might live and move again by the very power of a name. Moreover, as she looked upon her grandson, she saw little about him that was Crockett. Given always the possibility of growth and change, she yet could not see how the length and suppleness of the Crockett men could supplant or overcome his short, compact, almost square little body, his round head set close to his shoulders, his wide, thick knees. He must, ignoring Deborah and Nicholas, Silas and herself, have gone farther back for his lineaments and features. He might, of course, be a Winship like his great-grandfather, but as she studied him, she was more inclined to think that he was a Shaw, and if so, he deserved the name of those who had thus endowed him. Abigail had told her that the Shaws for the most part were stocky, thick-set people; and Solace herself as a little girl remembered Reuben, standing in the old church on a hassock for the hymns so that he might not look so short in contrast with his father and his brothers Nicholas and Silas.

Now that she had reached a place in her life from where she could look upon the world, not as a performer or participator within it so much as a spectator of it, the pathos rather than the tragedy of change came home to her, the steady resistless passing away of the sons of earth before the ever-rolling stream of time. And the sadness deepened when one realized that those who lived at any given present loved and hated, laughed and wept, failed or triumphed as the invisible chains which bound them to the past allowed them to do. Thus there was added pathos in the unconscious retaliation of the dead upon the living, revenge quite without rancour in the mere persistence of their natures. For those who had lived and were now dead controlled in large measure those who had forgotten or had never known them, Judah and

Amos in Silas and Nicholas, old Reuben Shaw, who had defied the ships of King George III, in this baby, removed from him by five generations. And since the wide-kneed Shaws, who had stumped about the Derby wharf and helped to give Salem its now dimmed glory, had sent back a memorial to themselves in the shape and features of her grandson, it seemed but just to Solace that his name at least should be an outward and visible sign of their insensible remonstrance against complete impotence and cessation.

Now that Fate had chosen to deal her its last cruel blow in denying her a daughter, Deborah had not cared a whit what name had been given to her son so long as no suggestion had been made that he should inherit his father's. That she could never have borne to call him or to hear sounding about the house. From the beginning of his life, except for her daily care of him, which she fulfilled to Solace's complete satisfaction, she left the decisions as to his early rearing almost entirely to his grandmother. She lived, as Solace was quite well aware, in the half-formed and never fully expressed hope that the future still held something for her far removed from Saturday Cove. And when, in Reuben's third year, after her own mother had died and the ties which bound her were loosening, she met a young artist who was summering in Saturday Cove, Solace saw as clearly as Deborah that a better way had opened for them all.

Deborah and the artist, whose name was Edward Sawyer, were decent about Reuben, never once suggesting that he should be left with his grandmother while they embraced a life they both wanted. The suggestion came verbally from Solace herself and silently from Reuben's complete dependence upon her. Solace, nearing seventy, felt the compensations rather than the inroads of age. She wanted to keep Reuben with her in the house of his ancestors where he belonged. He was clearly not Deborah's child in any but a physical sense, and Deborah was the first to recognize the fact. There was, indeed, almost gratitude in her recognition of it. Had he shown any of the traits that made her what she was or even a sufficient number of those belonging to Nicholas, she would not so willingly have left him in Saturday Cove. But from the start he was completely foreign to his mother, almost embarrassing to her in her lack of understanding of him.

He was a slow, sober child, quiet and orderly in his ways, not quick like Nicholas and Deborah at either comprehension or action. He would play for hours at some solitary game and pick up his toys when he had finished without having to be told. He was abnormally sensitive to reproof or punishment and seemed, to Deborah at least, quite without any vital spark which made most children disobedient or rebellious. Solace, watching him, could not herself discern those gifts within him which, Abigail had always maintained, came done up with the Crocketts and ready for instant distribution upon a waiting and subservient world. Perhaps for that very reason she loved him more, seeing in him an absence of those things which might have made life easier for him but harder for those who must live it beside him. And since, both because of what he seemed to be and because of the more settled character of the years in which he would live his life, time and chance could not presumably thwart and wound him as they had thwarted and wounded his father, her fears for him became less positive even in his babyhood than her sense of quiet protectiveness over him.

Deborah married when Reuben was four and went away from Saturday Cove, not to return to it save at long intervals and for brief visits. There followed her, quite at Solace's insistence, some of the furniture from the front parlour and more of the china from the dining-room cupboard—things which Abigail had left for Nicholas and which, Solace said, belonged also to Deborah as well. These, aside from their value in dollars and cents, which Deborah might some day need, would make her housekeeping in Boston easier. And when the things were crated and gone to the steamboat wharf and Deborah's last clothes had gone from her closets and the knick-knacks from her room, Solace, sitting in Abigail's chair and watching Reuben piling his blocks slowly and carefully on the worn rug, felt without the least feeling either of regret or of reproof, that the Crocketts and the Winships and the Shaws were now together, for better or for worse, just as they ought to be.

3

Reuben's childhood in Saturday Cove in the eighteen-eighties was far different from that of his father in the eighteen-fifties. In the first place, there were differences in the great house itself. Built and furnished by Amos Crockett as a wedding gift for his son in the last years of the seventeen-hundreds from the profits and products of foreign voyages and kept proudly in its original sturdiness and beauty by James and Abigail, who in their turn had wanted for nothing, it was now suffering the inroads of time and the reverses of fortune. It did not stand so squarely or so solidly upon its stone foundations as it had once stood. Its door-sills needed attention, and when a November wind took the last of the old leaves from the woodbine that all summer concealed the cracks and rotting wood above its white doorway facing the sea, it looked like an old house. The bricks in the terrace, which had formerly reached the first of its well-tended garden plots, were broken and missing; the garden itself had given place to the encroachments of the field, once a lawn; the orchard, so carefully pruned and cared for by Amos and James and Silas, was now perforce allowed to look after itself. The slope of its wide roofs now sagged in places, and the roofs themselves could have done with fresh shingles had Solace Crockett been able to see her way to anything but necessary patching as occasion demanded. The green shutters rattled now within and without their framework; their paint was spotted with white from the salt of many fogs; and from the outworn fastener of each there hung a stout cord to ensure its security in a high wind. The barn had done well enough for years without the repairs it sorely needed.

Within matters were much the same. The great hall with its double curving staircase reaching from front to back wanted fresh paint and paper as did the rooms opening from it. The cracks in the floors had widened, and the floors themselves sagged a bit here and there with the sagging of their foundations. The doors were the doors of an old house, loose and uncertain in their hinges and latches, swinging lightly to one's touch instead of substantially and securely as doors swing when their jambs and sills are kept in proper repair. The wood of the window frames also showed dry and dusty beneath the paint, which had a way of peeling off as paint will peel when wood is soft and crumbling from age. There were cracks here and there in the plaster of the ceilings which were not surprising since James had been the last Crockett to replaster them.

The rooms themselves, gracious as they were when the sun lay full within them or when a fire burned below their white mantels, lacked the freshness of other days. Judah and Amos, James and Benjamin still looked down upon Reuben staring up at them in the front parlour on Sunday afternoons. Their ships, except for the one which Deborah had chosen as her just portion, still hung upon the walls; Amos' paper of Versailles still showed its gardens and fountains; and the furniture, depleted though it was of some of its best pieces, still gave out its lustre when Susan rubbed it with oil on the palm of her broad hand. The dragons on Eliza Ann Shaw's firescreen were frayed and faded enough, but they still served as a curiosity for Reuben to point out shyly to his teacher when she came for supper twice a year on Saturday evening, and when Solace had warned him to remember his manners and not to be afraid to address their guest now and then.

"My great-great-grandmother made it," Reuben said slowly, conscious of his best clothes and of his new shoes that creaked. "She made it in Salem more than one hundred years ago."

And since Reuben had never known the house as it had been in his grandfather's boyhood and even in his father's, it seemed to him the most satisfying of houses. He conceived, in fact, a premature affection for it, seeing in it far more than the place of warmth and protection accepted by most children when they think of home. He never approached it through the field from the shore where he had been playing or came up its old driveway through the snow, which banked it almost to its window sills, without feeling a surge of pride throughout his body, not only because it was his home but because it was stately and beautiful. And when he and his grandmother came home together on Sundays from church and followed the path, where the grass now grew up through the gravel and clam-shells, to the side door beneath the lilacs, he always said to her no matter what the season:

"I think, grandmother, that we have the best house in Saturday Cove—no, I mean in the whole world."

Perhaps it was her recognition of this feeling in him that prompted Solace to open the front parlour on Sundays. She and Abigail had rarely opened it during Nicholas' boyhood, using the sunnier back parlour for their sitting-room. But Nicholas, at least during his father's life, reasoned Solace, had had small need of the better room with all the things it held, things which by their association and their worth might well impress a child with the graciousness and dignity of his heritage. Nicholas had known a wider world than his son could know, and he had had about him those who, by connecting him daily with the Crockett past, could pave the way for his Crockett future. Solace was glad as Reuben left his little boyhood and reached the age of ten that his future did not seem to burn so restlessly and yet so certainly within him; but she felt strongly that the past should be made clear to him before she had to leave him.

The front parlour served to this end. On Sunday mornings while his grandmother dressed for church Reuben studied his Sunday-school lesson at the polished table beneath the picture of Amos Crockett's ship *Mary* leaving Marseilles. He sat in a high-backed chair with his feet firmly placed on the floor so that they might not damage the chair rungs. He wore his Sunday suit of sombre dark gray, the tight trousers stopping awkwardly just below his knees and the jacket much cut away in front over the high buttoned vest. His low collar had been starched stiffly by Susan and tied with a bow-knot of black silk, and his heavy black shoes had gleaming copper toes upon them to keep them from wearing out too soon. He kept his Bible open on the newspapers, which Susan had spread to protect the table, and said the portions to be memorized over and over to himself in loud whispers until he thought he knew them unless his teacher should ask him too suddenly.

And why beholdest thou the mote that is in thy brother's eye, but considerest not the beam that is in thine own eye? or

Enter ye in at the strait gate: for wide is the gate, and broad is the way, that leadeth to destruction, and many there be which go in thereat:

Because strait is the gate, and narrow is the way, which leadeth unto life, and few there be that find it.

or, and most difficult to make any sense of even with the help of his puzzled teacher:

In the beginning was the Word, and the Word was with God, and the Word was God.

The same was in the beginning with God.

In addition to these prescribed verses or others like them there was always a temperance text, a backwash in the eighties from the tidal wave of the seventies:

Look not thou upon the wine when it is red, when it giveth his colour in the cup, when it moveth itself aright.
At the last it biteth like a serpent, and stingeth like an adder.

Finally there was always a lesson from his Sunday-school manual, which in the spring and summer was called *Almost Persuaded* and in the autumn and winter *The Lord God of Israel.* He did not much mind learning the verses or the lessons with their exhortations and threats, taking them as a matter of course and only feeling a shade of regret for himself when he learned that his father had not gone to Sunday-school, there being none in the Saturday Cove church when he was a boy.

"Didn't my father have to learn the Bible, then?"

"Yes, his grandmother taught it to him on Sundays and sometimes on week-days as well. She was far better than I am at teaching. She made verses and songs about the Bible stories and sang them to your father."

In spite, however, of Solace's descriptions of Abigail she remained a shadowy portrait to Reuben. There was no picture of his great-grandmother in the front parlour, and the album likeness which his grandmother showed him on Sunday afternoons did not impress her upon his imagination. His grandmother did better with his grandfather, although there was no portrait of him either. Indeed, from the very beginning of Reuben's memory Silas Crockett lived therein as did no one else, even his own father.

An old woman now, Solace lived most clearly in the past where even Nicholas was not. Nicholas was her present, too close and painful, especially when the past was ready and waiting to heal it. Sitting in the front parlour, she told Reuben endless things about his grandfather.

"Was he tall, grandmother, like my father?"

"Yes, he was tall and very handsome. He held his head high, and wherever he went everyone looked at him. He was strong, too. He could lift me and carry me ever so far."

"Do I look at all like him?"

"No, only you have his eyes and some of his ways."

"What ways?"

"Well, you are kind and thoughtful of me as he always was. And you love to think of going to far-away places. Your grandfather was forever planning where he'd go next, where he'd take me to."

"Did you like going to sea, grandmother?"

"Not at first. I was very frightened. But after a long time I learned not to be frightened."

"How did you learn?"

"By loving your grandfather, I suppose. He was not happy unless he was at sea, like all these others here and your father, too."

Reuben scanned the walls, looking at Judah and Amos, then turning slowly on his hassock to look at Benjamin and James.

"I suppose I'll go to sea, too, don't you, grandmother?"

She felt herself then tempering the thought which she and Silas and all the others in the room had given him.

"Perhaps so," she said, "but perhaps not. There are many other things to do besides going to sea, Reuben."

"There probably won't be sailing-ships when I'm old enough to go. But I might command a steamship and sail across the Atlantic ocean and other oceans as well. Then I'd see the places I study about. I'd like to see all the places, grandmother, that you and my grandfather saw."

On Friday nights from school he always brought home his geography book, standing it carefully against the firescreen so that it would be ready for Sunday. They always closed their hour after dinner in the front parlour with the geography book. They rested it upon the table and went through the maps together, one by one, beginning with the map of the whole watery earth, which stretched left and right over two opposite pages and upon which they could trace his grandfather's voyages from one hemisphere to the other. Then, once the courses of the *Southern Seas* or the *Solace Winship* or the *Four Winds* had been fully established in Reuben's mind, they turned to the other maps, which marked places neglected by the map of the whole earth, and gave his grandfather's several ports the attention they deserved.

Sometimes they played a game with his grandfather's cities and islands, straits and bays. They would both close their eyes tightly and count ten excitedly aloud, which had no point at all except that it added zest to things. Then Reuben brought his forefinger down at random upon any place at all and cried, "Ready!" Whereupon his grandmother must open her eyes and with no deliberation at all tell something about the spot upon which Reuben's forefinger rested.

"The Balearic Isles," said his grandmother. "They are in the Mediterranean, Reuben, as you see. The water is bluer there than you have ever seen it, and on that biggest island the people have built walls that go up and down the hillsides, even up and down the mountains—old walls built centuries ago. The walls hold up the olive trees, which shine like silver, and the people ride their donkeys there and gather olives in the sun."

"I should like to see an olive tree," said Reuben.

His grandmother opened her eyes a second time.

"The mid-Atlantic," she said. "So many things have happened there to your grandfather and me that I couldn't rightly choose between them. But if you move your finger two inches to the right, there's Marseilles. I've been there often. It's a fine harbour with mountains of rock all about it and all kinds of foreign people. Ships have sailed there for many hundreds of years, even the ships of King Solomon, so your grandfather once told me. They sell flowers, violets and roses, and queer shellfish on the quays in the spring. You hear all kinds of outlandish tongues there, and one can eat rolls of hard bread and drink wine at little tables out-of-doors in the sun."

"Did you ever drink wine, grandmother? I thought it was wrong."

She felt after nearly sixty years the crust of the French bread within her hand, saw the gleam of the sunlight in the red wine.

"Not in Marseilles, years ago," she said. "Only here, now."

When the short hour was over and his grandmother had gone for her nap, Reuben went to the tidy kitchen where Susan sat by the table, a white apron over her black dress. Susan always read on Sunday afternoons. She kept her Bible open before her, but she rarely read from it. She went to the Ladies' Social Library on Saturday evenings and procured upon the payment of five cents a book to last her until Wednesday when the library was again open. She had a few favourites which she read over and over, never seeming to tire of them. One was called *Tempest and Sunshine*, another *Thelma*, a third *He Fell in Love with His Wife.* Sometimes she was so absorbed in her reading that she did not hear Rebuen coming through the long hall. In later years he always remembered how she had sat bolt upright at the table, holding her book in both her hands, and how sometimes he had surprised tears in the hollows between her lower eyelids and her high, broad cheek bones. At fifty Susan had grown to more massive proportions than when she had shaken Reuben's mother at her bubble party. Her hair was gray, and she drew it straight back into a knot of the exact shape of a lobster buoy at the exact crown of her head, drew it so tightly that not a hair could ever relax; and she looked withal so scrubbed, so neat, so capable that Reuben always thought the tears must be a trial to her lying there untended while she read. He learned that it was *Thelma* which always brought the tears and had a secret urge to read it himself; but since it was kept high on the lamp shelf during its monthly visits and since Susan was always in the kitchen, his wish was never gratified.

When she had once recognized his presence in the doorway, she always put her book away (Reuben never guessed at what sacrifice) with her glasses in it to keep her place and began to make molasses candy. He always remembered the smell of the boiling molasses and butter in the warm kitchen and how a wad of it tasted when Susan to try it had dropped a bit from a spoon into a cup of cold water. When the candy was done, they pulled it together while his grandmother finished her nap.

They twisted it first into dark brown twists, soft and warm and likely to stick to one's hands if they were not well greased with butter. Then they pulled it between their outstretched arms, bending it in halves, sometimes again in quarters, watching it turn from brown to gold and finally to yellow. At the last, when it began to harden in their grasp, they pulled together, he and Susan, with their four hands, doubling and redoubling it until they could pull it no longer, until it was ready to be coiled in a great circle on the table and cut in pieces with a sharp knife. He ate it then, piece by piece, over his own book until Susan told him to stop lest he should spoil his supper.

And when the day was over and the twilight was darkening the meadows and the sea, he ate his bowl of pilot bread, stripped fish, and milk at the kitchen table and thought how fortunate he was to live in an old house where his great-grandfather and grandfather and father had lived and from where he could hear the sound of the tide as he fell asleep.

4

There was small sign of the shipyards left when the nineties were just around the corner and Reuben was thirteen. Grass and rank growth had covered them all; and when strangers who did not know Saturday Cove sailed into its harbour and saw the high banks above the shore and the vetches, wild lavender, and golden-rod that clothed their sand and clay, they little realized that below the soil nearest the sea there were remnants of wharves and docks and building platforms. So far as that went, only the older people in Saturday Cove itself remembered the docks well, the ships that had been built there and launched with the church bells ringing and everybody in holiday dress.

And now even the fishing-wharves were disappearing in their turn. The factory where packing had been carried on for a decade up to 1880 had gone, beaten out by larger plants eastward. Now what was left of it had been moved to the saw-mill yard where it served very well for the storage and drying of the planks, which were still sawn when the waters of the brook tumbled over the dam in the spring rains and joined the tide. The offshore fishing fleet had quite disappeared. What fishermen were left now sailed away to Eastport or Lubec, making these larger towns their base and coming home only when the best of the season was over.

Fishing, in fact, as well as shipbuilding had suffered from change. The great railroads now stretching across the country, although they carried much of the Gloucester catch westward in their new refrigerator cars, could quite as easily, after the development of the Pacific and Great Lakes fisheries, bring the over-abundant supply of Columbia River salmon and the fish of Lake Superior and Lake Michigan eastward to New York and Boston. The free importation of Canadian herring during the seventies and early eighties likewise crippled the activities of the smaller offshore fleets and turned the attention of many Maine village fishermen to other means of livelihood just now knocking at their doors. For by the time the nineties had reached Saturday Cove, it together with scores of other seacoast towns and villages was ready and eager to utilize a new industry—that of supplying the easier demands of a fast-growing summer population.

Master fishermen, who had weathered fogs and gales off Newfoundland, now cleaned and painted their schooners to take out parties for days of deep-sea fishing in the outer waters of Frenchman's Bay, or Passamaquoddy, or Blue Hill, or Penobscot. It was an easy and a pleasant occupation and brought hitherto undreamed-of profits without danger or hardship or even labour. Those who had in the seventies and eighties worked in the crews of such schooners, sharing profits dependent upon the runs of fish and their own luck and skill at catching and cleaning, were quick to discover a far simpler and more profitable means of living in the inshore fisheries near at hand. These strangers with good clothes and well-filled pockets, who were buying land at prices unheard-of and erecting cottages with native labour, needed fresh fish for their tables as well as lobsters and clams. Good grounds for trawling or hand-line fishing for cod and haddock were not far distant; there were few seasons when tinker mackerel did not run, turning the outer harbour to blue and silver; and any man whose back had well-nigh broken in hours on the Banks, rowing a dory or pulling a heavy trawl or coiling tubs of line in zero weather, counted it child's play to dig a barrel of clams at any low water, shock them clean, and sell them at ten cents the quart.

Reuben Crockett never saw a ship built or launched from Saturday Cove. That, seemingly the just and rightful portion of his long inheritance, was denied him. Nor in his day did a "trader" ever tie up at the wharf with marbles and tops and sling-shots on her dishevelled decks. Nor did he ever watch the boats of the offshore fleet bearing away for the Banks with their women folk crowding the pier in the April mist to bid them godspeed and a safe return. Even foreign faces in Saturday Cove in the eighties and nineties were almost unknown. Reuben, unlike his father, never saw dark, bearded men with rings in their ears, lounging about the piers, gabbering and gesticulating, while monkeys sat rakishly on their shoulders.

In fact, an incident which occurred in his thirteenth year made such an impression upon him that he thought about it for weeks afterward and boasted for days at school that it had happened to him. He and his grandmother and Susan one autumn evening were sitting in the back parlour quietly enough when a noise without of someone rapping against the window-pane caused him to raise startled eyes. There in the window between the bare lilacs and the light from their lamp was the shadowy black face of a stranger. He wore a red handkerchief knotted about his neck and was apparently in distress of some kind as they could make out from his frenzied gestures. Susan in her alarm was about to throw any object in the room at him; but when Reuben, trembling, had gone to the door at his grandmother's command, he proved to be harmless enough, wishing only to see the doctor to whom he had been misdirected. He came from Barbados, he said in his fragmentary, uncertain English, on a ship after lumber; and once they knew he was quite harmless and suffering from a broken wrist, Susan prepared him a good supper on the kitchen table. Reuben never forgot how he stood in a corner of the kitchen and stared at the stranger as he ate his food with his left hand, extending the painful wrist of the right before him. He was Reuben's one actual entrance in the flesh into the great world far beyond Saturday Cove; and although his excursions in spirit had been numberless, this seeing with his eyes and hearing with his ears outweighed all his more impalpable experiences.

The changes that Reuben saw daily in Saturday Cove did not, in fact, impress him at all, at least as changes. Their significance, destined to be so far-reaching in the next century, was quite lost upon a boy who had his chores to do and his lessons to get before he was free to range the now well-nigh deserted shores. He felt sorry that times were different, simply because his father's life as his grandmother, or more often as Susan, depicted it seemed more exciting than his own. He shared his grandmother's regret when the heads of seafaring families died one by one; he was sorry that they had taken with them the stories which they had sometimes told on the old wharves on Saturday mornings while the water slapped at the piers; but he little knew what was passing through her mind when she said:

"Captain Rufus Candage has gone, one of the last that held us to the outside world, once so close. I never thought I'd live to see the day when I was glad that your grandfather died a young man. He never could abide change."

Nor did Reuben for a moment realize that an era in coast history had closed when certain of the great white houses, which voyages to the Far East had built, passed one by one through the lawyer's hands to men from Philadelphia and Boston and New York. He was merely glad that their own need not be thus sacrificed, not because in his mind the dispensing with it would mean anything in the light of a long past, but rather because he would be desolate without it. And when the Boston and Bangor Steamship Company put on a daily boat to bring to Saturday Cove and points west and east those who were henceforth to determine the social and economic history of the coast, he in common with other village boys welcomed the innovation. It was fun to stand on the pier, now called the steamboat wharf, in the early June mornings, to watch the boat slip up to the gangway with her eager, well-dressed strangers crowding about the deck-rails, to see them drive away in buckboards and surreys to their new cottages among the spruces on the headlands or to the old houses in the village which they had bought. They brought business, Reuben heard the tradesmen say, kept money in circulation, gave employment to folks that needed it, and all in all were the best thing that had happened to the coast of Maine in many a long day.

5

When Solace Crockett saw her seventies running swiftly toward their close and recognized with the calm acuteness of women of her sort that her days were numbered, she sold her father's house to two maiden ladies from Boston. She did not want to sell it. But what, she asked herself and Susan, could Reuben do with two houses when there was not enough money to keep one even in passable repair? Moreover, if she died as she doubtless would while Reuben was still under the guardianship of some one or other, he would probably be induced to let it go and far less worthily.

She had had all sorts of dreams about the house even though she knew they were chimerical in view of her circumstances. She had wanted to give it to Saturday Cove as a library and museum. She would have liked to think in her last years of the downstairs rooms being used for books, which people might even linger over to read on rainy afternoons instead of selecting one and carrying it straight homeward. The upstairs rooms, she had imagined, might be the repository of manuscripts, log-books, records, old drawings, pictures and the like, which should preserve the history of a bit of the coast from carelessness, neglect, and ignorance. She would place there her father's plans of his fourteen meeting-houses, the specifications and figures of his lesser work, so that he might not in succeeding years pass entirely into oblivion. She would like to have had him remembered by the succeeding generations of Saturday Cove if only as a name. She would place, too, perhaps in her own room, the pictures of ships and the portraits of those who had commanded them. There were other families either in town or closely enough removed from it to be still interested who would be glad to contribute to such a collection. And later perhaps, even when the new century had half gone and not a square-rigged ship ran before the trades or the westerlies of either hemisphere, people would mount her father's winding staircase to her old room and look with respect and reverence upon the dignity and worth and grandeur which it held in trust within its walls. There would be other rooms for pieces of beautiful furniture, for bits of old china and damask, which people would be glad to spare from their family legacies, for shawls and other weaving and embroidery, made on either foreign or home looms by strange or familiar hands. All these things, carefully placed and guarded within the old house, itself a memorial of the days when men like her father laboured with faith and devotion for the very sake of labour, would perhaps halt time now and then, turn it backward upon itself, make those who looked upon them understand, if only for a moment, the sacredness of tradition, the long dependence of the present upon the past.

She had abandoned the dream long before it had been fully born; it died daily even while it was coming to life; for it was preposterous, even in its vaguest outlines. In the first place, there must be found in Saturday Cove a sufficient number of those in authority who, because they had been well nurtured by the past, recognized the value of its preservation. That task in itself was problematical. The old seafaring families who had in large measure made that past were fast dying out; for now that shipping was over, building and voyaging alike, there was little to keep later generations in Saturday Cove, if there was money enough to leave it. The very enterprise which had sent their fathers and grandfathers across the seas sent them, after school and perhaps college were over, to the offices, universities, and hospitals of larger centers where the leaven which they added, although taken from home, was not lost. And if, perchance, there could be found among those whom age, necessity, or sentiment had kept at home a sufficient number who might be depended upon to receive and administer her gift of the old Winship house, she must not for a moment forget that the gift was quite without endowment of any sort. Libraries and museums must not only be housed but run, she told herself, smiling at the secret foolishness which had given her such pleasure.

The Misses Peabody were school-mistresses of an old and excellent family. They knew and appreciated the beauty of the old Winship home, and they appreciated Solace Crockett as well. She was glad it was they who were to open and close the picket gate and clear the grass roots from the peonies in the front yard instead of a man from St. Paul, who had offered her a larger price. Since it must go, she told Susan, she wanted to sell it to New England people who would have a feeling for it and for the land on which it stood.

Susan agreed thoroughly with her mistress. She was not one, she said, to want a lot of new folks messing up a place to which they had no right. But since what was to be was to be, and these outsiders had come to stay, it was just as well to do business with the best of them, rather than with some scalawag from the West which, everyone knew, was full of folks not quite up to the mark of them that stayed to home. Furthermore, Susan said to the pump and the wood-box and to Seth Tucker under an oath of secrecy, if her eyes didn't deceive her, and they hadn't for fifty years and more now, it was just as well to get things settled up as they should be settled for Master Reuben and as soon as might be. She knew better than most, she said, when this world and the next met in a body's eyes, and although she was biding her time and keeping her counsel, she knew what she knew, and that was that.

Once arrangements had been made between Solace and the elder Miss Peabody, who shivered through Easter of 1890 in Saturday Cove, as to what was to be taken from the house and what left, once the lawyer had been seen and the deed drawn and the check signed, Susan put on an extra suit of winter underwear and spent two days cleaning out the Winship attic. The things which obviously might be of value—letters and books, odd pieces of old furniture, some great sheets of paper with drawings on them—she brought to the kitchen; and on the first warm day in April she built a fire in the stove there and fetched her mistress to make the necessary decisions for preservation or destruction.

Solace sat by the sunny window and looked over one by one the things which Susan spread before her. She could not bear to hurry over her task even though Susan's broad back, as she stood by the opposite window and looked out upon the brown orchard, registered impatience and vexation at the time she was taking. To look at certain of the papers before her, papers preserved by her father and recording sundry affairs of village importance in which he had been concerned, was like seeing for the second time some old play whose characters, costumes, and action, forgotten through the years, became once more familiar.

Among many others, all of which halted time for her, were two records of meetings held in 1821 of the Select Committee of the Saturday Cove Social Library. Her father, as scribe of the committee, had written the reports in his careful, precise hand. He had been forty-four years old then, she thought, a young man. The first, dated in March 1821, revealed "a dissension led by certain women of the town" who demanded a vote in the selection of books, hitherto ruled only by men:

This dissension having reached a point at which continued refusals seem ill-advised, the Select Committee has resolved to name this day of the aforesaid women one, viz., Mrs. Abigail Crockett, wife of Captain James Crockett, who shall have the right to attend meetings at her discretion and to cast one vote for or against the proposals of the said committee. She may have a proper voice in deliberation and discussion, but it is clearly recognized by all concerned that right of proposal of any course of action shall be withheld from her.

Solace could see Abigail at forty-six speaking a premature and unwelcome word for the rights of women. She knew as surely as though the dissenters had been named on the yellowing paper that Abigail was their self-appointed leader, saw her going about her kitchen and planning her revolt as she kneaded her bread dough or poured her candle moulds, the thought of the first Nicholas still new and painful within her.

The second record lent action to the play, increased a hundredfold the drama:

At a meeting of the Select Committee of the Saturday Cove Social Library held on the second of November, Anno Domini, 1821, it was voted to exchange certain books now in circulation for other books deemed and considered more useful and of better influence to and upon their readers.

viz.,

Humphrey Clinker, 2 vols. for *Miseries of Human Life.*

Tom Jones, 3 vols. for *Dr. Wood's Letters to Unitarians.*

Sterne's *Sentimental Journey* for *The Infant's Progress from the Valley of Destruction to Everlasting Glory.*

The Fool of Quality, 3 vols. for *Pure Religion Recommended as the Only Way to Happiness.*⋆

⋆The record of this exchange, with books accurately named and date exact, is taken from certain Maine village papers of the year 1821.

This resolution was adopted by the five members of the committee with but one dissenting vote, that having been cast by the newly allowed female member, Mrs. Abigail Crockett.

Solace, sitting by the table in the old house seventy years afterward, could see Abigail casting her vote with superb indifference as to its effect, and the consternation it must have wrought among the men of Saturday Cove responsible for the selection of its reading. She could hear Abigail's crisp, straightforward voice extolling the virtues and the values of novels before the scandalized committee, already regretting its forced decision to admit a female member. She knew how Abigail had laughed at home while she recounted to James her initial adventure into the affairs of men. Now no men could be found in the village save the præceptor of the academy and the minister who cared enough for what was read to serve on a committee; and the name had long since been changed to that of the Ladies' Social Library.

Solace had lived long, she thought, and had seen many changes. Reuben would see more. As she sat by the table, going through the books and papers before her, discarding some, giving others to Susan to pile in a clothes basket to be taken to the Crockett attic for safe keeping, she thought of the greater, more tenacious hold which a father's house held upon its descendants than that of a mother, always in reality *her* father's house. This house, which had in large measure given birth and nurture to the love responsible for Nicholas and Reuben, was now passing into other hands while the house of the male line remained. She herself had not for a moment considered selling the Crockett home, in spite of its better location and the more generous offers she had received for it. That must be handed down intact to Reuben for him to do with as he liked. Houses handed down by men to their sons, even to their daughters, assumed in some mysterious way a sturdier inheritance. One could say, "This was my father's house," "My grandfather was born here," "This is the old Crockett homestead" with a deeper and more continuous pride than one could refer to a mother's home, which at best, so far as a daughter was concerned, endured but for a generation and was never held seriously in the minds of men with anything but a passing sentiment. When a woman married, thought Solace, her hands cold and shaky in spite of Susan's fire in the kitchen stove, she transferred her allegiance to the house of her husband where her children were born. It was right, she supposed, and natural, but it was not always easy.

"Do you suppose," asked Susan, standing by the laden clothes basket with her arms akimbo, "that Master Reuben's goin' to have any use for all this cultch or for that matter any understandin' of it? Ain't it just goin' from one attic to another for another set of rats to gnaw on?"

"I suppose so," said Solace, laying the plans of Thomas Winship's meeting-houses on the top of the basket. She was thinking at that moment of how she had wanted to keep them spread out in cases in the upstairs room. "I suppose so, Susan. But I can't destroy them, foolish as it seems. They—they hold the thoughts of people. Reuben can do what he likes with them when he's grown."

"There are an awful lot of thoughts in this world," observed Susan, staring at the basket. "To my mind it's lucky they haven't all been wrote down. An' closin' up old places ain't good for nobody, their minds nor their bodies. It's an unhealthy business, if you ask me, which you ain't. I've got the front rooms all cleared out ready for them fussbudgets from Boston. I've saved every knick-knack and whim-wham accordin' to the papers that was drawn up. You ain't goin' to catch your death mosyin' about in there if I've got any say so. I'm goin' to take you home where it's warm and cheery an' there ain't no pneumonia in the very floorboards same as there is down here. Master Reuben an' I'll come back for this mess o' stuff when we get around to it."

Solace was grateful for Susan as they drove homeward through the April mud. Susan sat, solid and comfortable, slapping the reins over the back of the old horse. She was not to all appearances troubled by any sentiments at all; she was impervious to the way people had felt in certain chairs below certain mantels, to the ecstasy, the security, and the sleep which had stirred and comforted them in certain great beds at night. She apparently had been spared, or denied, the knowledge both that age in some persons accentuates rather than dulls emotion and that in the recollection of experience lies more reality than in the immediate experience itself. Susan would have an easier time of it in her old age. For one thing, her father's house had rightly descended to her brother, and her mother's house, which, of course, had never really been her mother's, had long since gone the way of all mothers' houses.

6

There was one major compensation in the disposal of the Winship home, major to Reuben and pleasing to Solace, who wanted to leave things shipshape for him. From the generous check, which had been received from the Misses Peabody, Solace set aside a fair portion for repairs on the Crockett house, which would be Reuben's, was already, as a matter of fact, in his name. Reuben always remembered that summer of 1890 when the carpenters and masons were at work inside and out; when the painters mixed and stirred their great buckets of paint, pouring the smooth, glossy liquid into smaller pails and mounting with them to the scaffolding where they scraped and painted with long, slapping sweeps of their brushes; when the paper-hangers bothered

Susan for hot water for their paste and spread their lengths of paper on long trestle-tables throughout most of the rooms in turn. It was a summer during which he needed and asked for no other occupation than to stand for hours at a time watching the men at work, the only difficulty being that he did not know upon whom to concentrate. He read that year in the daily paper from Bangor that a great World's Fair was to be held soon in Chicago, but that to him was as nothing compared to the delighted agitation that was his for a week when the carpenters allowed him to sit with them on the scaffolding of the roof and pound short, bright nails into the tops of fresh shingles, that smelled of new wood and must be placed carefully side by side in a straight line before the nails secured them with two heavy blows of the hammer. He wore a heavy apron of blue and white ticking and reached into its stiff pocket for the nails as he needed them, overlapping his shingles carefully and beginning on his next row with caution. When he was not helping, he went about, inside the house and out, taking delight in the mere presence of men who worked and talked with him, neglecting his playmates who seemed dull enough in contrast, fearful of his grandmother's and Susan's errands which might take him even for an hour from the scene of industry and labour. And every night when he went to bed, he considered seriously, for he was in the academy now and thinking uneasily of his future, whether it might not be better all around if he should embrace a trade rather than go to college as his grandmother wanted him to do, or even than to follow on in seafaring which seemed nowadays to offer little enough, even to boys with a long tradition within it.

Most wonderful of all during that fresh summer when every unspent day seemed awake and alive was the gradual transformation of the old house, not so much even in its outward aspects as, through them, in that inner character which made it what it was. Now it no longer slumped upon its foundations or sank beneath its sagging roofs. Instead it raised itself proudly like a person who, imbued with new courage, holds his head high and his shoulders up, or like one whom new clothes suddenly reveal in a manner transcending even the clothes themselves. It was though, thought Solace, it had been reanimated less by carpentry and brickwork and plastering than by the resurrection through them of the spirit which had lived a century within it. When she and Reuben after supper walked slowly through the field to the shore in order to turn back and look upon it standing there, they both felt, although they did not speak of it to each other, the intangible yet actual nature of its transformation.

Within it was the same. Judah and Amos, Benjamin and James, Abigail and Silas came back again with their old vigour once the rooms were spruce and new. Solace could hear Silas tearing up and down the stairs to fetch her wedding gifts and Abigail as a bride rattling her pots and pans as she hung them on her new kitchen walls in 1797. There was only one thing that she left as it was. That was the Versailles paper in the front parlour. One of the workmen, who knew more than the others and had a feeling for old things, said it would be a pity to strip that from the walls. They did not make such paper nowadays, he said, good for a hundred years and more. He could clean it with some new-fangled stuff so that much of its original freshness would come back. When he had finished with it, it did, indeed, look different beneath newly plastered ceilings and encased in freshly painted wainscotings. Solace was glad to keep it. Reuben would be proud to show it to people, she told him, ten or twenty years hence, to tell them that it came from France when Robespierre was making Paris a terrifying place and when noble heads were dropping one by one beneath the guillotine. She did not tell him that she herself would be glad to lie below it when her time came.

It came in September after the house was exactly as she had wanted to leave it for Reuben, after the scaffolding was down and the vines replaced and the furniture within all set to rights. The hay was cut, too, with Reuben now to bear a man's share in the labour, stowed away in the freshly painted and newly shingled barn; and the meadows were green again beneath the August showers and the fogs of the dog-days. August had been hard on Solace with its muggy, humid weather. Sometimes at supper Susan and Reuben had noted with alarm how her breath came quickly through her parted lips and how the beating of her heart became visible in her neck and beneath the folds of her dress.

She lay quietly in bed during the last few days, sleeping most of the time, now and again asking to have her pillows raised so that she might look out upon the harbour water. Reuben sat for hours beside her, placing his chair so that she could look at him when she opened her eyes. She seldom opened them as the days went on, but Reuben rarely left her, since there was always the chance that she would. He sat in the chair with his hands folded between his knees and watched his grandmother. At fourteen he was still short and stocky with compact, serious features, a nose shorter than those of the Crocketts, a mouth at once fuller and less decisive. He had the blue eyes and dark brows of Nicholas and Silas beneath his straight, dark hair, and only they gave proof that his thoughts were of any length or depth. He was an engaging boy, perhaps more through what he did not say or do than through what he did; but whatever he had within him was not obvious to anyone at all. Susan wondered often what was passing through his mind as he sat doggedly on beside his grandmother for hours on end, most of the day and half of the night; but she was not one for prying into the feelings of other folks, she told Seth Tucker when he brought in the milk, and probably no one would ever know.

When his grandmother quietly let her last breath go at sunset one September evening, Reuben as quietly left the room, crossed the field, and walked back and forth alone along the shore, now and then pausing to skip flat stones with practiced wrist out across the still water. Sometimes he got as many as six skips from a stone, Susan noted, as she and Seth Tucker waited outside for people to come to do what had to be done. He was the beatingest young one, she said, that she had ever seen, and she for one had never been able to make him out, much as she liked him.

7

Deborah came for Solace's funeral, and Reuben almost warily laid out his clothes and got himself ready for his mother. He had seen her but twice since he was ten, once in Boston on a long-deferred visit that had held more of embarrassment than pleasure, once for a few days in Saturday Cove. He met her at the steamboat wharf the morning she came. He had dreaded the meeting for hours, and it proved no easier than he had feared. He stood in his black suit at the top of the gangway as she came from the boat, his black cap held awkwardly in his hand. Susan had dyed his best clothes from navy blue to black. It was only proper, she said. The suit had shrunk in the process and made him look even more ungainly than he was. His mother said, "Well, Reuben," and kissed him on his cheek, which was wet from perspiration though the autumn day was cold. He could not seem to keep his face and hands dry, much as he mopped them with his black-bordered handkerchief.

He minded the stares of the people standing about far less than he minded the drive home with his mother. He could not think of one word to say to her as he drove her up the village street and along the shore road. She wore black, too, with a touch of white here and there about her, and she looked dainty and clean in spite of her journey. He replied as best he could to her questions, but his monosyllabic words and fragmentary sentences cracked with his changing voice and made him acutely miserable. Once at home it was no better, perhaps even worse. They sat together, seemingly for hours on end, in the sitting-room before the closed doors of the front parlour. It was hard for his mother, too. Reuben recognized that fact in spite of his own suffering and would have helped her if he could.

Deborah at nearly forty was lovely to look at, and Reuben in an odd, impersonal way was proud of his mother. He had even felt a momentary sense of pleasurable importance mingling with his fear when he had glimpsed certain of his school friends whose curiosity had drawn them to the wharf. She looked more like a summer visitor than a native. Her hands were soft and white with polished nails, and she moved about the old rooms with such an air of complete assurance that his own entrances and exits were accomplished with increasing torment.

It was not easy for Deborah to be back in Saturday Cove. In that Reuben was right. Only a decent sense of propriety, gratitude, and duty had brought her in response to Susan's telegram. The rooms in which she sat or walked about, the dead face of Solace in the front parlour, the field stretching to the shore, the bed in which she slept, the presence of her son—all these urged upon her an emotional response which she was unable to give them. The past was worse than dead to Deborah in that it held not even the sense of finality and acceptance which the death of things and experiences sometimes brings, a finality without remorse, an acceptance free from regret. It was not dead so much as blotted out, gone from her consciousness, dissolved and vanished, passed out of sight. The memory of her love for Nicholas became baseless and insubstantial even before she vainly tried to bring it before her. Reuben as its outward and visible sign was more an uneasy curiosity to her than anything else, entailing possible responsibilities from which she shrank as well for himself as for her. It was, would be insufferable, she thought, to have the past come hurtling into the present like some strange, almost abortive birth, unconnected by any affections or impressions, unrecognizable even by pain.

Deborah tried to break Reuben's embarrassed silence as they sat together, not because she had any real desire to know him as her son, but rather because the very tension of their aloofness became at moments unbearable.

"The old house looks very nice, Reuben."

"Yes, it does."

"It's a beautiful old place, I think."

"I think so, too."

"Your father was very proud of it."

"Yes."

"I hope you'll be able to keep it when you get older."

"I hope so, too."

"Have you thought of what you'll do when you finish the academy, made any plans for yourself?"

"No, not exactly."

"Did your grandmother ever talk with you about what she wanted you to do?"

"Sometimes she did."

There was always a point beyond which Deborah could not get with Reuben. When that point was soon reached, they sat again in silence.

Susan did not help matters during those trying two days. Susan was not one to forget past grievances, and she had neither cared for Deborah as a little girl nor expected much of her as a woman. Moreover, Susan was jealous both for the rights of Master Reuben and for those of her dead mistress in the front parlour. Knowing Deborah as she did, or at least assumed she did, she had what she considered her well-grounded fears. If Reuben's mother made up her mind to take Master Reuben back with her to Boston, Susan had already made up *her* stout mind to relieve it of certain opinions she held on the matter, opinions well substantiated by certain confidences given her by Solace Crockett herself. Susan was biding her time, she told Seth Tucker, and when the time came to speak, speak she would and to some purpose. She knew Master Reuben, his clothes, his appetite, and his odd ways; and before he was taken to Boston to live with ne'er-do-well artists, who cared not so much as a crumb for him, who would take what little he had (and the Lord knew it wasn't much) and who would fill the old house in the summer with Heaven knew what sort of idle daubers, she intended to have her say out. She intended also, she said, to keep both her eyes and her ears well open while Mrs. Edward Sawyer was in a house where she had never for one moment belonged; and she loyally fulfilled her resolve.

In all justice (or injustice) to Deborah, Susan might have been spared her agitation. Deborah had no desire to transport to Boston her unfamiliar son, who sat opposite her in the back parlour, not more ill at ease, she thought, than she herself. In point of sober fact, it was her possible duty toward Reuben which nagged at his mother. There he was, belonging to her, the fruit of a love which had once conquered her better judgment and of which now not a vestige remained, save now and again at rare intervals the uneasy sense that she had once made a mess of things.

When at last the two days were at an end and things were mercifully over, so far at least as their outward aspects were concerned, she spoke to Reuben as they sat together in the sitting-room. At the sound of her voice breaking the restless silence, Susan in the chair which she had moved to the open door leading from the kitchen to the hall raised her head like some great dog who hears strange footsteps drawing near his master's house.

"I've been thinking, Reuben, about what is best for you."

"You needn't. I'm all right."

"I don't like to leave you here alone."

"I'm not alone. Susan will stay with me. She told my grandmother so."

With a glance at the open door Deborah lowered her voice, but Susan caught the words.

"Are you happy with Susan?"

"Of course, I'm—I'm used to her."

"And you're not used to me. Is that it?"

"I suppose so."

Deborah gathered herself together as one gathers himself for a first daring plunge into deep water.

"You must know that I want to do all that I can for you, Reuben. I'm your mother after all. You're always welcome to come to Boston to stay with me. Your stepfather told me to tell you. The schools are better there, and it might be best for you."

Emboldened by his mother's temerity, Reuben found his own voice. Susan, listening, understood the cost of his words. She could hear him drawing himself slowly up on the cane seat and against the back of his grandmother's chair where he sat.

"Thank you, mother, and my stepfather, too. But I'd rather stay here in my own house where I belong."

Deborah, forcing herself to look at Reuben and see the matter through, saw with a start the eyes of Nicholas at the supper-table fifteen years before. She sought hurriedly for another question which should deaden a sudden, unexpected stab of pain.

"Are you sure you won't be lonely here?"

"Perhaps I'll be lonely sometimes, but not so lonely as in Boston."

There was a silence again in the sitting-room, a silence which, Susan knew, neither Deborah nor Reuben dared to break. As for he, she found all at once that there were tears in the hollows above her cheek bones, more tears than even Marie Corelli could bring forth. Feeling them there, she rose at once and bestirred herself, not without relief, to set her bread for rising during the night.

8

Reuben Crockett was never popular in the usual sense of the word among either his schoolmates or his teachers in the Saturday Cove Academy, but in an odd way he was prominent. Like Nicholas he never distinguished himself as a student, but unlike Nicholas he bent for hours over his studies simply because it seemed to him at the time the only thing to do. He kept from the beginning, when he had put his toys away without being told, a slow, meticulous sense of doing whatever was required of him whenever it was required and as well as he could do it. He made painstaking, correct translations of his Latin, which, although they would never fire any teacher by their spirit or originality, would yet satisfy by the fact that they were always forthcoming, exact and dependable. He did the same with all his other lessons, at school sitting quietly until he was called upon and then as quietly telling what he knew. Nor did he distinguish himself in school sports and games or at parties. Nevertheless, when games were to be played, he played them, and when there were parties, he was there.

His schoolmates liked, even admired him without exactly knowing why. Perhaps they liked him because he was kind, considerate, and fair, and admired him because he always seemed to know what he thought about things. When any matter for deliberation came up and preliminary discussions were held about the school grounds at recess, Reuben was never one for talk; but when a decision was about to be made, he was always ready with everything neatly placed in his mind and his opinion quite made up. Nor was he easily swerved from what he thought.

In church it was the same. It never once occurred to Reuben not to go to church, since he had always gone. He went every Sunday morning at half-past ten in his best clothes with a clean handkerchief in his pocket. He always led Susan in, down the main aisle to the old Crockett pew, the third from the front; and once she was seated and had arranged the folds of her black alpaca or foulard silk, he saw that she had a footstool for her ample, rheumatic feet. Then he sat at the head of the pew where James and Silas and Nicholas had sat, bowed his head when the long prayer was said, found the hymns for Susan and sang them unobtrusively, and always kept his eyes full on the minister's face during the forty-five-minute sermon, which sometimes ran into an hour or more without the slightest sign on Reuben's part that it was too long or dull. He stayed for Sunday-school, too, held now during the hour succeeding church. He had learned his lesson at home just as he learned his daily lessons at school and was comforting to his teacher, who had been forced to realize that the learning of Sunday-school lessons was now considered needless and supererogatory on the part of most of his class.

On Sunday evenings, leaving Susan in the kitchen with her old-time favourites, supplemented now by Anna Katharine Green, the latest Amelia Edith Barr, and the new success, *The Prisoner of Zenda*, he went to prayer meeting, sitting attentively in the vestry and singing *Work for the Night is Coming, Shall We Gather at the River?* and *Blest Be the Tie that Binds*. Unlike the other boys in the village, he did not at seventeen and eighteen see any girl to her doorwary, there to stand in half-embarrassed talk or to go into the sitting-room to finish with her family the Sunday afternoon supply of popcorn or molasses taffy. Instead he skirted the churchyard and walked home alone along the shore road.

Always in his walks home at night he stopped now and again to look off across the harbour to where the islands lay, dark, obscure humps when there was no moon, in moonlight pointed and sparred from their spruces and firs which were reflected in the shining water. Farther, on clear nights stretched the horizon, a pale line of light beneath the moon and stars. He liked to stand there at night and look seaward, with the crickets in August and September filling the air and in April and May the peepers from the marshes. He liked to stop even in winter before the ice closed in the inner harbour, note how the snow-covered fields fell downward until at the water's edge they became rhythmic, curving mounds of white above the high, black tides, and how, beyond, the sea spread out, dark, mysterious, and cold. He liked to imagine how others of his family had walked the same road homeward, had stopped as he stopped to look out upon a different harbour and a different sea, gleaming here and there with the lights of great ships at anchor and mirroring their dark yards and spars. Now except for the clear or obscured outlines of a schooner or two or of the smart, white hulls of pleasure yachts and sloops in summer, there was small evidence of ships when he had passed the inner harbour with the water slapping at the skiffs and dories of the local fishermen. The night was close about him; the air was fresh and free; and he was alone with his own thoughts, which from his childhood had never failed him.

Reuben's religious life was a matter of cogitation, not to say of controversy among the church authorities of Saturday Cove when, in 1894, at the age of eighteen he asked to be admitted to membership. So far as anyone knew he had made no public or even private professions of a change in mind and heart, which in that day by most brands of rural New England Congregationalism were held to be necessary preliminaries to the taking of such a serious and revolutionary step. He had, in fact, been conspicuous during the yearly seasons of revival by his apparent lack of emotional and spiritual fervour. He had never come forward to the seat of the penitents, had never risen when the call for Christians to stand had been sounded, had never given so much as a verse of Scripture to testify either to his faith or to the astounding transformation wrought by the grace of God within him. Yet here he was, without excuse or explanation, suing quietly for membership within the Communion of Saints.

The minister and the deacons comprising the church committee deliberated long and carefully over Reuben's request. There was no gainsaying that there were many things in his favour. He had the name of a moral and upright young man with no bad habits; he was a constant attendant at church; he was diligent in his business whatever it might be. The minister, although theologically not an exponent of initial grace, was half inclined to believe when he looked at Reuben during the Sunday morning service that by some special act of Providence it had been implanted in him, even although Reuben himself was not given to testimony and apparently was not in any way aware of the influx of the Spirit. It might be that with his baptism his tongue would occasionally become loosened, thought the Reverend Mr. Bentley, mulling the matter over in his troubled mind, and that he would no longer hesitate to declare in public the unsearchable riches of God.

Reuben, sitting uncomfortably before the minister in the old parsonage, quite unaware that in this very room his grandmother and grandfather, over sixty years before, had received holy instructions upon their approaching marriage, gave no sign either of his own consciousness of initial grace or of any loosening of his tongue. He made, in fact, but one thoroughly complete statement which, though it was not displeasing to his questioner, hardly contained theological implications.

"I should like," said the puzzled Mr. Bentley, "to learn what steps have led you to this momentous decision; in short, what has made you eager to ally yourself with the church of God?"

Reuben, embarrassed and perplexed, looked for a steady moment at the minister and then at the full afternoon tide, which before a strong southwest wind was rocking the dories about at their anchorage.

"I'm afraid there haven't been any steps, sir, at least that I can remember. I just think it's—it's the right thing for a young man to do."

But there was something about him sitting there, even with the nervous twirling of his cap in his hands and the inadequate answers which he gave to the succeeding questions, only half understood, that convinced the minister, who in turn set aside the uneasy objections of the church committee.

Reuben joined the church as unostentatiously as he had always attended it, and Susan, who had been saved early and had long since forgotten the ways and means of her rescue, found tears again on her face as she watched him go forward for his baptism and reception. She looked for no change in him although she knew that a change was expected after such a grave and significant step. She told her friends, whom she frequently met about the village or who sometimes came to sit with her for an hour in her bright kitchen, that Master Reuben didn't need any change in him, no matter what the church said. He might have his ways same as she had hers, but he was as good a boy as ever breathed the breath of life, and *that* she would maintain to her dying day.

Reuben did have his ways, accentuated within him by the very fact that he was not called upon to adapt himself to anyone but Susan. Above all else he liked things done as they had always been done, the same hours for bed-time and getting up, the same fish-balls for Sunday dinner, lamps in the same places shining through the windows in the selfsame, familiar shafts of light as he came home, apples in the same dish upon the table.

"What's become of the old dish?" he said to Susan when she made a change. "Did it get broken or something?"

He studied his Sunday-school lesson in the front parlour from nine to ten on Sunday mornings, and he always spent an hour there after dinner, sitting alone with his book. He had a way of walking through the house, looking at things, handling them sometimes. Whenever, urged by Susan, he asked his friends in on Saturday evening to play games, authors or anagrams, Boston or Jenkins Up, or to pull taffy, he liked to have the chairs in their accustomed places before he went to bed.

It was characteristic of him that he did not talk about his future with anyone at all. Not that there were many to talk with had he cared to do so. There was the lawyer, who had charge of his small affairs pending his twenty-first birthday and who each month dealt out to Susan whatever she needed for the running of the household and to Reuben the tiny sum allowed him for pocket-money. The lawyer had gone to school with Reuben's father and had come home, after reading in a Calais office for the bar examinations, to draw up deeds for the transfer of land and to take small fees from farmers who wanted insecure boundaries established. He understood Reuben as little as Reuben liked him. There was the præceptor of the academy, now called the principal, a kind, well-meaning man, who could not honestly say that any indications in Reuben's present glowed with a bright light for his future. There was his mother, who each year dutifully offered him a home and possible work in Boston and who each year received from Reuben a polite refusal. And there was Susan, who knew him too well to offer suggestions had she had any to offer and who was inclined to think that anything which Master Reuben decided to do would be done better than as though anyone else attempted it.

The natural result was that Reuben at nineteen, having graduated from the academy with no especial distinction, slowly made up his own mind as to his place in the years that stretched before him. He made it up during the long walks which he was forever taking by himself through the woods and along the shore paths. From money that he had saved from the amount allowed him he bought a small sailboat in the spring of the year that a decision must be made and spent hours sailing it in all weathers far beyond the harbour. Sitting in the stern with the sheet in his hands and watching with careful eyes the vagaries of the wind, he kept his mind busy on this possibility and that. There were few enough for him, and he knew it, knowing full well what manner of young man he was and how certain things were well-rooted within him for better or for worse. He thought seriously of college, which his grandmother had desired for him. There were many things against college, pondered Reuben, and few for it as far as he could see. To go to college meant the using of what money he had, perhaps even the mortgaging of the old house. It meant his bewildered entrance into a new and strange life among new and strange people, studies which had little appeal to him and, worst of all, the necessity for excellence if he were to succeed in any of the professions to which college inevitably led.

Reuben had no illusions about himself. At nineteen he knew far more about his own nature and worth than most men know at forty. He understood that he would never be a man to whom persons are unmistakably drawn, a man who succeeds in whatever he undertakes by the mere force of personality and an abundance of social gifts. He knew, for instance, that he could never sell things, either leaning across the counter of some city or even country store or going about from town to town with samples of cotton goods, clothing, boots and shoes in huge cases, which he sometimes saw in the small mercantile houses of Saturday Cove. The drummer business was booming in the nineties among the country towns, and many young men were embracing it. But to sell things, thought

Reuben, presupposed either confidence in one's wares or cleverness in hoodwinking customers, and above all else it required a kind of social urbanity, affability and neighbourliness which one had or one had not. Not a few young men in the nineties in Maine coast villages were giving up the idea of further education and a possible profession and instead taking up trades. Education meant money, which was scarce enough in most families, even the best, now that the old life had gone, whereas here at one's very doors was the ever-growing demand for carpenters and masons and paper-hangers to build and put in order the summer homes which were rising year by year. To learn a trade now meant good wages after the shortest of apprenticeships; and yet a certain stubborn pride within Reuben set summarily aside the notion, so alluring when at fourteen he had driven nails into the fresh shingles on his old roofs. He could not, he thought, without apology come up his driveway to his white doors with a tool-kit on his shoulders or stand in white canvas trousers, daubed with paint and oil and varnish, before Amos and Judah in his front parlour. He came of better stuff, he said to himself with a proud lift of his head as he trimmed his sail skillfully to get the best of the wind. And steadily as the summer days went on and the autumn loomed ominously before him, the knowledge came clearer to him that his work like that of his forbears must be with the sea and with some sort of ship that moved thereon.

Had he been differently situated, less alone in the world, even of a more venturesome nature, he might conceivably, though at that late day, have experienced under sail the life upon which his father had been about to enter. For there were still in the nineties sailing-ships here and there making the long passage eastward to Australian and Chinese ports, rounding Good Hope and Java Head, clearing the Sunda Straits, still competing through lower freight rates with the now triumphant conquest of steam. But Reuben in Saturday Cove in the mid-nineties knew little of such ships and no one who could put him in contact with their masters and owners. Nor did the Crockett name mean what it had meant in the seventies and fifties. Time and chance had smothered its magic. His immediate future at least must be nearer home among the smaller, steam-driven craft which were being built or renovated to take care of the steady stream of people, coming eastward from New York and Boston and points west with their goods and chattels to spend the summer months along the coast of Maine from Casco to Passamaquoddy.

Once his mind was made up, he went one warm day in late July to see the local steamship agent, who put him in touch with the Bangor office and who, a native himself of Saturday Cove and not unaware of the stuff that had produced Reuben, wrote a letter to anticipate Reuben's application. By the middle of August he was placed as ship's clerk on a coastwise steamer running daily except on Sunday between Rockland and points east to Mount Desert.

The steamer was a small one. She lay over every second night at the smelly, dishevelled Rockland wharf awaiting the arrival of the larger boat from Boston, which docked at five A.M. and transferred her sleepy passengers for their day's journey down the coast. Besides these and their baggage she carried every conceivable sort of freight, canned goods, farm machinery, wagons and sometimes horses, furniture, fish, and kerosene, fruit and grain, sugar and molasses, boots and shoes and Boston papers, everything in short that towns and villages off the railroad depended upon for their daily maintenance. She was a prepossessing craft, being a small wooden propeller with a length of only one hundred and twenty feet; but she was officered by decent and able men, some of whom like Reuben bore names once well and honourably known in deep-water traffic half around the world.

Now that he had settled the beginning of his future Reuben brought to his work the same trustworthiness and reliability that had characterized him from the start. The officers took notice of the way he did things and now and then gave him charges of responsibility not strictly belonging to his job. He was not without his ambitions and his dreams. When he walked through the noisy, fog-swept Rockland wharf-houses where dirty men were forever trundling freight-barrows, and the smell of multifarious cargoes mingled with the smells of grease and soot and harbour water, he thought how one day he might be transferred to the spacious, cleaner, newer steamers plying to Boston or New York or extending their runs farther eastward: the *City of Bangor*, for instance, or the *Frank Jones*, or the new steel propeller *Pemaquid*. He took pleasure in the very fact that he was helping to carry passengers who represented a larger life than he knew, men and women who had seen more of the world than he, boys who sometimes in city accents asked him questions as to this light and that island along their desultory course. He grew acquainted with the coast both in terms of navigation and of interest in its very loveliness. He never tired of the great curve of shore line sweeping up to Owl's Head, or of the perfect symmetry of Mark Island as they made the thoroughfare, the purple hills of Camden with Negro Island Light in their dark shadow, the blue sweep of Eggemoggin, the high green promontory of Eagle and the squat cosiness of Pumpkin, the spruces that back the great granite cliffs of Heron Neck, and the white lighthouse towers of Frenchman's Bay—Egg Rock, Bear Island, and Baker, warning mariners of the treacherous shoals and bars of the Cranberries. And on alternate nights when the *Matinicus* lay over in her Mount Desert port, he smoked his pipe, which Susan did not like but which seemed a necessity to a sailor's life, and wondered if Java Head and the peaks beyond Rio and even the harbour of Sydney, which his father had seen, were actually more beautiful than the tumbling Mount Desert hills rising darkly into the evening sky or growing blue as the dawn broke behind them.

9

He did not after all trouble Susan unduly with his pipe, since it was not often that he could spend a Sunday at home. When an occasional holiday intervened or a good trip on Saturday allowed him a few extra hours, he came by stage from the neighbouring railway station, now ten miles away. Saturday Cove itself was not on the route of his steamer. Susan always made it a point to be about the house on Saturday afternoons and evenings just on the chance of his arrival. She always watched him as he came up the driveway in his neat blue clothes and cap. She thought as the months and years went by that Master Reuben walked with a more decisive step as though he were growing quicker and more sure of himself now that he was in the twenties and had been promoted to an officership.

Susan asked no better thing than to keep the house ready and in order for his infrequent returns. It had become her home through the years, and she had no other. She had told Master Reuben when he once began to strike out for himself that her board and keep were quite enough for her. She had worked for forty years, she said, and had laid by a respectable sum from her maximum wages of three dollars a week. Reuben continued to pay her, nevertheless, his postal orders coming every month with the regularity of the sun; and Susan cashed each at the inside post-office window and then put by the money between the pages of the Family Bible that marked the Book of Joshua. She laid it away in that safe and secret place against the time when Master Reuben might be ill or in need.

She had quite enough to occupy her days. There was the cleaning of the house every week, the daily tidying up, the necessary cooking and washing. When her work was done, she knitted in the kitchen where the clock ticked on in almost perfect time with the tall one in the hall. She knitted Reuben's socks and wristers and winter gloves; and when a great plentitude of those was complete, she knitted sundry articles for a Calais firm, which supplied her with wool and paid her a small price for her labour. She could knit and read at the same time, and she still had her favourite books. Reuben kept Susan in touch with the outside world whenever he came home. He told her in the spring of 1898 of the latest developments in Cuba, and what he privately thought of Admiral Dewey, and how glad he was that a war for which he had small respect and sympathy was not calling for any number of young and able men. Susan was glad, too. She was sorry that the Cubans were starving; she would feed them if she could; but secretly she had no use for mixing up with a lot of outlandish folks who had nothing in common with good New England stock.

Each day she studied the wind and weather from her kitchen window, keeping an eye on the eastern horizon, and sometimes she walked about the house and into the meadows where she could better scan the heavens and the sea. In the fall of 1898 when the great storm of the 26th of November broke and ravaged the coast waters from Fundy to Cape Cod, she did not sleep at all. That Saturday morning had been exceptionally bright for November, a wind from the west bringing out clearly the islands and making the headlands on the farther shore of the harbour gaunt and distinct in their stern outlines of late autumn with winter just around the corner. There had not been the slightest hint of snow either in the morning air or in the sky. The rare and brief November sun had never shed a warmer light on the brown fields and meadows. She remembered afterward how at three o'clock the wind had suddenly shifted to blow from the northeast just as she had gone out to empty her soapy bath water over the brown, decaying leaves of the pie-plant by the side of the barn. Soapy water was good for pie-plant, Susan always thought, and every

Saturday she emptied a wash-tub full of it even after the ground had begun to harden a bit.

The wind increased that afternoon to gale force and by early darkness was shaking the shutters, slatting the bare branches of the lilacs against the house, and growing stronger every hour. At seven o'clock it was blowing a hurricane of snow. She did not go to bed at all that night. She thought of Master Reuben's boat, wondering if it had reached its Mount Desert port by five o'clock, knowing how, if it were late, it must battle against that northeast storm blowing dead against it.

She learned two days later of what that November storm had cost; and when Reuben came the following Sunday to eat a deferred Thanksgiving dinner with her, he talked for hours of it, his tongue so loosened that he paced her kitchen floor, talking, talking, while she did her dishes. Reuben's boat had come through all right—he was first officer of her now—though she had had a time of it at the last with the snow beginning at the approach of darkness and the wind beating her offshore. Just where the *Portland* had gone down, said Reuben, would always be a matter of sad conjecture. Some said off Boon Island Light, others Kennebunkport, still others around Race Point and High Head near Provincetown. Reuben's own theory was that she went down on Stellwagen Bank between Cape Ann and Cape Cod. At all events, he said, some bodies of the hundred and sixty-eight souls lost on her had drifted ashore on the Cape Cod sands as early as Sunday evening.

"And may the Lord have mercy on them all!" cried Susan, for once not minding the tobacco smoke curling about her kitchen from the bowl of Reuben's pipe.

No one on the Maine coast talked of much else that winter. Even the coal schooner *King Philip* and the Maine-named *Pentagoet*, which disappeared in the same terrible night with all on board, were frail rivals of the *Portland* disaster as subjects of conversation.

To Susan and perhaps even to Reuben himself it cast a new light upon his calling, proved that dangers had not passed with the passing of the sailing-ship, placed an added premium upon the hardihood and responsibility of those that officered and commanded boats through inshore as well as through deep waters.

"Come to that," said Reuben to Susan more than once on his succeeding visits, "there's a heap to learn about coast navigation. It's not just steaming along with all going well the way some people think. It's knowing every reef and shoal and sounding of the most tricky coast in all the world. It must have been a fine thing to sail in open water hundreds of miles on every side of you and get the most you could out of your ship. But maybe it's not such a poor job to know how to get through the islands of Eggemoggin Reach and Frenchman's Bay in a fog that's sitting thick on your very pilot-house."

Susan was proud of Master Reuben when he talked this way with his eyes glowing and the new braid on his blue coat shining in the light of her kitchen lamp.

Reuben was learning not only steamboat navigation in the late nineties but the history of it as well. He listened to the talk of the older men in the service, and, as his interest grew, he spent his off hours during the winter months in running down whatever records he could find in the various historical societies and libraries and in the archives of shipping concerns in Boston, Portland and Bangor. It seemed to Susan that he knew the ins and outs of each of the many short-lived companies founded on the coast for seventy-five years back and all the craft that they had floated. He had picked up odd drawings of the first steam-driven boats of the 1820's and even earlier, their wood-fired engines supplemented then by sail, and he liked to spread them out before her on the Sundays he was at home and explain their curiosities to her.

He liked to tell her stories of some of them. For instance, he quite endowed with magic the very day of Susan's commonplace and undistinguished advent into this world by identifying it with the burning of the *Royal Tar*, an early Maine coast steamboat, named after King William IV and bound from St. John to Portland. The 26th day of October of the year 1836 thus took on an unwonted glamour for Susan when she learned that even while her mother laboured in pain to bring her into the sin and suffering of this planet, where most folks forgot the Golden Rule every day they lived, a tragedy had been enacted on the sea only thirty miles away. The *Royal Tar,* Reuben told Susan, had carried besides her seventy passengers the singular cargo of a menagerie, having stowed away in her hold an elephant, two camels, two lions, and a royal Bengal tiger. The fire, which broke out shortly after she had left Eastport in the supply of wood stacked too near her boiler, was fed by a strong northwest wind; and the steamer with most of her passengers and all her menagerie suffered a merciless and cruel fate. Reuben's story had the odd effect of increasing Susan's respect for her own birth. That an elephant, two camels, a pair of lions, and a Bengal tiger, none of which animals Susan had ever seen, should have been swimming about in panic through the waters of Passamaquoddy Bay at the very moment when Susan was greeting this world with a cry made an immeasurable dent upon her imagination and enlivened not only her conversations with her friends but many a solitary hour over her knitting during the weeks when she did not dare so much as to hope for Master Reuben's return.

In the earliest years of his seafaring, when the closing in of the ice laid the *Matinicus* up for three months at least, Reuben had spent part of the winter at home. But as time went on and he rose slowly in his importance to the company, he began to find office employment in Bangor or Boston. This, Susan thought, was all to the good. Idleness, she maintained, was safe for no one at all, at any place, at any time; and she would far rather never see Master Reuben than to have him hanging about the stores and wharves of Saturday Cove like a lot of young men with no gumption whatsoever.

"I don't know what this village is comin' to," she said to Reuben, "upon my soul I don't. It's gettin' so that young an' old work only in the summer an' hang round air-tights all winter figurin' how they can cheat them that come here for three months so's to get enough out of 'em to live on the remainin' nine. It ain't healthy for all concerned. An' these new cigarettes the young fry's smokin' eat the linin' off their lungs and stomachs an' take away what little starch they've got left in 'em. Tobacco's a curse, if you ask me, Master Reuben, which you ain't. You stick to your job no matter where it takes you. I'll hold the fort here if it takes my last breath, as one general said to another in the Civil War which you can't remember, but I can, with my poor brothers so nearly starved that they've never been the same since."

In 1901 when the Eastern Steamship Company, a consolidation of all lines running east from Boston, was formed, Reuben left the *Matinicus* to become commander of the *Searsport*, the youngest man in command of any ship run by the new company. The *Searsport*, connecting with the Boston boat at Rockland, ran daily between that busy port and Saturday Cove. On Mondays, Wednesdays and Fridays she left Saturday Cove for Rockland; on Tuesdays, Thursdays and Saturdays she left Rockland for Saturday Cove. A sister ship, the *Searsmont*, took care of the alternate days so that each morning a boat left for Rockland and each afternoon a boat arrived in Saturday Cove.

Reuben had done well, and the new company recognized that fact. He might, indeed, have taken, instead of his captaincy, a first officership with the promise of quick promotion on the new and spacious *City of Rockland*, plying the main route between Boston and Bangor. But even although he had once dreamed of the larger boats with their nearer approximation to deep water, he decided to stick to the smaller, partly because he could not bear to give up the now familiar coast, partly because his command of the *Searsport* would mean Sundays and alternate nights at home.

When the decision was once made, he broke down all reserve and caution and sent Susan a telegram from the Boston office where he had been called to interview the heads of his company. Susan let it lie on the kitchen table for a full quarter of an hour while she sat staring at it in the still room, now reaching out her hand toward it, now drawing her hand back, unable for fear to tear it open. Once she had done so, she started for the village in the unusual heat of a September day to publish abroad the news that Master Reuben, like his forbears, was now commander of his own ship. When she had once come back at supper-time, hurrying along the shore road and up the driveway in an excitement that would not let her walk as a woman of her years ought to walk, she felt so odd and shaky that she had to lie down for an hour once she was in the house.

10

One Saturday afternoon in early October of the same year Reuben at Susan's back door met a woman, who remained constantly in his thoughts and behaviour for two years before he at last decided to tell her about it. Her name was Huldah Barrett, and she had come that fall from Machias to teach the grammar school at Saturday Cove. She was five years older than Reuben.

On the afternoon that she began to invade his consciousness Reuben had come home from the steamboat wharf for supper, secure in the thought of a good run from Rockland, a safely discharged cargo, and a reliable officer and purser remaining on board the *Searsport.* He had come up the driveway, surveying the old house critically as he walked. Some shingles on the western roof of the ell needed replacing, he noted, after the work in 1890 in which he at fourteen had had such pleasure. He was taking stock at that moment of his bank account and felt proud that now with no effort at all he could keep things in decent shape. The old place looked beautiful in the October light with the low sun streaming upon it. The woodbine above the front doorway was flaming red against the white clapboards. The whole house could do with a coat of paint, he thought, and when spring came round again, he meant to manage it.

Susan was dressing in her room above the kitchen when he opened the back door and went inside. She had been lying down for two hours as the doctor had ordered her to do, not because, as she had stoutly informed Reuben, she believed one word he said or had any patience with his tonics and nostrums, but because, once having been fool enough to go to see him, she insisted on getting her money's worth. She would be down directly, she called. There was a fresh squash pie in the pantry, and the coffee was on the back of the stove if he wanted a lunch before supper.

Huldah's knock came at the back door while Reuben, regardless of lunch, was walking about the familiar rooms. He opened it to see her standing there. He never forgot the moment, although she was neither prepossessing or in the least unusual in a worn brown jacket with leg-of-mutton sleeves, a shirtwaist with a high, boned collar that made red marks beneath her ears, a brown hat set high upon her undistinguished hair, and a wide and long brown skirt, to the stout brush-braid of which some fallen leaves were clinging. She asked for Susan.

"Is Miss Gray in?" she said.

For a moment Reuben was puzzled. He did not remember ever having heard Susan's other name, had, indeed, forgotten that she owned one.

"You must be Captain Crockett," continued this unknown caller. "I'm sorry to bother you when you're just home. I saw you coming ahead of me along the road."

She had a nice voice, thought Reuben, low and clear with a rise and fall in it that somehow made it musical. By this time he had recovered himself and asked her in.

"I'm afraid I don't know who you are," he said, leading her through the kitchen to the sitting-room. "I thought I knew everyone in Saturday Cove at least by sight. Maybe I'm growing old."

She laughed. She had a pleasant laugh like her voice in speaking, and her eyes laughed with her voice. They were gray eyes, Reuben noted, just off the blue, and they were frank and friendly. She put her gloves on the table—they looked worn and old—and sat down by the fireplace.

"There's no reason why you should know me," she said, looking straight at Reuben standing by the center table in his blue clothes. "My name is Huldah Barrett, and I've just come from Machias to teach the grammar school. My mother and I live in the second house below the church—the old Stevens' place, they call it. We've taken the lower rooms there and are keeping house. And right now I'm soliciting for the church supper next Thursday. I'm on the committee. Mother said she knew I'd be put on something directly, but I don't mind; in fact, I like it. We thought Miss Gray would be willing to make a marble cake. It seems she's famous for marble cakes."

"I'm sure she will," promised Reuben, looking uneasily toward the staircase. "She'll be down right away."

He tried to think of something else to say, but he could not seem to do so. Women were out of his line, especially strange ones who appeared unexpectedly. But he managed to sit down in the chair opposite her own, placing his cap, which he was still holding, on the table.

The cap had a star upon it above its gold braid and served to suggest her next observation which she hastened to make, sensing his own embarrassment and feeling sorry that she had forced herself upon him only for a marble cake.

"The whole village is pleased at your promotion. We heard about it at once from—from Susan. I think I'll have to call her Susan since everyone else does. I know some of the old people here and there who knew your father and grandfather. They're all proud of what you've done."

To this it was even more difficult to find a response.

"Thank you," said Reuben at last, relieved to hear Susan's stout tread. "It's very kind of you to tell me."

Reuben meant to go when Susan came in, but he kept on sitting there, as much because he found it oddly comfortable to have some one else in the house besides himself and Susan as because he did not quite know how to leave. He listened to ten minutes' talk on cakes, sponge and angel and marble, sunshine, moonshine, and lightning, Lord Baltimore and silver, nut, chocolate, and apple sauce, jelly-roll, cream pie, and the lowly one-egg. These were listed on Huldah's paper, and opposite them were the names of the artists, who of their exceeding charity were to mix, beat, and bake them for the Thursday night supper.

When Huldah rose to go, he rose, too, and led the way to the front door. It seemed more fitting that she should leave from that entrance. Susan, surprised, followed after them.

"I declare," she said, as Huldah turned on the first of the steps to say goodbye, "I declare if it ain't the beatingest thing the way the church folks have took you right in. But there—when a body'll work with a will, they'll always get the chance. Next thing you know they'll have you collectin' the minister's salary. I believe myself," she concluded with an appreciative look at her caller as she stood smiling under the old woodbine, "that it's because folks can't refuse you what you ask for. There's some that come here that I wouldn't stir up so much as a soda biscuit for, and that's a fact."

Susan talked about Huldah Barrett at the supper table that evening. She'd entered right into things, she told Reuben, and folks liked it. She sang in the church choir, played the organ for the opening exercises in the Sunday-school, and when the hymns were sung, didn't she come down from the organ and teach a class of unruly boys that nobody had been able to handle for a year? The scholars in the school liked her, too. Although she didn't put up with no nonsense, she made them feel to home with her somehow, went on picnics with them to the shore or the woods and called on their mothers and fathers.

She was thirty years old, Susan said, and didn't make a secret of her age like some silly women. Susan had gathered that her mother was somewhat of a burden, one of the spleeny sort that had indigestion when she didn't have rheumaticks, was given to fussing about these new things called nerves, and was forever running to the drug-store for something or other.

At church the next morning Reuben heard Huldah's voice in the choir. He spotted it just as soon as the service began with the Doxology. It was a good voice, clear and true, and she sang as though she meant the words. He stayed to Sunday-school for the first time in the seven years since he had left Saturday Cove, and while he sat in the minister's Bible Class to which he was assigned, he now and then glanced from the back of the church to the wing pews in front where Huldah was teaching her boys. They looked interested, he thought, and every once in a while they laughed at something she had said. Reuben could not recall ever having laughed in Sunday-school when he was young like that, and he liked it. At seven o'clock he found himself in the vestry for the Sunday night prayer-meeting. Here again Huldah was at the organ, pushing down the rasping pedals, arranging the white stops as she wanted them once she had glanced at the hymn to be sung. He might be mistaken in his memory, Reuben thought, as he walked homeward under the hunter's moon, but it did not seem to him that he had ever heard before such spirit in the singing.

When he had boarded the *Searsport* next morning and stood in the pilot-house edging her out from the wharf, making a close, safe circle of the harbour, and getting underway among the islands, he felt somehow a new interest flooding his life. He was almost unreasonably happy there in the autumn sunlight, watching the blue water part before his sharp prow, seeing the reds and yellows of maples and beeches and birches fire the high shores of the islands and headlands, feeling against his face the cold freshness of the October air. By noon, although the sun would still be shining, a haze would soften the now distinct outlines of rock-strewn points and white lighthouses, buoys, islands, and passing vessels. He loved the way that purple haze of autumn afternoons deepened and dimmed the shores and the sea, making the atmosphere drowsy, even slumbrous, urging upon a man time and desire to think and to take pleasure in his thought.

11

Reuben's courtship of Huldah Barrett was for a long time only in his mind. Except for the stout certainty of Susan and the active memory of his grandmother, women had heretofore played no part at all in his life. But now that Huldah had come into his thoughts, his mind suddenly opened in an odd way as though after walking through a shadowy and quite satisfying wood, he had come suddenly and without warning into the full sunlight of a summer field. He was glad that he had chosen to stay by the coast instead of steaming from Rockland to Boston and back again. He even saw at times in his decision the workings of some benevolent Chance. For now he was at home every Sunday, as well as alternate nights during the week, at least until the winter ice took his boat off her course.

It was months before he saw anything at all of Huldah beyond her presence at church, and she would have been startled enough had she known the part she was already playing in his life. It was not, in fact, until June after their meeting in October that he became so bold as to call upon her. Searching about for some reason or excuse which might explain his coming to the old Stevens' house, he discovered in a shop in Rockland a set of excellent photographs of some of the Maine lighthouses—Portland Head Light ringed with winter surf, the great shaft of Petit-Manan shadowy in thick weather, the lonely outpost of Saddleback Ledge, Matinicus Rock deep in January snow, the windblown spruces of Heron Neck, black behind its white tower. He selected eight of these and had them mounted on sheets of white cardboard. They would look well on the walls of her schoolroom. It was not at all a bad idea, he hoped she would think, to familiarize Maine children with their own coast.

When he came home one clear June evening and smelled the lilacs long before he had reached the house, he felt such an unwonted excitement within him that, quite contrary to his expectation, he showed Susan straight away the contents of the great package under his arm. He unpacked the pictures in the sitting-room and had them arranged on the white mantel above the fireplace before he called her in to see.

"For land sakes!" cried Susan, standing in her gingham apron with her stout red hands on her broad hips. "Are you goin' in for art, Master Reuben?"

"I thought," said Reuben, surprised that he felt no more ill at ease than he did before Susan's stares, "I thought I'd give them to Miss Barrett for her schoolroom, that is, if you think she'd like to have them."

He felt Susan's keen glance upon him and felt also at that moment the quick blood flooding his face and neck.

"Well, I never!" cried Susan again. "I snum, I never did!"

He knew Susan. He knew at once that she was pleased by his gift to Huldah. So was Huldah herself. Reuben sat on in the Barrett sitting-room for an hour with Huldah after he had presented his pictures with explanations of how he thought they might interest her children at school.

"I think it's a wonderful thing to know the world," he said, as he stood again before the pictures now on Huldah's mantel, "and I've often wished I could. But if you can't go to foreign countries, then I think it's a good thing to know the state you live in and a coast like this."

Huldah was direct and frank with Reuben in her delight over his gift. She should choose her favourite she said—she thought it was Petit-Manan, but she would have to sleep on it—and keep it on her desk in her own room there at home. It would help no end when she was correcting examples in cube root, which she thought the worst and most senseless exercise in all Greenleaf's arithmetic.

Now that he had opened the way and had not been repulsed, Reuben spent every Saturday evening with Huldah and saw her home from prayer-meeting on Sunday nights as well. The village began early to accept their keeping company and to talk about it with generous approbation, overlooking even the discrepancy in age. Reuben Crockett had never looked at anyone else in all his life, and now that he had, it was a good thing, might loosen him up a bit and make him more like other folks. As for Huldah, such a woman had not come to Saturday Cove for years, with ideas and standards that were fast slipping in a changing age. She was one in a thousand, and any man who could get *her* might count himself fortunate.

Reuben's entrance into her life was not without difficulties although the difficulties were a hundredfold outweighed by the compensations. Huldah's mother was not by nature a buoyant woman. She harboured, indeed nourished many ills both of the flesh and of the spirit, and she found occasion to speak of them during the hours that Reuben and Huldah spent playing with her the new game of *flinch*. Moreover, she looked warily upon Reuben's invasion of her life with her daughter, a life which she had until now assumed was to be entirely her own. She had a way of making them both uncomfortable in her presence, which resulted, once she was absent, in an extreme sense of comfort one in the other. Long before Reuben had told Huldah that he loved and wanted her, he had told her everything else he had ever thought, known or experienced in twenty-six years. Week by week he poured this flood upon her, unable to resist her interest, sympathy, and understanding in the eager questions and rejoinders by which she led him to talk about himself. Going home at night, walking rapidly in a peculiar sense of both physical and mental freedom, he would sometimes stop suddenly, find himself looking at himself as at another person, and wonder almost with panic in his throat at the things he had told to Huldah, intimate things about his thoughts and beliefs, his loves and aversions, confidences of his pride in his family and of the things he had longed to do and could not because of the changed and changing times, certain deprivations of his childhood which he was only now beginning to realize, old sufferings, new joys.

Huldah was one of the relatively few persons in this world who find life by giving it away, wholly and unequivocally. Upon her and others like her is the gospel paradox built and fulfilled. Whatever she received came flowing back, begotten, born, and nourished by what she had given. She did not have to wait many days for her bread cast upon the waters. She was an example, people said, to the young and undecided at the seasons of revival still held at the turn of the century, of the power of God and His grace in a human heart. This was undoubtedly true, although it was also true that God could not always find such a receptacle for His grace as was Huldah. Nor must Huldah struggle with misgivings for that grace, nor seize upon it like Jacob wrestling with the angel, as is the fate of some upon the long search for God. She had apparently in some mysterious way possessed it from the beginning, pressed down and running over. She loved God, at least partly because superabundant love was natural to her; and thus far in her somewhat circumscribed life, love for Him had not been rendered unnecessary, neglected because of other loves. When Reuben came in Huldah's thirty-first year, the necessity for God was well-established within her. She could not do without Him. With Reuben's entrance into her days and hours and minutes, she found much of her love for him in her love for God, and her love of God in him. But she did not recognize the new and mutual dependence of these loves, one upon the other, and would have been genuinely puzzled at any such suggestion, which in her time and place and by the people whom she knew was never even surmised.

Reuben felt sure that Huldah could not have been surprised when, after he had told her everything else in his world, he got around to telling her of his love. Nor was she. Nor was either of them unduly distressed over the apparent necessity of waiting for each other. They could wait more easily upon the certainty of a few untrammelled hours each week together than they could face the certainty of more trammelled hours with Susan and Huldah's mother to reckon with.

Susan alone presented no problem; it was Huldah's mother who was the stumblingblock. Susan was not drawn toward Mrs.

Barrett. She had small patience with her ailments or her whining nor yet with her possessive attitude toward her daughter. Susan would have "put up" with Mrs. Barrett; she told Master Reuben so every Sunday after 1903; but Reuben knew that Susan's "putting up" would be no flexible process if the four of them ever lost their common sense sufficiently to enter upon life together under one roof. And Reuben himself was frightened of innovations. He wanted his home as Susan had kept it and as Huldah and Susan could keep it together, not as Huldah's mother could and unquestionably would turn it topsy-turvey.

When all the trying realities of the whole matter had been once faced for good and all, as was Reuben's way, he and Huldah entered upon one of those long courtships of which most rural villages in New England and elsewhere bear record. By the time four years had gone by, Saturday Cove had ceased talking about it—the pity that two persons, one of whom was already in advanced years for marriage, could not spend their lives together, the once-persistent query as to whether Reuben Crockett might not do better with the odds so against him to seek elsewhere, the almost certain conjectures that unless time intervened and that hastily, the Crockett name was doomed to cessation with the death of Reuben.

Perhaps, indeed, Saturday Cove had been more anxious over their long-deferred marriage than were either Reuben or Huldah. As for Reuben, the very creation of love in his life was so overwhelming a thing that he could wait more patiently than most for its consummation. He could never become entirely accustomed to the way it heightened perceptions and experiences, forever bringing to shining points what before had been flat surfaces—the birds in spring when he left the house early to rejoin his boat, sure that Huldah would be at her door to say goodbye, the rugged outlines of the coast, his new understanding of the lives of the men with whom he worked, even the blessing of rainy days which seemed to him to halt time and give him a chance to live over his new life in his mind. Now the most concrete and repeated happenings put an edge upon themselves, cutting deeply into the succession of his days, things such as selecting with Huldah the evening hymns for church and, after church was over, staying behind with her to close the wheezy organ, pile the hymn books neatly, turn out the hanging lamps, and see that the old stove was safe.

At Huldah's suggestion Reuben became the new superintendent of the Sunday-school in 1904. He still retained enough of his old life to be surprised at the way he stood before the school, gave out the hymns for Huldah to play, and even made a few remarks of his own about the lesson to be taught in the various classes. These things now in his new freedom seemed natural and easy; and when in church he heard the minister read the morning lesson from the Psalms,

Bring my soul out of prison that I may praise Thy name,

he knew precisely what the words meant and understood that he now had no need to make the prayer.

12

Time as always kept its own counsel; but it was far kinder than anyone had ventured to expect. It was only six years instead of the twelve which the most sanguine had been lotting on when Mrs. Barrett's daily prophecy at length was fulfilled and she died suddenly at only sixty-seven from what she had always considered the least of a score of ailments. Reuben and Huldah waited six months to marry, though no one in Saturday Cove would have had a word to say had they not waited a week. In view of six years, however, six months seemed as nothing.

They were married in the church, largely because they both had a rooted feeling therein, partly because Reuben had a tenacious desire to follow, in so far as it could be managed, the way of those preceding him. The wedding was held late one Saturday afternoon in October after the boys of Huldah's Sunday-school class had swept the woods all the morning for autumn leaves, and at the close of a long day during which Reuben had been declared incapable with many guffaws by the officers and crew of his boat and allowed only to walk about the deck and watch the coast unfold from Rockland to Saturday Cove. All the men of Captain Crockett's boat came to his wedding, from the first officer to the meanest freight-trundler, marching solidly up the aisle, bronzed and shaved and scrubbed in their blue clothes. Huldah said she would always remember them, standing in the left-hand front pews at respectful attention. She had always known in her heart that Reuben's men had a feeling for him, akin to part of her own, and she needed no other proof. They gave Huldah and Reuben a silver soup tureen and a twenty-dollar gold piece and arranged besides for a week's wedding trip for Captain and Mrs. Crockett, fully paid for.

Susan stood by herself in the front pew on the right, her black alpaca freshened up by a gift of white gloves from Master Reuben. Behind her the church was thronged by the village at large. And although Huldah's dark blue mohair had been fashioned by her own fingers and her hat selected from drummers' samples at the local milliner's, although there was not the sign of a reception save that in the church vestibule and on the porch at the close of the service, it is safe to say that no Crockett and his bride, even in the old days, had ever received such manifold good wishes, genuine, superabundant, overflowing.

IV

Silas Crockett, 2nd

1910-1933

Silas Crockett, 2nd

1

During the short year that she lived with Huldah Crockett in the old house Susan was far more a friend than a servant. She loved Huldah as she had loved no one in her seventy-three years save Solace and Master Reuben. Huldah had a way of relying upon Susan which carried with it a kind indisposition to change any of Susan's long-established ways. When she and Reuben had returned from their week in Boston and settled in for their life together, Huldah took instant and careful note of the kitchen and pantry, the manner in which Susan stretched her dishcloth across the bottom of the agate pan, spread her drying-towels in the sun, and stood her scalded milk-pans against the well-curb. Within a day she had ascertained what stood on what shelves and in what order. She learned at what time Susan did certain things, never deviating for so much as a fraction of an hour from her steady course; and she had the sense to see that any suggestion of innovation in time or in method would not only disturb the even tenor of Susan's way, but would strike cruelly at the very roots of Susan's life itself.

Susan did not know how any man could have done better for himself than Master Reuben had done. On nights when she could not sleep because she felt heavy and uncomfortable in her insides, she lay in her bed and thought how well he had done, waiting there in the darkness for the morning, which was sure to hold a new excitement for her. Huldah might want Susan to dictate some new recipes while she wrote them down on some cards, which she was collecting in a wooden box almost precisely like the new-fangled catalogue recently acquired by the Ladies' Social Library. Since Susan knew so well the places of the books she liked that she could put her hands on them in the dark, she could not at first see the slightest sense in the new catalogue, for the purchase of which she had reluctantly given a quarter of a dollar; but once

Huldah had begun to collect recipes in a similar receptacle, arranging her cards under neat letters, C for cakes, P for pies, and M for muffins, Susan found herself, when she went for her books on Saturday, congratulating the librarian on being up-to-date. Huldah might want her skeins of wool held for winding or even offer to hold Susan's for her; she might have dropped a stitch in her knitting and want Susan to pick it up for her; she might want Susan to help her spread a pattern on the dining-room table, pinning it carefully to the cloth and figuring out the most economical way of cutting. Or she might at ten o'clock, when Susan invariably sat down by the window in the kitchen for a free hour before eleven o'clock and should start the dinner, come to ask Susan's advice about soliciting for a church supper or to find out exactly what she thought as to the wisdom of proposing to the Methodists a joint Christmas social. Or, once dinner was over and the afternoon was ahead, she might even suggest that Susan bring her sewing to the sitting-room.

Susan took Huldah one morning to the Crockett attic where sea-chests filled with log-books, trunks filled with clothes, and an old table piled with the plans of Thomas Winship's meeting-houses stood in order among numberless odds and ends of everything under the sun beneath the brown, unfinished beams and rafters. They went through them together so that Huldah might know precisely what was there and, in so far as Susan knew, what the things meant and to whom they had belonged. There were many things that Susan knew nothing at all about, things which Solace Crockett had never shown her. There was in one trunk what had quite apparently been a wedding outfit of white muslin and satin, merino and leghorn, gown and hat, cape and shoes.

"Muslin keeps like nothin' at all," Susan had said, showing Huldah the ravelled slits in the creases of the shirred and puffed sleeves.

There were shawls in another trunk, well wrapped in camphor and old newspapers twenty years back. They were beautiful shawls, obviously of some foreign make with tails of dragons and strange birds forming their coloured fringe, one shawl in dull blue, two in black. Solace Crockett had once imagined them placed on exhibition in the old Winship house.

"These must have been taken out not so long ago an' done up fresh," said Susan. "The papers say only 1889, but for the life o' me I can't call to mind when 'twas. I'm sure I never saw them before. But there, old Mis' Crockett was forever putterin' round up here, spite o' me. They're likely enough hers, or maybe they go farther back. Wool's not like muslin, an' these seem sound except for thinnin' a bit in the folds. Yes, it's likely they belonged to Solace Crockett in the days when her husband sailed the seas an' her herself for that matter."

"Solace is a lovely name," said Huldah, fingering the blue shawl.

Susan agreed with her.

"It's better than some they have nowadays, an' that's a fact," she said. "Gladys an' Sylvia, an' such like. An' in this case the name fitted. Mis' Solace Crockett couldn't ha' been a better woman. I used to often tell Master Reuben that whatever he lacked in a mother, or in a father for that matter, was made up to him in her."

"What was Reuben's great-grandmother's name on the Crockett side? I don't think I've ever heard him say. He talks about the men of the family, but except for his grandmother he doesn't say much about the women."

"Men don't," said Susan. "Now what was her name? I snum I've forgotten, though Lord knows I knew, same as gospel. She was old when I come to this village. She outlived Master Reuben's grandfather who was a fine set-up man. I remember him well. Ah, now I mind. 'Twas Abigail. That's what 'twas, but it's about as far back as I can remember, bein' more or less a stranger here till I was past twenty-five myself."

"That's a good name, too. Abigail."

"Well, it's not so fluttery as some, an' it comes from the Bible somewhere, don't it? At the minute I can't say where."

"Abigail?" said Huldah reflectively. "Why, yes, Susan. She was the one that got a lunch for King David when her husband Nabal had refused him."

Susan was refolding the shawls in fresh papers.

"That don't surprise me a mite," she observed. "Women are always feedin' men folks, in those old days as now."

It was a good, warm feeling, Susan thought, to find oneself thus necessary to another and younger woman, quite different from the way in which women felt themselves necessary to men. Men, thought Susan, trying to straighten it out in her own mind, expected women to do things for them, took them and their work for granted without so much as even realizing the extent of their labour and sacrifice. They could not help it; it was the way there were made, God help them! It was a new and thrilling experience for Susan to feel herself of value to Huldah, to know that she was understood and appreciated. She and Huldah within even a few months grew to have little secrets between them, women's secrets from which even Reuben was shut out. Sometimes the secrets had to do with Reuben himself. For instance, Susan and Huldah decided that Reuben was eating far too much pastry for his own good. Susan had been just on the point of proposing a change in desserts herself, she said, when Huldah consulted her about the matter; cup custards, Spanish cream, and baked Indian pudding were far more wholesome as occasional variants from the apple pie, which by some whim of Providence had seemingly been created principally for men; and they laid their plans straightway for the food which should be set before the unsuspecting Reuben on Sundays and on his nights at home.

Susan took untold comfort, not only in Huldah's prime housekeeping but in the knowledge that she thought and felt as

Susan did about most things. Young as Huldah was, and she seemed young to Susan, she had her feet firmly planted and moving in the right way. She was not misled or bamboozled, said Susan, into thinking that all the new rinktums now coming into this world would make folks happier or better. When Reuben in a reckless moment proposed having a telephone installed from the wires on the main road and Susan was wondering how she could ever endure the sudden, unexpected ringing of a bell through the house, it was Huldah who, with a quick glance at Susan's face, said it was not only unnecessary but useless. Huldah felt precisely as Susan did about the automobiles which were beginning to penetrate the coast, coming even to Saturday Cove. They frightened her to death, she protested. There was no pleasure in driving any more along the country roads when you were in constant terror lest the brow of a quiet hill should suddenly beetle with a great black object chugging toward one and emitting a vile smell. It had gotten so that you could not depend upon even an afternoon's drive without the probability of meeting one at least; in fact, you must drive with your left hand, keeping your right unimpaired and ready to wave it violently as a signal for the driver of the automobile to jam his unwieldy brakes and stop his treacherous vehicle before your horse should bound in frenzy into the wayside ditch. Huldah agreed with Susan, too, about the enormity of charging fifteen cents for a church supper of beans and brown bread which had heretofore always been free as salvation.

"It's an outrage!" cried Susan, chopping the vegetable hash with fury in her wooden chopping tray. "That's what it is, an' mark my words, no good will come of it. An' with the solicitin' just the same. You can't ask folks to stir up cakes an' finger pastry out o' their own pockets an' then expect 'em to hand over fifteen cents for what they're puttin' in their own insides. Used to be that church suppers was one big family with folks gatherin' in the vestry, all feelin' friendly an' to home. Now it's so everybody can come, Methodists an' heathen alike, an' there ain't the feelin' there used to be. Money's the root of all evil, as the Bible well says, an' the search for it'll be the ruination of the church, if you ask me."

Susan went to the village now only on alternate Saturday afternoons. She looked forward to these excursions largely because she knew that Huldah would lend a listening and sympathetic ear upon her return. The village, she said, was not what it once was. In summer it was messed up with people who didn't belong to it, who sat languidly in surreys driven by black men in livery, and who crowded common folks out of their way at the post-office window and in the village; in the winter it was filled with those that had nothing to do but speculate about their neighbours and listen to talking-machines which the whole world was going mad over.

Susan's moral character in the winter of 1909 through no fault of her own suffered deterioration, not to say debasement from one of these devices for the promulgation of unworthy thoughts. She had entered the dry goods store, she told Huldah, for the innocent purchase of hooks and eyes and a spool of white thread, number 50, when, having to await her turn, her ears had been assailed by a song, the like of which she had never heard before and prayed God fervently she might never hear again. The phonograph was sounding its blatant voice in a room at the rear and was obviously delighting some young listeners if one could judge from the squeals of laughter sounding even through the closed door. Susan had stood as though frozen to the spot, unable from very disgust to leave the place until she had heard the worst. The words, she told Huldah upon her return home, had lodged themselves in her mind for good and all, repugnant as they were to her, and the unwelcome tune kept running in her head. She had even found herself singing the cheap and horrid song as she ascended the hill:

Will someone kindly tell me?
Will someone answer why?
To me it is a riddle,
And it will be till I die.
A million peaches round me,
And I should like to know
Why I picked a lemon in the garden of love
Where they say only peaches grow?

If such things could lodge themselves thus securely in her old mind, asked Susan of Huldah, what effect must they have upon the young? Not that for one moment she was suggesting that love songs did not have their place, but why wallow in such unrefined music and thought and language when there were still to be sung, "When You and I Were Young, Maggie," or "Wild Roved an Indian Girl, Bright Alfarata."

Susan worried about the young in other ways, also; at least she took pleasure in dislodging her anxiety concerning them. She heard from all sides, she said, that the academy had fallen a prey to new ways and ideas. Not that the people who told her seemed overly concerned, but as for Susan herself she believed that the old had a responsibility toward the young. She understood, she told Huldah, that the scholars in the academy were rebelling against the studies they had always taken as a matter of course in Master Reuben's day and in his father's. Many of them did not want Greek and Latin any more or debating or reciting orations and poems on Friday afternoons, practices which, Susan had always assumed, were the mark of young ladies and gentlemen bent on making something of themselves in a world that sorely needed them. They were even tiring of spelling-bees. Instead they were wasting their time on publishing a school magazine, and even the girls were tearing about in indecent clothes at a new game called basket-ball. Taffy-pulls had quite gone by and playing games at one another's homes until ten o'clock on Saturday evenings as had been the order in Master Reuben's time. In place of these they danced until midnight in the village hall at least once every month with few to raise so much as an eyebrow at such goings-on. As a result, which anyone with any sense might see, human nature being what it was, there were things happening even to nice young girls which had never happened in her day, say what anyone would. Susan guessed she knew her own time and how decent young folks had always acted. She hinted these things darkly to Huldah as they sat over their sewing on Reuben's nights away; and Huldah at her side of the center-table beneath the lamp, even while she herself hoped that Reuben was remembering his winter underwear and taking care of his cold, knew that Susan was deeply enjoying her forebodings and the reception of them in a friendly ear.

There was something both satisfying and touching to Huldah as well as to Reuben in Susan's complete happiness with them. She took delight, they knew, in her condemnations and prophecies, finding ease in her uneasiness, tranquillity in her agitation. Times might be changing and, perhaps, for the worse, but Susan's days were fulfilling themselves and her care and labour receiving its just reward. And when in the late spring of 1910 she learned that a child was coming to Huldah and Reuben and that her hands were needed to make ready for it, her ways became more than ever the ways of pleasantness and her paths those of peace.

Nor did she worry overmuch about Huldah as she might well have done. To Susan the very contentment of Reuben and Huldah was proof against misfortune and disaster. They lived in such mutual dependence, received each day with such quiet pleasure in its beginning and middle and end, so clearly were asking for nothing of life except life itself, that Susan found herself also taking small thought for their morrow.

She never saw the baby. She died quietly one August afternoon when she had been out in the hot sun picking blackberries for a Sunday night supper. Huldah found her in her chair by the kitchen table, leaning over heavily upon it, her face and even her body strangely twisted out of shape. She ran to look for someone to send for the doctor and met Reuben coming up the driveway from the steamboat wharf. Susan was almost gone when they reached the kitchen. She could hardly speak, but they gathered that she would have told them something had she been able about someone named Joshua and about the baby.

"I'm trying to figure out about this Joshua," said Reuben in his slow way when Huldah came to sit beside him that evening on the porch. "I don't remember of her ever mentioning him before, and I'm sure her brothers weren't named that. I hate to think that there's anything she wanted done that we can't do. She's done so much for me all my life."

The August evening was cool and still with an early reminder of autumn in its shortened twilight and its clear, high stars. The windless air quavered with the hum of crickets and katydids, not as sometimes in a shrill, uninterrupted resonance but rather in high, monotonous tones that doubled back upon themselves, not separated and yet separable like the steady and yet intermittent pulsation of small, sharp saws pushed to and fro in wood.

"They say," observed Reuben, drawing his chair closer to Huldah's and taking her hand in his, "they say that when the crickets sing that way, not steady like, it means an early and a cold winter."

She returned the pressure of his hand.

"I don't care," she said, "early and cold, late and warm, it doesn't matter. Weather never matters now, dear, except for you, and I don't believe you mind either. Nothing matters except us together and all we have. I can't even be sorry about Susan. I'm glad. It's just as it ought to be. I like to think of her lying in there with all the house neat and tidy the way she liked it. She said just this morning when she'd finished the parlour, 'Well, it's done now for another week, ready for a wedding or a funeral or whatever else the good Lord sees fit to send us.' I can't help thinking He sent exactly what He wanted, and if that's so, then we can't do anything else but take it and be glad."

It was Huldah who an hour afterward thought of the Family Bible. She told Reuben later that she remembered Susan's peering into it from time to time and looking ill at ease when she was discovered. When they had taken it from the shelf beneath the table in the front parlour, they found Susan's money in a sealed white envelope which had obviously been changed from month to month. There were five hundred dollars in large bills within the envelope. Now that they had found it, lying against the words of the Lord to the son of Nun, words encouraging him to be strong and of a good courage and promising him rest from his labours, they understood to whom Susan in her last months upon this earth had wished it to be given.

2

Whether or not the crickets and katydids kept some infinitesimal finger on the pulse-beats of the cosmos and knew what they knew, the winter that year came early. After sharp October rains the leaves lost their unattained glory and fell in premature millions before high bitter winds. Huldah grew accustomed to sullen November skies long before November had come and Reuben to reaches of sullen, indifferent water. Early frosts denied the marigolds their last tenacious blooming, bright against their fading green in the bare garden.

True to her assertion, Huldah was careless of the weather. She always felt surprised when upon walking to the village she heard people complaining about it, and more surprised when it was borne in upon her that most of their irritation over it was because of her. They kept thinking of her, they told her, alone so much of the time in that great house way off there and in a condition where she might well be more upset than at other times. Some of them said there was not a night when Reuben was lying over in Rockland that they did not look for her light, glowing out there beyond the fields, before they went to bed.

When they said these things, even before she could thank them for their concern, she felt the almost pathetic unreality of their solicitude, a reality, of course, to them, to her in the new completeness of her life, unsubstantial, without foundation or form. Their worry, to which she could give no harbourage or even welcome, went fluttering through some void, dissolving at last into air. The thoughts which they sent to her at night, when they turned down their lamp wicks and stared through their darkened panes toward the old Crockett house, were like tiny pebbles thrown against her window, repulsed, powerless to arouse her from the deep, all-embracing security in which she lived. She rejoiced in the short days. Callers were not so likely to come when lamps must be lighted early, for, once a lamp was lighted, people began to think of supper though it was nearly two hours off.

In the evenings when Reuben was not at home she thought of him, inexhaustible hours of thinking above her sewing or knitting in the front parlour where she had taken to sitting on the nights when she was alone. She liked it there. She felt as though she were slowly becoming acquainted with the Crockett men, knowing Reuben through them and them through Reuben. Sometimes she had the odd sensation there in the parlour of their patronizing her a bit in that she came from more simple beginnings and had seen relatively nothing of the world which they had known so intimately. She felt half-relieved that there were no portraits on the walls of their wives. These she studied from daguerreotypes on the what-not and from pictures in the album where from their very position on her lap they made her feel less humble. She tried in vain to discover Reuben's features in the portraits looking so steadily at her. He did not look like his ancestors; except for his eyes she could not trace a similar lineament; and even his eyes lacked the spark and the humour of those of Amos and Benjamin and James. They were handsomer men than Reuben, that she must unwillingly admit, loving him all the more because he did not have their obvious masterfulness, urbanity, and charm. Nevertheless, she doubted if they had had many of the things that satisfied her most in him. Reuben rarely spoke of his mother, whom she had never seen, and she doubted also if he favoured her and her family. All in all, she concluded, Reuben had been specially made with his own special ways and virtues; and he did not need either voyages to China and Australia to bring them out or a portrait painter in London or New York to record them.

She could not get enough of thinking about Reuben. Sometimes she reproved herself for not reading more, keeping up with things, she thought, in the papers and magazines which she could easily get from the library. But now that the baby was but two months away, thinking about extraneous and irrelevant things was somehow difficult. Even though she read infrequently about profound matters like Canadian Reciprocity and the protective tariff, about strange ideas termed the initiative and referendum and recall, about the unrest in Russia where the common people seemed to think they were not getting their rights, such information was always eluding her or she eluding it. Before Reuben had come into her life, she would have grown pale with horrified indignation over the undignified and unprecedented goings-on of certain women who were actually trumping up absurd reasons why they and the others of their sex should have a vote like men. Neither such disgusting behaviour nor such cataclysmic demands now sat heavily upon her. Indeed, she could not seem to hold any of these things before her mind, try as she sometimes did. It was far easier and more satisfying to think of Reuben or perhaps not so much to think about him as to know the certainty of his love, to sit within the enfolding security of his presence.

On the days when he was due at home there was always the long making ready for his coming: the careful setting to rights of the house; the surprises for him in the morning baking; the fresh laying of the table for supper with the exciting question as to which china to choose from the wealth in the old cupboard; the scrutiny of her work-basket so that it might not occasion hunting for this and that when he was once in his chair and wanted her in hers; the concentrated watching for his boat when three o'clock drew near. First, the brown smoke staining the distant horizon, then the indistinct mound of grayish-white as though the sky itself had suddenly protruded just above the sea, the change from solidity and thickness to length and width, the slow taking shape of prow and pilot-house and smokestack, and at last the clear outlines of the boat, cutting the gray water below the brooding sky and the circling gulls.

Their evenings wanted for nothing. Even their desultory talk of unimportant things, the wind kicking up Fox Island thoroughfare, the new ways Huldah had found of disguising the taste of the milk which she hated, added to their sense of bounteous life, intact, inviolable, at last fulfilled. When the day had been long and cold with a high wind blowing up his nostrils, he told Huldah, and beating out his very breath, Reuben took pleasure in falling asleep in his chair at eight o'clock. Huldah smiled at him sitting there, his hands folded across his blue vest, his head, which was beginning to show gray about his temples, young though he was, slipping toward one side of the chair-back. Sometimes she took a few winks with him. In these last weeks her body had grown firm and hard. She seemed to herself compact and entire, holding everything within herself, sleeping and waking, food and work, love and gratitude, so that when sleep conquered, it did not fall upon her as it had always before fallen, but rather took possession of her from within, she yielding willingly to its sovereignty.

They always had a lunch at half-past nine. Huldah arranged a tray in the kitchen with a pot of tea and sandwiches. She used her favourite old cups from the cupboard in the dining-room. They were thin cups, almost transparent, white with tiny sprigs of palest green. They must be very old, she thought, but Reuben could not remember that his grandmother had ever said to whom they belonged before they came to her. The saucers still held traces of some foreign markings. Huldah liked using them and the tea-pot that went with them. She always used also one of the best linen tray-cloths which were in the house when she came; and when she had everything ready to take to the sitting-room, she picked a geranium blossom, with one green leaf to set it off, or a spray of oxalis and laid it on the tray. It looked bright lying there with the frail old china; it signified a special occasion; and Reuben never failed to notice it with appreciation and sometimes to say that no one but Huldah would ever think of placing it there.

Reuben always put an extra stick or two on the fire while Huldah was fixing the tray. In his spare hours he had been trimming and cutting away some of the useless limbs of the old apple trees. Dried well in the shed, they made an excellent blaze, flames which were often different in colour from those given forth by other wood—like the colour of rare November sunsets when after a dull and cloudy day the sun goes down in a clear green sky.

This evening lunch hour was a time for more desultory conversation or for none at all. Refreshed by their naps, they ate their sandwiches, drank their steaming cups of tea, and watched the fire. Reuben said now and then, neither minding that he had said it before,

"It's queer about apple wood—the hiss it has though it's dry all right."

And Huldah,

"It's got a smell, too, when you first put it on, almost like summer apples or the new leaves in the spring."

The drawn shades, the warm room, the light from lamp and fire shut them in in measureless content. Soon they would bank the fire in the kitchen stove, place the screen about that in the sitting-room, and go together up the long staircase to rest and sleep in the great front room facing the sea where others had loved and slept before them.

"Nights like this," Huldah often said, "I'm more glad than ever that we waited, Reuben. It couldn't have been so perfect if we'd hurried things and made other folks uncomfortable and ourselves in the bargain."

"That's right," Reuben answered, taking his last sandwich with a shade of regret that it was his last. "I always think a lot of trouble in this world comes from wanting to hurry up things before they're good and ready to happen."

3

Huldah Crockett was a religious woman, by nature, training, and practice. Which of these elements, now tenaciously established within her, was chiefly responsible for her feelings, her thoughts, and her behaviour, it would be difficult to determine even with the help of modern psychological research and discovery. There have been, and still are, countless thousands like her who daily and quite unconsciously give a stout and wholesome lie to the reputed fundamentals of New England Puritanism. Whatever were the imperfections of the inflexible thought of Massachusetts Bay in the seventeenth and early eighteenth centuries (and they were doubtless numerous) its heritage has unquestionably caused many a waste place to blossom and numberless minds and spirits to rejoice, if not in the Lord, then surely in those to whom the Lord has ministered in His ways past finding out.

Huldah rejoiced in the Lord, quietly, constantly, effectually. She loved Him, believed that she knew Him or at least was no stranger to His mercies, lived by Him. Whatever had been her contribution, before her marriage, to that spiritual reservoir which causes springs to flow in many a Valley of Baca, it was increased rather than diminished when she had joined her life to Reuben's. Reuben in Huldah's uncluttered mind was, naturally enough, the crowning proof of the loving-kindness of God, satisfying her longing soul and filling her hungry soul with good. What then, she asked herself, should she render unto God for His mercies? And her reply, translated into both thought and action, left little to be desired by those among whom she lived.

She was no zealot, having too much both of humour and common sense to want to run the lives and thought of others. The "goodly matter," with which her heart like the hearts of the sons of Korah overflowed, she kept to herself in so far as words were concerned. But since like them she honestly loved righteousness and hated wickedness, she had like them been vouchsafed an extra anointing with the oil of gladness.

She read her Bible daily, knowing by heart most of the New Testament, of the Psalms and Isaiah. This habit, begun as a pious duty enjoined upon children by parents and preachers alike in the eighteen-eighties, had become through years of practice a pleasant necessity, which she felt as binding upon her as the necessity for keeping her kitchen stove well supplied with fuel. She believed in its words and precepts, not merely as a guide to life but rather as the voice of God; and she took herself strictly to task whenever she felt that she had failed to live up to them. The Old Testament she read with sufficient humour to lighten its occasional darkness; the New she accepted simply and implicitly largely because her years of devout living by it had rendered unnecessary her understanding of it. Perhaps, indeed, although she had never heard of him, she was all unconsciously a disciple of Saint Anselm whose *Credo ut intelligam* has been the fountain of knowledge and the impregnable rock of faith to many spiritual minds of all creeds and in all ages.

She had certain unshakable convictions and lived by them. In this she was faithful to the highest inheritance of the best in Puritanism. She believed that in the love of God and of one's neighbour lay the secret to that abundant life which the Lord had come to give all people. Like the prophet Micah she held that men and women were not only admonished but required to do justly and to love mercy and to walk humbly. She held also that, unlike Micah, she and all others who would lay hold upon it had a new and more acceptable means of grace. She relied firmly and without question upon the gospel promises. When she read, *Ask and it shall be given you*, she never thought of doubting its truth any more than she thought of dictating the nature of its answer. She never doubted that all things, food and drink and clothing, would be added unto one who sought first the kingdom of God and His righteousness; and yet even while she sought both, she was not one to neglect her own share of the responsibility which the Lord, supplemented by the Apostle Paul, had made clear enough in a dozen places in her well-marked Testament.

In her the "old-time religion" was amply, in fact nobly, justified by its fruits. If the tenets and doctrines to which she unquestioningly gave her adherence can be torn from their high places by those who must know before they can believe, or swept out of sight by the searchlights of the new learning, at least the consequences of a faith such as hers remain inviolable, in themselves a truth of unassailable value whatever may be said or thought of its origin—the shadow of a great rock in a weary land. She was, in short, the kind of woman whose sons and daughters, themselves adrift on a wide sea of skepticism and unbelief, look upon with admiration and gratitude, knowing full well that whatever fastness they may build for themselves out of intellectual honesty can present no greater security or no richer resources than that which they have at least seen reared upon other and older foundations.

She had need of her faith and of her conviction that all things work together for good to those that love God when late December brought her son into the world. Both she and Reuben, protected from the thought of disaster by their happiness and by her perfect health during her carrying of the child, were ill-prepared for trouble. The doctor had been sure that everything was well, and the nurse, who had been on watchful duty a week in advance, had never seen a less perturbed patient.

The premature winter, Reuben said, was playing into the hands of them all. The harbour closed in early for the first time in years, a thin film making itself apparent before the first two weeks of December had spent themselves, increasing to ice under the bitter cold, ice so thick that even a windy tide could not crack it into bits. The cold held, summarily tying up the *Searsport* at the open Rockland pier and giving Reuben the chance to stay at home in the expectant, eager house.

Now he could enjoy his waiting, their quiet, unperturbed evenings, their bedtime lunches, and their long nights of sleep. His Shaw inheritance, at least on the female side, stood him in good stead. He was not bounding about the house like a Crockett, anxious to hurry things along, bristling with impatience and unwelcome advice. He could do the chores himself, going slowly and deliberately about his work in the morning and at night, filling Huldah's woodboxes, splitting her kindling, doing the milking with his lantern hung on the crooked nail which he had driven for Seth Tucker when he was a little boy. He liked the tingling air of the December mornings, the clear, cold skies, the swift fall of darkness. One day he took his axe and went to the woods beyond the marshes for a Christmas tree. He was foolish enough also to cut a tiny one for the baby, bringing it home in his hand with the larger on his shoulder. It was a perfect little tree, hardly two feet in height, and he made a standard for it in the kitchen with Huldah's shining eyes watching him.

He said as he worked:

"It's amazing, Huldah, how the firs and spruces are taking possession of all the headlands and the shore where they say the docks and curing-sheds were forty and fifty years back. Seems as though they grow up over night. When the baby's grown to half my age, this coast's going to be nothing but rocks and trees. I notice it, too, as I go along the shores day by day. My grandfather wouldn't know the place if he could see it, or my father either. Trees and summer visitors own this coast now and that's a fact. They're nice though, all standing quiet in the snow. There were a lot of blue jays squawking about. I wished all the time I'd had you with me this morning."

When the little tree was standing straight and firm on a white-covered table by the window and the big one was placed in the corner, and he and Huldah were beginning to string popcorn and cranberries in long ropes for decoration, he said, smiling at her:

"They say there's no fools like old fools. They always say it as though it shouldn't be, but I think myself it's just right."

She thought so, too, he knew as she went about trailing the popcorn ropes among the fragrant dark green boughs. She placed the white candles he had brought from Rockland on their tips so that there should be no danger from fire once they were lighted on Christmas Eve. The nurse, who had just come, watched them now and then from the doorway or from a corner of the room. She was a gaunt, middle-aged woman, practical and able, not too sanguine about life in general. She had helped to bring scores of babies into this world during her years about the countryside. She had brought them to homes that neither wanted nor could afford them, to merely tolerant families and to those who took them as a matter of course. She had never seen a household precisely like this one; in fact, she said to herself, she was in danger of becoming plain soft about these two folks if she didn't look out.

Huldah made a star from some silver paper she had and fastened it securely at the top of the baby's tree.

"It's such a little thing," she said, "that I don't think it should have any other decoration but the star and maybe one candle on the very front here."

Reuben thought that way, too.

4

The baby came on Christmas Eve just at the appropriate time to see his own tree, although he was as little concerned with it as those about him were concerned at the moment with him. In their indifference he was quite unconsciously as his first experience sharing that of a great-uncle of his born in the mid-Atlantic in June of 1831. He could scream, however, and he did.

It was Huldah about whom everybody was concerned. Things had not gone well with her from the night before when her pains had begun. All day long Reuben had sat by her bed, which had been moved downstairs and into the warm sitting-room with the Christmas trees. Now in the early evening he was still sitting there.

Logs blazed in the great fireplace, and Reuben sat much as he had sat by his grandmother when he was fourteen, forward in his chair, his hands folded between his knees, looking steadily at Huldah, who most of the time did not know at all that he was there.

Sometimes when the doctor and the nurse grew impatient with Reuben or found him in the way of things they had to do, they sent him out of the room. He obeyed them. It was not like Reuben to make a fuss, and anyway he was too dazed to remonstrate. Once they sent him to the telephone, which he had had installed so that he could call up Huldah on his Rockland nights to be sure that she was safe and well. They sent him now to call another doctor, who was to take the early train from Bangor unless in the meantime they told him otherwise. They hoped that Reuben would take a long time over telephoning and, as a matter of fact, he did. Twice they sent him out-of-doors, to get the air, the doctor said.

Reuben went out-of-doors unmindful of the cold. It was a perfect Christmas Eve. The deep snow lay everywhere, over the fields and meadows and marshes, over the reaches of the frozen sea, upon the ridges and hills toward the north. The stars were high and bright. The first time they sent him out the village lights were twinkling in all the houses. There were lights in the church, too, where they were about to have the Christmas concert with someone besides Reuben to call upon the children for their songs and pieces and someone besides Huldah to see that everything went as it should.

The second time he went out, the church was dark and still, and most of the village lights were gone. The wind had risen, and some low-lying clouds looked like more snow, cold though it was. He walked to and fro along the path to the barn, back and forward, forward and back. The packed snow creaked beneath his heels, and there was no other sound at all except that of the wind in the bare trees and of the naked vines slatting against the house.

When he had stayed out quite some time, Reuben went in through the back door to the kitchen. It was warm there, and on the kitchen table in a well-lined basket lay his son. He had been bathed but not dressed. He was wrapped in blankets and was squirming about within them. When Reuben drew aside the blankets and looked at him, he opened his eyes so suddenly that his father was startled. He was a long baby, Reuben saw, but he did not see much else, although he stood by him for fully ten minutes before he went again into the sitting-room. He even forgot that the baby was really a person with a name. Months ago they had named him Silas for his great-grandfather.

Just after midnight Silas Crockett, 2nd, was dressed for the first time in his life. One of the village women, who had come from the church concert and who had had six children of her own, dressed him. She was a friend of Huldah. Reuben, whom the doctor had again banished, watched his clothes put on him one by one. He sat quietly in a corner by the kitchen cupboard, but he could see each thing as the woman put it on, his tiny shirt, his petticoat, his slip with blue ribbons at the neck and sleeves. He seemed a little thing to wear clothes, Reuben thought. The woman who dressed him kept telling Reuben over and over what a fine baby he was.

"He's got a splendid head," she said. "And such lots of hair. I never saw such hair, and curly, too, I'll be bound. Did you have hair like that when you were born?"

Reuben did not answer her, for just then the doctor appeared in the doorway and beckoned to him. He followed the doctor into the sitting-room. He heard the doctor say:

"Things are looking up a bit in here. She's asleep now. When she wakes, I think we might even show her the baby. Why don't you stay out there and pay some attention to your son?"

Reuben went back then and answered the woman. No, he said, he did not think he had had any hair at all when he was born.

"Don't you want to hold the baby?" asked the woman.

"I might, at that," said Reuben.

When he had taken the baby in his arms, things seemed once more to come to life, the fire crackling in the kitchen stove, the baby's extra blankets airing on the clothes-horse by the fire, the outlines of the frost on the black window-panes, the steady ticking of the kitchen clock. The woman, once she had seen that Reuben had his son, took out her knitting and sat in Susan's old chair by the kitchen table.

Young Silas was sound asleep on Reuben's knees. His fists were folded tightly against the ruffles at his neck. His father could not have told that he was breathing had it not been for the beating of one tiny spot at the top of his head where his hair was thinnest. Yet he felt warm within his blankets, a warmth that penetrated through Reuben's thick clothes and made him suddenly comfortable there in the kitchen in Abigail Crockett's low old chair. There was a smell about him that Reuben had never smelled before, the smell of something new like spring, like warm April rain.

When the clock struck one, Reuben placed him carefully in his basket and without speaking to the woman, carried him into the sitting-room where the doctor and the nurse sat by Huldah. He put the basket as carefully on the floor by the fire. Then he lighted the one candle on the little tree and stood beside it while it burned.

He had suddenly thought he would like to tell young Silas later that he had had a Christmas tree all his own.

5

Christmas Day was well advanced along its slow, snowy course when Huldah saw the baby. She said she thought he was beautiful, and she smiled steadily at Reuben before she went to sleep again.

None of the doctors whom Reuben summoned from the larger towns knew exactly what had gone wrong with Huldah, but they knew something had, and they held endless conversations about it in the front parlour where Reuben kept a fire burning out of respect for them and their superior knowledge. She never walked again, though after a few weeks Reuben lifted her into a big chair which he had bought, with broad arms and wide pockets protruding from them where she could keep her sewing.

Young Silas in his earliest years grew so accustomed to seeing his mother in this chair and his father carrying her from her bed to it and back again, through the house on occasion, into the garden in summer, and sometimes even up and down the stairs, that when he began to play with other children he experienced a sense of surprise that their mothers could walk about, knead their own bread, and hang their Monday washing to their clotheslines. He was a lively child, and he grew fabulously, his father thought. The first day of every month, as soon as he could walk about, his father measured him against the sitting-room wall while his mother watched. He placed a ruler on the exact crown of Silas' head, moved it slowly back against the wall, and made a black mark there with a red pencil, which with the ruler was always kept for the explicit purpose on the end of the mantelpiece. Sometimes the mark was just the same, much to Silas' disappointment; again it had moved up the slightest fraction of an inch; and it kept on moving through the years until there was a tiny black ladder going up the wall.

"I don't see how we're ever going to paper this room again without breaking Silas' heart," his mother would say as he grew older.

He did not know so long as he was little that there was another reason against fresh paint and paper other than just his broken heart.

There was a woman named Sarah in the kitchen who did the work and looked out for his wants, bathed and dressed him, and kept a cookie-jar for him and his friends. Silas liked her; but there were many provinces in which she played no part nor for a moment expected to enter. She never gave him permissions or mended his clothes, heard his prayers or read to him. His mother did all these things, only turning over the permissions to his father whenever he was at home. Except for always sitting in a chair instead of moving about, his mother did all the things which, he grew up believing, boys' mothers always did. When he was only four, she taught him his letters, he sitting on a low stool at her feet, and at last to read by putting the letters that belonged to the anagram game into words and then with great excitement finding them in his father's old primer. She made him willing to eat whatever was on his plate by telling him about the starving Belgians and how glad they would be to have his oatmeal and milk and even his potato and cod-liver oil.

She got him off to school every morning, saw that his hands were clean and his hair brushed, heard him say his spelling-lesson over and over until there was not the slightest chance of his missing catchy words like *believe* and *obedient* and *misled*, made sure that he had a clean handkerchief and that he distinctly understood he was to come home immediately from school to report his presence and receive further permissions. She taught him rhymes about his grammar lesson, which made it more clear. One of these she had learned in school when she was a little girl:

> Three little words you sometimes see
> Are articles, *a*, *an*, and *the*.
> A noun's the name of anything,
> Like *ship* or *sailor*, *ball* or *swing*.

Adjectives tell the kind of noun,
As *great, small, pretty, blue*, or *brown*
Instead of nouns the pronouns stand,
Her head, *his* face, *your* arm, *my* hand.

She read to him for hours on rainy afternoons and every evening before he went to bed. He lay on the worn rug before the fire with his head propped up between his hands and listened to *Robin Hood* and *King Arthur, Twenty Thousand Leagues under the Sea*, and some old books upstairs that had belonged to his grandfather—books that were falling in pieces, that they pasted together and made new covers for—*Two Years before the Mast* and *Mr. Midshipman Easy*. When his father was at home, as he was every other night, he listened, too; and although he sometimes fell asleep in the most exciting parts, he seemed to be enjoying himself there with his pipe on the other side of the fireplace.

On every pay-day, which was usually the measuring day as well, his father brought him home a new book until by the time he was ten he had four full rows of them in the little book-case which his father made and which stood by his bed in his room upstairs.

"You really shouldn't do it, Reuben," his mother sometimes said. "He has so many already, and there's the library, you know."

His father was slow about answering, and he always said much the same thing.

"I like him to have books. There'll be a lot of things he can't have as he gets older."

He began to know about the things once he was ten. Not that he ever heard his father and mother talking directly about them, but they were borne in upon him in various ways. He began to realize that, beautiful as the old house was, it needed money, which they did not have, for repairs. Once when he was waiting early to walk with his father to the steamboat wharf, he heard him talking to some men who had come to work upon the roof.

"Do as little as you can," he said to the workmen. "Maybe next year we can make a decent job of it."

He knew from his father's voice that it hurt him to say the words, and he felt suddenly sorry as they went hand in hand down the driveway hill.

He saw Sarah sponging and pressing his father's captain's suit, using wet cloths, which the hot iron hissed upon and sent up clouds of steam, and then holding the coat and the trousers up to the light to see if the shine was still there. He saw his mother spending hours in turning the frayed collars of his blouses and setting fine patches in the knees and seat of his school trousers. More than once she said to him:

"Can't you be a bit more careful of your shoes, dear? Not scuff them quite so hard? New shoes cost money, you know."

The books stopped coming after he was eleven. They never mentioned the matter, but there were no new books after that year. Once when he was twelve and had been longing, too outspokenly perhaps, for a new sled with a ship painted on it, he caught the same hurt look on his father's face that he had caught when he had spoken to the workmen. When Christmas and his birthday came, two days in one, he found his old cape-racer with a new coat of fresh red paint and a new rope upon it. He said he liked it fine, that it could beat any other sled in Saturday Cove; but secretly he felt a bit ashamed when on Christmas afternoon he drew it over the crusty snow to meet his friends who were coasting in the fields.

Still for the most part he did not mind much. He knew he lived in the nicest house in Saturday Cove, except for those of the summer people. Much as it needed tending to, it was still the nicest. Moreover, it was a house to which his friends liked to come. They always took their caps off instantly they entered the door, and they spoke far more politely to his mother in her chair than they did to their own mothers, bustling about their own homes. His mother played with the boys, too. They got together all his toys and games and brought a low table which his father had made and which fastened to the arms of her chair. She played parchesi with them and chess-India and anagrams; and when they tired of those, there was literally nothing she could not cut out for them from strips of brown paper. Saturday evenings they always came and studied their Sunday-school lesson with her, though they never studied it at home; and after they had learned it and she had told them all kinds of stories to make it clear, she let them pop corn or on rare occasions (when he had been careful to save enough pennies) roast marshmallows over the open fire.

The boys liked his father, too, and looked up to him because he was captain of a steamboat. His father told them all sorts of things about the early steamboats along the coast: the very first in 1818 called the *Tom Thumb*, which had to be towed from Boston by a sailing-ship to the mouth of the Kennebec where she steamed up the river with all the people looking on in great astonishment; the steamboat *Maine*, which in 1825 was made from the hulls of two schooners with a paddle-wheel in the space between the hulls and a deck built above with odd deck-houses and space for courageous passengers. They never tired of hearing about the wreck of the *Portland* or about a steamer called the *Royal Tar*, which long ago lost a whole circus at once in their very neighbourhood.

In the year when he was eight and something called an armistice had ended the War and the summer people had gone to the cities, his father allowed him to ask six of his friends to go to Rockland on the *Searsport*, stay over night on board, and sail home the next day. He never forgot to be grateful to his father for that generous act and for what it did for him among his friends. They steamed along the November coast on the day after Thanksgiving when there was no school, saw all manner of boats everywhere, and were even allowed to hold the wheel and steer the *Searsport* with his father standing by in the pilot-house.

It was never dull for a moment for him in his house. His mother always knew what to do. When they tired of reading, they broke up long words like CONSTANTINOPLE and INCOMMUNICA-BILITY (which was difficult since it had no *e*) into smaller words, working briskly to see who could get the larger number in a given time. On Sunday afternoons they used Bible words like NEBUCHADNEZZAR and METHUSALEH. The trouble with young Silas' life was that there never seemed to be time enough to do all that they wanted to do. In the afternoons, while his mother rested or was in pain as she sometimes was, and he had been sent out-of-doors to play by himself, there were always the sea and the shore, flounders to catch from his father's boat and bring proudly home to supper, swimming in summer, stones to skip, and sometimes, when the sun lay on the full harbour, hours of lying in the July grass and wondering drowsily whether the same or different water came in each day and what it must have been like to sail away from Saturday Cove as his great-grandfather had sailed.

In spite of his health and activity he was a quiet, thoughtful boy, having something of his father in him as well as much of the Crocketts whom he looked like. He learned to speak gently in the house and to anticipate the wants of his mother. He learned, too, that it was possible to bear suffering without making others un-comfortable and upsetting the steady course of things. And above everything else he learned, when he was so young that he was unconscious of it, that his father and his mother were surrounded by a vast contentment in each other and in him, which not even the manifold anxieties of constant illness, of deprivations and of too heavy expenses could banish or make serious inroads upon. In fact, so deeply was this understanding grounded in him, enfolding all his days, that he felt suddenly embarrassed, perhaps almost afraid, when, as he grew older, he began to learn that many other people did not feel toward one another as they all felt in his house.

6

The past of Saturday Cove was a dark, uncharted blur to young Silas. In his own childhood, unlike that of his father and his father's father, he had no one who could acquaint him intimately with it. Out of its dimness, to be sure, there emerged now and then, under the stress of his father's stories or from the familiar yet unfamiliar portraits in the front parlour, faces and figures to whom he belonged but with whom he found it difficult to establish any close connection. Some of the things which these men had done he knew—that Amos had built the house, that James had fought with Chinook Indians; he liked to look upon the pictures of their ships; but they themselves were unreal to him. He knew what had befallen his grandfather off Newfoundland, and he felt more proud about it than sorry when he told his envious friends. In his day there was not left even a solitary voyager of deep water to tell the tales his father had heard as a boy.

Upon him as upon all others born in his day the present had swept too summarily, too suddenly, for him to realize clearly that there had ever been a past when things were different. Between the second decade of the nineteen hundreds and the years preceding it change had taken the aspect of a stout, immovable wall, reared almost over night to separate the new from the old—the new of motor cars and moving pictures, steam yachts and modern improvements, ready-made clothing, consolidated schools, easy prosperity, big business, from the old of horses ambling along the country roads, of fishing vessels leaving the snug harbour for the

Banks, of wells and pumps and home industries, of country schools and church socials and long evenings spent at home with one's family. Not that young Silas himself did not know many of these hang-overs; for that, he was fortunate in his parents and in his rural environment; and yet Saturday Cove had become so much a part of the new world that when at fourteen he saw the phenomenon of two past-minded Boston ladies driving a horse and buggy among the automobiles that thronged the coast roads in summer, he laughed as heartily at the spectacle as did everyone else. They sat so primly in the high wagon clucking to their horse; they looked so stubborn in their adherence to an outworn method of travel, that even the old who had at once more resignation and less courage were amused at their tenacity.

In the nineteen-twenties the village, in common with hundreds of others similarly situated and dependent entirely upon summer residents for their livelihood, retained few aspects of its former life. Only its old houses and its trees, its meeting-house, its academy, and its churchyard spoke of other times. One of its blacksmith shops had become a garage; the other, a market for articles in wrought iron, windmills and candlesticks, fire-irons, door-knockers, and lanterns. The sawmill no longer used the water of the stream, and the dam was overgrown with grass and weeds. Two prosperous red-front stores had beaten out the older establishments, and the mails now came twice a day by truck to a new post-office, which advertised the weekly movies on its red-brick front. The land on the west of the harbour, where the docks and the fisheries once were, had become the golf links of the new country club; and the craft which now rode the harbour water were, with few exceptions, the yachts and launches and sailboats of the summer colony.

To a discriminating eye the old houses, in spite of the fact that they stood much as they had stood for a hundred years or more, had suffered most from the pervading change largely because a house itself is forever inseparable from those who built its hearth-stones and once slept within its rooms. Many had been bought by summer residents, and although the houses themselves had gained in many ways by the transfer, those who had known them in earlier days looked upon them now with alien eyes. Some few families, like the Crocketts, still held on, dreading the bitter but inevitable end. Of those on the main village street, which now offered less desirable locations, one had become a summer inn, others had been shamelessly cut into tenements. The old Winship house, once the Misses Peabody were no more, had been sold at auction, passing to the local manager of the Atlantic and Pacific Tea Company, who was slowly paying back his borrowed capital by renting rooms to the chauffeurs and gardeners of neighbouring estates. Reuben Crockett was glad, he told Huldah, that the auction had taken place on a weekday when he was bound toward Rockland.

Reuben had his fears during the early nineteen-twenties. He wondered how long it would be before the Eastern Steamship Lines would take off the coast-wise boats like the *Searsport*. Already some had gone, and his own had become largely a carrier of freights. The company did not keep her so clean and spruce as they once had when she had brought or taken thirty or more passengers daily. She needed fresh paint and the refurnishing of her cabin space. Now that almost everyone who had once poked along from Rockland, taking pleasure in the landing-stages and in the coast itself, had an automobile, now that the Bar Harbor Express served the larger towns eastward, there were few enough to carry even in the heavy months. They had small time now for Reuben's slow journey.

So far as he could see, only the coastline remained unchanged. Even the invasion of trees, firs and spruces, pines and hemlocks, had not changed it so much as they had returned to their former sovereignty now that the docks were no more and the fisheries were becoming extinct. There it was, the coastline, Reuben thought, very much as it had been three hundred years ago when Champlain had sailed his unwieldy ship from Passamaquoddy to Penobscot. There it was with its shingle beaches and rocky shores, its ledges gaunt at low water, at high, slipping down into the sea; the herons in its quiet coves; the gulls shadowing its low, bright skies; the sandpipers running at the edge of its incoming tides.

Reuben knew every inch of it; and with his anxieties pressing hard against him and keeping him close to the living, nagging present, he found himself clinging to it as to something which must endure, outlast the passing of the old and the coming of the new, and prove triumphant over time and chance.

7

In the year that Silas was fourteen, tall and gangling and daily outgrowing his clothes, two events took place in his life which made lasting impressions upon him. The first was the death of his grandmother. It had been a surprise to him ever since he had known anything to know that he had a grandmother. He had never seen her and had rarely heard her mentioned at home; yet he knew that he had her and that she lived alone somewhere in Boston.

Sometimes on the first day of the month after the measuring had taken place and they were all together in the sitting-room in the evening, he saw his father and mother bending over columns of figures on his mother's table and heard his mother say:

"How much for Boston, dear?"

By that he knew that money went each month to Boston, and, since there was no one else in Boston whom they knew, he gathered quite easily that the money must be going to his grandmother.

It was one evening in late June that his mother told him his father had gone to Boston to bring home his grandmother's body for burial beside his grandfather in the churchyard. He felt as he went upstairs to bed that he ought to feel grief over his mother's announcement, but instead he felt only a pleasurable excitement and curiosity which was with him the next morning as he rose and dressed. How old was his grandmother, he asked his mother at breakfast, and why was it that they had never seen her? She was somewhat over seventy, his mother thought, and they had never seen her because she had not even known his father since he was little. He had been brought up by his grandmother, as Silas knew. No, Huldah had never known Silas' great-grandmother. Her name was Solace Crockett, and she had been a wonderful woman as Silas had often heard his father say.

"If she's never lived here," asked Silas, pursuing the exciting question over his oatmeal, "and never known father since he was little, why does he bring her back here to be buried? I don't see."

"She did live here when she was young," Huldah patiently explained. "She lived here most of the time and married your grandfather in the church here. She lived for some years in your great-great-grandfather Winship's house, the one with the white fence and the beautiful entrance. You know it, dear. After she married your grandfather, Nicholas Crockett, she lived here in this very house. Then when your father was four or five, I don't know exactly, she married some one else and went away. She painted pictures and lived in all sorts of places."

Silas was conscious then of a host of happenings from which he was shut out by the enclosing darkness of many years. Curious though he was, he was half-resentful of his grandmother, who had left his father when he was little but who was now usurping his time, adding to his worries, and casting even from the distance of Boston a strange and unwonted atmosphere over the great old house.

"I still don't see why they bring her back here," he said.

"I suppose it's because when people get old, they remember the places and the houses they lived in when they were young and somehow want to be brought back and rest in them. Anyhow the person who sent the telegram said your grandmother had wanted to be brought back here. She died all alone. Your father felt sorry about that."

Silas dressed early for his grandmother's funeral in his blue serge suit which was too small for him. He had gathered daisies and buttercups in the morning from the fields and blue flags from the marshes to fill the vases in the front parlour, which Sarah had cleaned and which now was swept with sunlight, its windows open to the June wind. His father's boat upon which lay his grandmother's body had docked at three o'clock. He had wondered while he dressed if it made his father feel strange to bring his mother's body home on his own boat, wondered just where his father had told the men to place his grandmother's coffin.

When the hearse came up the driveway, he was standing at the front entrance as his mother had told him to do. He and Sarah had moved his mother into the parlour, and she was sitting there waiting in a white dress among the few people who had come for the funeral. He studied his father's face as he helped some other men draw the black coffin from the hearse. He could not see that his father looked any different, only a bit more tired perhaps. Silas held the door open for the men to carry his grandmother's body into the parlour. They placed it below the Crockett portraits between the two front windows. Someone lifted the cover from the coffin, and his father stood for a moment looking into it before he went and sat beside Silas' mother in the corner by the fireplace. Silas joined them there, feeling odd and out of place even beside them.

The minister made a prayer, odd enough in itself, Silas thought, since he prayed for comfort for those who were left in sadness. They might need comfort because his father was anxious and tired and growing old too fast and because his mother worried about him, though she rarely showed it; but surely they needed no comfort in that his grandmother, whom they had not known, was dead. He read then from the Bible, his words sounding through the still room, out through the windows, and over the sunny fields:

For we walk by faith, not by sight.

There are celestial bodies and bodies terrestrial, but the glory of the celestial is one and the glory of the terrestrial is another.

There is one glory of the sun, and another glory of the moon, and another glory of the stars; for one star differeth from another in glory.

So also is the resurrection of the dead. It is sown in corruption, it is raised in incorruption;

It is sown in dishonour, it is raised in glory; it is sown in weakness, it is raised in power.

For this corruptible must put on incorruption, and this mortal must put on immortality.

So when this corruptible shall have put on incorruption, and this mortal shall have put on immortality, then shall be brought to pass the saying that is written, Death is swallowed up in victory.

Something happened to Silas as he heard the words, something more strange even than the minister's prayer. A door somewhere in his mind seemed to have swung wide open for a moment, allowing him dimly to understand that that which the minister was reading had really relatively little to do with the still figure in the coffin, that instead it had to do with all people and all things everywhere, with him and his mother and father, with days and hours, weeks and months and years, with the sun and moon and stars, with the assured faces of the Crockett men so alive on the walls, looking down at his grandmother who was dead. It was but a momentary perception; the door swung to again before he could hold it open; but he was always to remember in after years the odd and new experience of light thus flooding his thoughts.

Then with the swift closing of the wide-swung door in his mind he knew that the funeral was over and the people going away, that his father had risen and expected him to rise also.

"I should like to have you see your grandmother, Silas," his father was saying. "I don't want her to be nothing at all to you."

Silas felt an odd sensation in his long legs as he stood with his father looking down upon his grandmother in the old room. Even now he towered above Reuben, and his grandmother seemed somehow far below him. She wore a black dress, he saw, with some soft white lace about her throat. She had her hands folded and on the fourth finger of her left there was a wedding-ring. He wondered as he looked whether his grandfather had placed it there or the other man whom she had married and whose name his mother had not told him. She was a lovely old woman, he saw, nor did she look really old even in death. Her face was smooth, and her hair, though it was white, curled upon her forehead.

When he turned away, he met the blue eyes of James Crockett looking steadily at him. At the moment young Silas was puzzled as to just which one James had been and whether he had ever known the Deborah Crockett in the coffin between the open windows.

8

In early September of the same year at the close of Silas' first day in the Saturday Cove academy, he came hurrying home from school, eager to tell his mother of his new studies. He had begun his Latin that very day and was declining *mensa* as he followed the shore road to the driveway. Most of his friends were not taking

Latin. They thought it a useless thing even on the small chance that one would go to college; and now that many colleges were no longer requiring it, it had small, if any, point at all. Silas, however, was taking it; his father and mother had had no question about it. All the Crocketts had studied Latin, Reuben had said, at least until they had gone to sea; and he took an odd pleasure, Silas could see, in having Silas do as the others of his family had done.

Silas was always excited by anything new or strange, whatever it was. It was fun to look ahead in his Latin grammar and see letters written by people named Pliny and Cicero which he would soon be able to read. He stopped now and then on the road to turn the pages and gaze at the unfamiliar words which, centuries ago, Roman boys had used to call to one another.

He had been so engrossed upon leaving the academy that he had not noticed his father's boat, tied up already at the wharf. He was surprised as he followed the driveway, where the maples were already turning gold and red, to see a mammoth car before the door with a chauffeur sitting at strict attention behind the wheel, and to hear through the open windows his father's voice talking to someone in the front parlour. He went into the house through the side door expecting to see his mother as always in her chair in the sitting-room. The chair was empty, and he was again surprised when through the open door he saw her in the parlour. She was almost never carried in there, at least without her own chair; and he understood at once that something unusual and most important had caused the innovation.

"You may come in, Silas," his father called. When he was once in the room and face to face with a large gentleman who wore immaculate but rather showy clothes and a diamond ring on the third finger of his right hand, his father said,

"This is my son. This gentleman is Mr. Schwartz, Silas."

"You don't say so!" exclaimed Mr. Schwartz, extending a heavy hand toward Silas. "Your boy, is it? He's a tall fellow all right, all right."

Silas sat down by his mother. Callers, especially of Mr. Schwartz's sort, were such a deviation from the normal course of things that he was puzzled as well as surprised. Moreover, he had the odd feeling that Mr. Schwartz had been there before, although he had never seen him. He sat well back in his chair, his hands folded across his ample front, the calf and shin of one leg placed so high upon the knee of the other that one foot stood out at right angles with the rest of him.

"Well," said Mr. Schwartz, once Silas was seated and a silence had fallen on the room. "We might as well get back to where we started from, don't you think? I'll just go over my offer again so's we can have it all clear just as though 'twas written down, so to speak. I'll give two hundred and fifty dollars spot cash for the oldest of the lot. I'm not saying it's the best, but it's the oldest. The one alone there on the other wall is the best. The London fellow did a better job than the Paris, and the subject himself—James Crockett, you say?—was a handsomer man, at least he sat better, more natural-like for a painter to work from. If I was buying him alone, I wouldn't stop at four hundred though I said three fifty was my limit. And if you'll reconsider the matter and sell the four of 'em, I'm ready with fifteen hundred dollars. You'll make a better deal, see, to let them all go at once, and if you do, it'll be like letting the family go together to keep itself company, so to speak."

Another and heavier silence hung over the room once Mr. Schwartz had spoken. Silas looked at his father sitting quietly in the corner opposite Mr. Schwartz. His face was in shadow so that Silas could not see it clearly, but he saw with a start how white his father's hair really was though he was barely fifty. Reuben had folded his hands between his knees in their old, familiar position, but they were not still as usual. Instead he was moving them back and forth, his fingers holding tightly to his knuckles as he moved them.

"Maybe the wife has an idea," suggested Mr. Schwartz. "Ladies have the vote nowadays. Let's have her say."

Silas glanced at his mother beside him. She was looking at his father instead of at Mr. Schwartz.

"It's not for me to decide," she said quietly. "I want what my husband wants. The portraits are of his family and belong to him."

Reuben found his voice then.

"I don't want to sell them at all. I feel—" He was about to say that he felt like a traitor to the Crocketts, but since he could not say it before Mr. Schwartz, he interrupted himself. "I don't know anything about portraits, but it seems to me I've heard my grandmother say that the one of James Crockett at least cost far more than the price you name, more than three times that, in fact. Even if I didn't need the money at all, I'd feel better to think I hadn't sold my family portraits for less than they are worth."

Mr. Schwartz smiled at Reuben, nodded his large head sagely, and placed his hand with the ring on it upon his raised knee.

"I see. Sort of loyalty to them that are gone beyond recall? And not a bad feeling at that as feelings go. I don't doubt for a minute but what your grandmother was right. No, sir, I don't. But the way I look at it is this. A fellow that's having his face painted is willing to pay for it. It means more to him, see, than it means to a man like myself who's interested in the art more than in the subject. And oil paintings aren't like some things, furniture, for instance, like some you've got in here, that increase in value with age. The cleaning and retouching of these is bound to be considerable."

Silence again fell over the room. Silas saw an odd quivering seize his mother's hand extended on the arm of her chair and placed his own warm, brown one upon it.

"I might," said his father, "be more—inclined to part with them if I could be sure where they were going, where they were to be hung."

He spoke slowly, and Silas knew that his words were costing him no end.

"Well," said Mr. Schwartz, "it's hard to say as to that. But I'll tell you what I'll do. I'll give you a man's promise, and that's my own, yes, sir, to tell you where they go if they leave my hands one of these days. Who knows but what this boy of yours, who, I take it from his looks, has a head on his shoulders, may buy them back some day when he gets into big business, steel or oil, say. He looks good enough for Wall Street, to me."

Mr. Schwartz ended his words with a chuckle and an admiring stare at Silas.

His father stared at Silas, too. He thought he must speak to him in spite of Mr. Schwartz.

"You've never known the portraits as I used to, Silas," he said. "But I'm sure you'd hate to see them go."

Silas raised his head then and looked straight at his father. He knew that the time had come when he must help his father out. Things must have come somehow to a head, he knew. There must be some terrible need of selling the portraits or else his father would not for a moment have considered it.

"I don't mind much, father," he said. "Honest, I don't. I don't mind at all if you think it's best. I can always remember what they all look like."

Mr. Schwartz's hearty laugh then sounded through the room. He slapped his knee delightedly.

"You're a philosopher, young man!" he cried. "You've put the gist of the thing in a nutshell. It's remembering things in this old world that counts."

Reuben rose slowly from his chair.

"You're sure," he said to Mr. Schwartz, "that the names and dates will be kept on them just as they are now."

"They will," said Mr. Schwartz with another slap upon his knee. "A man's word for that, too." He went about the room then, peering at the brass name-plates that were attached to each of the solid, gilded frames. "Let's see. James Crockett—he was a good-looking fellow and no mistake—Amos, Judah, Benjamin. They sure did use the Bible in those old days, now didn't they? And your name's Silas, young fellow. Well, now, what do you know about that?"

Reuben carried Huldah back to her chair in the sitting-room when Mr. Schwartz began to take down the portraits after he had written the check with his gold fountain pen. None of them stayed in the parlour to see the portraits go. When he had them safely in the great car, he came in to say a hearty goodbye to Reuben standing firmly by the table, to Huldah in her chair, and to young Silas. They heard his car backing about and swinging down the driveway.

Huldah was tired, she said. She thought she would rest an hour if Reuben would place her on her bed. And she thought that Reuben and Silas might as well take a walk before supper. It was a lovely evening, and the wind had fallen.

Silas and his father went down through the field, over the stone wall, and through the familiar meadows to the marshes. Then they skirted the shore, rounded a tiny cove where a brook came down to the sea, and walked toward some low brown ledges which they both liked and to which they often came. Reuben spoke but once to Silas. It was in the meadows that he said what he had to say:

"I've been worrying over this for weeks, Silas, with this man pestering me. He came last summer, and he's written me three times since then. I thought I'd never let them go, but I came to it. First I thought of some of the furniture, those old tables and things. But they won't fetch much money. I went into that, too, and besides we've got to have those things to use. You're getting older now, and you'll have to know how things are. Things have been getting bad, with your mother and your grandmother and all, and I'm not so young as I was once. I've had to put a mortgage on the house. I did that years ago. I could sell it, there's plenty that want it, but I can't bring myself to it, at least not now. With taxes coming due and a note at the bank, I had to do it, Silas. I'm sorry, for your sake."

Silas felt a lump rise in his throat. He picked a long blade of grass, which the July haymakers had left standing, and chewed it to make his voice steadier.

"Don't you worry, father," he said. "I think you did just the right thing. Honest, I do."

It was quiet on the ledges; the tide was just coming in. It was a soft day, not sunny, but fair. The sky was swept with low, still clouds with spaces of light between. Two old deserted fish-houses stood above Silas and Reuben among the blueberries in the rough coast grass. The steps were still standing at the threshold of one, and above its sagging, half-open door was a rusted iron horseshoe, put there years ago for luck, thought Silas. One of the nails that held it had disappeared so that it had swung downward, spilling its good fortune. In a crevice between the rocks close by where they sat there were the frail shells of sea-urchins tangled among the brown and golden seaweed. Silas picked up two or three of them and studied the rows of tiny, jewel-like knobs on their rounded sides. The knobs increased in size as they mounted the shell, small ones at the bottom, fat ones in the middle, small again at the top, encircling the hole which looked like the chimney opening of some curious little house. He liked to hold the pale green shells in his hand, to see how some of them had taken on a purple colouring from the wet kelp and sand. The sea lavender was at its best, clouds of colour all along the high beach between the ledges, its thick, pulpy leaves now turning a brilliant red. Sea goldenrod grew among it, spikes and stars of deepest yellow.

It was nice to sit there quietly with his father. Reuben lit his pipe. The tide was coming, covering the clam-strewn flats. Schools of tiny fish made sudden ripples and eddies in the shallow water near the shore. Sandpipers scurried along at the water's edge, running helter-skelter for some distance, then giving an odd flutter as they turned to run back again.

As they looked at all things there in the still, early evening light, a fisherman came along the shore with his clam-hoe and laden basket. Like the sandpipers he, too, walked at the water's edge. There seemed somehow, Silas thought, something sad about him as he followed the shore with the coming sea before him and the soft skies far above.

9

The last years of the nineteen-twenties were prosperous ones, at least away from Saturday Cove; and, so far as that went, all those who had to do with the constantly increasing flow of summer visitors felt the prosperity, the storekeepers, the proprietors of the inn and the several boarding-houses, the owners of the village garages, which now had increased to three. People from the cities had money to spend and they spent it. They built new houses and bought old ones. They collected antiques, were avid in their eagerness to snap up all the old things they could, ship pictures, sandwich glass, old china, chests of drawers, Boston rockers and ladder backs, four-posted and spool beds.

Reuben and Huldah sold some things from the old house whenever matters tightened up as they frequently did and cash had to be had, but they hung on to all they could. Silas, in the academy and leading his class, worked in the summer. He mowed the lawns of the less pretentious houses which kept no gardeners of their own, trimmed the walks, and was proud of his money.

They had set their hearts on Silas' going to college. He liked his books and was good at all his studies. He had a secret desire to be a doctor in some thriving coast town if he could find such a one. Portland, perhaps, he thought, where he would not have to leave the sea but could look out upon it from his office windows. He did not talk about this dream at home.

The furnishings in one of the great front bedrooms which Reuben and Eliza Ann Shaw had given to Abigail Crockett as a wedding gift in 1797 sent Silas to Brunswick for a year, or at least they broke the back of it, and he worked for the rest. The head of some museum bought them. He was a decent man; he knew their worth, and he gave what they all thought a breath-taking price for the lot—the canopied bed, the chests and mirrors, the fire-irons and warming-pan, the beautiful, slender chairs with Eliza Ann Shaw's needlepoint still intact on two of them.

Silas loved college, and when he came home at Christmas and Easter and told them all about everything at meals or in the sitting-room, they all thought they had never been happier even with the knowledge that his next vacations must be spent elsewhere, in another house. For they had at last come to selling. Reuben saw no other way out. In a few more years, he said, the house would be falling to pieces over their very heads. He said, too, and Huldah and Silas agreed with him, that it was almost more fair to the house itself to sell it rather than to keep it in its present condition, which would have distressed the Crocketts dead even more than it distressed the Crocketts living.

"At least," said Reuben when they had at last come to it, and the buyer, a man from Philadelphia, had sat with Reuben for a long hour with the lawyer and the banker in the private room of the new Saturday Cove bank, "at least all them that are gone won't have cause to be ashamed of it any longer. They're going to put money into it, fix it up tight and fine, and they don't plan on changing it any at all except for bathrooms and such. Mr. Wilson's got good ideas, with all his money, and I'm glad we're selling it to him."

The bank had virtually owned the house, and Reuben did not get much for the actual buildings; but the remaining furnishings, except for some things they kept for Silas, and the fields and meadows brought a decent price, so that Reuben felt more secure in his mind than he had for years past. It was well for him that he did, for the *Searsport* made her last trip in the fall of 1930. She was no longer necessary to the coast, had, in fact, for months been running at a loss.

Things had begun to look bad throughout the country by that time, and men with work were holding on to it. After Reuben had taken the *Searsport* to Rockland for her last trip, skirted the familiar headlands and islands, soft in the October haze, whistled for the landing-stages, saluted the light stations, looked out from the pilot-house upon sea and sky and shoreline, he spent days in interviewing men here and there, looking for a new job. He was an excellent captain; the company dealt generously with him; but he was not so young as he had been, and, moreover, dead jobs could not be resurrected after all. He found at last eastward where the fisheries were still doing a respectable business a ferry-boat that needed a pilot. It was not what he wanted, but it would do because it had to do.

They moved late that fall during some warm Indian summer days to a village fifty miles down the coast. They had rented a house there, a small house in a field sloping to the sea. The house was old and had nice roofs, Huldah said, when Reuben had made it ready for her and some friends had driven her there in their automobile. It had a square, squat chimney in the center and a big fireplace in the small sitting-room. Reuben had put their own old things about the house which had been freshly painted and papered by the owner; and once they had placed her in her chair by the sitting-room table, she said she thought it the cosiest of rooms. Reuben had remembered all sorts of details, a dish of apples on the table, some geraniums in the windows, and flowers in all the vases.

10

Silas left college in the spring of 1931. He said, sensibly enough, that there was small wisdom, especially during bad times, in using the little money that had been laid away for a rainy day in paying college bills for him when he was strong and well and had two hands of his own. He said, too, that if things kept on as they surely were tending, a college degree might be a greater hindrance than a help. Better get work while work was to be had, he said, any work at all. He was still young. Lots of fellows left college and then went back to finish when they were long past twenty-five. He said this last, looking steadily and a bit uneasily at his father and mother, wondering if they understood as he did that he should never go back.

He found a job straightway, but he did not take it for a week and more. It was not what he wanted, and he spent days in pacing back and forth along the shore through the wet April grass and the clinging April fog trying to bring himself to it. The hard-headed, keen-eyed manager of the great herring factory three miles away had told him that if he had any sense at all in these times, he'd snap it up like a gull diving for herring refuse. The manager said, too, that if a fellow with any guts at all came into his factory and was willing to begin at the beginning with none of the flimsy notions which one got at college sticking in his head, there was a chance to rise.

"If you look about you," the manager had said, eyeing young Silas in the dingy office of his factory where the machines whirred and clattered to the right and left and the gulls darkened the small windows, "if you look about you, I say, you'll see that this business is about all that keeps this coast alive just now except for rusticators that are losin' all their money and are bound to lose more. I ain't sayin' that you're not different from some that begin with beheadin' herrin'. All I'm sayin' is that jobs are scarce and that they're goin' to be scarcer. Twenty or twenty-five cents an hour don't seem any great shakes I know, and you've got to step lively at the start to get that much, but a job's a job, and I keep a weather eye out all right for fellows above the common lot that's got any stuff in them."

Silas had thanked the manager, whom he liked in spite of his bluff ways, and turned to go out into the fresh air and away from the persistent smell of fish—fish dead and rotting, fish in the holds of many boats clinging to wharves and awaiting their turn, fish cooking, fish drying, fish in oil. Then the manager had called him back, looking at him keenly and not unkindly as he said:

"There's something else I'd like to say. I know how this idea sits uneasy in your insides just now. I began myself bailin' herrin' from the weir pounds out yonder and shovellin' 'em at these very wharves into baskets to go to the cannery. I've done every step of this business myself. Maybe I don't know much about anything except herrin', but there's few men livin' that know any more about herrin' than I do. But that's not what I was aimin' to say. The people that work in this factory aren't any Canucks or Eyetalians or even Irish. They're fine coast-of-Maine stock. Every man-jack on my rolls, and women, too, has a good English name attached to him. Their families did better things years ago in these parts and in other parts of the world, too, just as yours did, I take it. But this coast has changed. I'm tellin' you, and you've got to keep pace with bad times, no matter how it gripes you."

Silas had not gone straight out and away as he had intended. When he left the manager's office and went down the steps, slippery from fish scales and fog, he wandered across the wharves to their very edge where the herring boats, just in with their morning freight, were lying at the piers. Men deep in their holds, literally knee-deep in a silvery, opaque sea of fish, were shovelling herring into baskets, which were taken by overhead carriers to the cannery. They were silent men in hip-boots and heavy shirts and trousers stiff with fish scales. They bent their backs and raised their bare, brown arms beneath clouds of gulls, screaming and swooping above the boats, diving for mutilated fish and for other refuse, which were thrown over the sides.

Within at the cutting tables boys and girls were severing with seemingly one motion of their sharp knives the heads and entrails of fish and throwing the bodies into boxes to be carried to the washing and the brine vats. Other boys and girls, men and women dipped the fish from the brine vats to inclined stands over which streams of water were playing. They worked methodically and swiftly; there was a rhythm in their certain movements there in the great room with the noise of the tide against the piers beneath their feet.

Silas went upstairs where the cooking flakes stood and where still other men and women spread them with row after row of clean fish, placed the orderly, laden flakes on racks and rolled them into the oven to be cooked by steam. The drying room next with its Ferris-like wheel steadily rotating around and around with workers to remove from its great arms the flakes already dried and to insert the never-ending fresh supply. He thought he had never seen fingers move so fast as the fingers of the girls and women in the packing-rooms, picking the cooked and dried fish from the flakes, sorting them into lots with quick glances at their size, laying them closely and neatly in the small rectangular cans. He stood a long time by one man who was covering the oil-filled cans, placing the thin tins on them with both his hands as they automatically passed by him to be sealed with the sealing weight, not able to risk a moment of inattention or of fumbling lest the whole process should be thrown out of its necessary even course.

These men and women, he thought, looked like decent, self-respecting people. They were clean, and their faces were ruddy from the fresh sea air. When he went downstairs and out again to the piers, nudged by the jumble of the fishing-boats, the sun had burst through the April fog and was tipping the wings of the gulls with silver.

After a week of studying the new coastline in all sorts of April weather, he took his job and stood with the others of good English names at the first of the fish-tables.

11

Reuben's new work was dull enough in comparison with commanding the *Searsport*. All day long, every half-hour, he backed the dirty brown ferry-boat from the wharf of one fishing town and took her across the bay to the wharf of another. The water that he thus unadventuresomely steamed upon was strewn with the wreckage and the refuse of the factories along the shore. It had none of the clean, fresh smell of the sea that encircled the islands of Penobscot Bay or of the thoroughfare off Rockland.

But at fifty-five Reuben was glad of any job at all. He looked far older than fifty-five. His hair was white; he had grown more thickly set with the years; and he stooped a little as he walked home at night along the country road carrying his tin lunch-box. But there was still the excitement of reaching home, of telling Huldah all the unimportant things that had happened, of hearing what sort of day she had had, how she liked her new neighbours, and whether she had been made comfortable under the ministrations of a new woman in the kitchen.

Huldah always seemed to have had a good day. She was interested in a thousand things. She liked the new minister, who came to see her every week and who had gotten into the habit of laying before her the problems of his far-flung parish. Her neighbours could not be kinder. One was teaching her a new crochet stitch, and another was exchanging geranium slips. She and Reuben had endless conversations about their garden, bending over gay seed catalogues in the fall and winter, deciding what they should place here and there, climbing nasturtiums and scarlet runners over the woodshed, new tiger lilies to give courage to the old on either side of their door-rock.

She had made an almost immediate friendship with the visiting nurse, the nicest girl, she said. The visiting nurse had annexed Huldah to her regular weekly rounds. She had an idea that she could make Huldah more comfortable by raising the legs of her chair just a trifle and by rubbing her legs and back twice a week with certain motions which unquestionably relieved the pain she sometimes had. Huldah looked forward to the stopping of her Ford in their rock-strewn driveway. No one knew what good it did her, she told Reuben, to have the nurse come in, good for her body and her mind, too. She had even thought that when the next fall came, and Miss Sewall might easily change her boarding-place, they might ask her to take their unused front room. The extra money would help out, and, what was more, they would enjoy her in the house.

Reuben liked the nurse and so did Silas. It was amazing how soon even Reuben took to calling her by her first name, which was Ann. She was only twenty-three, but she had a head on her shoulders, Reuben said, and good common sense. When she came home at night after a long day about the countryside, she would eat a late supper by their sitting-room fire with Silas to fetch things for her from the kitchen. She always had things to tell them about what she had done since morning.

"My word! What a day!" she would say with a laugh, stretching out her long, fine hands to the blazing logs and looking neat and lovely in her blue dress and white collar.

It surely was a day, Reuben thought, his own labour seeming paltry enough in comparison. She went everywhere; she had three villages on her route and all the hills and valleys, points and islands between them. There seemed to be nothing she could not do. She could deliver babies on kitchen tables in out-of-the-way farmhouses, cheer along crippled children, make bedridden old men comfortable, go to the schools and tell children how to brush their teeth and to drink more milk instead of eating doughnuts and pie for breakfast. By the time she had been with them a month they knew all her patients, old Captain Alley on the island four miles out, who refused to have his windows open at night, a young boy in the fishing village, who was dying from an accident in his father's boat and who knew it, Mrs. Nevells, who in spite of all Ann could say or do, *would* give her baby paregoric or vanilla to keep it quiet.

"And I must say at that," said Ann, leaning back in her chair and extending her damp, shoeless feet toward the fire, "I might be running for the paregoric bottle myself if I had a shiftless husband and four babies under five years old!"

She could laugh about her work; in that lay her salvation, Huldah said. She had short and curly fair hair, and she had a way of running her fingers through it just as she was about to tell them something funny. She could be sad, too. Sometimes she came home so upset by something that had happened in some outlying place where the people were distressed over poverty and no work that she could hardly eat her supper.

"It's hard," she would say at these times, "not to think that life is pretty ironic and futile after all. I'm glad I'm here with you. It helps no end. I can't begin to tell you how much."

It did help. That was certain. One could not see Reuben Crockett carrying Huldah from her bed to her chair, morning and night for months on end without casting aside at least a part of the weight of the unintelligible world, without reconsidering the question as to whether life is necessarily ironic and futile. For Reuben, now as at the beginning, the mystery, even the miracle of love, lay in the very fact of its creation in the world, the very way it could lay its revealing and transforming touch upon the common things of a man's life. Once that creation in his own life had been grasped and at least partly understood, the rest followed as necessary acts of gratitude, as loyalty to a sort of unfaltering remembrance. One seeing Reuben and Huldah was tempted to declare with the ancient philosopher and apologist that the glorious and overwhelming truth of a thing is proved by its seeming impossibility.

Silas early fell under the wholesome spell of Ann. In fact, he fell so suddenly that the morning after she had arrived to stay with them, he awoke to find himself aware of such a new interest in the house and in the world that he sang on his bicycle all the way to the fish factory. He did not even fall in love, he thought, when he began to sort out things in his new and freshly furnished mind. He simply awoke that first morning to find himself anchored there.

From the first she was more his companion than he her slave, subservient though he was. Reuben was frequently startled at the nature of their conversations. Sometimes when they sat together over a late supper in the dining-room on warm spring and summer evenings, Reuben would hear them talking of everything under the sun, intimate things, the details of a birth somewhere, which she was relating to Silas quite as though she were talking about the food on the table, discussions of unfortunate situations in the district, which Reuben had been accustomed to think of as "immoral" and never under any circumstances to mention to a woman.

"It seems queer to me," Reuben would say to Huldah. "If I didn't know her, I'd say it ought not to be. Times have changed, I know that well enough, and I suppose young folks have changed with them. Imagine you and me talking about such things when we sat together years ago!"

Huldah's laugh sounded in the quiet room, the kind of laugh, Reuben thought, that he had heard with Susan in the Crockett sitting-room thirty years ago.

"It's better this way," she said. "And as I remember it, dear, you and I talked about most everything under the sun only not in their words, perhaps. Young people haven't changed, at least in the real things. They're all right. I think they have a better chance to be happy when they can talk things over like that. If Silas and Ann can have the kind of life we've had, I couldn't wish for anything better."

Silas and Ann were happy. There was no doubt about that. Ann could make a romance even out of packing fish. On half-holidays from the factory and in the spring and summer evenings he drove her about in her car. Sometimes he even helped her with her patients. He was deft and quick with his fingers; he should have been a doctor, Ann said.

Under her influence he awoke and blossomed like the green bay tree of the Psalmist. He laughed and sang and tore about the house, was forever thinking of things for them to do, places for them to go. He seemed now to be letting loose a store of energy which he had seemingly never possessed before in such measure. He was going up by leaps and bounds in the factory, earning more money each month. He wore his clothes well, now that he occasionally had some new ones, was so tall and handsome and well set-up that Reuben was puzzled, at times, in fact, a bit dismayed in the midst of his pride and pleasure.

"He's not a bit like me," he said to Huldah more than once. "He's all Crockett, I guess. I shouldn't wonder if he was like the old Silas we named him after. My grandmother used to tell me when I was little about how handsome he was and what a fine figure he cut all over the world. Ann was saying just the other evening from those books she's been reading how people take back sometimes for their appearance and their traits. I guess Silas has taken back all right."

Silas wanted for nothing as he and Ann drove over the country roads above the sea. In spring the lambkill filled the pastures, deep purple in the evening light. They heard the peepers from the marshes and watched the moon rise beyond the islands and throw into sharp relief the dark St. Croix hills. The white-throats eastward stayed longer than they had stayed in the woods and pastures above Saturday Cove. Silas and Ann heard their plaintive whistling, their running fall of notes as they ate their supper on summer evenings in places they had discovered and to which they liked to return. Ann knew and loved the coast. She had been brought up upon it; her people, too, had sailed far seas; and all its aspects and moods were familiar to her, the pale skies of November brooding over land and water, the quiet of October haze, the way the low light streamed over everything in the spring, outlining all with itself.

Here farther eastward the coast was different alike from that about Saturday Cove and from Ann's home at Merrymeeting Bay where the deep waters of the Kennebec and the swift shallows of the Androscoggin join to meet the sea. Its blue hills and ridges for the most part lay back from the shoreline, far back beyond miles of flat and desolate country, swept by east winds and low-lying fog in late fall and early spring, covered by drifting, swirling snow in winter, in summer receiving the hot sun full on its stretches of blueberry land, now with the herring its chief source of livelihood. The blueberry fields were lovely, constantly affording surprise that such seemingly barren wastes with few trees could be so beautiful. In the spring their fresh growth was starred and whitened by countless tiny bell-like blossoms of palest green, packed so closely among their thick stalks and small, pointed leaves, that when a low wind passed over the fields there was almost a resonance in its sound. Early summer brought out the hues of old country wines in the new berries, the reds of Burgundy and Bordeaux; in August the ripe, blue clusters, large and rich from frequent autumn burnings, made the long reaches of the land blue above the longer blue reaches of the sea before them. Men and women worked among them with their rakes and baskets, bending low over the bushes as peasants bend in older lands above older soil. And when the harvest was over and September had come, the fields flamed red and purple for weeks under the early frosts.

They roamed over the fields, eating handfuls of the berries, marvelling at their size and flavour and at the bloom that lay upon them like the gray silvery haze of the approaching fall.

"When I first came down east here," said Ann, "I missed the higher coastline and the nearer hills. But now I'm not so sure that it isn't just as lovely."

Silas poured from his hands into hers a hundred and more berries, the biggest he could find.

"I know," he said. "I felt that way, too. But it's the coast anyway. I couldn't live inland. Some part of me would be dead. So long as it's the coast, I guess it doesn't matter."

12

Reuben fell ill in the summer of 1932. He had caught cold in a spell of damp weather in June, and he could not seem to throw the cold off. It was really not so much that, said Huldah wisely, as the coming to a head of an accumulation of worries that had long been pressing against him. It seemed as though now in the first real illness he had ever had, everything which had ever caused him anxiety came back to sit beside him and to show its dark face. He was not an easy patient. Not that he fussed or fretted or disobeyed orders. Those things might have been simpler to handle merely because they were more tangible. It was his still brooding and his omnipresent, silent discouragement that troubled them most.

When he could get up from bed and sit in his chair, it was no better. He had the old house on his mind and it stayed there, solid and substantial as it doubtless now was under its new owners. He forgot the stark necessity which had commanded him to sell it. If he could only have looked ahead into the future, he kept saying, could have foreseen that Silas would do well in spite of leaving college, he might have been able to hold on to it. He never wanted to see it again, he said, but he would like to know how it had fared, whether the same woodbine framed its doorway, the small lilacs stood by its door-rocks. He was plain homesick, Ann said. That was the matter with him.

It was her proposal that she and Silas drive to Saturday Cove and see the house. Silas like Reuben had not wanted to go back, but with Ann, as with God, all things were possible. They went back on a Sunday in July, driving away from more open water past sheltered coves and bays until they saw in the near distance the tumbling Mount Desert hills.

The quiet of a Sunday afternoon was upon Saturday Cove when they reached it. The old village street beneath its elms was drowsy enough as they drove past the white meeting-house and churchyard.

"My great-great-grandfather built that church," said Silas. "Father has some old plans somewhere or other marked with his name. We must look at them some time."

They went along the shore road toward the old house. The day was still and the gulls rested quietly upon the full water. When they reached the driveway, stretching immaculate in its raked white gravel up the hill, they found a new white fence and high gate enclosing the house and fields. The fields were no longer bright with daisies and buttercups, hawkweed and Queen Anne's lace. They had been carefully graded, sloping now almost to the water's edge in lawns set about with new trees.

Silas felt odd and lonely within him.

"I don't think we'd best drive in, do you?" he asked. "I feel out of place some way. I think we'd better leave the car and walk. It will give us time to think what we'd best say when we get to the door. After all, they may think that just because we owned the house once is no good reason why we should ask to see it."

They left the car accordingly on the shore road and opened the great gate, which bore beautiful lamps of wrought iron upon its high posts. They both felt uncomfortable and out of place though they did not say so to each other. They walked slowly up the wide driveway that now had no trace of the encroaching plantains and the sorrel which Silas remembered. The lawns extended on either side of them, smooth and undulating with perfectly kept grass. The old meadows on the left as they drew near the house were no longer high with a ripening crop of hay. They had been made into a small golf course with tiny flags hanging idly at their posts in the windless air.

The great house itself was relatively unchanged at least in outward aspects although to Silas, because of its very perfection, it retained little that had once belonged to the Crocketts. A wide terrace of brick now extended across the front, gay with chairs and tables, doubtless homelike and comfortable to those who now looked upon the sea where near the shore some pleasure craft lay jauntily at anchor. Below the terrace stretched the gardens almost to the water's edge, formal gardens of well-kept borders with delphiniums and tall foxgloves and every other kind of July flower graduating in size to the tiny plants that edged them, beautiful gardens, one must in all fairness say that. A fountain played in a pool halfway down the perfect expanse of green which formed the center, and the falling water was the only sound on the still afternoon.

The barn was a barn no longer. It had become a garage where shining cars stood on new cement floors. The woodshed had quite disappeared. A walled kitchen garden had taken its place. And beneath the old elm trees at the entrance to what had been the meadows some low white buildings stood, immaculate in fresh paint and new shutters, servants' quarters without doubt, Ann said.

They stood for some moments at the point where the driveway ended and the terrace began, wondering what would best be their next move. They would gladly have escaped then and there, had not the memory of Reuben's tired, troubled face persisted in their nervous minds.

"I don't think," said Silas at last, "that they could mind just letting us go inside for a minute. Anyhow we've got to ask. I can't go home and tell father we didn't."

They crossed the terrace and mounted the steps to the old doorway. It was set about on either side by carefully trimmed cedars and lower evergreens, all neatly clipped. The woodbine had vanished, and not a trace of the old lilacs remained. He raised the new brass knocker and sounded it against the freshly painted door whose whiteness gleamed in the July sunshine. Ann, beside him, took his hand for a moment before the door opened.

A servant stood in the doorway, an elderly man stately in black clothes. He stared inquiringly at Silas, and Silas nervously removed his hat, which obviously to the man before him was the most unfortunate of gestures.

"I'm sorry to bother you," Silas said. "I used to live here—all my life. My father owned this house and all my family. Would it be possible for us just to come in the hall and see if it's as it used to be?"

The man in black straightened himself perceptibly. He stood in the exact center of the old doorway and did not move aside as he looked at Silas.

"I'm sorry, sir," he said. "I'm afraid not. The family is away, and I have my orders."

Ann saw Silas' head rise higher on his shoulders, and a red flush spread over his tanned face.

"I'm sure they wouldn't mind," she began. "It's not for ourselves that we ask. Mr. Reuben Crockett, who sold the house to Mr. Wilson two years ago, is ill, and he wanted us to come back and see it so that we might tell him about it. Perhaps you don't understand. The Crocketts built and owned this house, and it means a lot to the ones that are left."

The butler had turned his gaze from Silas to her. This was doubtless an extraordinary and perhaps an exceptional occurrence, but in these days, when somebody was always wanting something or other, an old and tried servant must remain firm.

"I quite understand, madam," he said. "As I say, I'm sorry. I'll report your calling to Mr. Wilson. Perhaps some other day you might come again? I'm sure if you wrote ahead it might be managed. All I can say is, I have my orders."

"Yes, father," said Silas that evening. "They're keeping it up first rate. You'd be pleased if you could see it. The view is just the same, and they've made a lovely garden in front of the house."

"There used to be one there," said Reuben, "when the Crocketts were prosperous. I remember my grandmother saying how when she was young the garden almost filled the old field. I'm glad they've put back the garden. What about the vines and the lilacs?"

"They looked fine. And the doorways are just as they were, the big fan and the sidelights and all."

"What about the barn?"

"It's just the same, only, of course, there are cars in it now. You couldn't expect a barn to stay a barn in these days."

"No, of course not. I don't suppose they have much use for the hay in the meadows. Give it away most likely to anyone that will cut it for them. I made hay in those meadows for years on end. I remember how I liked those days. A fair crop did you say?"

"The meadows looked splendid," said Silas.

Reuben's face looked brighter than it had for weeks.

"I suppose, of course, they've taken the old paper off the front parlour? I hoped they wouldn't, but there—you can't expect them to feel the same way about old paper like that."

"They haven't touched it," said Ann quickly. "Silas told me all about it going over, how it was old French paper of 1793, but I never dreamed it could look so well. They have all sorts of clever ways of restoring those old papers nowadays."

"That's fine," said Reuben. "I do feel better about things. Were there any of the old things in the same places?"

Silas found his voice.

"The hall looked just the same," he said. "The old sconces and all, and the staircase. I know you'd have been pleased, father. After all, it's the Crockett house, and it's fine to think it's being kept up the way it ought to be."

"I am pleased," said Reuben. "It takes a load off my mind. I don't want to see it myself, but it does me good to hear about it. You say Mr. Wilson wasn't at home? That's too bad. I thought him a good sort of man with all his money."

"I'm sorry he wasn't there," Silas said, holding Ann's hand tight in his. "But the man who showed us about was—very polite. We didn't get his name."

"Did you go upstairs?" asked Huldah. "I loved those big rooms facing the sea. Your father used to carry me up there, you remember, though I'm sure he shouldn't have. 'Twas a long climb up that winding staircase."

"We didn't like to ask for too much," said Silas, "with Mr. Wilson away and all."

"That's right," said Reuben. "I'm glad you didn't. After all, it's their house now, and we don't want to seem to lay claim to something that's not ours any longer."

Silas stared at the wall above the fireplace where Amos Crockett's ship *Mary* was leaving Marseilles. He wondered if his heart would ever stop beating in his throat, and how soon he and Ann could get away and walk along the shore under cover of the summer darkness. And then Amos' ship *Mary*, sweeping from Marseilles, swept clear his bewildered vision.

"I someway feel it *is* ours, father, just the same," he said, his voice ringing clear and firm. "I thought today we'd done the best thing we could possibly do by selling it as we did. There isn't a Crockett that ever lived who couldn't be proud of the way it looks now. We've—we've kept it by letting it go."

"Yes," said Huldah. "You're right, Silas. I'll tell you what it makes me think of." Her face was shining. "It makes me think of that place in the Bible that says you lose your life once you try to save it, but that once you are willing to let it go, you keep it forevermore."

13

Silas and Ann went back to Saturday Cove in the spring of 1933. They were happier as they followed the coast road than during their last journey over it. They were going to be married in the fall. Ann would keep on with her nursing for a time at least, and together they would make out famously, they thought. So did Reuben and Huldah. Until Silas and Ann could see their way to a house of their own, they would all live together as they had done for two years now. After all, the happiness they had already had was a sufficiently sure foundation for that which they knew awaited them.

It was on Memorial Day that they took their journey, partly because it was a free day for them both, partly because, as Huldah and Reuben often said, it was difficult to observe Memorial Day as it should be observed when a new home had taken one away from the familiar churchyard of the old. The sentiment surrounding the thirtieth of May, common to all rural New England, was deeply rooted in Reuben and Huldah, and, if placed less securely in Silas and Ann, was, nevertheless, there. From childhood, Ann in her home, Huldah in hers, Reuben and Silas in Saturday Cove, they all had been accustomed to gather in the morning of the day with the members of every village household to place flowers on the graves of the family lots. That no one for two years had thus remembered and honoured the Crocketts in the Saturday Cove burying-ground had distressed Reuben and Huldah; and they had eagerly concurred in plans to repair the neglect and continue with the old custom.

Silas and Ann had heaped the back of the car with flowers, lilacs from their present doorway in place of the branches that Silas had once gathered, apple blossoms from their few old trees, wild plum and cherry from the pasture slopes. It was a perfect day, clear and shining, and people were busy in the cemeteries of the small villages through which they passed. Even the now unused and neglected family graveyards, which still marked the fields of once isolated farms, showed flowers placed at the foot of slanting, moss-grown stones within their enclosures of rusted iron or white pickets.

The old graveyard before the church was mown and sun-swept when they reached it in mid-morning. New flags marked the graves of those that had fought in any one of the six wars which Saturday Cove had known. Jonas Norton had his flag and Sergeant Peasley and Lieutenant Simpson theirs, although Silas had never so much as heard of any one of them or had the slightest inkling as to the part that two had played in the circumstances dictating his life. He was pleased that old Amos and James Crockett had their flags, which fluttered from the small sticks holding them in the earth, although, as he told Ann when they filled their pails from the cemetery well, he could not for the life of him tell her, even from the dates which sometimes embraced two conflicts, what wars they had fought in. The sombre, half-obliterated inscription that marked Amos' stone, so dulled by time and weather that they had to trace the words with their fingers, could not tell them that he had commanded a privateer against the monstrous aggressions of King George III. From the pious sentiment on James Crockett's not the most buoyant imagination could have pictured him at fourteen, receiving in his surprised face the warm brains of a man shot on Captain Nicholas Danforth's rebel ship in the year 1781. Indeed, one might rather have concluded that James was given to contemplative piety! Nor could Silas and Ann know that Abigail Crockett had smiled more than once in her later years at the verse which her time and place had held entirely appropriate for James.

Ann read the verse aloud as they placed their flowers by the stone:

Beyond this narrow vale of time
Where bright celestial ages roll
To scenes eternal and sublime
Religion points and leads the soul.

"He must have been a serious man, your great-great-grandfather."

"I don't know," Silas said. "I don't know anything about him except that he went to sea like all the others and then owned the shipyards here. He was a handsome man from his portrait. I remember that."

She was studying the stones.

"They all seem to have gone to sea and some never to have returned. Here's one sacred to Nicholas, who died of fever in Africa, and to Reuben, who was lost at sea. And to Nicholas, too, your grandfather. He was young to be buried off Newfoundland as it says. Imagine having had a grandfather who died at twenty-five! Perhaps we'd best place the wreath your mother made by Silas' stone since you were named for him, but I'm rather drawn toward Nicholas myself. Do you know how it happened that he was drowned so young? Was it a wreck or something?"

Silas was filling the jars and cans from the pails of water which they had drawn.

"I'm afraid I don't know very much about any of them," he said. "It seems wrong, standing here among them, not to know. But I don't. I know my grandfather was frozen to death in his watch when he went on a fishing schooner. It seems as though I ought to know more about him since it was only sixty years ago. And I know my great-grandfather Silas was a handsome man, too, and sailed all over the world with my great-grandmother Solace there. She brought up my father. I know that. He says she was a wonderful woman."

"They all had nice names," said Ann. "Abigail and Solace, Mary and Deborah. I like them."

"I remember Deborah. She was my grandmother. She married Nicholas, and then after he died off the Banks, she married some one else. You see she died only ten years ago. I remember the funeral, but I never saw her until I looked at her in her coffin in the front parlour of the old house. She lived away somewhere, and they brought her home. I remember what an impression it all made on me when I was just a kid."

"Susan Gray," read Ann. "Who was she? Not a Crockett, surely. 'Faithful friend and servant,' it says."

"I know about her," said Silas. "She brought up my father after his grandmother died. She must have been a good old soul; funny, too, from the things mother tells about her. She left me some money, which she hid away in a Bible. We saved it for college, but we had to spend it long before."

When they had once placed their flowers on the graves and Huldah's wreath by the memorial stone to Nicholas, they stood together looking at them in the roughly mown grass. The sun lay bright and warm over the churchyard; the wind bent the trees and grass, such sun as Abigail Crockett had delighted in, such wind as Judah and Amos, James and Benjamin, Silas and Nicholas would have welcomed in their taut sails.

"Maybe it sounds silly to say it," said Ann, "but what makes me feel bad is, not that they're all dead, but that we can't know how they felt about things while they lived. Of course, they must all have done as we do. Silas must have loved Solace and Nicholas, Deborah, just like you and me. They probably did foolish, lovely things the way we do, gave each other presents, and sometimes had broken hearts. That's the sadness in it, I think, that we stand here and don't know. If it hadn't been for all of them, I keep thinking, I shouldn't have you now."

Silas kissed her. She was leaning against the stone sacred to Nicholas, who had paid a grievous toll for other kisses long ago.

"I know," he said. "That's why I'm glad we came here. People say the past is dead, but it can't be. I feel it coming back whenever I see a dingy old schooner like that one out there beating along the coast."

When they had finished with their work, they walked through the old churchyard, reading the quaint inscriptions, seeing the old devices on the stones, anchors and full-rigged ships and coils of rope. Near the entrance to the yard they came upon an old stone fallen backward upon the ground, broken at its base, cracked, half-overgrown by grass. They bent over to decipher it.

"It must be one of the oldest here," said Ann, dropping on her knees beside the broken slab. "Look, dear, it's to three children that died all at once, probably in one of those terrible epidemics they used to have, diphtheria or scarlet fever. One of them was named Silas. Wait till I make it out. It's the oddest of them all."

She read the old inscription slowly, her fingers helping her upon the fallen stone:

In life they were pleasant though transient their bloom,
Their dust now divided now rests in the tomb,
But in Eden forever their spirits shall shine
With a beauty transcending a bloom that's divine.
So, strangers who pause here and neighbours who stay
To contemplate sadly our frail, sinful clay,
Take heed, look toward Him who hath power to save,
And grace to sustain thee through Death's chilling wave.

"It's hard to realize," she said, "that people ever felt that way and believed those things. Life must have been full of fears with death from all sorts of unknown causes so close on one hand and the anger of God on the other."

Silas watched her there in the grass by the old stone, her hair shining in the sun, her quick face almost anxious, as quick faces often are. In an odd, half-formed way he felt it somehow right that she should be here with him, they so alive among the

Crocketts, who had made their love possible. So engrossed was he in this satisfaction that he did not reply to her words.

"And still, I don't know," she continued. "Sometimes when I get going over it in my own mind, I think how much more secure they were then, with all their terrors, than we are. They were clinging to something that they knew existed. They weren't forever wanting something—God, I mean—and then finding themselves almost compelled to give Him up because of this new discovery and that. At least they had convictions."

"So have we!" cried Silas sharply, startling even himself. He stood by the old grave in the wind-blown grass looking seaward, his face suddenly alight. With Ann's words and in the sureness of her love for him, there had swept over him a flash of understanding, clearer than that years ago at his grandmother's funeral when the opened door in his mind had swung suddenly shut. Now, whatever of mental darkness and confusion might follow, he knew, for that moment at least, that the way was broad and straight before his face.

"So have we," he said again. "All the things we've learned can't take away what's rooted in us through generations like these around us and through this coast and sea. Believing in a thing doesn't mean that you've got to understand all about it first. That's where our generation makes its mistake, it seems to me. I think believing in a thing means hanging onto it because you know it's good and, even when you lose faith in it for a time, still hanging on to what it did for you when you had it. Do you know, Ann, I believe that truth is a much bigger thing than just what you can prove in your mind about it?"

"Maybe," said Ann. "When you talk like that, darling, I feel sure of it myself."

She still knelt on the grass, looking up at him. There was in his face and bearing more conviction even than in his words.

What was lost to her in one was made up abundantly by the other. She had never seen Silas so alive and glowing. Her love quickened, increased, flowing in boundless streams straight from her to him there in the quiet churchyard. Looking out from his eyes, standing firmly in the poise of his head were unchangeable things—the daring of Amos and James, the humourous wisdom of Abigail, the steadfast devotion of Solace through years of fear, the faith of Silas and Nicholas hanging to fast-dying sail with the world against them, the secure and patient ways of Reuben, the unshaken and glorious reality of Huldah's love for God. Ann did not know them for what they were, but she saw them there—the substance of all things hoped for, the evidence of things unseen, the everlasting triumph over time and chance.

"You look like a prophet, dear," she said, "standing so straight and looking out to sea like that. Like Moses and Isaiah and all the rest having visions in holy places. They always marked those places with stones, and ours is marked already. Only, when times are better and we're rich, let's come back and have this old stone raised up as it ought to be. I don't want the little children forgotten in the grass, even though they are in Eden. It's a big stone. It must have been an important one years ago."

THE END